Condemned
to Repeat

Condemned to Repeat

A Randy Craig Mystery

By

Janice MacDonald

RaveN
STONE

Published by Ravenstone
an imprint of Turnstone Press
Artspace Building
206-100 Arthur Street
Winnipeg, MB
R3B 1H3 Canada
www.TurnstonePress.com

Turnstone Press gratefully acknowledges the assistance of the Canada
Council for the Arts, the Manitoba Arts Council, the Government of
Canada through the Canada Book Fund, and the Province of Mani-
toba through the Book Publishing Tax Credit and the Book Publisher
Marketing Assistance Program.

This novel is a work of fiction. Names, characters, places and incidents
are either the product of the author's imagination or are used fictitiously,
and any resemblance to actual persons living or dead, events or locales, is
entirely coincidental.

Printed and bound in Canada by Friesens for Turnstone Press.

Library and Archives Canada Cataloguing in Publication

MacDonald, Janice E. (Janice Elva), 1959– author
    Condemned to repeat / Janice MacDonald.

(A Randy Craig mystery)
ISBN 978-0-88801-415-3 (pbk.)

    I. Title. II. Series: MacDonald, Janice E. (Janice Elva), 1959–
Randy Craig mystery.

PS8575.D6325C66 2013   C813'.54   C2013-902241-4

This is for Sharon and Steve Budnarchuk,
of Audreys Books, who have done so much
for Canadian writers and Edmonton readers,
and especially me.
Thank you for preserving the magic
that is the bricks-and-mortar independent bookstore.

Condemned
to Repeat

1

It was a good thing Rutherford House was within walking distance from my apartment, as there was next to no desk space for me to actually spread out and work there. While I had been invited to use a desk that was set discreetly in the back of the gift shop in the basement, there I tended to be interrupted by someone wishing to purchase a vintage-like pocket watch or a painting of a grain elevator. I had tried to pitch in to help out, but had made the cash register seize up twice before the manager of the House agreed that it would be more advantageous to everyone concerned if I were to conduct my prime work from home.

After all, it's not as if you can sit down in too many places in a historic site like Rutherford House, except the restaurant. Everything in the House is an artifact, either actually belonging to the family of the first premier of the province or authentic to the time period. I sure didn't want to go down in history as the girl who broke Alexander Rutherford's library chair.

In effect, I owed my present job to the insights and dreams of two separate premiers: Alexander Rutherford, who had the vision to create a university that would stand among the best in the world, and a more recent resident of the office, Ed Stelmach, who through the combination of his rural ties and innate sense of fair play, was instrumental in promoting an even playing field for all Albertans. The same governmental impetus to provide common access to services across the province was creating a need to have museums and historic sites accessible to all, and it was my job to concoct a reasonable facsimile of an actual visit to Rutherford House. While I wasn't going to be able to provide the scent of furniture polish or old leather-bound books, or the creak of floorboards in the kitchen, I was doing my best to find a way for Sherry in High Prairie or Murphy in Milk River to have a virtual Rutherford House experience. My own feeling was that success would come from increased interest in actually visiting the House, since to me there is just nothing like knowing I'm standing where those before me have walked. However, we are a widespread province, a people who determine journeys in how many hours they take, not how many kilometres they span, and gasoline prices being as volatile as they were, who was I to make people stir from their front stoops? Further to that, far be it from me to question a government contract.

The Friends of Rutherford House were the folks who were presently signing my cheques. They'd hired me to design and facilitate a virtual museum website that would underline the House's importance in the firmament of historic sites of Alberta. It got complicated a bit, though, because I was being paid from a project grant funded entirely by the provincial Ministry of Culture. On top of that, I got tapped every now and then to pitch in as a part-time employee of the House, which offered more money and what I was telling myself was a better way to get a feel for the pulse of the House. If I was going to be honest with myself, though, the extra monies were going to really help out with Christmas gift buying.

Tonight, for instance, the week after Thanksgiving, I was working on-site, but not in the capacity I had been contracted for. I had succumbed to the flattery of Marni Livingstone, the manager, and was signed up to be part of the Evening of Illusion, the Rutherford House way of getting the jump on Hallowe'en activities this year. A candlelit dinner and entertainment by a magician, followed by a mystery theatre enactment, was the basis of the event. Marni was perpetually short-handed at evening events, and so I had agreed to be part of the crew. Who knew, it could be fun, and Marni was offering more than minimum wage for one evening's work. Mostly we were there just to guard the artifacts and make sure no one decided to take a nap on Cecil Rutherford's antique bed.

I got to the House, situated on the eastern edge of the university campus, at five, which was an hour ahead of the time the guests were expected to begin drifting in. The sun was hanging red in the river valley across the street, lighting up some ominous dark clouds dramatically, and aside from a couple of joggers heading down Saskatchewan Drive, I had the scene to myself. Not for long, though. The event had sold out, according to a phone call from a delighted Marni earlier that day. And justifiably so. She'd put a lot of effort into organizing it.

There would be appetizers and drinks offered, then the magician would perform in the front parlour. After this, the party would adjourn to the Arbour Tea Room, where the meal would be served. During the meal, a murder play would be enacted, and clues placed on a bulletin board in Premier Rutherford's study for post-prandial perusal. The guests would write down their guess of who the murderer was on an entry slip, which would be tallied up while the actor playing the detective walked them through the denouement. The winner received a coupon for high tea for two, and everyone went home happy. Three or four of us would stay to clean up, after having monitored the House during the play. It was practically guaranteed that at least seven people would write down "that tall woman with the braid guarding the hat collection" as their guess for the murderer, even though I would have told at least forty people who asked that no, I wasn't part of the mystery itself. This was not what I'd signed up for, but on the whole, it didn't matter. Rutherford House got under your skin really quickly and I felt sort of territorial, wanting to make sure the furniture and artifacts remained safe and scuff-free.

I was excited to watch the magic show, too. Marni had been thrilled to book Stephen Dafoe for the event. Dafoe da Fantabulist had been a huge draw around Edmonton in the early '70s, when he was just a young teen. He had probably appeared on the Harry Farmer TV show as many times as Edward Connell, the keyboard prodigy. Not as flashy as some of the other

Canadian magicians of the era, like Doug Henning, Dafoe was renowned for his close-up work and his ability to make a deck of playing cards do pretty much whatever he wanted it to do, and what most people would consider impossible.

Magic had always fascinated me. Of course, I still had to really focus when tying my own shoes, so I had no idea how rope tricks worked. I would likely be amazed by illusions a ten-year-old could replicate with one viewing. Some of the other workers weren't as jazzed as I was to hear we'd be seeing a professional magician.

"He was at the Magic School a while back," sniffed Jossie, one of the tea-room waitresses, who was barely in her twenties from what I could gather, way too young to sound so jaded. "I've seen his show."

From her I got the sense that Mr. Dafoe was a prickly sort, so I was hoping that I wouldn't be stationed anywhere too close to his show area. The last thing I wanted to do was wreck a magic act by barrelling through the room at the wrong time. And I certainly didn't want to telegraph something inappropriate to the audience. As my boyfriend Steve said, I had a face that would lose any poker hand; I could not keep a bland expression to save my life.

They really needed to come up with better words than "boyfriend and girlfriend" for people in their forties. "Partner" was too ambiguous, "lover" not ambiguous enough. Steve Browning and I had been together, more on than off, for the better part of a decade now, and though we were considering cohabiting on a regular basis, I was still too enamoured of my tiny vintage apartment to make the leap. Instead, we installed toothbrushes in each other's homes and considered ourselves committed exclusively to each other, which most of the time was fine by me. I wasn't one of those girls who had doodled wedding gowns in the back of her binder during chemistry class. In fact, I would have been the one looking quizzically at the over-foaming beaker, or trying to live down the slight explosion. It wasn't just love of literature that had led me to English literature in university. An outrageous lack of absorption for anything scientific made the choices much more limited to begin with.

In the context of Rutherford House, home of the first premier of Alberta and president and founder of the University of Alberta, the whole concept of "university" took on historical meaning and seemed much more up my alley. Knowledge was considered of value in the abstract, or to make you a more valuable citizen and member of society, in the days when Rutherford and his cronies sat in this leather-lined study and envisioned the future down the road. Students would be educated so they could dream a new tomorrow, not in order to walk into better-paying jobs.

If only I hadn't been quite so willing to buy into the concept of the liberal arts education for education's sake, I might by now have a condo overlooking the river valley, a tidy sum accruing in an RRSP, and a dependable source of income. Instead, armed with an MA in English literature, a quiver full of useful computer and audio-visual skills, and some handy recipes using lentils, I had managed to gypsy my way through four and a half of Shakespeare's stages of man, and all I had to show for it was a banjo, several hundred books, a small Jane Ash Poitras painting, and a laptop computer that was probably out of date the week after I'd bought it. Still, if you were of a mind to measure out life in coffee spoons, I have indeed had my share of coffee.

My last gig of writing for a university website had been mostly wonderful, though there had been some associated troubles. References from Dr. Fuller and the Centre for Ethnomusicology had been what had landed me this contract, which was a shared project of the Province of Alberta, the University Archives and the Friends of Rutherford House. In 2011, the brick house on Saskatchewan Drive had celebrated its one-hundredth birthday and the City had commissioned a book about the house itself, stemming from research and interviews with surviving Rutherfords, neighbours, fraternity boys who had been members of the Delta Upsilons, who had used the house later, and early members of the committee to turn it into a historic site. The interest in this book had led to the concept of a virtual museum website, bringing Rutherford House to the world. The website I had helped to create for the folkwaysAlive! folks in the Department of Ethnomusicology had been my ticket to this job.

So far, I had read the book, several transcriptions of interviews that hadn't made it into the book, and a coffee-table book about Achnacarry, the home of the Camerons in Scotland, after whom Alexander Cameron Rutherford had named his own Alberta castle. I was slowly getting a feel for the place, and I certainly had a delight in entering the House and being surrounded by the atmosphere of another era, right down to the smell of ginger cookies wafting in from the back kitchen.

A dark SUV pulled up as I was looking out the window of the study, and out stepped a man in his late forties or early fifties. He stood for a minute, taking in the House. I understood the feeling. There was just something so right about the impressive symmetrical construction of the place that wasn't something one came across too often in Edmonton, which was more a place of split-levels and ranch bungalows. The stranger with whom I now shared an architectural affinity straightened his shoulders and turned to the hatchback of his car. He pulled out the first of what turned out to be six plastic tubs, which he stacked in two piles on the sidewalk in front of the vehicle. Stencilled on the side of the tubs was the word DAFOE.

The magician had arrived.

2

tephen Dafoe was not really what I had expected from what Marni had told me about him. First off, since he had been such a child prodigy and local icon, I sort of expected more ego to be emanating from the man. Instead, when I went out to the curb to see if I could help him with his equipment, he introduced himself with a bright smile and a firm handshake.

"I'd love some help. You know, most magicians have assistants just to help schlep equipment. Fishnets and a Vanna White presentation arm are incidental."

We propped the front door open with one of the bins and began hauling the rest in, straight to the kitchen hall. We were going to have to close one of the public doors for this event, which had already been agreed to when they were negotiating Dafoe da Fantabulist. The mystery event actors had been a bit miffed that they wouldn't be able to lead participants up the maid's stairs at the rear of the House, but I figured they'd find a way to get by.

By this time, Marni had arrived to introduce herself and determine what extras Mr. Dafoe was going to require. Luckily, he provided for his own animals, so water and a plate of food kept warm till after his show was all the sustenance required. The mystery players would eat with the group of participants, jollying them into the fiction of the evening. Dafoe would be entertaining prior to dinner taking place, then would recuse himself and the dinner theatre would begin.

The gist of the evening was that a group of magicians were having a reunion, ten years after the terrible accident that had killed the Great Guilfoyle's assistant. Guilfoyle had taken to drink and was now a mere shell of himself. Three other magicians had returned, ostensibly to have an intervention, to keep him from tipping over the edge, but there were various hidden agendas. Two of them were hoping to steal his greatest trick, The Disappearing Dame. One of them wanted the Great Guilfoyle's patronage, because his name was still a known factor in Las Vegas, and his protégé would have more doors open to him. One of the other magicians' assistants still carried a torch for Guilfoyle and there was a hint that they'd possibly had an affair. Another assistant was certain that Guilfoyle's late assistant had had an affair with her husband. And finally, a writer hoping to write a sensational true crime book had insinuated himself into the gathering.

I was impressed with Marni's foresight to hire an actual magician to set the scene and create the aura for the evening. This way, the audience would be buzzing with that "how'd he do that" mind tilt that always happened to me after a good magic show.

This event was completely booked, which was totally a tribute to the actors hired. In the relatively short time I'd been working around the House, one thing I had realized was that the level of promotion of events was pretty paltry. Secretly, I had a feeling Roxanne, Marni's counterpart with the province who oversaw the historic site aspects, was willing these things to fail. Her view was that people should just appreciate the fact that we had these lovely resources being preserved for us. Marni would knock herself out to get events organized, to help promote the House. But for some reason, all the energy went into the creation of the event; putting out advertising became almost an afterthought. As a result, the board of directors for Rutherford House were seriously considering pulling special events from the roster and focusing their energies entirely on the tea house and tours.

Marni had something to prove with this event. Two or three of the board members had apparently signed up for the mystery dinner. Luckily, thanks to Marni's decision to hire actors from the talented crew who populated the Die-Nasty Live Soap Opera, the improvisational theatre that had flourished for over two decades in town, word was getting around and tickets were selling.

Once it was learned that Die-Nasty actors were involved in a mystery dinner theatre, the phone had rung off the hook and tickets were gone within a day. With any luck, the theatre lovers would become House patrons and this would be exactly the sort of cross-pollination that Marni had been hoping for all along. If she could prove that these events promoted the House, her programming would live to serve another term.

There is just nothing like a little job-on-the-line pressure to bring up the pitch in someone's voice. Today, as everything came to a head, she was beginning to sound like Topo Gigio. Already, I was regretting agreeing to help her with the set-up. Another couple of hours of shrill was going to send me to the ibuprofen bottle. Pasting a plastic smile on my face, I nodded and agreed to bring up more chairs from the basement, and then to set out the candelabra table centres for the tea room, to match the set-up in the Rutherfords' dining room. The mystery elements at the dinner could be stymied by the popularity of the event, since the guests would be eating in three separate areas, the dining room, the glassed-in sun porch, and the inner room of the tea house. Still, savvy actors could create events in each room to bring out the necessary information.

I love mystery dinners. The aspect of having to listen carefully to each actor, who was salting his or her dialogue with hints or clues, then setting everything you had heard against what was on the clue board and coming up with a solution, has always appealed to me. I had treated Steve to one once, though, and he hated it. Although the steak dinner had been terrific, he had felt the entertainment to be more like work than play. Personally, I think it was because he guessed wrong and didn't win. His defence was that, since they were actors, they all seemed to be lying to him.

Marni didn't think it was necessary for me to be at the rehearsal process for the actors, so I wasn't altogether certain how the evening was going to progress. The only thing I knew for certain was that the victim was going to be played by Tanya

Rivera, because she had to be across town at the Mayfield Dinner Theatre for an eight o'clock curtain. The concept was that Miriam Stewart, playing one of the magicians' assistants, would lead people upstairs to the Rutherfords' bedroom and discover Tanya's body in the long walk-in closet. They would cover her in a sheet and lead people downstairs to wait for the "police detective," who I was certain would be dressed in a trench coat and homburg.

Once everyone was downstairs, I was to give Tanya the high sign and she would sneak down the maid's staircase and out to the side driveway, where her car was parked. From there on in, photos that had been already posed and shot would be used on the clue board.

In movies, time is often treated in a montage format, so that before you know it, days or hours have passed and all the people have arrived and put on running shoes, or built a barn, or got into the shape required to box for glory. While it never quite rings true to viewers, I swear sometimes it just happens in real life. Although I don't recall hearing an Oscar-worthy song playing, between bringing in Stephen Dafoe's plastic totes and being given the final pep talk as a group by Marni before the doors were opened on the evening's event, time seemed to fly by in a blur. People arrived, props were placed where required, a bulletin board was set up in Mr. Rutherford's study, and the dining tables were set and ready. Dafoe was organized to perform at the west end of the front parlour, to a standing audience. After his half-hour show, the patrons would disperse to their tables. Two actors would eat in the dining room, one at each table in the inner part of the tea room, and two more in the sunroom addition. Those places were marked reserved. The rest of the seats were up for grabs.

Marni looked us all over. The actors playing erstwhile magicians and assistants were dressed in various combinations of tuxedos and fishnets and satin. Dafoe, in contrast, was wearing a loose corduroy suit, looking more like a junior high social studies teacher than a magician. The three of us assigned the tasks of keeping visitors out of restricted areas and away from artifacts were in the standard white shirt, dark skirt, and tights.

The actors had all been introduced to us and seemed very nice. Tanya Rivera asked me to take her through the path she'd have to creep along in order to leave unobserved. As we walked up the stairs, she asked about my job, seeming genuinely interested. With her BBC English accent, almost anything she said sounded gracious, and I found myself describing the goals of the website historical project in more detail than I usually offered.

"Of course, working on history is supposed to help us speak with the dead, but I don't think they had this in mind. It's fun, though, to participate in these sorts of events and I think they will likely attract more people to the history of the House as a byproduct than anything I might put up on the website."

"It's true what Woody Allen said, isn't it," Tanya mused. "Ninety per cent of success is just showing up. Anything that makes people talk about Rutherford House, or brings people to it, is good news for Rutherford House in general."

"Right, so Marni's special events concept is one I can really get behind. It's just that I'm not too certain the board feels the same way. This evening may be the breaking point. At least we have a full house of participants. If everyone who is here tonight tells two people, and they tell two people…"

"As I recall, this results in a screen-ful of people with shiny, flippy hair," Tanya deadpanned, and I laughed.

"Well, whatever it takes," I said. "Here, madame, is your closet. Lovely and spacious and dark and creepy. Just what the director ordered."

"Eww, yes, well what do you expect when the director is your husband?" Tanya laughed. "Mark knows I hate enclosed spaces. Do you think we could keep the door ajar?"

"I think, honestly, we would have to if we want anyone to even look in here. There are several doors that will be closed and locked to the public, so they could overlook it entirely if we don't call attention to it. The only problem is that, from the way the house has settled over time, the door's inclination is to swing shut."

"Hmmm, perhaps I should wedge one of my shoes in the jamb, keeping it from closing completely. And the sight of a jewelled satin slipper should be anachronistic enough in this room to bring the perspective this way."

"That sounds good to me. How soon after the dinner do you have to slip away up here? I can make sure there is no one on the stairs."

We plotted her retreat a bit more and settled on some hand signals to let me know when she'd be on the move from the dinner table and when she would have to lie doggo in order to be found by Miriam and the trailing crew.

Once the play logistics were all satisfactorily organized to Marni's specifications, I was sent back to help Stephen Dafoe as best I could. From what I could tell, he had everything under control, but he didn't seem to be intent on shooing me away, so I hung around.

He had set up a tripod table at the end of the room, centred so he could stand to either side or behind it. With Marni's permission, he had drawn the west curtains. I guess it wouldn't do to have some anthropology student from the Tory Building wandering over and peering through the window to steal a trick. To be generous, it might have had something to do with sun glare.

Dafoe himself had changed from his corduroy outfit into tuxedo trousers and a swirling jacket that was almost a cape; it was fitted at the front, but swung from the shoulders into a wide back. The collar stood up, and shone with a satin finish. The reflection from the satin highlighted the arch to his eyebrows and made his eyes seem blacker. Perhaps it really was true that clothes made the man.

He noticed me staring at him and smiled, which really didn't do all that much to put me at ease. It was a carnival smile, half-amused, half-cruel. It was a smile that was looking for the next sucker.

"Magic is what people want it to be, Randy. I may call you Randy?" I nodded, once again ruing the fact that my face was, as my boyfriend Steve would say, more transparent than glass. "If we hope to deliver illusions to the masses, we must dress the part, which is danger. No one trusts what they cannot explain, and what you cannot trust, you fear. Ergo, if we open the door to fear just a bit from the beginning, we have set the stage for the audience to buy into the whole experience."

"Maybe you could just get a rabbit with fangs," I suggested, trying to lighten the mood. The chill in the room couldn't entirely be the fault of the ancient boiler. Dafoe laughed, and with that the illusion disappeared. He once again seemed like the nice man whose rubber storage boxes I'd help schlep in a couple of hours ago. Almost done his preparations, he pointed out a few things. On a hat stand to the right was hung a wizard's cape, a top hat, a furled umbrella, and a cane. To the left was a purple box on wheels with green and blue and gold question marks painted all over it. These, he said, contained his illusions. From the table in the centre, he would perform what he called "close magic," which used cards and water.

As he said "water," he pulled a goldfish bowl, complete with placid orange fish, out from under his coat and set it on the table. Startled, I laughed and clapped, and Dafoe produced a short Prussian bow.

"That was wonderful! Marni actually wanted to know if you needed me for anything—to hand you things or make sure people are standing in a certain formation, that sort of thing."

"I'm not sure I brought along the sequined costume," he began, and then laughed again at the horror of my reaction. "Relax, I was only joking. I appreciate the offer, but," and he swirled his cape around for effect and turned his face once more into the devilish mask, "I work alone."

If that wasn't a curtain line, I had never heard one. I did my best heel-clicking bow to him in return and left the room.

3

I was on my way upstairs, where Roxanne had sent me to close off the door to Marni's office and the adjacent door to the attic, where we kept all the extra artifacts and seasonal props like Canada Day bunting, to make sure no one went rummaging about in those rooms during the event, when I heard the front doorbell jingle. People had begun to arrive. I hurried down the stairs, carefully re-hooking the velvet rope stretched across from newel post to newel post, to help Jossie, the waitress, deal with the coats. We had a coat rack on wheels for the event, because we were pretty sure the Arbour closet wasn't going to suffice. Earlier, I had helped stick the double tags of numbers on each hanger, and now we dutifully took jackets and raincoats, and handed the owner one of the tickets. Marni had told us that the service was free, but that if we were to set out one of Mrs. Rutherford's pretty cut-glass bowls near the closet, we might receive some tips by the end of the evening. I noticed Jossie had found a suitable bowl and even primed the well by setting two coy twoonies and a loonie at the bottom. She winked at me, and we continued to work until it seemed like the entire house was full, and the coat closet smelled of a damp flock of sheep in a soggy forest. It had started to rain while we were setting up, and I hadn't noticed, really, until the first sodden visitors had begun to arrive.

This sort of weather wasn't enough to dampen Edmontonian spirits, though, and none of us had worried that it might keep people from coming to the event. After all, it had been such a mild autumn so far. A little rain was nothing to people who lined up in -20°C weather on Boxing Day to get door-crasher specials from The Brick. Edmontonians kept shovels and Kitty Litter for added traction in the trunks of their cars throughout the winter, along with survival kits in case they got stuck. In the last couple of winters, record lows had been broken (along with record highs—the weather really was unpredictable) and there had been no discernible exodus from our fair city.

When I had been studying for my MA, I attended a conference on Canadian literature. I recalled some phlegmatic undergrad asking the panel why it seemed like all Canadian novels had such a focus on the environment. I think it had been Professor Dick Harrison who had drily replied, "Canadians respect the weather because here the weather can kill you." It was true, but like any adversary, if you had a healthy respect for it, and made preparations with it in mind, you could live a pretty pleasant life.

More umbrellas were arriving than usual. In fact, I had noticed recently that more Edmontonians were using traditional umbrellas. Maybe we were experiencing more constant rain, or maybe they were tired of replacing cheaper collapsibles that stripped themselves backwards in an up-gust of wind. Jossie offered to run upstairs and grab another umbrella stand while I stayed on duty for more outer gear. You know you're working in a historic building when you have access to more than one umbrella stand. I was just hoping she wasn't going to come downstairs with an ancient elephant's foot. I'd seen one of those at the Victoria and Albert Museum once and didn't want a replay.

I needn't have worried. I doubt Premier Rutherford would have allowed such an unenlightened object into his house. He had been a forward-thinking visionary of a man, perhaps not as effective a political animal as some might have wished for, but a decent man with such wonderful ideas that few could stand in his way. There was a story of him luring Henry Marshall Tory from the east to what was then a huge meadow along the side of the North Saskatchewan River and saying, "I want to build a great university here and I want you to run it." Rutherford was not an easy man to say no to, and Tory became the first president of the University of Alberta, with the only truly "ivory" tower on campus named after him.

The large bamboo basket, which Jossie had finally returned with, soon filled up as well, but just as we were considering using a cauldron from the kitchen, a bell rang in the front staircase area, and we realized that the evening had begun. Sure enough, as we filled in behind the rear of the crowd, Marni was standing on the stairs, where so many speeches had been made, explaining the logistics of the evening to eager, upturned faces. Everyone seemed prepared to have a lovely time, except perhaps for the short, old woman glowering by the entrance to the study. Her squatness was made even more obvious in contrast to the tall elegance of the two men near her, one university-aged and the other an older gentleman. I wondered briefly if she could be one of the actors, already in character, but although both she and the older man looked familiar, I knew she hadn't been milling about earlier in the afternoon. She was a guest, not a helper. I made a note to myself to ask Marni if she knew who it was. Maybe she wasn't actually annoyed with anything, either; she could be a person whose face actually had frozen the way our mothers warned us about when we pulled ugly looks at them. Giving her the benefit of the doubt, I squeezed around the crowd to situate myself at the inside edge of the parlour door, telling myself it would behoove me to be able to retreat easily when having to go help Tanya, but knowing it was just a matter of my really wanting to be able to observe Dafoe da Fantabulist's act, which Marni was about to usher the crowd in to behold.

The magician was nowhere to be seen, but since I'd entered the room, he had erected a screen, made of a shimmering black curtain, which covered the back wall. People began to stream into the parlour, but in an orderly fashion, with no one moving forward past the glittering golden rope that had been placed straight across the floor in front of the magician's area. As the room began to fill, we became aware of a soundscape that had started so softly, I doubt any of us could say when it had actually begun. Almost familiar orchestral music, which toyed with recognizable themes but veered away just as you were about to name the piece, started to swell; and, just as magically, the chattering in the crowd fell silent.

Cymbals crashed in the music, and the shimmering curtain shuddered and suddenly there stood Dafoe, looking even more diabolical than I had noticed before, due to a cleverly positioned low light from somewhere near his tiny table, which made his eye sockets deepen and his cheeks cadaverous. I heard a couple of people gasp in surprise, and I knew that this was going to be a great magic show.

As the fish he'd magicked for me earlier swam about in his little glass world, Dafoe made decks of cards fly about, fanning them to show each and every number and suit, and then re-fanning them so that they were all the queen of spades. He pulled eggs out of the ears of people closest to him, broke them into the fish bowl, produced a wand to stir up the mess, and covered the bowl with a silk cloth. Tapping the bowl three times, he pulled away the cloth and displayed a small cage holding a happy little hamster running on a wheel. Before anyone started worrying about the fish that had been swimming with albumen a short time earlier, Dafoe excused himself, coughed politely and removed the fish from his mouth, then placed it in a sparklingly fresh bowl of water. People were applauding wildly before he even approached what he had told me were his actual illusions. He moved toward the hat stand and, taking the top hat, he pulled out a placid rabbit, two more hamsters, and a budgie, who politely sat on a tiny perch I had not previously noticed, built onto the top of the hat stand. Pushing the hamsters into separate cages and holding the rabbit under his arm, its long legs dangling as if it was a stuffed animal inured to being hauled up the stairs to bed, Dafoe continued to pull things out of the hat, only this time they belonged to people in the room. A pink, sequined cellphone was snatched back by a woman in the front. A wristwatch was dangled before a man who had to check his wrist to prove to himself it was actually gone. Keys were claimed by a young Asian man, who blushed for no reason I could think of, unless it was just the embarrassment of being singled out. When Dafoe pulled out a bra covered in Day-Glo green shamrocks, though, everyone laughed and no one stepped up to admit it was theirs. Feigning puzzlement, he stuffed it back in the hat and retrieved a bouquet of pussy willows, which he presented to an older woman with a sly wink, as if to say it was a fair trade for the lingerie she wouldn't own up to. More applause ensued.

Donning the swirling, long cape, Dafoe moved the tiny table behind the curtain and pulled the question-marked box on wheels to the centre of his stage. Turning it around and around, he demonstrated its construction. It had a latch at the top, which held up a side of the box. When undone, the side came down to show an empty box within, painted a dull black. Into this box, Dafoe placed the top hat. He re-latched the side, turned the box around twice, tapped it with his wand, and opened it up to show the hat had disappeared. He continued to do this with all the props—the hamster cages, one by one, the fish bowl, the tiny table, which folded as you lifted it up, and eventually, even the lop-eared bunny that had been draped over his left arm the entire time. Dafoe then removed his long cape, folded it into a compact square, and placed it into the box, disappearing it. Standing now on a stage containing only the hat stand with the budgie and the umbrella and the mysterious box, Dafoe silently took the umbrella off the stand, led the budgie with his finger onto his shoulder, bowed his clipped little half-forward bow, opened the umbrella towards the audience, setting off a poof of smoke, …and disappeared.

The place went wild with applause.

4

As Marni was ushering people into the dining areas, you could still hear them muttering and exclaiming about the amazing performance they had witnessed. I heard Mark Meyer, with a true professional's timing, move immediately into character as the MC of the magicians' reunion that was the heart of the mystery dinner theatre. People began to laugh and respond to the various actors at their tables and the party was soon in full swing. No one noticed the nondescript man in the brown corduroy suit who had come through the back door to help take down what was left of Dafoe da Fantabulist's set. After standing near the entrance to the parlour to be sure the dining room curtain was drawn, I nodded to him the all-clear and went up to offer help with the rubber containers that apparently had been behind the shimmery curtain the whole time. Dafoe calmly pulled open the parlour curtains and nonchalantly closed one of the windows. Between us we carried the containers to the back hall and set them in the kitchen room with the backdoor access. Marni had told me to offer the magician a meal, and he was happy to accept. I could only imagine the energy it took to perform such a concentrated and precise show. We sat in the maid's parlour up the back stairs and ate our food with our plates balanced on our knees. I didn't have much time, because I had to be ready to get Tanya spirited away to her corpse scene, but it was pleasant to see the return of the ordinary man with the nice manners. Like most westerners, we made the requisite remarks about the lack of early snow, and he mentioned how good it was to have another month of clear highway driving, since he lived out of town. He told me he had witnessed a car accident near the St. Albert Trail on his way here, and that led to a polite argument over whether or not the right lane could be considered for slower traffic when in the city. We deliberately talked about anything but magic, although he probably knew I was bursting like a little kid to ask him how he'd disappeared all his equipment. Man, if I could clean house with one of those boxes for just an hour!

Mostly, though, we talked about the House and about my project. Dafoe seemed really interested in the House itself, saying he'd never actually been inside before. I was thinking that Marni might be right on the money with her special events. All it took was to bring people through the door and the genial atmosphere and accessible history did the rest to charm folks into learning more about their own past. It was that sort of philosophy that had also built and maintained Fort Edmonton Park, the city's tourism jewel.

I excused myself from Stephen Dafoe and headed down the

stairs to keep an eye out for Tanya. Any minute now, she and Mark were going to stage an argument that had to take place in all three dining areas, after which she would be heading upstairs to get into place. It was my job to make sure no one saw her head upstairs.

From where I stood at the edge of the foyer, I could see into the dining room and straight down the hall that led to the Arbour restaurant area. The staircase in all its splendour rose before me, and the parlour, which now held no vestige of magic, unless you consider upright pianos to be magical even when they are not white and not in the middle of parks, lay to my right. Tanya came out of the dining room and around the newel post and deked up the stairs to take her place in the master bedroom closet, giving me a quick thumbs-up on her way. I removed the velvet rope from its hooks on either newel post, to allow access to the upper floor. Neil, the actor who was playing the murderer, was going to slink over to the parlour and stand out of sight next to the piano for a count of twenty, until we all heard Mark shout, "Hang on a second, where's Tanya?" and that would be the cue for the guests and actors to get up and move about. Right on time, the action moved forward and the game was afoot.

I moved against the tide toward the breakfast nook. It was also our cue to clear away the dinner plates and reset with dessert forks. We would be serving coffee and dessert as the actors did the big reveal and tallied up the ballots cast by the patrons to see who had come closest to guessing the murderer and the reasons for the crime. People were still milling about a bit, and I

Janice MacDonald

wove in and out, carting dirty plates down the steep stairs to the kitchen and coming up with the crumb broom and pan.

Guests were certainly getting into the spirit of the game. The House rang with the thumping about of feet, and I had a sudden idea of what it must have sounded like in the years when it was a fraternity house. I gingerly moved one woman's open purse from the table to the seat of her chair, marvelling at her general trust in her fellow man. Of course, perhaps there was nothing of value but tissue in her purse, merely what one supposed Queen Elizabeth kept in hers.

Taking another tray of dirty dishes downstairs, I noticed Roxanne sitting at the till-desk, reading. I suppose someone had to man the gift shop, since it was open to anyone passing through to use the washrooms, but it was annoying to see her doing nothing while I navvied. Better yet, I was scolded by the chef, who told me that we had to hurry up or they'd be returning to unset tables. I wasn't totally sure what he was talking about, since most of the tea-room area was reset, but on my next trip upstairs, I peered into the dining room, where I had thought Jossie had been doing much the same as I.

It was still a mess, with dinner plates at each place. While I had presumed we'd been working in tandem, she had apparently skyved off and wasn't pulling her weight. I cursed, thinking she had probably got caught up in the game, and conveniently decided her role was to guard things where the fun and action was, leaving the menial tasks to me. Never mind the fact that I had signed on for this for the extra cash, she was getting paid for her time as well and should be earning it.

There is nothing like righteous indignation to set me to work at a fierce pace. Muttering under my breath about pretty undergrads with far too much of a sense of entitlement, I had the dining room bussed for dinner plates, swept, and set for dessert in record time. I did a double-check of the breakfast nook and was just peering into the sunroom to assure myself I hadn't forgotten anything when the screaming began.

5

It was coming from upstairs, and I grinned at the fact that I had been startled, even when I had expected it. Tanya's "body" must have been found, artfully draped into the master bedroom closet. The sound of footsteps racing up the front stairs confirmed my suspicions. Pretty soon we would hear Mark Meyer declaiming, "She's dead. My beautiful assistant is dead," and the whole crowd would be ushered back down to the parlour for a visit from the constabulary, played by Andrew MacIvor-Smyth. I had seen him in the basement, dressed in a trench coat and flipping through a coil-bound notebook, too preoccupied by reviewing the clues he had to highlight to do anything but smile and nod as I went by.

I looked around for Marni, as I intended to complain to her about Jossie. I knew this evening had to go well in order for special events to continue at the House, but bussing tables wasn't what I had been hired for. While I wasn't averse to pitching in, being left to do all the menial chores still burned. She would be told that her junior staff was not pulling their weight. So what if I didn't get invited out for drinks with the wait staff? Honestly, what could we possibly have in common, anyhow?

As I waited for the patrons to come back down the stairs, it occurred to me that something was wrong. For the first time since the beginning of the evening, the timing was off. Mark still hadn't called out his line, the thumping about and thrumble of voices upstairs was still happening, louder and shriller than before, and the screamer, who had finally ceased her high-level alarum, sounded as if she was hiccoughing and crying, which seemed a bit much even for the actors involved.

There was another thing. The locus of all the sound was coming from the wrong side of the house.

I took one look at the front vestibule and knew I would never manage to push my way up there, so instead, I took a shortcut through the passage beneath the main staircase and ran up the steep maid's stairs at the back of the house, the ones we had intended to sneak Tanya down right about now. I eased past the maid's sitting room, where I had eaten with the magician, and noted a dirty dish sitting on the floor. Picking it up reflexively, I moved into the upper hall, where most of the guests and actors were standing, alternately stricken or puzzled. The crying seemed to be coming from the guest room, directly across the hall from the master bedroom, where the focus should have been.

Curious, I pushed forward; and, dressed in my apron and carrying dishware, I must have registered as official enough to warrant the movement. People stepped back, and I soon found myself in the sunny bedroom with the yellow ceiling, which Mrs. Rutherford had had painted in order to bring cheer to any guests of the House. Marni was standing with her arm protectively around a young woman who was convulsively sobbing quietly, and behind her a small knot of people stood in shock, staring toward the guest bathroom. I had to step fully into the room to look in the direction they were all aimed at, and when I did, I almost dropped the Limoges plate in my hand.

Lying in the bathtub, in a hideous pantomime of spa relaxation, was Jossie Jaque. She had one shoe on, and the other was lying far under the claw-foot tub as if it had been kicked there. Her apron was askew, and the front of her blouse looked as if it had been ripped. An arm dangling over the near side of the tub showed marks near her wrist akin to a bruise, and her nails were broken. The worst thing, though, was her eyes, which seemed to be looking with horror through the open doorway toward us. Her head was twisted at an unrealistic angle, and even from here I could see that she was quite dead.

I am not sure how long I stood there before I processed the fact that Marni was saying my name. I pulled my eyes away from the horror before me and turned toward my boss.

"Randy, would you please go downstairs and call the police?"

Shaking myself aware, I nodded. I was about to leave the room, when some of the senses that must have rubbed off from dating a policeman for so long kicked in.

"Marni, perhaps we should get everyone downstairs and out of this room and make sure that no one leaves before the police get here, too."

She looked at me and I could see in her eyes the weariness and woe that would mark the next few weeks for us all. Nothing can rule your life like being stuck in a murder investigation, even peripherally. Just ask me about it.

"Good idea. I will move everyone out of this room. Please have the actors help you seat everyone in their dinner places, and perhaps Chef can serve dessert while we await the police."

On the surface, it may have sounded cavalier, but I could see the value in keeping everyone calm and carrying on, as it were. Besides, if they were all seated, we could keep track of them better. I ran down the stairs and grabbed the telephone in the hall, hoping 911 would have GPS coordinates to Rutherford House, because I was in no condition to give them directions.

The operator put the call through to the police immediately. I explained the situation, requesting as many officers as possible to help with the rather large group of patrons in the House, and then signed off. I was told to be at the front door to identify myself to the detectives and officers on their arrival.

As soon as I hung up the phone, I ran downstairs with the plate I'd pulled from the maid's room and grabbed the cellphone I rarely used but now always carried from my purse, which was tucked away in the cubby at the back of the kitchen.

I needed my own personal cavalry. I hit speed-dial and called Steve.

6

Steve got the gist of what I was saying without too much extrapolation. After all, he knew where I was working, and I'd gone on at length about the whole mystery event two nights earlier, when we'd been out for dinner together. Making sure I'd already put through the emergency report, he told me to follow their directions, praised me for thinking to secure the crime site, and warned me to be careful till he got there.

"If everyone is sitting at their places at the table, you've got to figure the murderer may still be there. Do not hide yourself off in any hidden alcove. Be seen, be with people, and keep your back to the wall till I get there. Love you." And he hung up the phone.

Trying to follow both his and the 911 operator's instructions, I positioned myself in the front hall, by the door to the vestibule. From here I could see through the glassed doors to Saskatchewan Drive, which soon would be awash in blinking red and blue lights. I could also see the entrance to the dining room and the breakfast nook, and the hallway leading to the back exit.

Most of the guests were now on the main floor, and I asked them to return to their seats, as the police would be arriving shortly. Mark and Tanya were coming down the stairs, arm in arm, with Tanya dangling her beaded shoes from one hand. She caught sight of me and hurried forward to hug me, likely seeking comfort from a familiar face in all the chaos. Or maybe she just hugged everyone.

"Oh my lord, can you believe this? I was just lying there and when that woman began to scream, I almost had a heart attack. There was something just so appalling about feigning death so close to where a life was actually being taken, I am just shaken."

"You're probably in shock. The police are coming right away, though, and Marni wants us all to go back to where we were seated for supper, if you can manage that. That way, we can try to maintain some sense of calm for the rest of the guests and preserve any clues for the police."

Somehow, my words transformed the two actors in front of me. It was as if I had uttered "the show must go on" in some grainy black-and-white '30s musical. Both of them seemed to grow an inch or two; squeezing hands, they smiled at each other gamely and separated to their set places. I breathed a sigh of relief. With these two troopers exuding grace over the tables where they sat, I was pretty sure we would be able to avert any hysteria or demands from the guests to leave before the officials got here, and we could then hand off everything to the trained professionals.

The ambulance arrived first, followed by a lit-up police car and an unmarked sedan, which pulled up behind it. I stood in the open doorway, explaining to the paramedics that the victim was very likely beyond their help, but directed everyone upstairs to the guest bedroom.

Behind the two uniformed officers came a man and woman in street clothing. She was wearing skinny black jeans and a tailored camel jacket over a black turtleneck, with a black satchel strap crossing over her chest. He was in jeans and wearing a windbreaker over a blue-and-orange-striped polo shirt. They showed me their identification, even though I had actually met them once before, at Steve's office Christmas party. They were Detectives Nancy Gibson and Joe Howard, from the south-side division, the same precinct out of which Steve and his partner, Iain McCorquodale, worked. While I knew I would have been teased severely by Iain for getting myself involved in yet another spot of trouble, part of me wished it had been that duo heading things up in this situation. At least I would know where I stood.

I explained as briefly as I could the set-up of the evening, and what we had done to contain the guests, so that the police could speak with them all.

"Do you have a reservation list showing all the names of the people here tonight?" asked Detective Gibson.

"I'm sure there is a list, but I am not clear if everyone is listed or only the people who purchased the tickets. There were no place cards at the tables, if that's what you mean. We just knew we had a full house of sixty guests and six actors. Then, of course, there was Chef Bryan downstairs with Brad, the sous-chef, and

Kathy, the dishwasher. Roxanne Bachan, the chief interpreter, was downstairs, too. Marni Livingstone, the city manager, was here, along with Jossie and myself, and of course the magician, Stephen Dafoe."

Detective Howard picked up on the last name and likely my shift in tone.

"Magician? Is he still here?"

"Now that you mention it, I haven't seen him. We ate supper together up in the maid's quarters, to avoid the crush downstairs, and I had helped him move some of his totes into the back hall, so that he could load his car while dinner was still happening. Maybe he'd just left, before any of this happened."

"We'll need to get his contact information, at any rate," said Detective Gibson.

"I'm sure Marni has it for you," I responded, wondering where the heck Marni had got herself off to and why she wasn't the one dealing with all these questions. "Do you want me to see if I can find her for you?"

"Actually, if you wouldn't mind, we would appreciate it if you would help us conduct an initial viewing of the crime scene by pointing us in the general direction and then introduce the uniformed officers to your boss for help coordinating the interviewing of the guests."

"Sure, no problem. You'll want to go upstairs and to your left. The guest room is the front room to the right of the balcony area. She's in the tub in the guest-room bathroom."

"Wow, a private bathroom in a house this old?" Joe Howard looked impressed.

My history-nerd gene kicked in. "Aside from, arguably, the McGrath Mansion, Rutherford House was the premiere house in Edmonton for much of the early twentieth century. Built in 1912, it featured indoor plumbing, a stained glass skylight, Grecian colonnades, and an open sun porch that was later glassed in to protect against the western winds. As you can see, because it was built of brick from the newly formed Riverdale Brickworks, it stood apart from its wooden, stuccoed, and shingled counterparts. The private bath for guests, who often stayed for several weeks visiting from down east, was considered in the best diplomatic taste."

Detective Gibson grinned. "I didn't expect the guided tour, but thanks."

I blushed and began to stammer something about finding the other officers when Steve walked in the front door, causing both me and Inspector Gibson to light up. Inspector Howard stepped forward to greet him.

"Steve? I thought this was your night off?" he asked, shaking my boyfriend's hand.

Steve smiled grimly and nodded toward me.

"Hi, Joe. I see you've met my girlfriend, Randy? I'm really just here for moral support. What would you like us to cover for you?"

I walked back down the staircase, giving him a quick hug, as the detectives moved upstairs toward the crime scene. Telling Steve about our set-up of offering the guests coffee and dessert to keep them calm, I asked if he thought I should be offering the same to the waiting paramedics and uniformed officers.

"They'll be busy, I think, but it couldn't hurt. Take me to your boss, Marni Livingstone. I am going to have to see if we can set something up in the library or parlour, to streamline the interviews."

Marni turned out to be downstairs with her staff, concentrated on loading trays full of mini-trifles and sending them up the stairs with Kathy, who had shucked off her rubber apron in exchange for a waitress's cotton striped version. I introduced her to Steve, who informed her that the rest of the police had arrived and that he was merely helping out with the interview process to keep the guests from becoming too restless.

To my surprise, Marni, who had always displayed an almost glacial grace around me, actually turned and hugged Steve, whom she had only met a handful of times before this. Shock and trauma do strange things to people. She offered us a folding table to set up in the parlour, as she thought the library might be too overwhelming for some of the guests.

"It might be like being sent in to see the principal, with all those heavy leather tomes," she remarked, and Steve agreed. He and I schlepped the table up and clicked the legs in place. Marni had followed us with two business-like folding chairs. While it was anachronistic, it would suffice.

Steve and the officers sorted out a system. While he interviewed people singly in the parlour, one of the officers would direct people to Steve and the other would hand out pens and statement sheets for those waiting to fill out and sign. It was my job to bring them back to their places and settle them in with another cup of coffee or tea. It ran like clockwork, and Steve had soon worked his way through all sixty guests. Checking briefly with the detectives upstairs, he made an announcement that the guests could now leave, thanking them for their cooperation. Marni chimed in with apologies for the curtailment of their event and handed out vouchers for two-for-one high tea, which, I knew, was the only offer she had printed up. I guess it was better than nothing.

Only the actors were left. Tanya had been asked to call the Mayfield to have her understudy take the show there, since the detectives didn't seem to care about theatrical traditions. As a result, perhaps the theatrical tradition of some young girl getting her Ruby Keeler moment was happening across town even now.

One by one, they were sent in to see Steve, and their interviews took quite a bit longer than the guests' had, I suppose because they were observant by nature and had covered more area of the House than the average guest had done. Pretty soon, though, they too were putting on their coats. Steve had asked Mark to leave the clue board up, mostly because the detectives upstairs hadn't had time to get the entire lay of the land, but also because it might contain information about the general movement around the House that evening.

Marni saw the actors to the door. Mark stopped in the vestibule and seemed to be very concerned about something. Marni patted him on the arm and nodded, but he didn't seem particularly placated. Tanya pulled on his arm, and reluctantly he followed her out into the dark.

Now the only folks left in the House were staff, police

personnel, and one dead girl. I shivered. It was as if the presence of all the other people had been a buffer against the horror that a dead body always instilled in me, but now the memory of her lying broken in the tub upstairs filled my head like a nasty movie reel running on a loop. I caught sight of the medical examiner's team carrying the black-bagged remains of the same person I had earlier spent quality time with, hanging coats and storing umbrellas. You didn't need a Dali picture to feel surreal when having to wrap your mind around death. I could feel my legs buckling; luckily, I was next to the Rutherfords' low-slung settee in the parlour. I sat there, trying to remember to breathe deeply, trying to remember to feel grateful for the ability to breathe.

Steve came into the room and sat down beside me. He had wrapped up the interviews and had a bit of a confab with the detectives in charge, who then took over the staff interviews. The medical examiner and photographer were packing up their toolkits and leaving. The actors had gone, some of them choosing to leave their costumes and props in a bin next to the clue board, which I supposed Mark was going to come back to collect the next day, after the police were through with the House and things were back to normal.

Ha. From experience, I knew that once murder has been let in the door, nothing ever goes back to normal. Steve patted my back, which he had been stroking rhythmically, the way one does to a baby one is trying to put to sleep, and I knew it was time for my interview.

7

The table and chairs were still set up at the end of the room, where Dafoe da Fantabulist's magic show had wowed the crowd only a few hours before, though it seemed like it had been weeks. Weeks without sleep. I sat across from Detectives Gibson and Howard, who still seemed relatively composed, probably drawing on invisible coping skills to do this sort of job day in, day out.

Not that there are daily murders in Edmonton, of course. Or daily murders anywhere in Canada, for that matter. But somehow, perhaps, that was worse. Coping with the dreadful, when one had to do it every day, might eventually become second nature. To come face to face with the horror of violent death perpetrated on another, when it didn't happen as a rule, had to be a shock to the system, even if you were a hardened detective. I knew Steve didn't ever take it lightly, and I was sure these two didn't either. They only looked calm and collected.

Nancy Gibson took my statement from the pile.

"I know you have been busy helping us with our investigations this evening, and probably didn't get as much of a chance to fill in the blanks when you were writing down your statement, so I wonder if you'd mind if we were to tape this interview, and we could get someone to type up your statement tomorrow and you could come down to the station to sign it then."

I had been in a rush, getting people more tea to keep them calm, ushering them in to see Steve, finding their coats when they were allowed to go. Steve had initialled their coat tags, a way I had thought up of identifying them as being free to leave. I had taken the police-statement form with its self-copying paper beneath that everyone had dutifully filled out and jotted down bullet points, trying to lay out the timeline the best I could. A more fulsome statement would undoubtedly be better. I nodded, and as she turned on her tiny digital recorder, said, "Yes."

After asking me to state my name and address and purpose for being in Rutherford House that evening, Detective Gibson asked me to detail the events of the evening, both as they should have gone and as they actually played out. She and Detective Howard, who probably had a pretty good idea of the timelines after having interviewed Marni, Roxanne, and Chef Bryan, and having glanced through all the statements Steve had taken, let me talk, guiding me gently every now and then with a more probing question.

They were particularly interested in anything Jossie might have said to me while we were hanging coats. Did I notice that she seemed nervous or worried about anyone who had arrived as a guest? Was she in any way pensive or unlike herself? Did I notice anyone taking particular interest in her as they handed over their outerwear? Feeling as if I was somehow letting them down and proving myself as blissfully unobservant as Dr. Watson, I kept shaking my head and answering no to most of their queries.

They were also interested in my dealings with the magician, for whom Detective Howard had left a message on his home phone to make arrangements to meet the next day. I tried to recall for them what we had talked about over our shared supper in the maid's sitting room, but as far as I could tell, it had been me asking questions about the various venues at which he had performed magic, and our mutual discussion of whether or not this would be an easy winter, which was mostly what Edmontonians fell back on as a conversational gambit with strangers.

Eventually, I answered every possible question they could throw at me. Standing up a bit creakily, I stretched and yawned, excusing myself immediately. Detective Howard grinned.

"It's late, no worries. Good night. We'll see you tomorrow down at the station."

Just outside the parlour doors, I found Steve with Marni, who was waiting to lock up the House once the detectives packed up their table's worth of gear.

"We can clean up in the morning. I am just too bagged to do anything more than set the alarm tonight."

I hugged her, and she, who was always so entirely professional, hugged me back. She looked exhausted, as if the evening had drained three years of her life. It had been up to her to find Jossie's emergency contact information for the police, which would be Detective Howard's next call. I didn't envy him that conversation at all.

Steve had been giving her some tips on how we should operate in the days to come.

"There will be gawkers and reporters, and it's a toss-up who will be the most annoying," he grimaced. "Take tomorrow to clean things up and put things back to normal. Once you are reopened, if people ask, just tell them it is a tragic occurrence for your staff personally, whom you do not want disturbed, and a sad chapter for Rutherford House. Don't get drawn into anything, just tell people that it is a matter for the police at present. That should stop anyone legitimate in their tracks, and you can just ignore more persistent idiots."

"So, we are allowed to set things back to rights, upstairs, I mean?" I asked, meaning, of course, the guest bathroom, which would have to be cleaned of all the grey fingerprint dust and muddy footprints and last vestiges of a young woman I barely knew.

Steve nodded.

Marni still looked shell-shocked.

"I don't think we can leave something like this to the Bee Maids. We have such a strict hands-off-the-artifacts policy with them, how are we now going to expect them to scrub up blood and dust? No, I'm going to have to do this myself."

"I'll help you," I found myself volunteering. I just could not imagine Marni having to come in here alone and tackle the task. I saw Steve smile at me, whether because he was touched by my generosity of spirit or amused at my inability to walk away from vulnerability, I wasn't sure.

Marni and I made plans to meet up in HUB the next morning for coffee, and then tackle things together before a general staff meeting she was going to call at two. The detectives joined us in the lobby, and, after Marni had locked the doors and checked the alarm lights, we all went out into the damp October night together. Although the rain must have stopped while we were serving dinner, the sidewalks were still wet, and there were puddles reflecting the street lights all the way down the road.

I was happy to take a ride home from Steve. He pulled into a parking spot on the street and walked me to my apartment. Once we were inside my door, I began to shiver.

Steve ordered me into the shower, the hotter the better, even though it was past one in the morning and I was sure the pipes would wake up the old man who lived next door. I sluiced the sweat and fear and horror off me as I slowly began to warm up. Wrapped in a fuzzy bathrobe and a hair-towel turban, I padded out through my miniscule bedroom to discover that Steve had made tea and toast that he had brought into the living room on a tray. I sat down beside him, so close that I could feel his heat, and reached for a piece of marmalade-covered toast.

"You need heat and sugar for shock, and then you need sleep, Randy," he said, pouring me a cup of green tea, which was all I had in the house these days. I cupped my mug with both hands, loving the warmth pulsing through my fingers, and sipped at the too-hot tea. "How you get entwined in these situations, I will never know. What is it about the jobs you choose that makes you on the scene for murder?"

"I honestly have no idea. After all, it's not as if anything I do is remotely dangerous or edgy. It's not as if I go looking for it, either, though I'm pretty sure Staff Sergeant Keller thinks that's exactly what I do, like I'm some sort of ghoulish groupie who hangs on at murder sites."

"Oh God, Keller's just going to love this," Steve sighed.

"Maybe it will be okay, since it's not your case," I said hopefully."

Yes, I'm sure that will make all the difference to Keller," Steve laughed.

It really wasn't fair of Steve's boss to hate me so much. It's not like I obstructed police justice or, heaven forbid, caused murders to happen. I just had a knack for being in the wrong place at the right time. And it wasn't always a bad thing. In the past, I had been of some small aid to the police in their investigations. And of course, I would have never met Steve if a university student of mine hadn't been murdered. Talk about silver lining, storm cloud.

You know that phrase, "It's an ill will that blows no one good"? It took me a long time to realize that what it meant was that, no matter what happens, someone profits by it. All my life I had been parsing that sentence as a description of a particularly bad wind that indeed was evil to all ("What is that? That? Oh, that's an ill wind, the sort no one likes!"), rather than saying it would have to be a terrible wind that didn't benefit someone somehow. I guess I had been too used to all my grandmother's phrases, which were always so negative, to realize that for once she was trying to tell me to look for the bright side to things.

So murder had once brought me Steve. I wasn't sure he

would care to be thought of as a silver lining, but he had helped me through several other situations I'd found myself snagged in. But what had murder brought me this time? Was this wind, that had whipped through a seemingly placid workplace intent on raising its profile as a historic museum and tourism destination celebrating its centennial, going to do anything more than destroy? What good could trail in the wake of the murder of a young girl on the brink of adult life? Why the heck would someone kill anyone there, with more than seventy people milling about and ready to walk in on the act?

Nothing made sense except the warmth of the tea and the crunch of the marmalade-tart toast. I ate, brushed crumbs from the front of my robe, and then Steve walked me to my bed and tucked me in.

"Aren't you staying tonight?"

"I wish I could, but I can't. I have to be at the station early and I didn't bring anything but my phone and my gun to the House this evening. I'll set your alarm for eight thirty, and you can just roll out of bed and go meet Marni for nine thirty as you planned. Sleep well, Randy."

He kissed me, and turned out the lights.

I was asleep so quickly I am not certain I even heard the door close.

8

Aside from a few persistent puddles, the rain had dried up overnight, and it was looking to be a crisp fall day as I loped along toward HUB Mall to meet up with Marni. I had brushed my teeth and hair, but that was about all the grooming I was capable of, having slept hard and woken disoriented.

Since we would likely be scrubbing away police residue, I had deliberately chosen my more faded jeans, which thankfully were clean enough to seem "casual Friday" professional. A sweatshirt under my leather jacket was almost warm enough, but I was glad I had grabbed a scarf and mitts on the way out. Weather in Edmonton was always deceptive. We were the location that the layered look was invented for. By noon, I would likely be passing undergrad boys wearing board shorts and tank tops.

Marni, too, had chosen to dress for housecleaning rather than wear her usual professional garb. While she normally put her hair up in a simple chignon, today she was sporting a ponytail. She smiled as I walked up to the table in front of the breakfast place. I set down my coat and went over to order an egg sandwich and hash browns, figuring I deserved some carbalicious energy for the task ahead.

When I sat down, I noticed Marni was finishing off the same meal. Great minds think alike. As I ate, she filled me in on her plans. She had sent an email out to the whole staff, those who had been there last night and the rest, giving a brief summary of the situation and asking that everyone who could make it be at the two o'clock meeting in the House. Seeing as how the fall and winter part-time staff tended to be composed of students fitting in an odd shift here or there between classes, I wasn't totally clear how many people to expect.

She and I would clear up the evidence of the crime scene and the police presence, and try to set things back to normal from the mystery event as best we could. The more we could smooth things over physically, the less likely staff who hadn't been there last night would be to grieve the loss, or so we figured. Of course, I wasn't certain how many of the staff members knew each other well, let alone Jossie. There were never more than three or four people in the House any time I had ever been there during a normal shift.

We dawdled over our coffees, though. Neither of us wanted to be the first to head toward the crime scene. With a look and a shrug, we got up in unison and trudged together down the length of the mall. Exiting down the stairs at 9201, one of the stairwells of apartment doors, we went in the back door of Rutherford House, Marni entering the alarm code on the anachronistic plastic box inside the door. Apparently, the board had spent two hours discussing the addition of the alarm system, worrying that it would detract from the authenticity of the site. A series of burglaries in the area, around the same time as the Garneau Grabber had been operating, had swayed the vote in favour of security, and the insurance rates had gone down considerably as a result.

Security had done nothing for Jossie Jaque, of course.

Marni found us rubber gloves and buckets in the back of the basement kitchen. We filled them with hot water and Pine-Sol, then hauled them up two sets of stairs, trying not to slop over. The bathroom where Jossie had been found was a very confined space, but there was fingerprint dust everywhere, on the door frame, the sink, the mirror, and of course all around the tub itself. Marni decided to start with the walls, and I began with the porcelain, meaning the tub and sink. Guests of the Rutherfords had to use the same toilet facilities as the family, which was originally a water closet near where the staff offices were situated now, but apparently it was no problem to run pipes for a tub and sink to the guest room.

Getting the grey dust off the tub was easy. It was scrubbing the small patch of dried blood, which contained a few long brown hairs from where her head had hit the side of the tub, that made me nauseous. Like a Polaroid photo, her body reappeared in front of me, lying like a broken doll flung into the tub. I sat back on my heels and gulped air, trying not to be sick.

"Randy, are you all right?" Marni had stopped swabbing the door jamb and was looking at me.

"Yeah, I'll be okay. It's just all a bit much."

"I hear you. The police called her folks last night, but I am going to have to telephone them later today, and I just cannot wrap my mind around what I am going to say to them. After all, who would think that working as a waitress, hanging coats and pouring tea, would be a dangerous occupation? It's not even as if you have to worry about drunks and letches, either. Everyone who comes here is on their best behaviour."

"What did you know about her? As a person, I mean?" Perhaps talking about Jossie-the-living-person would erase Jossie-the-dead-body from behind my eyelids.

"Like most of the kids who work here on a part-time basis, she was a student. She wasn't a history major, though, which is sort of odd, because that's who we usually get. History majors and actors. I think Jossie was actually planning to go into museum curating, which was why she had taken the job. She saw it as a win-win thing, make some pin money while in school, but gain a little on-the-ground training in the general day-to-day of running a museum."

"I didn't know that. Was she useful in that respect?"

"To tell you the truth, if she wasn't such a hard worker when it came to the events, I would have likely figured out a way to get rid of her. She was just too useful, if you know what I mean. It's like every time I turned around, there she was, with a question about why I was doing something or had I ever tried doing something else. Not to speak ill of the dead, but it's not as if I was getting paid to train her in museum studies. At first it was kind of flattering, because God knows no one else thinks my job is in any way interesting. But after a while it got a bit tiring to always be answering questions."

Marni pushed a stray strand of hair behind her ear.

"Funny, eh, to be tired of questions? When all we do is answer questions about the Rutherfords and the House all day long?"

I smiled at her, and wrung my cleaning cloth into the hot water.

"No, I get what you're saying. Sometimes, when people ask questions about your methods and actions, it saps your energy. If you just do what you do, you're like a machine, clicking away. Once you have to concentrate on your movements, they get bigger in your head—heavier and harder. No wonder you feel tired. Those sorts of questions are not the same as the general House questions at all."

"That's it, exactly. So, while I'm shocked and horrified that she is dead, I can't pretend she was my very favourite person, and that somehow makes me feel even worse."

I patted Marni's shoulder with my rubber-gloved hand and moved past her to scrub the sink. Pretty soon, we were both scrubbing the tiled floor. We took our grimy water to the toilet and then refilled our buckets with hot clear water from the once-more shiny tub. One more clear rinse of the floor removed the gritty powder from the grouting, and we backed out of the bathroom to tackle the footprints of the police in the room itself.

The table and chairs in the parlour were taken back downstairs, and Marni had begun to vacuum the lobby while I moved tables back into their regular placement in the sunroom and breakfast nook. I was just coming upstairs with a tray of salt-and-pepper shakers for the tables, when I heard the vacuum cleaner go off and Marni opening the door. I poked my head into the lobby to see Mark and Tanya speaking with Marni.

"We've come to clear away our stuff," explained Mark. "The detectives called me this morning to say we could remove the clue board, since they'd taken pictures of it last night."

I nodded to Tanya, who seemingly took a moment to recognize me. I guess I didn't really look anything like the woman in black who had been detailed to help her the night before. Today, I was without makeup, wearing a green sweatshirt and jeans, with my hair in a ponytail. I was more like a forty-something *Bye Bye Birdie* extra than an efficient Mrs. Danvers. To her credit, she smiled anyway, and then followed Mark into the library to clear away the actors' materials.

Marni looked at her watch, and then rewrapped the vacuum cord onto its pins.

"Once we get the library put to rights, we will be pretty much done. I think we should get staff to meet in the dining room. People will be arriving in the next ten minutes or so. Could I get you to go down and get the kettle ready for tea? Several pots of plum and elderberry tea, along with some of the scones reheated in the microwave should do us."

Nodding, I headed downstairs to do Marni's bidding. It occurred to me that I would have to be pretty clear on my job specs from here on in. I didn't mind pitching in for her because of the unfortunate circumstances, but I had been hired to write and research for the virtual museum, not to work as a waitress or cleaning lady. If I bent too far, it would be my own fault, because managers like Marni were perfectly capable of learning to consistently expect what had been delivered to them once or twice.

I wasn't sure if staff meetings were conducted formally, but I opted for a more casual concept. As the kettle boiled, I brought up napkins, side plates, and a handful of spoons and knives. Another trip with a tray of teacups and raspberry butter pots, and I was ready. All that would be required was to pour boiling water into the ten teapots I had loaded and ready in the kitchen, and I wasn't going to do that until the staff actually arrived. This was a specialty tea house, after all. Someone would be bound to complain of over-steeped tea.

I started to pour hot water into the pots as I heard the bells ring on the front door. People were arriving. I checked my watch to note that it was still only quarter to two. There's just nothing like a devastating incident to get people to work on time.

I hauled up the tea tray and smiled at Brad and Kathy, who were already sitting in the dining room. They were tea house kitchen staff. Roxanne, the head interpreter, was shrugging off her coat in the hallway. Chef Bryan was at the door, speaking with Marni. We were still waiting on three servers, two part-time interpreters and Harold, the man who did the bookkeeping and ordered stock for the gift shop. Marni had said that every one had agreed to come in, which was why I was shooting for a dozen of everything for this meeting.

I hurried down to pull the brown paper bag of scones out of the microwave. Not having the time or desire to bake something fresh in the midst of cleaning up crime scenes, we'd pulled some frozen scones from the freezer and set them to thaw. Dribbling a bit of water on the outside of the paper bag before microwaving returned them to their piping hot status, and I shook them out onto three serving plates.

Now, everyone had gathered upstairs. I set the scones down in the centre of the table. People were already helping themselves to tea. The seat at the head of the table was empty, tacitly reserved for Marni. I wiped my hands on my House apron and took a place next to Harold. He smiled at me and whispered, "You were here last night, right?" I nodded, and he was about to say something more when Marni came into the room, having locked the front door and reset the Closed sign in the window.

"Thank you all for coming. Before anyone starts to worry, you will all be paid three hours for your time today," Marni announced to nervous laughter. She sat at the head of the table, and although I had seen her just an hour earlier, grubbing about in cleaning gear, she was now glacially managerial. Somehow, while I was schlepping teacups, she had smoothed and pinned up her hair, changed into a cashmere pullover she must have had on hand in her office, and tidied her makeup. Every face at the table was turned to hers, rapt. Management skills include the little things, like dressing for success, which is why I would likely die an academic freelancer.

"I wanted us all to get together to bring everyone up to speed. I was trying to be circumspect in my email to you earlier, but for those of you who weren't here at the mystery event last night, I am sorry to tell you that it ended in tragedy and one of our own, Jocelyn Jaque, was murdered and found dead in the guest-room bathtub. We will, of course, be trying to underplay this event in any tours that happen, although I am afraid the news will leak out. About sixty guests at the event either saw the body or heard about it, and they all knew where the police were focusing their attentions. It is up to us not to let this overshadow the rest of the history of the House. While tragic, this will eventually be only another incident, not one we will bring up immediately, though we will likely respond with accurate information when it is known to us."

She took a deep breath.

"The police have taken statements from everyone at the event. They may want to take statements from the rest of you as well, or those of you who knew and worked with Jossie."

Roxanne raised her hand.

"Yes, Roxanne?" Marni asked drily. There was no love lost between these two, I had noticed in the relatively short amount of time I had been working at the House. Marni was a City of Edmonton employee, commissioned to make the House, the tea house, and the gift shop a profitable concern along the lines of Fort Edmonton Park. Roxanne, on the other hand, was a provincial employee, hired by the Ministry of Culture to oversee the care and maintenance of a registered historic site and educate visitors to its importance. She didn't concern herself with the general day-to-day aspects of keeping the House afloat, which was probably why she had refused to do anything for Marni's mystery event the night before except sit like a lump in the basement gift shop.

"I had very little dealings with any of the tea house part-time staff, as you know. I don't see how my statement last night was of any use. I didn't know the girl personally and hardly even knew what she looked like. Since so many of your staff are part-timers, they might not be able to offer much help to the police."

"Jossie was the same age as me, only taller and with long straight brown hair," volunteered Chloe, who sat across from me.

"She had the face of a Byzantine saint," stated the second dishwasher, Jimmy. I looked down the table at him, a middle-aged, dark-complexioned man, and wondered at the imagery. I also wondered what normally quiet Jimmy had done for a living in his home country before heading to the riches of North America.

"I am sure the police will offer you all a photo to examine, should they decide to interview you. Thank you for mentioning that, Roxanne," Marni said politely. "In the meantime, we have to determine our timetable for the coming days. I have been informed there may be a police presence in the House from time to time, which is not something we will be able to control. We may wish to cordon off the guest room, though we were given permission to clean away the residue of the police investigation, which Randy and I managed to accomplish this morning." She nodded down the table to me as she mentioned my name, and for some reason I felt Roxanne glaring at me.

"So, I'd like, with your permission, to set the tea house work schedule for the coming weeks as usual, but warn you that we might have to close on a dime if the police determine they require the premises. Likewise, we have to maintain tour hours with an eye to having officers coming and going. Officers in uniform and detectives showing their ID will, of course, not be charged admission."

I almost laughed, but I guess it had to be said. Roxanne and her minions were sticklers for making people pay their $4 admission. It was a sore spot with Marni, especially when they tried to halt people obviously only coming through for lunch at the tea room.

"People will very likely be asking you all about the murder, as they read about it in the papers or hear about it on the news. When you reply, please remember you are a representative of Rutherford House and the dignity it stands for. If you can turn their curiosity into more visits, all the better. But, we do not want this turned into a Firkin House situation, by any means. Am I clear on that?"

Everyone nodded. The Firkin House was one of the historic houses that had moved to Fort Edmonton Park, and it had a reputation for being haunted. The provenance of the "ghost" was unclear, and most of the stories had likely arisen from the amount of time the house had stood empty and lonely on Saskatchewan Drive before being moved to its present home on the Park's 1905 Street. Interpreters at Fort Edmonton, many of them connected to the Rutherford House staff in one way or another, despaired of being able to offer accurate historical information when visitors only wanted to know if they had ever seen a ghost.

Interestingly enough, the Firkin House was situated right next door to the first Rutherford House in Fort Edmonton Park. Made of wood and various add-ons, the first house was still quite impressive, but had nothing of the grandeur afforded by the second house, this brick mansion where we all now found ourselves.

We had been steadily demolishing the scones as Marni spoke, and as the meeting dribbled to a close, most of us stuck around to clean up after ourselves. Roxanne and her two interpreters, Dawne and Arlene, did not lower themselves to such a task, of course, leaving us to clear their teacups away as they convened in the front hall. Trying to be charitable, I supposed she was giving them their work schedules, but casting a glance back up the table at Marni, I saw that the slight had not gone unnoticed.

This whole arrangement of running of the House by two different parties made for quite a bit of friction, as far as I could see, although the veneer of polite, early-twentieth-century tea-time etiquette tried to gloss over it all. Well, what was Canadian history without a house divided now and then? Just as long as we didn't get stuck in another referendum.

I helped tidy by bringing the dishes downstairs, then considered my duties complete. After all, I'd been in early to do grunt work, while all these other folks were going to get paid the minimum three hours for coming in for a short meeting. They could do the dishes. I grabbed my coat and headed back up the stairs, intending to say my goodbyes to Marni on the way out.

The interpreters were no longer in the hallway, but I could hear voices coming from the dining room.

"Greta Larsen spoke with me last night." That was Roxanne's voice.

"Yes, I thought she might. I spoke with her and her grandson briefly when they arrived," Marni was responding, her voice having taken on the same tired tone it always had whenever she was speaking with Roxanne.

"She is not pleased with the situation, you realize."

"Roxanne, I don't think anyone is pleased with the fact that a young woman was murdered. I spoke with Walter Karras last night, too, and he assured me the board is not going to be holding me responsible for this. As chair, he will be informing the rest of the board. The police are involved. Let them come up with some conclusions as to what has happened before you and the Greta Larsens of the world begin assigning blame, please."

I decided this was a conversation I didn't want to break in on. My role as contractor was tenuous enough, given that I was being paid by the province but had been brought in and ultimately hired by Marni. I had been walking the tightrope of trying to be equally pleasant to both of them. While I had to admit I liked Marni better, I couldn't afford to play favourites when it came to holding down the job.

I let myself quietly out the front door and walked home along Saskatchewan Drive, then up the path behind the High Level Diner. On an impulse, I popped into the Diner to pick up two of their breakfast muffins to go. If Steve stayed over tonight, I could heat them up and slather them with butter for a splendid breakfast in bed.

Since I had spent most of the morning housecleaning elsewhere, it seemed too much of an effort to do anything but tidy up the pile of newspapers and clear away the dishes in my own sink. I had an urge to pamper myself and ran as hot a bath as I could stand. The parallel between Jossie's last resting place and my bubbly tub were a bit close, but I sank into the water grate-fully, stalling only briefly in that moment of burning breathless-ness when one tries to get used to the heat before stretching out into a position that was sort of creepily similar to the dead girl's.

Why had she been upstairs in the guest bathroom, anyway? Her particular job had been to hang coats and keep people from touching artifacts in the parlour once the game had begun, after we'd reset the tables. I was the one who was supposed to follow Tanya upstairs and mind that things stayed all right there. Of course, Jossie's body had been found before the participants had really been given a chance to spread through the house.

So, where was Jossie supposed to be during the dinner and table entertainment? Had she been busy being murdered while I was just a few metres away, eating my dinner in the maid's parlour with Mr. Dafoe, the magician?

I would have to ask Steve what the timelines really were. She certainly didn't look stiff, lying sprawled in the tub, but I hadn't touched her. I wasn't overly sure how long it took rigor mortis to set in, anyhow. Everything happened more quickly than it should on shows like *CSI*, and that was where my basic expe-rience with dead bodies came from. Well, that and stumbling across them every now and then.

The bathwater was beginning to cool off. I contemplated turning the hot-water tap back on with my semi-prehensile toes, but decided I should probably just get out and dry off.

Clad in a tee-shirt and old yoga pants, I curled up in a corner of my sofa with my laptop to check my email and determine my schedule for the next day.

While going in today to help Marni out had seemed a sensible enough idea, doing so had eaten up my Sunday entirely, and I had deliberately set out a steady schedule to follow on this project; if I didn't push myself to be done by January, it would not be monetarily feasible. Besides, I was hoping to snag a couple of courses at Grant MacEwan in the winter term, and needed to be cleared to jump into them, given the word.

Tomorrow, I was to start a week-long session at the Archives, which I'd booked almost a month back. I had likewise hired a car for the week, since the Province of Alberta Archives was out in the southeastern back of beyond, where buses ran on the hour and lunch spots were sparse. I was planning to pick up the car and slot in all my run-around necessities this week while I had it, including a long overdue trip to the Superstore for food and pantry supplies. For the next week, at any rate, I was going to be continually on the move.

Steve knocked on the door while I was on the phone with the car agency. He let himself in and waved back at me. While he was kicking his shoes off, I finalized my plans to pick the car up downtown, which would be easier to get to by bus, I figured.

"I still cannot believe you budgeted for a rental car."

"Well, I thought about it, and the commuting time would be more than double if I were to rely on rapid transit for this week. Besides, I figured I would also fit in a trip to the Ukrainian Village next weekend to see more historic sites of the same time frame. Do you feel like going out of town for a spin?"

"What sort of mileage do you have to pay on this car?" Steve asked skeptically.

"No mileage at all. Just a flat rate per week and bring it back with a full tank of gas. I took out the set rate of insurance and I booked the guest-parking stall for the week with the landlords. I'm all set."

"Good enough. Are you hungry at all, Helen Wheels?"

My stomach grumbled loudly enough for us both to hear, as if in response. Sometimes, the body is just there to keep you honest.

"I'm starving. Do you want me to whip something up here? Or did you have other ideas?"

"Well, I was thinking we could head over to the Old Spaghetti Factory, but you look pretty comfy here."

"Which I take to mean, I am too grubby for a nice place. Give me three minutes and I can be ready. By the way, I popped into the Diner for muffins for breakfast tomorrow, if you have a mind to stay over."

"Yum. I think I could be persuaded."

Steve sat and clicked through the channels on my television while I changed in my tiny bedroom, the door three-quarters shut mainly to be able to access the closet behind it. I kicked off the yoga pants into the bottom of the closet and pulled on a pair of grey-blue trousers I'd purchased for a song at a Bay Day last spring. A heathery-grey cashmere twin-set I'd found two weeks earlier at the Value Village was a perfect match. One quick brush of my hair back from my face and fastened into a clip, and I was ready.

I came out of the bedroom with a pair of socks in my hand. Steve whistled.

"Randy Craig, you do clean up nicely," he drawled.

"This is the sort of look I am hoping to adopt while dealing with archivists and historic-site people, what do you think?"

"I think you are edging very close to sexy librarian."

"Don't you think I would need to get glasses and put my hair up for that?"

"We can make do." He came toward me and hugged me. I laughed and, after kissing him on the nose, pushed away from his embrace.

"Let me put on my other sock, and don't forget you promised me spaghetti."

"Right you are, my lady." With a flourish, he bowed, and opened the door. "Your carriage awaits."

I grabbed my purse and keys, and turned off the lights on my way out.

9

The Old Spaghetti Factory was part of a long-standing chain of restaurants known for setting up in historic or re-gentrifying areas. The chain had begun in Oregon, but soon after expanded to Vancouver's historic Gastown, Winnipeg, and then Edmonton. Ours had been one of the cornerstone businesses in the Boardwalk, a reconstituted downtown warehouse that had become a building full of boutiques, an arcade, and various funky restaurants in the '70s. The arcade, wicker emporiums, and head shops had disappeared, but a couple of the restaurants were still there, along with the wooden sidewalk. The Old Spaghetti Factory was a glorious hodgepodge of antiques. The tables were all different, the bar was fronted with the intricately carved sides of a European hearse, and a full-sized streetcar sat in pride of place in the centre of the restaurant. That was my favourite place of all to sit. Eating at a table in a vintage streetcar satisfied the same urges in me that had made the now long-gone Buffalo Bill's Western Village restaurant my favourite place as a child. There, birthday parties of children would have their meals served in alcove rooms made up to look like saloons and jails. There was another Spaghetti Factory out at West Edmonton Mall, and I had to admit I chose to eat there whenever I was caught at the mall—partly for the mizithra cheese, which the menu vowed was the same as what Homer had eaten when penning the *Odyssey*, and partly for the sanctuary of old and funky amid all the mirrors and marble that was the mall.

You know you are getting to be a regular when the waiter smiles and leads you straight to the table in the streetcar. It's moments like this that give me a double-sided sensibility. At the same time as I'm feeling all "Norm!"-happy à la *Cheers*, I get the nagging feeling I probably spend too much money eating out. I tell you, it is not easy living with the voice of your parsimonious grandmother in your head.

Since it would be equally small-minded to complain, I busied myself with slicing up the loaf of fresh bread the waiter had left with the menus and slathered garlic butter on a piece, glorying in its melting into the warm bread.

We had each ordered a glass of wine, me deciding it was still warm enough out to warrant a Pinot Grigio, and Steve debating the merits of two different Australian reds before choosing what the waiter suggested. All conversation ceased as our meals arrived, and I barely heard the music playing in the background over my small moans of delight. I had been hungrier than I realized, and the food was gone before I knew it. I debated whether or not to accept the bowl of spumoni ice cream, with the vague consideration that if I walked home across the High

Level Bridge, I might work off a third of the calories. In the end, I decided to opt for coffee, like my responsible boyfriend.

We were finishing our decaf before Steve actually said anything about my day. I had had no particular desire to discuss it prior to now, which probably said more for my previous lack of food than anything else.

"So how did it go? Was it hard to go back into the House?"

"You know, it wasn't all that problematic. I'll tell you what was hard—getting fingerprint powder out of grouting on all those little tiles, that was hard."

Steve laughed. "I know; that stuff is pervasive. I swear it's in the seams of my clothing forever. I wander the world sort of like Pigpen from Peanuts."

"I feel weird, too, that I feel sort of distant from it all, even though we had been talking to each other earlier that evening. Maybe it was just that I didn't know her all that well, so her death wasn't the blow that it could have or probably should have been. She was just one of the young staff that seemed to be around from time to time. They all work part-time hours around their classes and such. The chilling thing is trying to figure out when exactly she died and how long she was lying there. After all, I was eating my supper upstairs. Maybe she was being killed while I was filling my face. That's the part that really bothers me."

"What about the part where it could have just as easily been you?" Steve looked very sober. "That's the part that really bothers me."

"Do you think so? Do you think she was just killed because

she was in the wrong place at the wrong time? It had nothing to do with who she was, herself? Somehow that seems even worse."

"Randy, pick a lane. Either you want the girl to have been a hapless victim or you want her to be somehow involved in something so shady she gets herself killed. Which is it?"

"Hapless victim, I guess, though that really does make Jossie a total non-player, doesn't it?"

"Seriously, you have to examine either scenario. Don't close yourself off to either, or you might miss something in the investigation."

"I take it that is the royal 'you' you're using there; I'm not about to poke around in this. Your boss would throw me in jail. I am sure he's thinking about it right now, if he's seen me on the statement list."

"Oh, probably," Steve smiled. "But somehow you do seem to be involved, and I want you thinking, not getting involved in the investigation, but thinking all the time. Because if it is something to do with the House, and not with Jossie herself, then you could be just as much in the line of fire."

"When do you think the detectives in charge will figure out which it is?"

"They will be questioning the girl's family this week, and her friends, trying to piece together her life apart from being a waitress at Rutherford House. In the meantime, they'll also be poking into the workings of the House, to see whether it was something to do with her particular connection there. I think they'll likely also look into the backgrounds of the theatre troupe and the magician."

"Has anyone talked to the magician yet, do you know?"

"Joe Howard was hoping to question him this morning. Dafoe lives just out of town, past St. Albert. The medical examiner is still working to narrow down the time of death, but I wouldn't be surprised if your dinner with him doesn't exonerate the both of you."

I sighed. This was going to be another long, ugly process. The situation at the House, where everyone walked on eggshells trying not to annoy each other, was going to expand exponentially. And walking into that gorgeous, wood-panelled foyer, not one of us was going to feel safe for quite some time to come.

People were starting to fill up the restaurant. The dinner hour seemed to be gaining speed. We relinquished our seats and paid up, easing ourselves out past a sizable crowd waiting at the door.

Steve drove me home down the hill behind the public golf course, where we could see people delighting in an extended season due to the mild autumn, across the Groat Bridge and up Saskatchewan Drive past the Faculty Club, the sprawling Biosciences Building, the rock garden planted by the Geology Department in front of the Earth Sciences Building, and around the parking lot. We passed the Tory Building, and there was Rutherford House, its red bricks glowing in the glow of the street lights. There was nothing but calm emanating from it, no evil aura. I could not imagine Jossie's death had anything to do with the House.

A few twists and turns down one-way streets and Steve had pulled up in the guest slot behind my apartment.

"Are those breakfast muffins still on offer?"

"Oh lord, how can you think of food after a meal like that?"

"I can think of ways to work it off," he leered seductively. I laughed and we headed back into the apartment together.

10

I had set an alarm so that neither of us would sleep in. Steve had to be at the precinct by eight thirty and I was planning to pick up the car from the downtown office by nine and be out at the Archives for ten. We showered together, to save time, and as I was towelling off, I smiled to think of what I considered to be intimacy. It wasn't roses or whispered promises; it was the sharing of regular activities that created the sort of togetherness I valued.

I was making coffee when Steve came into the kitchen, "all Brylcreemed and Lavorissed," as my grandmother used to say. A clean, handsome man on a sunny October morning—what more could a girl want?

Steve offered to drive me downtown to the rental office, but I didn't want him to clock in late and I would be fine on the bus. He kissed me goodbye, and I tidied up the table quickly before popping into the bathroom to brush my teeth and apply a quick brush of mascara. I wanted to look my best. After all, today I would actually be meeting the archivist.

In my experience, librarians and those who guard the gates of any realm can be very prickly and must be handled with care. They identify with their role of guardian very seriously and can make snap judgments over whether you are the right sort of person to be handling their grails. Because I was going to be heading to a place that was climatically controlled—where I would have to sign in to see every single document and artifact and would have to wear white cotton gloves the entire time doing so—I had to look my best.

The advent of laptop computers was a great thing for the historical researcher. Most archivists would let one in with you for note-taking. In the good old days when I had been freelancing before returning to university, they would frisk you for ballpoint pens before you could receive any files to peruse.

I looked at myself critically in the mirror, checking to see if there was anything I could alter or enhance in order to make a great first impression. My thick hair was braided back in one long braid. My skin, which had never let me down through puberty, still showed the few freckles which usually faded in the winter, but would eventually stay year-round as age spots, I supposed. There weren't many lines in my face, more due to high cheekbones than proper sun avoidance. I was wearing a loden-green pullover under a black leather jacket cut like a blazer, with a thin pink-and-green scarf wound around my neck. My dark jeans were clean and pressed; I should pass inspection with flying colours. I grabbed the satchel containing my laptop, wallet, keys, water bottle, and granola bar, and headed out to catch the bus.

The woman at the car place had my paperwork ready for me, although she seemed a bit confused to be dealing with a female Randy. I am sure it had been her on the phone when I had called the week before. Who knows, maybe I have a male-sounding voice on the phone. My register did skew to alto when I sang in choirs. I had all the right ID, and most importantly, a credit card stating I was Miranda Craig, which seemed more compatible with her sense of who I should be, so soon I was fitted with the keys and paperwork to a shiny green Kia Soul that some minion had kindly parked outside the kiosk while I'd been inside.

I took a few minutes to ostentatiously set the mirrors and figure out where the signal lights were. Then I clicked the little switchblade key into the starter, and off I went, zooming across the city toward the Province of Alberta Archives.

It had been several years since I'd driven in the city, but one of the great things about Edmonton is that the streets are numbered on a logical grid, so that if you are given an address of say, 8107-50th Street, you would know that it would be to the southeast, since the centre of town was 101st Street and 101st Avenue, and the numbers got larger the further west or further north you went. Sure, every now and then they threw in a named street, or a neighbourhood full of circular drives and culs-de-sac,s where you would require GPS, a map, and a cellphone to use when you got hopelessly lost. But on the whole, you could usually navigate from just the address given.

The Archives were out in what was mostly an industrial end of town on one of the few named streets out that way, Roper Road. While I had gone along with Steve the fall before to get his new car speakers installed at a nearby business, I rarely had reason to go out this way. I was nervous of overshooting the proper turnoff to the Archives and finding myself heading instead toward Sherwood Park, which was a trick I had done years before when IKEA had first been out in that direction. However, a lovely, large sign on the corner announced the presence of the Archives ahead to my right, meaning I wouldn't even have to worry about crossing aggressive traffic to get there. I loved it already.

I was relieved to see a large, rather empty parking lot. I pulled into a slot and tried to remember how to lock the car with the buttons on the keyfob. One press of the lock button produced an audible click. Two made the car beep at me. Oh well, I guess I deserved that.

Hoisting my heavy satchel onto my shoulder, I took a deep breath and headed to the Archives. Not terribly shy by nature, I am still a bit awkward when it comes to meeting new people, especially if I have a chance to over-think things. If Steve happened to introduce me to someone we ran into somewhere, I would be fine, able to talk and produce appropriate chit-chat off the cuff. It was when I knew I was going to meet people that I would tend to over-rehearse things in my head, running possible conversations through to their logical conclusions to see if there were any potential traps for faux pas. This tended to make me feel stilted when actually meeting the people, as it all felt like some sort of shabby déjà vu.

I walked through the double set of glass doors, setting off a muted bell.

A large counter of blond wood, like the front line in a doctor's office, sat straight ahead. From behind a half-wall of shelves came the archivist. I introduced myself and he smiled.

"Ah, yes, Randy Craig, from Rutherford House. It's lovely to meet you. I am Alastair Maitland. We are a little short-staffed this week, as our administrative person is in Las Vegas seeing every Cirque du Soleil production she can get tickets for. If you wouldn't mind filling in and signing this research agreement, I'll give you this ID card, which is good for a year. Then I will show you to our locker area, where you can hang up your coat and lock away everything but your laptop and pencil. No cameras allowed in the reading room, I'm afraid. The lockers are a quarter, but you get it back at the end of the session. Do you need a quarter? No?" He bustled me through, after checking I'd filled everything in to his satisfaction.

"Once you're through here to the reading room, you're in my territory. This is where we keep the catalogues you can browse to see which archives you might want to request. In the meantime, I took the liberty of pulling a few you were mentioning over the phone, so I can bring those to your table right away."

I was so charmed by the pleasantness of this dapper little man that I completely forgot to be nervous. Plus, his proactive interest in my project tossed all my rehearsed conversations into the hopper, leaving me to be happily spontaneous. I dumped my coat and bag in a locker in the anteroom he showed me, and followed him through another set of doors into a quiet reading room with several tables in the centre of the room and single carrels lining two walls. The far wall, across from the one containing the door we'd just come through, was lined with windows, letting in the sunny eastern sky.

Mr. Maitland noticed my glance at the windows and immediately assured me they were treated glass which wouldn't allow sun glare to come through and damage any of the papers being examined, something that hadn't even occurred to me. He nodded approvingly as I set down my laptop, deciding to commandeer the table closest to the window, just in case a horde of researchers raced in behind me. I was just settling into position, having brought up a blank Word document, when Mr. Maitland returned with the first box of papers.

"The guest books and diaries of Mrs. Rutherford are in this box. I also pulled the archival material from the Delta Upsilon fraternity, who used the House between 1940 and 1969, as I thought that material might be of use to you." He leaned in, slightly conspiratorially. "My father was a Delt, you see, so I just naturally assumed you'd be including that in your survey of the House's history."

I assured him that the website would indeed focus on the Delts and their place in university history. On the whole, I was not that bothered by having to deal with a fraternity, because as fraternities went, the Delta Upsilons seemed to be far and away the most upstanding and clean cut of the lot of them, very egalitarian and open. The one thing that could get you automatically ousted was a drop in your grades, so the whole party-boy, wild-hazing-snob persona that hovered over so many of the Greeks were totally absent from the Delts.

I thanked Mr. Maitland, wondering privately why he hadn't

followed in his father's footsteps and joined the frat, but feeling it was likely too early in our relationship to be asking him those sorts of questions. Whatever the case, the Delts could wait. I was excited to be getting my hands on Mattie Rutherford's diaries.

Much was known about Alexander Rutherford, but I thought it would be nice to get a sense of the woman who had used and cherished the lovely china still used in the House, and who had the happy idea to paint the guest-room ceiling yellow to make guests feel as if they were always waking up to a sunny day. I pulled on the white gloves Mr. Maitland had left me and opened the cardboard banker box he had placed on the table.

In the box were a series of blue leather volumes, each one the size of a small pocket bible. There had to be thirty or more of these, all the same. I ran my finger over their nubby spines, counting thirty-three. Slid into the end of the box, alongside, were five cream-coloured ledger books, which turned out to be the guest books. Mrs. Rutherford would ask each guest to sign his or her name and the date of the visit. Several visitors left small messages, as well. It was a charming tradition, and one the House still used today. Although I had stopped signing in once my contract had fully taken hold, I could see from flipping through the book that several women signed in almost weekly, every time they came to tea. A Mrs. Lister and Mrs. Oliver, whom I assumed to be neighbours, seemed to be regular visitors.

I opened my laptop and pulled up a new document in order to create a list of names of visitors I might want to research a bit more, to see if they warranted sideline web pages of their own on the site. Not all the signatures were legible, of course. Bad penmanship and blotty fountain pens were not a researcher's best friends. Still, within a matter of an hour, I had a list of thirty or forty names that were either strongly reoccurring or historically interesting, enough so for me to delve into with a bit more effort.

I leaned back from the table and stretched, trying to recall the physio exercises I'd been given to keep my shoulder mobile. I'd suffered from a frozen shoulder due to a bicycling injury a year earlier, and needed to be more consistent in my exercises, especially if I was going to insist on hunching over a computer most days. I looked up at the large institutional clock on the wall and realized it was almost lunchtime. My stomach growled, as if to underscore that discovery. As I was still the only person in the research lounge, I figured Mr. Maitland wouldn't mind if I left my materials on the table for a quick break. I closed my laptop and carried it through to the locker area to pop into my bag and shrugged into my coat, taking a quick look to see if I'd left anything behind.

Mr. Maitland was working at his computer terminal at the front counter when I came out of the reading room. He mentioned two or three good places for lunch a bit further west on 51st Avenue, agreeing that leaving the materials on the table was quite all right.

There is something about digging into the past, even if it is just on paper, that makes you long for red meat. I turned the car in the direction of the Fife N' Dekel deli and treated myself to a smoked meat sandwich and a huge slice of cherry pie, which was obviously made that morning on the premises. Since I was far away from delicate documents, I felt free to pull a pen and notebook out of my bag, so I could try to organize my week to come.

I had booked archive time for the entire week. From the looks of things, I was going to be able to fill that time completely. Aside from the catalogues, my morning had been taken up entirely by the guest books. I hadn't been through any of Mattie Rutherford's diaries yet, and the fraternity box might lead to other names to pursue. The catalogues I'd browsed showed several Rutherford collections of papers worth a look, and a whole slew of photographs donated by his daughter, Hazel McCuaig. So, my days were likely packed from here through Friday. If I had to, I could likely manage a personal chore or two before the Archive's ten o'clock opening, or after Mr. Maitland kicked me out at four. Otherwise, it would have to wait for the weekend. And by weekend, I meant Sunday, because I'd already decided I was going to have to get to the Ukrainian Village on Saturday. Like Fort Edmonton Park, the village was only open for school tours during the week after the Labour Day long weekend, but there were still Saturday and Sunday hours listed for limited access.

Steve had agreed to go with me to the Ukrainian Village. It was another historic park, with a slightly different, more rural focus on the immigrants from Eastern Europe who came across Canada by train to secure land for themselves and a brighter future for their children. It would be interesting to feel the difference between how the rural Alberta immigrant was living around the same time as Alexander Rutherford was building his brick mansion.

And then, after all that running around, I was going to have to turn in my lovely little green boxy car, which had already charmed me into seriously thinking of saving up for one of my own. It would take a hard look at parking fees and gas prices-per-litre to bring me back to my senses after this week of luxury, I figured.

By one o'clock, I was back. Mr. Maitland smiled at me as he buzzed me through to the inner sanctum.

"If you like, Randy, you are more than welcome to bring your lunch with you in future and eat it in our lunchroom. It's not usually open to researchers, but there is no one else presently registered to come in, and as I seem to be manning the ship alone this week, it would be no imposition at all. I normally eat my own lunch between twelve-thirty and one-thirty, and would be happy to have company if you like."

I was really touched by his generosity, and also thankful. Bringing lunch would save a heap of money, and it was getting too chilly to go out and sit in the car to eat.

I was back in the reading room by one-fifteen, fighting my way through Mattie Rutherford's diaries. While her penmanship was "copperplate excellent," she had a tendency to use abbreviations I couldn't always decipher. Most of her days, in the beginnings of the diaries, were taken up with household matters. Then, there was the building of the House, on which, I was happy to see, her husband consulted her in many aspects. It was she who pushed for the guest bathroom, the sun porch and the skylight. There had been apparently a tense time arguing between Doric and Ionic columns for the front porch, but she professed in her diary to be "happy with Alec's choice."

I read diaries most of the afternoon, taking notes from time to time, and citing the date. Perhaps these could be set in, overlaid on photos, a line or two in a cool *handwriting* font to enhance the personal feel for visitors to the website.

Around three forty-five, Mr. Maitland popped into the room, a regretful look on his face. I smiled at him to let him know I wasn't holding him personally responsible for my having to leave, although I could see why he might have learned to steel himself against resentment when kicking out researchers. He told me that I could store the boxes on the shelves near the door, if I was still interested in using them the next day.

"Anything you're done with can be set on the table here, and we'll re-shelve them in the archives before the next day."

Since I had nothing I wanted to turn in, I set both boxes on a shelf. After stopping at the front desk to sign out, thinking of shades of Mattie Rutherford's guest books, I headed to my little green chariot and pointed it toward home.

It took me almost an hour to get there. I began to suspect that a week's worth of rush hours would be enough to turn me off the idea of owning my own car. Of course, I had found CKUA on the radio and was grooving to a Good Lovelies tune while waiting at yet another red light, so it wasn't all bad.

Lazily watching the world from behind my windshield, I spotted someone at the corner of Whyte Avenue and 104th Street who looked familiar. I focused a little bit more and tried to place the rather miserably-annoyed face squished on top of a navy peacoat and under a grey tuque, an outfit that might have been a good combination on a sailor on leave but didn't at all suit the little woman wearing it. As she turned to speak to the young man beside her, I remembered where I'd seen her before: it was the old woman who had been standing next to the two tall men and looking so grim at the mystery evening. One of the men had been Walter Karras, the chair of the board. The other had been this same young man. I wondered who they were. Marni would know. Just then the light turned green, and I was forced to move forward and put all my attention back on the traffic. While I might not have made it home on foot faster, I wouldn't have been much later than I was. My thoughts on buying a car retreated back on the list where they normally lived, somewhere under "spend a year in Malta" and "buy a red Mixmaster."

I kicked off my shoes inside the door of my apartment and turned on the small television before heading into the bedroom to change. Steve had bought me the tiny flat-screen TV the previous Christmas and equipped it with a PVR so that I could record and keep tracks of programs I might want to watch. After several years of my not watching any TV, it was an effort not to become hypnotized by the advertisements, but I had finally worked out a system where I watched the news at a set time of day and recorded most everything else I wanted to see so that I could view it later and race through the ads with my skip button.

The news reports had got hold of the Rutherford House murder right away, working on every angle they could over the weekend, and it was still the second story from the national news desk. They weren't releasing Jossie's name yet, which made me wonder if Marni and the police had managed to contact her parents, who were supposed to be spending a three-week holiday in Europe. That wasn't a call I would want to either initiate or receive.

The anchor was saying that police were still questioning witnesses who had been at the House that night for an event involving magic and entertainment. Great. It was starting to sound as if Jossie had been sacrificed at a theosophical séance.

I came back into the living room and aimed the remote at the television. I'd had enough reality for one day, present or archival; I wanted utter escape. I scrolled through my recorded selections and clicked on a Masterpiece Contemporary offering about love in the wilds of Wales.

The next thing I knew, I was creaking awake from a slumped position on my chesterfield. The television had turned itself off, and the living-room lights were blazing. Checking my wristwatch, I noted it was two in the morning. I was sleepier than I was hungry, so I turned off the lights, peeled off my watch and clothes, and crawled properly into my bed for the rest of the night.

The next morning's alarm hit me hard, but at least I didn't have to worry about where I was going. I packed up a proper lunch for eating with Mr. Maitland, sorted through my satchel for laptop, power cord, pencils and notepad, wallet and car keys, and whipped up the Craig version of an eggy-muffin breakfast, which replaced bacon with thin slices of tomato and used whatever bread there was to hand, which in this case was a whole-wheat wrap. On reflection, any resemblance to a fast-food breakfast sandwich was entirely in my mind.

Brushed and flossed and shined into a semblance of morning business shape, I got into the car about half an hour after I thought the regular rush hour should have died down. After all, the Archives weren't open to the public till nine.

Edmonton was getting to be a lot bigger of a city than I usually gave it credit for. Morning rush hour, which started around seven, was still in full throttle when I eased out into it around eight-fifteen. I decided to relinquish my place in the stop-and-start parking lot that was Argyle Road, and ducked into a Tim Hortons parking lot. A large double-milk coffee and the newspaper would be a better idea than battling rush hour. Not having been a driver for so many years had me feeling sort of spooked. Aggressive drivers used to get me nervous anyhow. Now they were aggressive in huge SUVs. There was a long line of cars waiting in the drive-through, but not a terribly long queue of people inside, I was relieved to find.

The doughnut shop had several papers on hand. I picked the *Journal*, assuming that since we don't get a Sunday paper anymore, any coverage of the murder would have taken place in yesterday's paper. But you never knew.

It must have been a slow news week. A picture of Rutherford House was still on the cover, over the fold. As I'd heard in movies about journalism, "if it bleeds, it leads." While Jossie hadn't technically bled out, I guess they weren't going to quibble as long as she was young and pretty and dead.

Again, Jossie's name wasn't listed; she was described as an

employee of the Rutherford House staff, engaged at an evening event put on by the House. They were reporting that more than sixty people had purchased tickets to the "Magical Mystery Hour" and described it as a dinner theatre sort of event, which was far closer to the mark than the television news had managed the night before. Police were investigating and nothing more could be offered at this time.

I wondered if Marni had given them the number of attendees. I reminded myself to call her or possibly email her from the Archives, to see if she had a list of all the people who had been at the event. I was still wondering about the identity of the grouchy little woman I had seen on Whyte Avenue.

The traffic was beginning to slow down and the Tim Hortons was beginning to fill up with older, rather loud men who all seemed to know each other. I took both of these things as signs that it was time for me to go. Looking longingly at the showcase of freshly-baked doughnuts, I headed into the parking lot and pointed myself once more toward the past.

11

Mr. Maitland was at the counter discussing acid-free photo album choices with an older woman when I got there. He nodded to me, but continued patiently to explain the differences in the three choices the Archives shop stocked. Satisfied, the woman pointed to the mid-level choice and Mr. Maitland rang up her sale. She smiled at me as she left, and I wondered what sorts of memorabilia she was planning to preserve, and hoped that whomever she intended to hand it off to would truly appreciate it.

Mr. Maitland ushered me into the reading room, tutting over the crunch he was feeling by having an employee absent with a sick child. Normally, the Archives apparently buzzed with all sorts of workers, but this week had been the chosen time of vacation for several of the technicians and conservators, and the thought was that they could limp along for one week with their normal weekend skeleton staff. However, with this latest call in, the whole system was being manned by Mr. Maitland, the head reference archivist, and a retrieval technician who was in only mornings. As I hung up my coat and shoved my bag into the locker, he announced he would be shutting the gift shop for the rest of the day.

I mentioned that I had brought my lunch and he inquired whether I would like him to put it in his fridge for the morning. I thanked him and handed over my polyvinyl zip bag. I headed back to the same table I'd commandeered the day before, detouring to the shelves to retrieve the box of Mrs. Rutherford's diaries. Before I opened the box, I whipped an email off to Marni, asking her if I could see a list of the folks who had attended the magic evening. I was hoping one of the names would bounce out to me as the angry woman. I was about to close my email program when a new email popped up from Steve.

Subject: Gibson and Howard need you

Hey Randy, can you take some time today to come over to the station and fill out more of a statement for the detectives in charge of the Rutherford House case? They have some questions about the timelines, and whether you have any insights into some of the witnesses and connections between them. Let me know when would be an okay time for you.

Love,
Steve

I was pretty sure most requests from the police didn't sign off that way. I was grinning as I returned an email saying I could be over at the south-side station at two-thirty, if that suited them. I left the email up and got an almost immediate return from Steve acknowledging the time as just fine. I was about to open my Word program and settle in to reading the first of Mattie's diaries when another email popped up. This time it was Marni, with the list of ticket holders to the event. She had also attached a list of the actors involved in the dinner theatre and the names of all of us on the staff. I looked at my own name staring back at me and wondered just how much blood-pressure medication Staff Sergeant Keller was going to need when he looked at it.

I scanned the list of guests and checked especially the women's names. There was one that stood out: Greta Larsen. Where had I heard that name before?

"She's on the Historic Sites Advisory Board and, if I'm not mistaken, the Friends of Rutherford House, too," answered Mr. Maitland, who had appeared at my table with another box of material.

"Ack, I am sorry. I didn't realize I was talking out loud."

"Now that is a real researcher tic, talking to yourself," Mr. Maitland chuckled. "Be careful, Randy, or we'll have to put your name on a chair as a full-timer!" He turned to leave, but I wanted to pick his brains about this Greta Larsen a bit more.

"Ms. Larsen, do you know her personally?"

"We've been at some of the same meetings," he nodded.

"Could you describe her to me? I am not sure I'm putting the right name to the right face, if you know what I mean."

"Oh you would know her, if for the simple reason that I don't think Greta Larsen has smiled in the last three decades. She is the most ill-tempered person I have ever seen. Now, my sainted mother would likely have tried to explain her grimaces away with excuses of ulcers or scoliosis pains, but I have heard Greta talk to people, too. And she is just plain mean." Mr. Maitland offered up an angelic smile that no one could ever take for ill-temper, and left the reading room.

So the woman I had seen in the lobby of the House and then again on Whyte Avenue had to be Greta Larsen, member of the board. She had been standing next to Walter Karras, the chair of the board, so that made sense. Could that have been why Marni had been in such a tizzy just before the dinner began? Because one of the board members there checking up was renowned to be nasty? Was the board really that focused on what events were happening at the House, or was Greta Larsen just being a busybody? Or was she simply drawn that way, as Jessica Rabbit would say, and only attending because she was a fan of close-up magic?

Regretfully, I closed my email program and turned my mind back to the job at hand, immersing myself in the world of the historical personages who had actually inhabited the House. Today's bout at the Archives was already going to be cut short if I had to head to police headquarters to go over things once more with Detectives Gibson and Howard. I needed to hunker down and get to it.

Mattie Rutherford had a charming flow to her diaries. While the earliest one began as a strict accounting of what she was seeding in the garden and when, the entries expanded quickly into a record of her thoughts and observations of the world around her. She adored her children and enjoyed the company of her friends and visitors from the east. She admired her husband intensely and approved of all his dreams for a civilized and forward-thinking province and city. I sketched out the bare bones of a potential web page devoted to Mrs. Rutherford, which included a sprinkling of a few of her quotes, and perhaps a shot of some of the pretty sketches of her garden dotted in her diaries.

By the time the noon hour rolled around, I had listed volumes and page numbers for several requests for photo reproductions. There was a form for this purpose on the Archive website; I populated the boxes and sent it all over the universe to land on Mr. Maitland's computer in the central foyer. Might as well get started on the requests now. This way, too, the images could be sent electronically, so that we could later insert them, with acknowledgement, straight onto the website and avoid any degradation to photo quality due to scanning or over-processing. My budget for this sort of thing wasn't huge, but the cost per page wasn't astronomical, either. I also had to admit, no matter how precisely, gracefully, and clearly one wrote, a photo was not only going to capture the imagination of the viewer better, it would also in the long run net a freelancer more money. I had once been contracted to write a short piece about a vacation destination for the Alberta Motor Association magazine and, on a whim, sent in five photos I had taken while holidaying. Their purchasing of the photos had more than doubled my take on the assignment.

Mr. Maitland popped his head into the reading room to suggest we break for lunch. He smiled at the stacks of blue diaries piling up in front of me as if to say he knew I'd find them of interest. I leaned back to stretch and felt my back crack in protest of the length of time I'd been sitting still. I was ready. If I took a half-hour to heat up and eat my soup and sandwich with the little archivist, I could still work for another hour before packing up to go see the police. As there was still no one but me in the hall, I left my laptop and paraphernalia the way they were and followed Mr. Maitland to his lunchroom.

A round table with a couple of magazines sat in the centre of a room with only a simple high window in one wall. Along the opposite wall was a counter and cupboards, with dark melamine surfaces. A sink, microwave, and fridge were fitted into this as well. In between was a short wall on which hung a small bulletin board, a large government-issue calendar, and a framed cross-stitch of the famous Santayana quote, which I supposed had to be the archivist's mantra: "Those who forget the past are condemned to repeat it." I commented as much to Mr. Maitland, who laughed.

"No, our mantra would have to be, 'Those who collect the past are condemned to re-shelve it.' I have a soft spot for that picture, though, as it's my mother's handiwork."

He opened the fridge to produce my lunch bag, along with several plastic containers of his own that he set out, just so, on the counter. A loaf of bread and a butter dish were pulled out of the cupboard to the left of the fridge, and while I heated up my cabbage soup in his microwave, Mr. Maitland put together a fresh sandwich from a selection of cold cuts, lettuce, and tomatoes. He offered to make me one as well, but I explained that my wrap would be enough lunch for me.

We brought our food to the table and sat down in companionable silence. It took Mr. Maitland half of his sandwich before he broached a subject I figured he'd wanted to ask me about all morning.

"I've been reading about the terrible happening at Rutherford House," he began.

"The murder, you mean?" I didn't mind talking about it with him. After all, I was going to discuss it within feet of Steve's boss, who hated having me involved in things, in just a couple of hours. I might as well talk it over with someone I liked, and get my mind straight about whatever it was I was going to say.

"Yes, I take it you were there?"

I filled Mr. Maitland in on the general layout of events and where and what Jossie and I had been doing that night. He was properly shocked to learn how young she was, and how similar her tasks for the evening had been to mine, which was something I hadn't really considered till he pointed it out.

"It sounds as if it could just as easily have been you strangled in that bathtub," he stated, in a shocked tone.

"Her neck was broken, she wasn't strangled," I corrected, but his words hung in the air, and, in spite of myself, I shivered. Until that moment it hadn't actually occurred to me that I might have been in danger that night.

"I'm sorry, I've upset you," Mr. Maitland said, filling a rather awkward silence. He began to clean up his lunch detritus and I did the same.

"I have to leave early today, so I'd better get back at it. Mrs. Rutherford's diaries are fabulous," I told him and thanked him again for letting me share his lunch zone.

"It's my pleasure and please consider this an open invitation," he said. "It's so nice to have someone to break bread with."

Feeling re-energized, I headed back in to read though another diary. There was going to be no way the website could feature everything about each Rutherford, all the fraternity boys, every visitor who stayed overnight, as well as all of the individual ladies of the Canadian Federation of University Women who fought to preserve the House as a historic site, so my research path would have to be more bumblebee than beeline. I pulled a diary at random out of the box, setting one of the Archive's cardboard markers in the space I'd removed it from.

Mattie Rutherford didn't date each diary page, but merely denoted the day of the year at the top of each entry. She seemed to have written the year in the front fly-leaf of each book and then carried on, assuming she'd spend just one year within each binding. The first couple I had skimmed through were from 1906 and 1924. I flipped to the front to see what vintage this book was, but the numbers were smudged and I could only see the "19." If I was well-versed in my Rutherfordiana, I could possibly suss out the year from context. I wondered if I was up to that challenge yet.

It was worth a try, more so because her writing was clearly legible throughout and even a little larger than in the past volumes, making it easier reading. I decided to stick with this diary until it was time for me to head to the police office.

Once again, she spent a bit of time discussing the children, who seemed to be an utter joy to her. Both were intelligent and curious, and Cecil seemed to be a devoted brother to Hazel. Hazel had sent a letter from the Ladies College she was attending in Toronto and had promised to write to Cecil next. Mattie and Alec attended the church picnic together and Mattie brought along four loaves of fresh currant bread and strawberry preserves, which were enjoyed by all. Alec was busy with a case involving several people near Lacombe and had had to travel back and forth twice for depositions. Mattie was worried that the new maid was homesick as she was certain she had overheard her crying for several nights when she herself awoke with leg cramps and had to walk them out on the cold floor.

August 15. —I'm not certain S. is suitable. I had no idea who or what Mattie was referring to, with her penchant for abbreviations. "S" could have been a person, a thing, or even a place, such as the Strathcona Club. I was going to flip back to see if one of Cecil's friends' names started with an S, or if Mattie had mentioned an "S" anywhere within her own circle of friends. However, one glance at the wall clock and I realized I would have to put a move on it if I was going to make it to the southside cop shop by two o'clock as I had promised.

I slid the diary back into the box, leaving the cardboard marker beside it so I'd find it when I returned, trotted the box over to the shelves, and quickly packed up my satchel. Saying a quick goodbye to Mr. Maitland, I hurried out the door to the parking lot.

12

The police station where Steve worked was probably pretty much like any police station across North America, though there wasn't quite as much bulletproof glass in the lobby as I'd noticed in the movies. I wrote my name on the sign-in list, showed the desk officer my driver's licence as identification, and was given a visitor tag with the number 66 on it. He pointed me toward the bank of moulded plastic chairs along the wall, and I went there to sit and wait.

My wait wasn't long, which was just as well, as the chairs had obviously not been moulded with anything resembling comfort in mind. Steve showed up to take me into the inner sanctum. Noticing the number on my visitor tag, he laughed.

"Keller's going to want another 6 put on there for you!"

"Very funny. I'm nervous enough about potentially running into him. Do not joke about that to me. I can just imagine what he'd say."

We turned a corner, and who should be right there but Steve's superior officer, Staff Sergeant Keller. The tilt of his eyebrow told me he had likely heard every single thing I had just said. I could feel my neck and ears starting to burn into what would be a full-fledged blush in a minute or two.

"Ms. Craig. I am sorry that we have to meet again under such circumstances. Please accept my condolences on the loss of your colleague and thank you for coming in to help us with our investigation." He nodded his head in that same crisp way Christopher Plummer perfected in *The Sound of Music*, and continued down the way we had just come. Steve and I looked at each other in astonishment. Who had replaced Keller with a placid clone, and what had they done with the real Staff Sergeant Keller?

"He had a month off, and there was some speculation it was health-related," Steve whispered to me, as we headed down the hall. "I got the sense he was pacing himself a bit differently, but maybe he has had a whole new mind change."

"Like what? He went up Leonard Cohen's mountain and found nirvana? Or his doctor told him not to get het up over insignificant bugs like me, for his angina's sake?"

"Hell, I don't know, Randy." Steve sounded a bit exasperated, as if filling in the void left by Keller's lack of animosity. "It's not a social club here. He didn't come back from his time off with presents for all of us and vacation photos."

"Really? Cops don't do that?"

"Well, maybe some of us do, but I don't think anyone would expect it of Keller. No fraternizing with the lower ranks is more his style."

Steve opened a door with a frosted-glass panel on the top.

"Here we are. Joe, you've met Randy before at Rutherford House. Randy, Joe Howard."

It was odd to be going through introductions as if we were at a party, but courtesy was Steve's middle name and somehow he made it work. Detective Howard and I shook hands and he thanked me again for coming in to help them with the investigation. I took a much more comfortable chair by his desk. Steve squeezed my shoulder in farewell and left us to it.

Detective Howard had me read through the statement I'd made the evening of the murder, to see whether there were things I wanted to add or correct before signing it. Reading it brought all the memories of that night flooding back into the forefront of my mind, making me wonder, as a side thought, just how much compartmentalizing I did on a regular basis. As it stood, the statement seemed accurate to me, so I took the pen offered and signed and dated my statement. Detective Howard, who had been doing some sort of Internet search, or perhaps playing mah-jongg on his computer while I read, now swivelled his chair toward me and focused his full attention on me. He asked me if I'd mind being taped during my interview and ushered me into an interview room that was just the tiniest bit claustrophobic. He set out an old-school tape recorder, spoke the date and time, identified himself, named me, and rattled off the case number. Then he stopped the tape, rewound it, and listened to whether or not it had taped. I smiled. He shook his head at me.

"I lost vital testimony my rookie year by forgetting to hit 'record.' You do that once, you check every time for the rest of your career. I am not sure whether I'm looking forward to us going digital, if we ever get new equipment in here, or not. It'll be one more thing to worry about, if you ask me."

"Wow, no kidding." I settled into the chair and Howard started the machine once more.

"You are not quite the same level of employee as the deceased, in the hierarchy of Rutherford House, are you?"

"Well, no. Technically, I suppose I am not so much an employee of Rutherford House as of the foundation that supports it. I am under contract to design and write the virtual museum website that is going to accompany the centennial book recently published about the House. I was just pitching in to help, because the manager, Marni Livingstone, was short-handed that evening."

"Were you being paid for your efforts?"

"I sure hope so. I think Marni was going to write it up as an honorarium, rather than set me up with an employee number. That was how she paid the magician and the actors, too."

"The magician, Stephen Dafoe, is who you are referring to, correct?"

"Dafoe da Fantabulist. That is how he billed himself, and it was written that way on his storage bins. All six of them."

"Had you met Mr. Dafoe prior to that evening?"

"No, but I think Jossie had seen him perform somewhere before. It may have been she who suggested him to Marni, who put the entire evening together. Marni thought the actors' production of a mystery-dinner show set around a magicians' reunion was good, but would be stronger if a real magic act was part of the event. None of the actors could do more than fan a deck of cards, so she went outside to hire Mr. Dafoe. And it was great. All the guests were still buzzing as they went in to dinner, and the theatre worked so much better, I think, than it would have otherwise."

"Tell me how things ran at the dinner."

I took him through the various steps, trying to remember if at any points I had seen Jossie where she wasn't supposed to be, or anything else that seemed out of place. Howard sensed what I was doing and broke in to tell me to just describe it as I saw it in my mind's eye, and not to worry about analyzing things as I went. I guess, having had to go through this sort of exercise a few times more than the average citizen, I was more self-aware of what was expected of me.

You would have thought that, with the number of times I'd actually given a statement to Steve or his colleagues over the years, I would be a master at detailing my recollections and reflections, but maybe that never becomes a learned behaviour. I tried to just hit a mental replay button, but even such a short time after the event, some things were fuzzy, and I said so.

"Shock and trauma will do that to a person," Howard nodded. "Everything gets coloured by the ending you already know is there. You're doing fine, though. So, the paying guests had sat down for the meal and you were helping the magician clean up."

I went back into my part of the evening. I had gone down to the kitchen to get meals for Mr. Dafoe and myself, and had carried them up the maid's staircase to the maid's parlour. We had eaten there until the time I was to act as sentry for the actress playing the body to slip upstairs with no one seeing her. I saw that happen, and saw the play-acting murderer move into place in the study, from my place in the foyer. Once the guests were on the move, I was back in service, cleaning tables. I had assumed Jossie must have been doing the same thing, but I couldn't actually see her from where I was working. I then found out the dining room hadn't been cleared and had to race to do it myself.

"So, guests are milling about, some of them in the parlour where the clue board is, some of them in the library where two of the actors are talking and possibly giving clues. Some of them may have gone upstairs by this time, but for certain, we have Tanya Rivera up there in the master closet and Dafoe the magician in the maid's parlour, unless he has already gone home. You are in the restaurant area, cleaning tables. Who do you actually see when you are taking plates downstairs and bringing up dessert settings?"

I thought about it with my eyes closed.

"Marni was downstairs talking to the chef when I went down with a bus pan full of dirty dishes. I saw the actor playing the detective sitting in the alcove of the gift shop, waiting for his cue. Roxanne was down there, too, reading a book. I was certain I saw Jossie carrying dishes down the stairs from the dining-room area, but then the chef chided me for not getting things reset properly, and I noticed all the dessert dishes for that side were still waiting down there. When I went upstairs again, the dining room hadn't been reset at all."

"Did anything else unusual stick out for you? Something out of place, someone where they shouldn't necessarily have been?"

"Well, some of it was a bit of a blur. Normally, when I am in the House, it's just me and a couple of interpreters and three tables of people having high tea. It was as if the fraternity boys were back that night. The House was packed and people were all talking and thumping about. Nothing really stood out. Well…"

"Yes?"

"There was an older woman there who didn't seem all that jolly. She was talking to Marni at one point and seemed really sour."

"Did she do anything unusual?"

"Well, not really. I think she may be a board member who is purported to be opposed to special events taking place in the House. So I guess she was checking up on things. Come to think of it, maybe she was just annoyed because she felt she had to attend, in her capacity as board member, something she didn't find entertaining or appropriate."

Detective Howard made a note, with the tape still running.

"Tell me a bit more about the magician. What did you talk about when you ate dinner?"

"He mostly asked me about my research and work at the House and about the House in general. He was interested in the time period, he said. His family had come to the area around the same time as the Rutherfords, he said, but I got the feeling they were in a different tax bracket. I really wanted to ask him about how he managed some of his illusions, but was too shy to do so. So the conversation mostly went where he led it."

"How did he feel about the actors pretending to be magicians?"

"I don't think that bothered him. I saw him talking to Mark before the event started and got the sense he was giving him some tips on banter and presentation. He really is an interesting person, not the sort of person you would suspect of even knowing a card trick, let alone the amazing stuff he did."

"How so?" Howard seemed genuinely curious about the magic, rather than merely leading an interrogation.

"Well, he came in all dressed in browns and earth tones, and gave off a vibe of being anything other than a performer. I helped him bring in his totes and he was very polite and thanked me. When he was in the middle of his act, he was mesmerizing, a totally different person. You would swear he was a matinee idol, that kind of looks. I have no idea how he did that, with just a change of clothing. And then, after he disappeared, the little brown-suited man reappeared and you wouldn't have looked at him twice on the street."

"And you left him in the maid's parlour?"

"Yes, he was still eating. I had finished and heard the cue for helping the actress, so excused myself. I think I promised I'd be back with desserts, and I never did that. He must have let himself out, because when I went upstairs to see about the screaming, I just found his dishes sitting on the floor of the maid's parlour."

"Could he have let himself out one of the back doors without setting off an alarm?"

"You would have to ask Marni that. I know there was a way to turn them off and that Mr. Dafoe had sorted out with her a way of his disappearing through the parlour window, so I think he may have let himself back in one of the back doors. And the actress, Tanya, was going to head out the back way after her 'body' had been discovered. Maybe the alarm stayed off. Hey, are you thinking someone from outside could have come into the house and murdered Jossie?"

"Well, they would have had to go up the maid's staircase and walk past you and Dafoe in the maid's parlour in order to place themselves in the guest room, somehow luring Jossie up there in order to break her neck and toss her in the bathtub. We're not ruling out an outsider, but logic dictates that the murderer was already in the house."

I couldn't help myself; I shivered. "Do you think it was Jossie the murderer was after? Or did she just get in the way of something else? Do you think murder was the purpose? Or was it incidental?"

"Right now, we are keeping an open mind about any and all possibilities. If you have any other thoughts about that evening, feel free to call me at any time. Here is my card. You can leave as detailed a message as you like. The voice mail goes to me alone."

I pocketed Joe Howard's card and stood up, glad to be released from the tiny taping room. The air in the main office, which had seemed laced with eau de testosterone on my way in, seemed a lot fresher now. Steve was standing near Nancy Gibson's desk, shooting the breeze while waiting for me. He smiled as he saw me, and my heart lifted, making me realize how anxious I'd been feeling. I couldn't imagine being a real criminal herded into an interrogation room, if this is what "helping the police with their inquiries" felt like.

"Hey, kiddo! Did Joe bring out the brass knuckles?"

"No, just a rubber hose," I countered. "So, is that all you folks need me for?"

"For the time being," Detective Howard said, coming up behind me with the tape recorder still in his hand. He transferred it to his left hand and stuck out his right for me to shake. "Thank you for your help today. I hope you won't be leaving town without telling us."

"That's okay. Unless you consider going to the Ukrainian Village for an afternoon leaving town, I'm not going anywhere. And come to think of it, I'll be taking a police escort with me."

Detective Howard smiled. "I think the Ukrainian Village can be considered within the boundaries of accessible contact."

"All right then." I turned to Steve. "You are still free to join me in a jaunt out there, aren't you?"

"I am. Why is it you are heading out there, again? Rutherford doesn't sound like a very Ukrainian name to me."

"Well, they've set their re-enactment timing around the same time as the Rutherfords were building the new house and he was so focused on building the university. I thought it would be a nice parallel to denote how different country life was, even within the area, to highlight the splendour that was Achnacarry"

"Achna-what?"

"It means 'place near the fish weir' in Gaelic. Achnacarry was the name of the ancestral home of the Rutherfords, so that was the name of the brick house."

"Okay, so that's not pretentious."

"Not if you think about it from an early-twentieth-century mindset, which, let's face it, was a late-nineteenth-century frame of reference. Everyone named everything. Heck, people still name their summer cottages. Just drive along the road round Pigeon Lake if you don't believe me."

Detective Gibson spoke up. "These bozos all name their cars." She nodded her head in the fellows' direction.

I laughed with her, seeing the wounded looks on Steve and Joe's faces. "I rest my case."

Steve shrugged philosophically, willing to cede the argument to me. That was one of the many things I loved about him, his lack of a need-to-always-be-right gene.

"Let me make sure I'm still free for Saturday, before you leave."

"That would be great. I'm going straight home now, since it's too late to go back to the Archives. I really need to pick up where I left off tomorrow."

He smiled at me, knowingly.

"I have a feeling you want to drive out to the Ukrainian Village, right? As in taking your rental car?"

"You better believe it, buster," I laughed. "I am turning into a true-blue Alberta girl. Next thing you know, I am going to be buying a straw hat and a pickup."

"Rodeo Randy, now that I would like to see."

Walking back through the halls and joking with Steve made the building somehow less authoritarian and stern. When I was finally out in the parking lot, clicking my keyfob to let myself into the little green car, I realized my shoulders felt an entire three inches lower than they'd been on my way into the building.

In order to take full advantage of the wheels at my disposal,

I stopped off at the H & W green grocers, tucked away off any regular bus route on 34th Avenue, where I picked up five bags' worth of vegetables and fruit for under $30. It really was fun to have a car.

13

Popular wisdom says that it takes three weeks to form a new habit, which is why so many gym memberships languish after ten days and people find that twenty-one-day marker something to celebrate, if they ever reach it, when they first quit smoking. It is alarming to me, however, how quickly I can move into a routine. I was waiting in the parking lot of the Archives the next morning, lunch packed and pencil and laptop ready, when Mr. Maitland appeared at the front doors to unlock the treasure trove. He saw me and waved, holding the door open for me, as I walked toward him.

"Randy! Nice to see you again. Looks like we're going to have a sunny day, doesn't it?"

"I am hoping the weather lasts. I'm planning to head out to the Ukrainian Village Saturday, and I'd like to take some photos."

"From what I hear, the weather is supposed to hold steady for the next five days."

I wonder why it is that meteorologists can predict five

days into the future, weatherwise, but no further. Is that Siberian High, which seems to be known further south of us as an Alberta Clipper and which the Russians probably call a Mongolian Gust, so predictable that it can be seen five days in advance? Or are they still just guessing?

It didn't take much of a guess to predict today's forecast, though. Mr. Maitland was right, it was going to be a gorgeous day as Edmonton days went, sunny and bright and dry. Though we were all bracing ourselves for the possibility of a pre-Hallowe'en snowstorm that would wreak havoc with all the children who had been planning thin and filmy costumes, which would then have to be covered over by snowsuits and too-small winter boots from the season before, this sunny Indian summer we were experiencing was to be appreciated. The autumn winds had not yet arrived to denude the trees of their golden glory and the sun through the yellow leaves made everything glow a little brighter.

I followed Mr. Maitland into the warm, beech-lined foyer and resigned myself to an indoor stint. The daylight would still be there at four o'clock, although it was shortening into evening at the rate of about two minutes a day.

Once in the reading room, I took the box of Mrs. Rutherford's diaries to my favourite table and reached in for the one I'd been reading before heading off to the police station. I flipped to the middle, where the mysterious S had been mentioned. There was nothing in the previous few pages to denote who S might be. I read on from the cryptic entry. A few pages later, another entry seemed to clarify who S was, even as it opened up a new mystery.

I am certain it was on my nightstand. S. was downstairs throughout the morning, blacking the stove, so if she had a hand in things, surely there would have been a smudge. Hazel and her friends were off to the lake and I cannot imagine Alec moving it without telling me. I haven't said anything to him about it. Surely it will turn up.

Okay, so "S" had to be the maid. But what was Mattie missing from her nightstand that she couldn't mention to Alec and wasn't sure she wanted to blame on the maid? Something precious, like jewellery, that she had inherited or Alec had given her? Some important document or book she had been reading?

I was assuming there had to be some value attached to whatever it was Mattie was missing; otherwise she wouldn't be writing about it. I wondered where she kept her journals, so that the maid couldn't read what she was saying. Or maybe the maid simply couldn't read. It was possible that someone working as a servant in the early twentieth century would have only rudimentary schooling, or perhaps be an immigrant just learning English as a second or third language. Of course, there would have been other people in the house, almost constantly. Two maids could be housed in the second-floor rooms; Cecil's wife, Helen, lived with them throughout the war; Hazel came back from college and lived there till 1919, when she married. Relatives from down east came to visit and stayed for weeks at a time. Ladies came for tea and to knit for the war effort. The house was, by all accounts, a hub of activity. Given that, I really began to wonder where Mattie could have hidden all her blue-bound books.

I have gone through all my drawers and the hamper from the attic, to no avail. If it has gone missing inadvertently, somehow it has lodged itself where no one can see it. I fear, however, that it has been taken, leading me to distrust those around me. I am unsure whether my new-forged vigilance is making S. more clumsy, or whether it is a manifestation of her guilt. She bumps into tables and stammers so that I find myself speaking more sharply to her than I have ever done. I am inclined to let her go, yet fear that to have her leave before I retrieve my property might mean it is lost to me forever. Alec is too preoccupied with his present case to notice my nerves, which is probably for the best, as I am not certain I would wish to divulge the loss to him as yet.

This was fascinating. If I only had some inkling of the year this diary covered, and who "S" actually was, I hadn't seen a listing of all the maids in the centennial book, but it was possible I had overlooked it, because after all, they were only maids. Wasn't that a Chesterton observation? That people never noticed the ordinary person in a uniform they expected to see, so they never mentioned a postman or a milkman walking through a crime scene, because they faded into the scenery. Maybe the maids were the same way. The focus was so much on the Rutherfords, and yet how many of us could identify with the upper echelons of early Edmonton society? How many people to visit the website would be more fascinated with the young immigrant serving girls who worked their knuckles red in the hopes of a better life in a new land?

I exchanged pleasantries with Mr. Maitland while buttoning up my coat, waxing on about my ideas of promoting the maids as a result of reading Mrs. Rutherford's diaries, but realized he probably had to endure conversations like this all the time. I grinned ruefully and made my goodbyes.

14

I wasn't sure the Friends of Rutherford House would be all that keen on affording much space on the website to the maids of the House, but since they were letting the frat boys have a strong presence, I figured I could make a case for it as a sidebar sort of linkage. I had spent the rest of the evening thinking about S and the other maids who had inhabited the two small rooms upstairs in the back of the big brick house. The more I thought about it, the more I believed I had my through-line into the website. I made a note to check on whether there were names listed in the account books for maids' wages. Perhaps I could make a list of names from that.

There was a real case to be made for highlighting the under-classes within this virtual museum, anyhow, since part of the grander purpose was to make historic resources accessible to all areas of the province, which was a diplomatic way of saying people who couldn't afford the time and gas money to drive halfway across the province to visit in person. Maybe some of those virtual visitors would get more out of seeing how the servants lived than the first premier of Alberta.

I was eager to get back into the diaries today so that I could cover some more of the fraternity rosters and a bit more of the CFUW minutes on Friday, my last full day at the Archives. Mr. Maitland waved at me as I entered the foyer. After taking only a few minutes to pop my lunch into his fridge, I soon returned to the box of Mrs. Rutherford's recollections.

I had to admit, it was the hint of a treasure hunt that had me hooked, as much as the humanizing aspect of the maids' stories becoming clearer to me. I couldn't wait to get back into deciphering the diaries to find out what it was that Mattie Rutherford had lost. Was it lost forever? I picked a diary at random from the half of the box I'd not yet perused, but the only mention of maids at all appeared in the next-to-last entry.

G. left today. I made certain to help her pack, making a great show of folding her clothing for her, telling her to sit while I did so. Could not refuse my offer to drive her down to Walter's ferry this afternoon. Her young man was meeting her on the other side of the river. She seemed less than grateful and more taciturn the closer we got to the river. Certainly, she might have considered the consequences of her actions before this. I am just as happy to be rid of her. The MacQuarries have a girl whose younger sister is looking for a position in town. Also from near Lamont. She is arriving for an interview on Thursday. Till then, I shall play the navvie.

I closed the diary and picked up the next in the box. There was nothing but listings of who was at various afternoon events.

The book after that had a few notes in it, often quoting things Hazel had written in her letters home from Ladies College. No more mentions of lost objects or truculent maids.

It was fun to eat lunch with Mr. Maitland, as I couldn't imagine anyone else being kind enough to let me blather on about interesting comments in diaries, especially about the maids and Mattie's suspicions about them. He did seem taken with the idea of focusing on maids on the website, understanding immediately my feelings that too many people had been sidelined in the vision of Canadian history. Of course, he might have just been being polite.

I beavered away for another few hours, and then packed things up. Poor Mr. Maitland was nowhere to be seen. I sure hoped his assistant didn't decide to extend her vacation. He certainly had his hands full.

On Friday, I ate my lunch earlier than Mr. Maitland and got back to work as soon as I could. I flipped through the diaries, scanning rather than reading each and every word. It wasn't till the seventh volume that my eyes hooked on another entry.

This book was very clearly marked "1923." The entry in question was June 15, and it was the use of initials once more that grabbed my attention.

Cleaning the sitting room for the new girls. Found a loose floorboard, under which was a knotted handkerchief full of crumbled petals. Signs of a sad little romance left behind. Wonder which girl dreamed on her wildflower bouquet, then left it forgotten? My guess is it was B. Cannot imagine S. or G. as so sentimental. Had Stanley come nail down the board.

So, Mattie had found the maids' hidey-hole and, in her prag-
matic and sensible manner, had sealed it. It made me wonder,
though, if another hidey-hole existed, somewhere in the House,
where "S" had managed to secrete the missing item, the loss of
which had worried Mattie so. And it also made me wonder if
something like the thought of hidden treasure was behind the
tragedy during the magic evening at the House.

I put the diary back in the box, intending to place the box on
the "To Be Refiled" shelf. First, though, as an obsessive-com-
pulsive tic, I ran my fingers over the spines of the blue books,
counting them as I went. Frowning, I counted again, more
focused. Thirty-two. I was sure there had been five guest books
and thirty-three diaries in this box when I had first begun my
research. Which one was missing? Was one missing? Maybe I
was getting as bad as Mattie Rutherford, imagining things being
ferreted away by a mysterious "S."

I checked the clock on the wall. It was almost time for the
Archives to close to the public, and I didn't want Mr. Maitland
held up on a Friday afternoon on my account. I could see him
on the other side of the window, pleasantly trying to shoo people out of the Archives store, without seeming to rush them.

I checked the side of the box, but it only said "Mrs. Mattie
Rutherford, Diaries and Guest Books," leaving me uncertain
whether or not I had miscounted in the first place. I had only ten
minutes, too little time to ascertain whether a particular book
was missing. Something occurred to me, though, and I hauled
the diaries out of the box, piling them in four stacks. Hurriedly,
I opened the fly-leaf on book after book, seeing the date written

clearly on the front inside cover. Each of the thirty-two volumes had a clear date.

Not one of them had a smudged, unreadable date.

The volume dealing with "S" and the missing item was gone.

I pulled my bag and coat out of my locker, trying to figure out what to say to Mr. Maitland when I saw him in the lobby. However, when I got out there, the grille over the gift shop area was pulled and locked and there was no sign of him. I presumed he was back in the vaults locking up. I let myself out, intending to email him from home concerning the missing diary.

15

It was a novelty to be picking Steve up at his house in my car, instead of the reverse. I had driven through Tim Hortons on the way, and because I was not used to such things, had at first given my order of two large coffees with double milks into the garbage receptacle rather than the microphone. While there were likely several baristas laughing at me on their CCTV, I was not the one wearing a funny little hat pouring coffee that morning, so in my mind I was still ahead of the game.

We drove out of the city on the Anthony Henday Drive ring road and peeled off toward Saskatchewan. The stubble in the fields was peeking out like an old man's beard. The windbreaks between the farms were more bare of leaves than the trees in the city, and somehow it made the life of a rural Albertan seem that much braver in my imagination. The only thing worse than being cold and alone over winter in the vast parkland that was north-central Alberta would be being cold and alone and mauled by a bear in the mountains. Or anywhere, come to that.

Being mauled by a bear in the Whitemud Creek Ravine would be equally terrible, but far less likely.

"Which would you rather, Steve? Freezing to death on a winter road or being mauled by a bear?"

"There are no other choices?"

"What do you mean?"

"Well, as deaths go, having an aneurysm during an orgasm would likely be my first choice."

"Ha! No, you have to pick between frostbite and bears."

"Okay, I would rather freeze. I understand you feel bizarrely warm just before you die, which accounts for why they often find people who have frozen after removing articles of clothing."

"There is that. I don't suppose you feel anything but terror and pain before a bear eats you."

"There are not that many cases of bear deaths that I would worry about it, you know."

"Oh, I know that. I just don't intend to sleep in anything except a cabin or a hotel when I'm in the mountains. I think sleeping in a tent is sort of like offering them a burrito."

"Why are we talking about bear maulings, anyhow?"

"I was just thinking about how cold and lonely it must be to live in a farm in the winter."

"Ah, of course. Makes perfect sense."

I smirked at his teasing, but since the sign for the Ukrainian Village was just ahead on the right, instead of forming a retort, I just sang, "We're here!" in my best *Poltergeist* voice and flicked on my turning signal.

There was plenty of parking in the gravel lot outside the

Administration Building. I guess an outdoor historic park is not the first thing you think of on an October weekend for amusement, unless there is a corn maze involved. People were probably already contemplating the various indoor water parks or the Galaxyland amusement park at West Edmonton Mall as their getaway destinations. That suited me fine. Crowds were not something I sought at the best of times, and I wanted a chance to take some photos of the various buildings here, in case I could use them as contrast for the website. Part of me was hoping for a suitably dressed young girl who would pose as a potential maid heading into the city for employment at the House.

We pulled up near the Admin Building, and I hauled out my backpack.

"What's in there?" Steve asked.

"Sandwiches, bananas, and another thermos of coffee, so keep hold of your Tim cup. I figure we may need sustenance by the time we get to the pig farm at the far end of the Park."

"Have you been here before?"

"Once, when they were first starting out. It was the hottest day of the summer and one of the interpreters was in a tiny little kitchen making pickles over a hot stove. My mother and dad were visiting and both of them spent the rest of the day reliving their childhoods for me, along the lines of walking-seventeen-miles-to-school-uphill-in-a-snowstorm stories. Is this your first time here?"

"Yep. I've been to Fort Edmonton and Heritage Park and out to the chimneys at Rocky Mountain House, but never made it here. There's a Ukrainian house in Elk Island Park, too, isn't there?"

"Yes, but nothing like what you're going to see here. No, put away your wallet, I am getting this."

I bought us two tickets, and promised Steve we'd look through the gift shop on the way out. He had spotted a rose-covered scarf he thought his mother might like.

We passed through the back door of the building and ambled down the causeway over a reedy marsh and into the past. To the right was the iconic building from most prairie childhoods, a grain elevator. Steve was thrilled to go inside and see how every-thing worked. He pushed on the levers to change the grain bins and jumped up and down on the floor that was also a scale. The young man minding the area smiled at Steve's city-boy enthusiasm, but managed to stay in character as Orest Simchuk, United Grain Growers officer. Steve tried to ask him about what was happening for farmers today with the dismantling of so many elevators, and what he thought it was doing to the sense of place for small-town Albertans, but Orest refused to step out of character and merely acted surprised to hear that other elevators were being torn down.

That was the one thing that bugged me about historic parks that chose to enforce the time period for their interpreters. I ended up having to work hard to place the facts I was learning in my own sense of historical perspective, and in some cases, I would end up feeling as if I was a trespasser into the homes of strangers. I preferred the way Fort Edmonton did it, with inter-preters playing their roles, but happily willing to break character if you asked them a fiddly question or two.

Still, the young folks of the Ukrainian Village knew their material, and as long as you didn't push it, they were quite accommodating. Steve was also taken with the small steel jail cell in the front room of the policeman's home.

"How would you have taken to that in your parlour, Randy?"

"Are you getting a hankering to be a small-town constable... in the last century?"

We strolled up the road that took us past the newcomer's sod house dug into the ground, which I had to admit was surprisingly cozy and reminded me greatly of Mr. Mole's house from *Wind in the Willows*. At the next farmhouse, where thatching was taking place on the roof, I asked one of the young women if I could take her picture. I asked her if she thought about going to the big city to work as a maid, and she smiled and nodded. In her made-up historic world, two of her sisters had already moved to Edmonton to work as chambermaids and were sending some money home to their mother. She was hoping to go live with her older sister in a year's time.

This was the sort of community from which the Rutherfords' maids had likely come. There was no point in talking to the girl there about photographic rights for the use on web pages; she would likely try to tell me I was possessed by a devil for mentioning such bizarre things. I figured I would discuss it with someone back at the Administration Building.

Steve was finished talking thatching with the fellows up on the roof, so we moved along to see the pigs. Three young pigs, maybe a year old, trotted about while a large sow lay on her side in the shelter of the rough-hewn sty; a middling large pig stood close to the fence. I noticed a couple of sticks leaning against the side of the fence between us and the placid animal, and handed one to Steve. Together, we leaned over the fence and scratched the pig's back. Delighted, grunty drooling noises were our reward.

One of the fancier houses was placed nearer the school and church, but even with its two storeys and wide front porch, it had nothing on the grandeur that was Rutherford House. It was much easier to see, amid the rural examples of the early twentieth century, just how spectacular the House must have been. Now, compared to places down east in Ontario or Quebec, where everything was older, statelier, and made of brick, or even Winnipeg, which was what westerners called central Canada, and what folks from Ontario lumped in with the prairies, Rutherford House was nothing out of the ordinary. Several houses on Winnipeg's Wellington Crescent dwarfed the house I'd been hired to celebrate. But here in the brash, raw West, Achnacarry must have gleamed bright with promise that civilization was truly on its way.

Steve and I sat on a bench in the sun near the gas station with its antiquated pumps and bizarre metal signs for soft drinks that no one remembered. We had to squint at each other from behind our sunglasses, but it was getting a little too chilly to sit in the shade. I was very happy he had made the time to come out with me. Although we could see a few people strolling about, it was enough off-the-beaten-track that one had to really choose to come out here. It would have been a very lonely proposition, otherwise.

"Have you ever thought of living in a small town?" I asked Steve.

"Not really, but I can see the advantages. It would be nice to walk to wherever you had to go, to know people by name, and deal with them on a daily basis instead of feeling so anonymous in grocery stores and post offices. And it would be great to have a big yard with room for your own garden and a place for kids to play."

"Really? You like to garden?"

"I didn't say that. I like to eat fresh vegetables. I figure that there is a bustling, industrious small-town wife in this fantasy who is doing all the things required of the lifestyle."

"Aha! Yes, well, here I was considering the fellow who would be shovelling that long expanse of driveway and supervising the septic-tank truck driver and teaching all those kids to skate and drive cars."

"Face it, we're as urban as it gets." He stood up and held his hand out. I took it and let him pull me to a standing position. We picked up after our makeshift picnic, dusted ourselves off, and headed back toward the Administration Building.

"That sandwich was good, but it's a shame their restaurant wasn't still open. I could really go for some pyrogies."

"Just watching all that activity makes you think you can eat like a farmhand, eh?"

Steve laughed. "I guess so. Those fellows were really working up a sweat, too."

He went off to price the scarf for his mother while I spoke to the woman in the glassed-in office. I explained who I was and what my project was, and that I might wish to use some of the photos I had taken for a contrast and connection to Rutherford House.

As both sites were considered Provincial Historic Sites of Alberta and overseen by the Ministry of Culture, she could see no problem with the use of the photos. The interpreters all signed contracts that allowed their photos to be taken and used at the photographers' discretion, which I supposed made sense when you were working in a tourist haven. I thanked her, took her card in case I needed to contact her, and went to find Steve.

He was at the till, sheepishly buying not only a scarf, but two painted wooden pysankas, or Ukrainian Easter eggs, and a pair of pysanka earrings, which he presented to me.

"It seemed like a nice memento for the day," he said.

They were lovely, intricately patterned in black and white and red, emulating the stylized patterns stencilled and wax-resist coloured onto delicate eggs, from which the inner yolk and albumen had been blown out a tiny hole in the bottom. This was the true Ukrainian icon; no wonder there was a huge version on a pedestal in Vegreville. It ranked as one of the greatest of those "world's largest" roadside attractions.

I popped the hooks of the earrings out of their paper card and into my ears.

"Thank you," I said, and leaned up to kiss him, to the shy delight of the young woman behind the till, who probably thought people in their forties just wrote sonnets to each other for erotic release.

We walked hand-in-hand back to my rental car, and settled

cozily into its warmth from the sunny parking lot. It was a forty-minute trip back home, but Steve had suggested we head for an early dinner downtown, so I was keeping my eye peeled for the turnoff to the Victoria Trail rather than the Henday.

"So why are you so interested in the maids of Rutherford House all of a sudden? Are you looking for something to add to the research already done? Or is there something about a particular maid that has your interest?"

I told him about Mrs. Rutherford's diaries, her distrust of one of her maids, the loss of something she wouldn't mention in the books, and almost as an afterthought, the fact that one of the books had disappeared.

"Are you sure?"

"As sure I can be. That particular book had the date badly smudged, as if liquid had got on the fly-leaf. You could see the first two numbers, but not the second two. And not one of those diaries in the box yesterday had that fly-leaf."

"Did you mention it to the archivist?"

"We had been talking about the diaries and my interest in the maids over lunch a couple of days earlier, but on Friday afternoon, Mr. Maitland was busy with some folks in the store when I let myself out. He's been short-staffed the whole time I was there, so I didn't want to disrupt him. I am planning on calling him next week, to talk to him about it. But you know, part of me is just in denial, or was, until I mentioned it to you. It must have been him removing it from my research grasp, right? After all, who steals a diary that is almost one hundred years old?"

"Someone who is looking for something they don't want

other people to find first?" Steve supplied. "After all, someone cared enough to kill someone at Rutherford House. I don't think we can overlook the connection, Randy. You need to mention this to the archivist and to Detectives Gibson and Howard."

I sighed.

"You're right. I was just hoping it was nothing, you know? For once, I would like to be totally uninvolved."

Steve laughed. "Sure thing. I have a feeling you want to be so uninvolved that you were going to head in to the House looking for the floorboard Stanley nailed down in the maids' sitting room, when, tomorrow? Or were you going to be really reserved and mature and wait till Monday?"

"Damn your perspicacity, Steve Browning."

"And bless your little gumshoes, my dear. Just don't get all girl sleuth on me and go do this on your own. Do not forget, there's someone out there who takes whatever this is seriously enough to kill. I don't want him or her setting sights on you next."

I shivered. "No, me either."

16

I had only one more day with the car, or technically twelve hours, if you wanted to get picky. My contract was to get it back to the lot by six with a full tank of gas. While my plans had been to drive to Fort Edmonton Park and tour the other Rutherford House on 1905 Street, walking around yet another historic park with costumed interpreters trying to engage me in make-believe just seemed like far too much work for a Sunday. Instead, I found myself sleeping in for the first time in ages, then padding about my apartment making a grocery list.

Treats, when you are young, consist of presents and toys, or splendid outings. As you get older, treats realign themselves into more mundane and useful considerations, like being able to venture to a grocery store for a substantial shopping expedition. My biggest goal of the day was to drive to the closest Superstore to stock up on canned goods, cleaning supplies, and fresh produce, and then come home by way of the M&M Meat Shops for a box of frozen chicken breasts. The glory of having wheels was not going to be used up by merely ferrying me back and forth to the Archives. This little car was going to be put to use. I was seriously considering a quick jaunt out to IKEA as well, but the sad truth was that my apartment couldn't actually contain one more BILLY bookcase; I was going to have to cull some books instead.

Next weekend would be soon enough to visit Fort Edmonton Park, and if I couldn't coax Steve into coming along, I could always catch a bus at the South Campus LRT Station and walk in to the park from the bus stop on Fox Drive. Apparently, there was a shuttle that operated, but only during the peak summer tourist hours. As they were now focused on school groups who arrived in their own buses, solitary carless visitors had to leg it in along the river valley path running under the busy Quesnell Bridge, each step taking them further and further away from the twenty-first century and back into the early days of Edmonton, first as a trading post, then a settlement, and eventually a city.

I hauled my purchases, including a new mop and doormat, out of the hatchback, unpacked a dozen more bags than I could have ever carried home on foot from the local Safeway, and filled up my depleted cupboards and rather empty fridge. I still had some time before I had to take the car back, so I called Denise to see if she had time for a get-together.

"I am in the midst of marking research papers, and have torn out all my hair. Yes, please, rescue me!" was her response on the phone. I promised to be over within twenty minutes, and grabbed the paperwork for the car rental along with my satchel and keys. Denise and I could have high tea or an early supper or whatever you called eating when it occurred between lunch and dinner, and I could take the car back on the way home.

Denise, my best friend since grad school days, had been moving up the tenure-track mountain and was now officially an associate professor. In another year, Routledge was going to be publishing her book on father-daughter relationships in Shakespeare, and my guess was she was going to be bumped up to full professor status. As far as I could tell, they had better up the ante pretty quickly or they might lose her entirely. In the last while, Denise had been having a long-distance relationship with a fellow Shakespeare scholar at Vanderbilt University. There were probably a lot of nice colleges a whole lot closer to Nashville who would jump at hiring a well-respected, published scholar like Denise.

Maybe it was just that whole prophet-not-being-recognized-in-their-own-home-town sort of thing. Denise was unusual in that she had been hired straight from the moment she finished her PhD. Most departments tended to hire from someone else's student pool, in order to maintain some sort of cross-pollination. Or perhaps there was a quota on just how many full professorships a department could engage. Whatever the case, Denise was to my mind the epitome of what a university professor should be—dedicated, curious, and engaged, and most of all, amazingly classy.

As if to prove my point, she walked out of the tidy house she had purchased in Parkallen, dressed in a grey leather jacket over dark jeans and a green turtleneck. Her black leather gloves matched her boots, and her tam and matching scarf held black, grey, and green lines in the wool, tying the whole ensemble together. She had likely just grabbed it out of the closet as she saw me drive up, but I would have had to plan that look for half an hour.

"Ooh, isn't this fun! Randy Craig at the wheel. How have you enjoyed having a car this week?"

"It's been amazing. This is an entirely different town, depending on how you get around in it."

"Isn't that the truth? I am constantly amazed at the various circles alive within this place that I am totally unconnected to. A student will make some reference, or I'll read something on the news, and whole vistas will open up. For instance, did you know that raves were still happening here?"

"Denise, I had no idea raves ever happened here. In fact, I only figured out what raves were about a year ago."

"See! You are proving my thesis over again."

We drove to the gallery district on the north side of the river, over by 124th Street, at the end of Jasper Avenue. For someone almost preternaturally slender, Denise had an extraordinarily sweet tooth and was opting for tea and pastries at the Duchess Bake Shop. As far as I am concerned, all bakeries should have a restaurant component to them, because sitting in the midst of all that yeasty, sweet deliciousness was the metaphorical icing on the cake. The real icing wasn't bad either.

Denise ordered a London Fog, pea soup, and a brioche. I opted for the beef and barley soup, but went along with her choice of drink and pastry. We sat ourselves close to the wall. Bright and airy, the Duchess had large windows facing the street that made you feel as if you were part of the display behind glass cases. Passersby on their way to a matinee at the Roxy Theatre looked in, very likely salivating at the thought of trading places with us.

"So how goes the battle of the website?" Denise asked, daintily wiping flakes of pastry from her lips with her napkin. It was as if she had tacitly determined to resist talking about the murder, for which I silently thanked her. "Is it easier or harder to focus on researching one specific thing, rather than all those singers and recordings?" She was referring to the website writing I had done for folkwaysAlive! at the Centre for Ethnomusicology.

"In a way, it is easier. There is more of a structure to hang things on, with the chronological history of the family, then the fraternity, and finally the push to make it a historic site. But, you know, it's not that easy to humanize it, even with all the people involved, and that's what really needs to happen. There have been books about Alexander Rutherford, and the centennial book about the House itself covers a lot of interviews with people who had some connection or other to the house or the Rutherford family. I'm not trying to reinvent the wheel with the stuff people will find on the website."

"Do you envision the people coming to the website as the same people who will have read the book? Or is the focus to attract a different set of people, who might not have toured the House or read the book beforehand?"

"There's the million-dollar question for sure. My theory is that they overlap in a way that makes me worry about overkill of some material. Some of the folks on the board would probably like to see everything replicated online. And I am pretty certain the interpreters would like the website to just offer the hours of operation, so that they can work their own personal magic on visitors to the House, without having to deal with people who already know a little 'something something' before they get up the stairs."

Denise wrapped her fingers around her tea mug. "Well, according to reading I've been doing lately on advertising and promotion, the best way to pull someone into caring about anything is to personalize it. People will spend more charitable dollars saving one Rosalita with her big sad eyes than they will if you tell them that over a quarter of a million children in any particular country go to bed hungry every night. So, you need to find your personal hook, and my money says it probably isn't Alexander Rutherford himself."

"I think you're right," I nodded. "He was by all accounts a very impressive man, but there is something dry about that focus. I have been reading Mattie Rutherford's diaries, to find a way into her as a personality, and I'd been thinking of focusing on the kids, but of course they were both technically grown-ups by the time the Rutherfords moved into the brick house. Having read my way through the diaries, I think I may introduce the maid's role in a bigger way."

"A maid! Oh, I agree, that's your hook. Bring in the groundling interest, with the lower-caste element. You can play the whole *Upstairs Downstairs, Downton Abbey* card. Have you found any former maids in the interviews?"

I tried to see the list of interviewees in my mind, closing my eyes and running mentally down the page. Looking back at Denise, I shook my head.

"You know, I don't think there were any listed. And that is so odd. Why hasn't anyone come forward and identified themselves with that role?"

Denise shrugged. "I can't imagine it would have been the most prestigious thing to admit, and if you were a child or grandchild of such a person, would you automatically tell the world that your grandmother had been servant, even to a family such as the Rutherfords?"

"I don't know. My mother has always mentioned that her great-grandfather was the head gardener at Stoneleigh Abbey in England with great pride."

Denise laughed. "Well, there are two things happening there. First off, your mother is falling into the great Canadian habit of noting that any connection to the British Isles somehow carries a cachet of great import and, secondly, being head gardener of an estate would be on a par with being the matron of a large hospital or the director of a foundation these days. But to be a housemaid to a well-to-do family out in western Canada in what is just barely a province? Not so much."

I licked my finger to pick up stray bits of sugary pastry off my plate. "You may be right. So, if I am going to create her presence on the website, she would have to be an amalgam of what was probably several girls over the years."

Denise nodded. "Yes, and using her as the entry persona, you will have created someone outside the family and not totally familiar with the society in which they move. In a way, you are creating a first-time visitor to the House. Of course, your visitors would be more educated in general, and probably more sophisticated, but their lack of specific knowledge could be mirrored in the maid's outsider status, making it easier for them to gain entrance to the story."

Denise looked so happy with her pronouncements that I insisted on picking up the cheque and treating her for helping me clarify the patterns in my mind. Truth was, my task wasn't going to be quite as simple as scouring the archives for more information on the Rutherford maids. I had a feeling Mattie Rutherford didn't want all that much found. And if I was right about the missing diary, she had someone still watching out for her interests today.

17

I had dropped Denise off and delivered the lovely little car back to the rental shop with an hour to spare. As I walked back up to Jasper Avenue, it occurred to me my choices for getting home were threefold. I could walk five blocks east and catch a bus in front of the *Edmonton Journal* building, which would drop me around the corner from my apartment. I could pop right down into the Corona LRT station and get off at the University station, leaving me three blocks from home. Or more sensibly, I could walk five blocks to the High Level Bridge and trudge the half-mile edifice home, working off the Duchess pastries in the process. On the whole, the subway was the most appealing. I turned in that direction, but was happily waylaid by the sight of the burgundy window awnings of Audreys Books.

I don't really ever need a good excuse to visit Audreys, but this time I had one. If I was going to get a handle on the maid persona as my fictional host to the website, I needed to do some reading. Nodding at the pleasant young woman behind the till,

I crossed past the banks of enticing new releases and bestsellers that crowded the front of the bookstore and headed straight for the Canadiana section next to the history shelves. I was looking for one particular book, *All of Baba's Children*, by Myrna Kostash, but was open to finding anything that would illuminate for me the life of the Ukrainian immigrant to Alberta in the early twentieth century. Kostash herself was of Ukrainian descent and had made a livelihood of researching and writing her roots and those of her ancestors. Her first book was the one I was searching for. I had owned a copy once, but had a vague recollection of loaning it out to someone who had likely packed it away with his books when he took a post-doc at Memorial. Academics are like magpies, only the shiny objects they steal and hoard are usually books.

I found it, along with a couple of other books on the subject. Flipping through a highly-illustrated, coffee-table-sized tome, I came across several of the propaganda posters the Canadian government had sent out to lure broad shouldered farmers from the breadbasket of Europe with the promise of cheap land all their own. I wondered how many second and third sons packed up their belongings the day they saw that ad.

Aware that I had to carry home whatever I bought, I put back the big hard-covered volumes and took Kostash's book, an overview of historic sites of Alberta, and two other smaller paperbacks to the till. I didn't dare wander the stacks, or I'd end up with two mystery novels, the new Trevor Cole, and box of magnetic fridge poetry. I wasn't safe on my own in a bookstore, especially this one.

"Did you find everything you were looking for?" the young woman asked me and I nodded. She placed my purchases in a burgundy bag and I exited toward the LRT steps across the intersection.

My phone was ringing as I got in the door to my apartment, and I dashed for it without turning on the lights, bumping my shin on the coffee table that had not moved an inch in the seven years it had been mine.

"Randy?"

"Hey, Steve! I just got in."

"I have been trying to call you on your cellphone. Why didn't you pick up?"

"Really? I had it with me in my purse." I rummaged into the front pocket from where I had just dug my keys. Yes, my phone was there, but as I pressed the button to unlock it, I realized that the ringer was set to silent. Sure enough, there were several missed calls, message notifications, and text messages lit up on the face of the phone.

"Oh rats, it was on silent, I'm sorry."

"Randy, the point of getting you that phone was so that you could be accessible to the rest of the world, most specifically, me. It doesn't work if you don't have the ringer on."

"Do you want me to listen to all these, or are you going to tell me what you wanted? I was out with Denise and then taking the car back." I didn't figure I needed to admit I had also been spending money in a bookstore.

"I just wanted to make sure where you were and to find out whether or not you had heard."

"Heard what?" I suddenly was tuning in to the grim tone of Steve's voice.

"The archivist at the Provincial Archives was found murdered this afternoon."

There was a fuzzy noise beside my temples, and I sat down unceremoniously on the edge of my sofa.

"Mr. Maitland? Murdered? But I eat my lunch with him."

"Randy, I am so sorry."

"Steve, I don't think I can talk on the phone at the moment."

"I am coming over, as soon as I can."

I don't recall hanging up the phone, or how I made it to the washroom, but the shock of hearing that another person I'd been so recently connected to was dead acted like ipecac on the system. Luckily, there was something in my stomach to throw up, because the retching would probably have occurred anyhow. I am not certain why the verbal news of Mr. Maitland's death would hit me harder than actually seeing Jossie dead in the tub. Did it have something to do with being alone when I got the news, instead of seeing her through all that puzzling mayhem? Or was it linked to my feelings for each person? Maybe it was Mr. Maitland's kindnesses to me, or the vision of me leaving him on his own at the end of the day on Friday. All I knew was that the news hit me hard.

By the time Steve arrived, I had cleaned myself up and was lying on the chesterfield with a cool washcloth over my eyes, trying to restore some equilibrium.

"I'll make you something to eat," he offered, but I couldn't bear to think of food, so instead he produced tea and toast, the international offering to weak stomachs and shock victims. We were both sitting on the sofa, my knees now bent and my toes wedged under his thigh for support and warmth and solidity.

"He was the loveliest man, Steve. It's like he was the most perfect person for the job, as if he was himself a cog in the machine that was the Archives. I cannot imagine him gone."

"All I can say at the moment is that I was relieved to hear you weren't still working there this weekend," Steve answered, patting my knee. "When the call came through, I was scared to death."

"No, I only had the car this week, so I did all my Archive stuff earlier, though I was intending to head back to discuss that missing diary with him next week." I sat up straight, bringing my chest to my knees. "Steve, you don't think Mr. Maitland was killed because of anything to do with the Rutherford House research, do you?"

"It's hard not to make that connection when Jossie Jaque was killed at Rutherford House itself just a week ago. Regardless of the fact that *Maclean's* magazine had dubbed us the murder capital of Canada a few years ago, Edmonton is just not the hotbed of crime they wanted the country to believe. When two cases occur with no clear suspect and a possible link, we have to examine the link. And that link is…."

"Rutherford House," I interjected.

Steve looked at me, and I was about to apologize for interrupting him, but he squeezed my knee and continued.

"What I was going to say was, that link is you."

18

The death of Alastair Maitland, found bludgeoned in the lobby of the Provincial Archives, was front-page news in both papers, and made it below the fold in *The Globe and Mail*. The general idea was that Mr. Maitland had been set upon by a petty thief; the till in the shop area had been broken into and emptied. One of the newspapers was tying it to some thefts in the Mill Woods area and linking it to the rash of robberies perpetrated by a group of teens in hoodies, who apparently had been swarming convenience stores, demanding money and goods while threatening to beat up the proprietor or wreak havoc.

If that was the case, I was thankful that whoever it had been had not gained access to the archives themselves. It seemed that Mr. Maitland had been in the process of locking up on Friday evening and had already set the combination lock to the climate-controlled warehouse. The thieves would have had to beat that information out of him, since he was so protective of the materials. I shivered as I realized that quite possibly they had tried.

Such a nice man—I still couldn't wrap my mind around the thought that he was gone. I had been looking forward to heading back there to talk to him about the missing diary.

That was a lie, of course. I had not been looking forward to it in the least, as part of me was suspicious that he had removed the diary himself, so that I couldn't see it again. Somehow, there was a connection between Mr. Maitland and the murder at Rutherford House, but I was buffaloed if I could see it.

Steve had suggested I write up a statement about being in the Archives to do research on the Rutherford House website, so that it could be added to the file on Mr. Maitland's murder. That way, any link that might be there would be acted upon. Although I knew Staff Sergeant Keller, seeing my name on yet another open file, would likely spew coffee all over the report, I wrote a short statement and sent it by email, not wanting to make the trek to the station for so marginal and voluntary a report. It would also nicely avoid the risk of running into Keller face to face.

Meanwhile, I still had work to do on the Rutherford House website. I had spent most of Monday just trying to regain equilibrium, and started slowly on Tuesday morning, by remaining at home to read through the books on Ukrainian Albertans I'd bought and download the photos I had taken when we'd been out at the Ukrainian Village. That trip now seemed like months ago. Nothing like a murder now and then to really screw with timelines. Huge shocks to the system tend to reinforce Einstein's theory that time is indeed the most relative of measurements. I looked at the pictures Steve and I had posed in together, which he had taken by extending his long arm to get us both in the frame. We looked so relaxed, even though we'd been dealing then with the death of a young woman. But that had seemed so random, so disconnected to me then. I knew that were I to take a similar photo today, the skin around my eyes would be tight, the brow furrowed, the nasolabial folds on either side of my mouth far more pronounced. Death was closing in around us, and I had no idea why.

I dragged myself over to the House on Wednesday morning. It seemed like forever since I'd been there, cleaning up after Jossie's murder. In reality, it was just ten days ago. Ten days and another death.

Marni was in her office, I was told by Roxanne, who was manning the front door, but she wanted to see me if I came in today. That was fine with me, as Marni was the person I had come to see. Not only did I have to report to her where I was at with the research, I wanted to run by her the idea of a maid persona to introduce people to the site. Since the folks here were so tied up in the personalities of the Rutherfords themselves, I wasn't sure how much buy-in I was going to get, but something about the idea of the vaguely anonymous character of the maid drawing in the casual Net surfer had a real appeal for me, and I intended to fight for it.

I also wanted to get some pictures of the maid's areas so that I could use them for a better connection to the text I intended to produce. *Up the Back Stairs* was my working title so far, even though I had been assured by several egalitarian interpreters that when there were no guests in the house, the Rutherford maids were allowed access to the main staircase. None of them ever sounded ironic when stating this, either.

I clomped up said staircase to get to Marni's office. She was at her desk, staring at her computer screen when I got to the doorway, but turned to me immediately. She looked terrible. Dark circles defined her eye sockets and her hair, which was usually tidy in a French roll, hung limply to her shoulders, tucked behind her ears, which were without jewellery. It suddenly hit me that Marni had known Mr. Maitland. Of course she would have, they were in the same line of work. No wonder she looked like hell. If I thought I felt bad, I could only imagine how she was holding it together.

"Oh Randy, how are you?"

"Hanging on," I said. "What about you? Mr. Maitland was a friend of yours?" It was a stab, but a fairly positive one. Bull's eye. Marni's eyes filled up with tears, threatening to flood.

"Alastair and I go way back. We were in grad school together, and of course, there were always curatorial workshops. We didn't socialize much, but he was always there, you know?"

I nodded. Other people's grief makes me uncomfortable, not because I don't want to validate it, but because I am so terribly worried I might inadvertently say the wrong thing.

"I only met him last week, but he was very personable and nice. I really liked him."

Marni yanked a tissue from the box on her desk and dabbed at her eyes.

"God, I must look a sight. Sorry. The reason I wanted to see you was that I needed to warn you that one of our board members is not too happy with the whole idea of an interactive website and has made her feelings known to me. Her argument seems to be that offering too much on a computer site negates the need to visit the House itself, and may remove the government's sense of urgency to maintain funding. After all, if they can just run a virtual museum, perhaps they could board up the actual site and save on upkeep. She is talking about bringing it up at the next meeting of the board in a couple of weeks' time, and I wanted you to be prepared for that. I was also wondering if you would have anything by that time to produce for the board, to show them the project's scope?"

"In two weeks?" I squeaked. "That's pretty short notice. I can mock up some of the material, but I have barely scratched the surface of my research, and what with the Archives being closed as a crime scene, that end of things has been put on hold."

"I'm not saying anything has to be completed. I just thought that if we could have you present something to the board to counter Greta's bad-mouthing of the project, there'd be a chance to maintain it. Otherwise, there is a possibility she could stop things in their tracks."

Greta Larsen. How on earth did I know Marni had to have been talking about her?

"What about my contract with the Friends?"

Marni looked worried. "That's the problem. There is a condition in that contract that the board has to approve all aspects of the project. If it gets voted on and there isn't the support of the board, we may have to enact the kill fee. Which is not something I want to do," she hurried to add.

"Wow. Well, I had better get cracking then."

"Was there something you wanted to talk about?" she called, as I turned to head out into the upper hallway.

"No, nothing that can't wait till after the board meeting ultimatum, I guess. Sorry, Marni, if all I have is two weeks, I don't have time to talk."

Two weeks. How was I going to get things organized enough in a linear fashion to create a mock-up of the website by then? I knew I had an opening, and I had some ideas of how to progress through the Rutherford years into the fraternity days, but the thought of making a presentation to a negatively-minded board filled me with dread. Bloody Greta Larsen. What was it about that snarly-faced woman that made her hate my project? And why was she so determined that Rutherford House not be as celebrated a historic site as Head-Smashed-In Buffalo Jump or Stephansson House? Damn, the Brookes Aqueduct had more of a web presence than Rutherford House.

I popped down to the Arbour Tea Room to grab a bite to eat. A table of three women and another two tables of couples were seated in the sunroom area, but luckily there was no one in the breakfast room portion of the restaurant. I plunked myself into the two-top tucked in around the wall, so that should someone glance casually into the area, they wouldn't spot me. I had no desire for Roxanne to head over and try to winkle out any information the police might have neglected to tell her. I had no desire for anything more than a scone slathered in raspberry butter and a pot of Earl Grey tea.

I had two weeks to justify my existence. There would barely be enough time to track down the site builders, let alone get my vision laid out for them in any sort of translatable manner.

When we had worked together on the folkwaysAlive! website, Judy and Linda, the designers I had been paired with who were both working on their master's degrees in computer science, had realized I was never going to get my head wrapped around much more than rudimentary HTML, so they decided that my laying out my ideas and content in a storyboard manner would be the easiest to follow and translate onto the web. I produced a notebook that looked like a treasure map created by the Jolly Postman when I was through. There were pages taped into it that unfolded downward to show scrolling areas, and envelopes glued into places where sidebar information and hyperlinks had to occur. My miracle workers, who had since graduated and formed a company together called the Black Widow Web Works, then took this hodgepodge and turned it into a working website that opened and worked smoothly on every computer platform you could imagine. Contracting out to them had been part of the deal, and I had even worked sane, civilized deadlines into the project. When you have two fancy degrees on the wall, you should no longer be sleeping under your desk with empty pizza boxes for a pillow, trying to meet crazy deadlines.

Now it looked as if I'd be asking the impossible again. I hauled out my cellphone and texted Linda, giving the gist of what to anticipate. Within five minutes, I had a response.

"No bigE. Meet nxt 2sdy, J Xed week 4 U."

Translating, it sounded as if the Widows would be able to accommodate the quick turnaround. If I could get materials ready enough for next Tuesday, which gave me just under a week to prepare, then I would be ready for Judy, who had blocked off the entire next week of her timetable to deal with my issue. I texted back that this would be great and I would get to them by one o'clock on Tuesday and then tucked my phone back in my bag before Roxanne caught me. She was a real stickler about anachronisms in the House, and since she couldn't chide paying customers, she saved her wrath and took it out on staff.

I scribbled sketches into my notebook as I drank my tea. If we were to start with a view of the House, and be welcomed in the front doors with a sweep, we couldn't begin with the maid's story. That is, unless I had two or three different linkages from that front-door splash page. I could have one link that showed Mattie Rutherford coming to the House when it was finally complete. I could have another link that gave us the servant's voice, and then took us around to the side door and up the maid's stairs. I could also have the voice of a young man who was starting out university on the promontory above the North Saskatchewan River and joining the Delta Upsilons to forge life-long friendships and business connections. Each one of these stories could unfold from the opening page.

If the Widows could build me a shell that included an opening page and a sketchy follow-through based on those three storylines, then I could present it at the board meeting and show the value of an interactive site. The province and the board shared the aim of getting people aware of their local history and interested in the preservation of historic sites. That a website could engender this sort of interest, leading to more visits to the physical site, had to be a no brainer. Marni had certainly seen that when she hired me.

I wondered if Greta Larsen actually stood for the whole board, or whether she just personally had some bee in her bonnet about the Internet. For all I knew, other members of the board had been against the project all along, too. There was likely no way of knowing before the meeting, unless I spent time researching every other board member. In ordinary circumstances, I might have, but I had a deadline to meet.

I paid for my tea and scone and left the breakfast room. There were still three hours till the House closed for the day, and I had my work cut out for me. Since the Archives were closed and I wouldn't be able to purchase any photos for the Widows to use in their presentation, I was going to have to provide the pictures needed.

Although I had taken a photography course in my teens and used to know my way around a darkroom, I had never pursued my early fascination for photography. My camera was barely one step up from a digital point-and-click, but it did have some interesting features and a solid zoom lens. I had a great photo of the front of the House from the street already; what I needed were some shots of hallways and rooms that the Widows could manipulate into a virtual tour.

It took me a while to cover the main floor because I had to change my settings from colour to sepia on every shot. I wanted the website to be able to bleed out of the look of old photographs into modern-colour reality and back. By the time I got upstairs, my system was up to speed and I managed to capture a 360-degree view of Cecil's room, the Rutherfords' bedroom, the sitting and sewing area, the guest room, which was no longer cordoned off by the police, and Hazel's pretty room. I shot the maid's staircase both heading up and going down.

I took some time in the maid's sitting room and bedroom. If I wanted an entire thread following a young, anonymous girl from the country, I would need to flesh out her particular world. I shot the view directly down from her window, since she would have been looking out toward trees and houses, not the backside of the Humanities Building. Finally, I slipped off my shoes and lay down on the narrow iron bed, to approximate the start of her day. For such a thin mattress, the bed was comfier than it looked. There was no way I could make any sort of claims that the Rutherford maids weren't well treated; from this angle I could see that the maid's bedroom was slightly larger than my own bedroom in my small apartment a few blocks away.

My eyes gauged the wood floor, which looked solid and unbroken with no possible loose board for hiding treasure under. The baseboards might be a better possibility, though the ones visible all seemed to be of one piece. Would someone risk the noise of dragging their iron bed frame away from the wall in order to hide something from the mistress of the house? Was it worth looking?

Of course, the bed might have been against the other wall when she was the maid. I rolled off the bed to look underneath it.

In keeping with the time frame of the museum, a metal chamber pot was stationed under the bed, but nothing else, not even a dust bunny, could be seen. The coverlet hung down on either side of the bed, making it very dim, but it looked as if the baseboards were of a piece on that wall as well. The excitement that had built up as a result of my conjecture deflated just as quickly, and I knelt in the middle of the room on the small braided rug and considered the impossibility of what I was doing. With a deadline looming that could mean my livelihood for the next four months, I was searching for clues to what Mattie Rutherford had written cryptically about in a missing journal I couldn't even get into the Archives to search for. I felt like an idiot.

I was pushing myself oh-so-gracefully up off the floor into a standing position when the door behind me swung open with a bang against its stopper, causing me to shriek and twist around.

Roxanne was standing in the doorway with a look that could have shut down the most defiant rebel, one of which I certainly wasn't. Put her in a wimple and she could have been a kick-ass Mother Superior. Put her in a nurse's uniform and even McMurphy would have taken his medicine.

"Why was this door closed?"

I felt like a preteen boy caught spending half an hour in the bathroom. I stammered my response, which likely made me sound even guiltier than I felt.

"I was taking pictures from the maid's point of view, Roxanne. I just wanted the idea of what she would see, waking up in the morning."

She stood there, resolute. "Do not close any of the doors in the House which are open. Do not open any doors in the House that are closed. Is that so very difficult to understand?"

There are very few things I hate more than condescension. Well okay, genocide, bigotry, blatant non-environmentalism and the neo-conservative dismantling of the social safety net in favour of trans-global corporations were slightly higher on my list, but condescension was right up there, about ten times higher than off-leash dogs. And that is probably why I answered Roxanne so snappily, something I realized in hindsight I shouldn't have done.

"Why thank you for reminding me, Roxanne. As a professional contracted to provide you with more visibility, I guess I just had more pressing things on my mind than adhering blindly to your petty regulations. As it is, I don't think my closing the door momentarily has stopped any of your countless visitors from seeing this priceless view, has it?"

The shock of being given back some of her own acidity may have been what made Roxanne step aside out of the doorway and allow me clear passage into the hallway. On the other hand, my irony might have been lost on her, as it is for so many Mike Judge fans, and she just wanted me out of there. Whatever the case, the exit was presented, and I lost no time making myself scarce. I was still feeling the frisson of looking for something someone didn't want me looking for, the maid's hidey-hole.

If there was such a thing. Having combed the Spartan space on my own hands and knees, I wasn't so sure. Grabbing my coat off the rack in the lobby, I made my way out the front door, the bell spring signalling my departure. I had till next Tuesday to shape up a design that would pacify the board and save my contract. I didn't have time to waste on a treasure hunt. And when it got right down to it, I couldn't imagine one of the Rutherford maids getting her hands on anything that would cause the death of two good people. It was a false trail, like one of those red herrings set out in mystery novels to keep readers occupied while the detective juggled all the clues into place.

I gave myself a shake and headed for home. History was not going to write itself.

19

Steve being tied up in the Archives investigation turned out to be a good thing for my schedule. I managed to crank out what was for me an amazing output toward my website notebook. I walked into the Black Widow offices on the following Tuesday, confident that I had enough for Linda and Judy to spin some of their trademarked magic.

I wasn't wrong. Judy was particularly entranced with the idea of a Ukrainian maid leading the viewers through the history. I hadn't realized that she, with a last name like Thompson, was of Ukrainian descent.

"Ha, all you have to do is poke the average Albertan and you will find all sorts of roots. My grandmother was a Lyzaniwski. Really, this is great. I think we can cobble something together for your deadline, no problem. You do have all the printed matter on a flash drive for us?" With her huge eyes and short dark hair, she looked like a slightly manic pixie.

"As per orders, and all labelled in harmony with the notebook. I really appreciate this."

Linda, the ethereal redhead, ushered me graciously to the door, where my coat hung on an upscale version of a coat rack. Their offices, located in an old building on trendy 104th Street just off Jasper Avenue, were up two flights, but I didn't trust the elevator, so I clomped down the stairs and headed to the Sobeys on the corner to buy a few groceries before popping into the LRT station to take me across the river.

This supermarket had wedged itself into the downtown core to capitalize on the condos and lofts that were springing up all over the area. While not as large as most of the grocery stores in less dense neighbourhoods, it catered to the lunch-hour shoppers from the surrounding office towers who were looking for just one or two things to stuff into their kitchenette fridges till it was time to head home for the day, and to the urbane condo dwellers who alternated between trying quinoa-stuffed Cornish game hen recipes from *Gourmet* magazine and stirring up a box of Kraft Dinner before heading out to the clubs.

For me, it was just the place to pick up a butcher's foam tray of pork chops, a lemon, and a plastic clamshell of huge strawberries from California. I was always totally motivated to eat locally until I hit the fruit-and-vegetable aisle. *Canada's Food Guide* surely couldn't expect me to eat five to ten rutabagas a day, now could it?

I was hoping Steve would be coming by for supper, as I hadn't seen him the entire week I had been racing to put together my web notebook for the Widows. I would be hard pressed not to quiz him about Mr. Maitland's death, since I felt so personally affected, having really liked the man. And of course, he would have nothing to tell me about Jossie's death, as that wasn't even his case, let alone the complication of my being a witness in the situation and the whole piddly ethics thing. God knows what we would find to talk about. We might as well take the pork chops straight to bed.

My salacious joke made me laugh out loud, causing a young man with distended earlobes stuffed with black lab corks and a dotted line tattooed from the edge of his eye to his mouth to look at me in alarm, as if I was some sort of weirdo. You would think that by now no one would pay any attention to anyone laughing or talking out loud on the train, since so many people had a Bluetooth gizmo attached to their ear or were speaking loudly into a receiver on the line of their smartphone earphones. Still, it didn't do to be pegged as crazy; the mentally ill were only marginally less disdained than the obese in today's society, since it was no longer fashionable to publicly hurl epithets at immigrants or homosexuals.

The not-so-silent majority were always going to find someone to place beneath their heel, I supposed, though why hatred was such a burning need for the human psyche, I still had not been able to answer to my satisfaction. Hatred was, after all, such a self-destructive emotion. I wondered whether someone had hated Mr. Maitland or Jossie in that concentrated, specific white-rage way, or whether they had merely been in the way of someone's greed or need.

Steve said that money, sex, or an escape route were the three main compulsions to commit violence. Since I couldn't imagine anyone trapped in either the Archives or the guest bathroom at Rutherford House, I had to assume we were concentrating on money and sex. Well, who wasn't?

I must have giggled again, because Mr. Self-Mutilation gave me another troubled look. I studiously sorted out the plastic handles on my bags, and headed up to wait for my stop by the automatic doors.

I wondered just how much the police were connecting the two murders. After all, the main connecting point, as Steve had pointed out, was me. Other than the fact that I had known both victims and had been in the same buildings with them within twenty-four hours of their deaths, the only connections were that both those buildings were owned by the Province and each housed items that had once belonged to the first premier of Alberta.

I called Steve and left a message for him to come over for supper on his voice mail. I heard back from him almost immediately, and we settled on a seven-thirty dinnertime; that way he wouldn't have to head back into the station after supper. Knowing I wouldn't get to eat till more than two hours past my regular mealtime, I made a pot of tea and a huge sandwich for lunch, stuffing everything I could find in the fridge between the slabs of bread. Feeling like Dagwood, Jughead, and Wimpy combined, I put all my focus into the sandwich before me. The time it took to eat my way through the layers of cheese, shaved turkey, sprouts, lettuce, tomatoes, cucumber, mayonnaise, and mustard was therapeutic, sort of like yoga or meditation. My mind, released of the worry that had been spinning in a constant loop, had emptied itself while focusing on opening my jaws wide enough to clamp down on the sandwich without spilling the contents all over my plate, table, and lap. Zen and the Art of Deli Eating.

Conventional wisdom has it that one should never eat a big meal and then go lie down if one wants one's body to use up the fuel one has just ingested, rather than storing it in one's hips and belly. Wisdom, however, hadn't been clocking twenty-hour days trying to get the website notebook together, so I decided to listen to all of my crying muscles and brain cells that were begging for a nap. I considered setting my alarm, but figured that it would be so much more satisfying to just sleep as long as I needed, and if Steve got here before that time was up, so be it. He had a key, and pork chops can be ready in five minutes.

I hung up the linen blouse and black trousers I had been wearing to meet with the Widows, pulled on a fleecy top and my sweats with U of A embroidered at the thigh, and crawled back under my covers for a nap. What luxury, to be able to immediately indulge in sleep in the middle of the day. This was truly the freelancer's and contract worker's ultimate reward. We may never have the ability to retire on a pension, but napping on a Tuesday afternoon was something most CEOs and executive directors were never going to experience.

I thought about writing myself a note to ask Steve whether they had looked at the "To Be Refiled" shelves in the Archives, but figured I would remember to do so without one. Dumb me. Sleep took over, and I was out like a light.

20

By the time Steve arrived, I was awake, had splashed water on my face and the dinner started. The light was waning, and I noticed one or two miserly snowflakes trying to start something outside, but they gave up with a stern glance from my direction. While I have nothing against snow in particular, I dislike its arriving too early. Not only does it make everyone's winters that much longer and harder to bear, it really knocks the stuffing out of the little kids who want to Hallowe'en in fancy costumes. I am not sure why mothers didn't just promote warm costumes, like Yeti and sheep and rabbits, made from the same material mall mascots were constructed from. That way it wouldn't matter whether it snowed or not, and the kids would be cozy, trick or treating all over the neighbourhood.

Steve shivered as he entered my apartment, shaking off the chill he'd brought in with him.

"I don't know. We might be seeing the last of fall this week," he announced with that tone we all take when discussing the weather, the one that sounds like, "hear me? I have no idea what I'm talking about."

"Really? I want it to hold out for another two weeks at least. Just long enough to get all the candy, bats, and plastic cauldrons out of the stores, and all the tinsel and singing trees into the aisles."

"I've already seen Christmas stuff in the stores."

"Have they marked down the little candy bars on sale yet?"

"No, but it won't be long now. Speaking of, what's for supper?"

"Pork chops, apple sauce, and salad. If you want carbs, you'll have to have a slice of bread. I was going to do potatoes, but I had a nap instead."

"I thought you looked a bit fuzzy. Did you get the web designs in today?"

"This morning. I took them downtown and came home and sort of crashed. It's been such a push. Of course, now I have a week of waiting till the Widows get back to me and the board meets to decide my fate."

Steve smiled around a forkful of pork chop. "You'll be fine. After all, they've already determined a website was necessary, or else they wouldn't have had the contract for you. It's just this one woman, I bet, using the murder at the House to have another kick at a project she alone didn't want happening. Mmm, these are good."

"I hope that a) you're right about there only being the one person who is opposed, and that b) she's not the sort of person who runs roughshod over a committee. Let there be strong-minded people on this board!"

Steve laughed. "So you have a week. What are you going to do with yourself?"

"Oh, I still have tons of research to do, so I'll keep on until I'm told I can't. No point in getting way behind in the project if they do give me the green light, and I will be charging for this week, anyhow." I picked up the pork chop bone and gnawed on the bits of meat that wouldn't come politely. "I was thinking of calling up Fort Edmonton Park and getting dispensation to head down there this week, since I never got around to heading down there the same weekend we hit the Ukrainian Village."

"Are they still open? I thought everything closed down after their Harvest Festival."

"Actually, they are still open weekends to the public for quite a few weeks into the fall, and they are open on a daily basis in the fall and spring for school groups. One of the servers at the House, who also does work at the Selkirk Hotel down at the Park, says there is more in the way of volunteer action and houses open during the week for the school kids at this time of year, and access to the inside of the old Rutherford House is what I really need. I think there are even whole weeks that schools can book to go to the Fort daily and immerse the kids in what it would be like to learn from memorization and scribbling on slates, after drawing water and chopping firewood and doing chores before school."

"Not a bad lesson to learn right there, that school wasn't always the cakewalk it seems to be now."

"Steve Browning, I just for a minute there spotted you as a

grandpa, poking your cane for emphasis and telling those young folk what's what."

He had the grace to laugh. "I suppose I'm getting there. For me, though, it's not so much a difference in the scale of difficulty between schools now compared to when I went, as much as it is the air of entitlement of the students I notice when I do school tours. For one thing, hardly any of the little kids actually walk to school anymore, and once they've stopped being dropped off by SUVs parked in the middle of crosswalks, they are clogging up school parking lots with their own cars. And they all assume they'll be heading off to university or into a career that will eclipse their parents' work. And I think, where are they getting these ideas? More young people are finding themselves staying at home longer, or going back to live with their parents, because they can't afford to live on their own, let alone buy a house. So what's with the attitude they're slinging?"

"Who knows? Maybe it's that whole competence with tech-nology aspect to their lives. They've spent their whole lives hear-ing people say how easily little kids pick up computers and new products. That could give them the edge of superiority, in that every time you turn around there is a new version of things."

"It's wild, isn't it? And, you know, do we need it? I was just reading about a museum run by the National Trust in England. It's a row house and photography studio of a famous photog-rapher who died in 1988. He and his wife didn't seem to have remodelled or upgraded from when it was first built, post-war, and it's all preserved as a tribute to the 1950s. There is no big stove or fridge or double-glazed windows, just a hot plate and a larder, but there is running water, electricity, a good old dial-up telephone, and furniture made from solid wood and dense upholstery, and it all looks serviceable and long-wearing."

"So?"

"So, it made me think that, given a radio and a newspaper delivered and possibly an upgrade to a colour television, a person could survive perfectly well using all the things I could see in the displays. There is very little we actually require that has come about in our lifetimes. Most everything we have around us is a time-saving device or a luxury. Aside from, say, the polio vaccine, what invention would you say has made the world a better place?"

"Spandex."

"Really?"

"You have no idea. But seriously, I hear you. The more I delve into the past or spend time in Rutherford House itself, the more I wonder about that sort of thing. Of course, a project like mine would be impossible without a computer, and my laptop has made going to the Archives so much easier, since there is no need to bring in a pen or anything that might mark up or damage any of the artifacts."

"But an artifact still went missing."

"Yeah, I think so. God, who am I going to tell about that?"

"You put it in your statement. We can take it from there. If you are not absolutely certain how to identify it besides it not having a clear date marked on it, I'm not certain how we're going to track it, but it may turn up in another box."

"I hope so. Not that I think it has anything to do with why

poor Mr. Maitland was killed, but I hate to think that somehow I contributed to messing up his legacy of organization."

Steve was spooning out some more salad onto his plate. I hopped up to get the apple crisp I'd popped in the oven at the beginning of the meal. I had three of them in the tiny freezer compartment of my fridge, given to me by an elderly neighbour down the lane who made them from the apples on her lovely tree in the backyard. I had helped her last month by climbing the stepladder and filling up buckets, pans, and an old baby bath full of apples; and she had later presented me with enough ready-to-freeze desserts to last me well into the winter. I had ten more piled in my corner of the apartment's communal chest freezer in the laundry room.

Steve oohed at the smell of the warm cinnamon and brown sugar wafting toward him, and I spooned a massive helping into a cereal bowl for him, topping it off with a scoop of vanilla ice cream.

"This is fantastic," he murmured between spoonfuls.

"I know. Just nothing like harvest bounty."

I was still halfway through my dessert when Steve, finished, hopped up and began to clear the table. His belief was that the cook never cleans up, which is one of the reasons I so enjoyed cooking for him. While he ran hot, soapy water into the dish-pan, I continued to chew my dessert.

"So, aren't you worried that if you add the earlier version of Rutherford House into your virtual visit, you'll siphon off visitors to present-day Rutherford House by sending them to Fort Edmonton instead?"

"Well, this website is meant to promote more visits to Rutherford House, and Fort Edmonton already seems to lure its fair share of tourists and return visitors, so there's that aspect. Mostly, I figured it would do me some good to see some of the other houses of the era that they've amassed on 1905 Street, as well as walk down 1885 Street and get a sense of what was there when Alexander Rutherford built his dream home. History hits us in its relativity, right? We have to see what was there before, compare it to what would have been amazing then about this new thing, and then set it into context with what we know now. If we were to just take Rutherford House as a big brick house on Saskatchewan Drive, we might not get the full import of what it means to Edmonton and the university and our past. After all, there are other big brick houses all over Edmonton."

"Well, not that many, when you think about it."

"What do you mean?"

"Well, most of the brick seems to have gone into businesses and factories, while stucco went into wood frame houses. Brick houses always seem to me to be a more eastern thing. Maybe brick was more plentiful there, or trees less plentiful? But I think Rutherford making his house of brick was a real three pigs sort of thing, just like the Magrath Mansion over on Ada Boulevard, or some of the big houses on Valleyview Point and off River Valley Road by the zoo. Built of brick to last and to be a cut above the run-of-the-mill houses in the rest of the city."

"You may be right. I should check the Edmonton brickyard and see if there is anything in the Archives that shows how much went to private homes."

Steve sat back down with a cup of tea for each of us.

"This was nice, thank you."

"That sounds as if you can't stay."

"I really can't. I do have to be at work for seven, but there is also the connection to the case; there is no way I want anyone saying that our relationship might somehow jeopardize the integrity of the police work in searching for Mr. Maitland's killer."

"Is there any chance of my getting back to the Archives any time soon?"

"How does slim to nil strike you? Seriously, we are still dealing with it as a crime scene, and having to examine everything with white cotton gloves on is making for a slow and painstaking process."

I shrugged. What can you do?

"Have fun at Fort Edmonton, soaking up flavour. Maybe, by the time you present and hear back from the board, all this will be cleared up and you can get back to the land of musty documents."

We watched a bit of the news and an episode of *Justified*, the Elmore Leonard television show that featured a modern-day gunslinging sheriff in Kentucky, which seemed plausible enough that I wondered if we in the Wild West should be suing our Blue Mountain cousins for encroachment. True to his word, Steve shrugged on his coat around ten o'clock and headed home, leaving me to brood about just how I was going to fill my week, and just how involved I actually was with the deaths that were populating the periphery of my world.

That's the real trouble with afternoon naps. They leave you way too wide awake in the evening, when the grim thoughts appear.

To counter it all, I stuck a glass of milk in the microwave, drank down the warmed result, and went to bed.

21

The next day, as soon as I was coherent, which for me meant showered, breakfasted, dressed, and moisturized, it was time to call the Fort. Luckily, there was now a year-round staff presence right on site. I explained my request and situation to the woman on the phone, who suggested I come down with identification, a copy of the contract with the Friends of Rutherford House, and $18, which was the standard admission fee for an adult for the day.

She specified that there would be no professional interpreters available to me, as the only ones hired year-round were assigned specifically to school classes. There might be two or three volunteer interpreters on site, and therefore some of the buildings would have activity within them, but only until four o'clock, with the exception of the Selkirk Hotel, which was an active hotel with a bustling restaurant and bar for much of the year.

This all sounded great to me, and I assured her I would be down to see her within the hour. Knowing I would be on my feet all day and outside a lot, I decided to opt for warmth over style. I loaded my laptop and camera into a backpack, along with a bottle of water and all the ID the Fort office would require of me, and tied up my runners. It was still mild enough for just a light jacket, so I pulled my jean jacket over the Superman hoodie I was wearing. I figured that my runners, with their air-pocketed arch supports and polymers, were so anachronistic to begin with that I didn't need to worry about my Kryptonian leanings. Besides, the historic park reached into the '30s as it wended its way back through history. Maybe they would find some connection to the Canadian boy who had drawn the Man of Steel.

I took the train from campus to the South Campus station and after squinting at several small maps, determined which bus to catch down Fox Drive that would actually let me off before the bridge to the ginormous mall. I was glad I had taken the bus, since the walk to the Park gates from the bus stop was still about half a mile. I popped into the Fort office, a modern building set to the right of the train station that acted as the entry gate and gift shop. The woman I'd spoken with on the phone greeted me like an old friend and processed my application for "historical research visitor" efficiently. I was given a lanyard with a plastic ID pocket, into which she slipped the card she'd made, and which she told me to wear visibly. This would allow the interpreters to gauge that I was not a teacher accompanying one of the classes of students (they had their own ID), nor a guest of the Selkirk Hotel. Most of all, it tagged me "not an interloper." I would be accorded access to all the open buildings. She said that if I could return the lanyard at the end of the day, it would be filed for a period of two weeks for my use.

I wondered how many other scholars spent two weeks of their research time in a historical re-enactment park, but nodded and smiled and signed where she told me to sign. Eventually I was sent back down the path toward the train station, where in regular summer hours one caught the vintage steam train to ride to the far end of the Park, to be deposited at the glorious replica of the palisaded Fort. Visitors would begin their visit to Edmonton in the fur-trade era, circa 1854, and then make their way back through time toward the near-present, along 1885 Street, catch a tram on 1905 Street, turn the corner at 1920 Street, then head back, past the celebratory midway, and out through the souvenir shop. It was a great concept.

However, at this time of year, the train apparently was not running. It was a good thing I had already shaved some time off the commute this morning. Instead of waiting for the streetcar with a group of very noisy nine-year-olds, I opted to walk backwards in time into the centre of the Park.

The Ferris wheel and tents of the midway looked lonely in the late fall morning. As entertainment on the prairies in the '30s wasn't on anyone's curriculum, they closed down early and were not part of any of the school tours. It was a pity, since the hand-carved horses of the carousel were things of beauty. I wondered, though, if they could compete with the high-tech, hand-held entertainments that today's youth possessed?

I moseyed down the boardwalk along 1920 Street. To my left, the first mosque in Alberta shone in the sunlight, while Mellon

Farm to my right was dwarfed by the Blatchford airplane hangar, next to which was housed a model of Wop May's famous bush plane. The newest addition to the Park was the replica of a movie theatre. Sarah Bernhardt and the Marx Brothers had toured through Edmonton on the Pantages circuit, and so it seemed fitting to have added the theatre, which soon became a cinema. The Park had commissioned a company from the States to provide a historical experience, complete with snow falling on the heads of the viewers, but most of the fun seemed to be watching old movies, which ran on the hour, and the occasional live theatre produced for short runs in the evenings. As it was right next to the Selkirk Hotel, a lot of people had been booking into the hotel, so they could enjoy a theatrical evening, drinks in the hotel bar after, and a slap-up breakfast the next morning. It was like getting away on vacation right in the heart of the city. All the fun, none of the jet lag.

I turned left when I got to the hotel, heading south down 1905 Street. This was where I wanted to spend my time, where most of the buildings arranged by era were the actual buildings, trucked to the Park from their original locations. The old Rutherford House was somewhere up ahead on my left, according to the map I'd picked up in the train station. I passed the post office, pausing to take a picture of the fire hall and the china shop across the street. The Masonic Hall ahead of me had a short-order counter and tables set up on the main floor, in case visitors got hungry. Right now, I could see twenty-some children clogging the tables, filling out workbooks, wriggling around and generally making more noise than necessary. I didn't think I'd ever get hungry enough to join them.

The first house after the Masonic Hall was the Firkin House, the one that was rumoured to be haunted. It didn't look haunted from where I was standing, but at any rate, determining its relative lack of ectoplasm wasn't my mission. I was far more concerned with the house beside it, the original Rutherford House. The verandah would have been the biggest selling point for me, but I could sort of see how this house wouldn't be quite majestic enough for the premier of the province, let alone the president of the university. This was a house that had been added on to two or three times, as I had learned from my research, but the signs were not readily obvious from the exterior. I walked through the picket-fenced gate and up the stairs, hoping the door would be open.

It was unlocked and the interior of the house was warm, indicating that someone was stoking the fire and at work somehow within. The smell of molasses cookies was also wafting through the air from the back kitchen. Following my nose, or perhaps my stomach, which gurgled appreciatively, I was about to make my way toward the back of the house.

"Hello?"

"Good day," came a small voice from the left and down around my knees. I twirled, startled to see a small, dark-haired boy dressed in a period costume of a boiled-cotton shirt, suspenders, knee pants with woollen stockings, and lace-up boots. He was on the floor, playing jacks, which I had thought was a girl's game, but he was so dexterous and fast that I figured any girl competing would lose whatever she'd been betting. Seeing me, he scooped up his little metal game pieces and rubber ball, and stood in one fluid motion. The toys went into his pocket, and he thrust out his hand.

"It is nice to see you. My mother is baking cookies, which should be ready soon. Would you like to see the rest of the House?"

"Hi, there. Sure, I would love to see the rest of the house." And so, with the smell of cookies drawing me back into memories of my own childhood, the boy, who couldn't have been more than four or five years old, left the rather ornate parlour he'd been playing in and pointed out the library of the premier across the hall.

We took the tortuously narrow stairs, which he assured me were very luxurious for the time, up to the second floor. I looked at him, trying to determine whether any of the cavorting and loud children down the road would have understood the word "luxurious," let alone had the presence of mind and aplomb to use it in a discussion with an adult they had just met.

"My name is Randy. What's your name?"

"Well, I am supposed to say Cecil, because that was the name of the Rutherfords' son, but I don't have a younger sister, so it seems sort of silly to pretend to be the family when we don't fit the numbers. So I say my name is Jasper Peacocke, and I was named for the mineral, not the town or the hotel on 1885 Street. People always ask me that. Jasper Peacocke is my real name."

"That's a real name, all right. Nice to meet you, Jasper. How old are you?"

"I will be six this coming Christmas. And no, it is not essential for me to be in kindergarten with other children my age."

"It isn't? I didn't know that was compulsory."

Jasper sniffed. "Well, that is the other thing most people ask me—why aren't you in school, little boy?" His voice took on the screeching tone of a raptor, and I got a sense of old ladies like large owls, swooping down on him.

"What do you tell them?" I didn't really care if he went to school or not, but there was something compelling about his intensity and seriousness that just made me want to continue to hear him talk. He was obviously precocious, in that way of bright children who spend the majority of their time with adults rather than other children.

"To them I usually just say I'm not old enough yet and they leave me alone." He looked up at me with a candid grin. "And then they usually get all freaky about my vocabulary."

I laughed. For a five-year-old, Jasper Peacocke had a pretty good bead on human nature.

"Truthfully, the real reason is that my father is a cinematographer, and we travel a lot, so I haven't gone to a playschool yet. My mother and I go along with him and have adventures and experiences wherever we have been. We are back home for a while and so we have been volunteering at the Park this summer, so I can learn about history, and develop communication skills."

"And become a killer jacks player."

Jasper nodded, acknowledging the compliment. "I am even better at hoop rolling, and a dead aim with a slingshot, but the

Park administrators don't care for that because they say it might inspire other children to commit violence."

I laughed, thinking of the various shooting games available to children outside the Park's boundaries that were far likelier to incite anti-social tendencies.

Jasper looked troubled, but I assured him I was not laughing at him.

"This was Hazel's room," he intoned, as we stood in the doorway. Obviously, Hazel's room held no interest for a young boy, in that it was decked out in Victoriana femininity. I am not sure it would be of interest to a young girl of the twenty-first century, either. Cecil's room, on the other hand, awakened what sounded to me like a bit of hero-worship in Jasper.

"Cecil went to war in 1916 with the British Royal Garrison Artillery. He was just married, but he served till the end of the war and then came home to Edmonton and became a lawyer. These were not likely his jacks," he said, producing the little metal x figures from his pocket, "but he probably played with similar toys when he was young. He was born in 1890 and had a sister when he was three years old. I am an only child." That last bit sounded a tad wistful.

"Are people allowed to touch the things on display?"

"In some rooms you can, but if there is a rope across the doorway, you are only allowed to lean in and look around." He led me back down the narrow hallway. I could really see from the inside how the house had been added to. It didn't have the gracious lines of its brick counterpart on Saskatchewan Drive. The hallway around the staircase was narrow and a little treacherous. A maid with too big a load of laundry could probably take a bad spill down the stairs if she wasn't careful.

Speaking of the maid, her room was the next one that Jasper showed me. Like the other bedrooms, once you descended a few stairs, this one too had a rope across it, but you could walk through to the back stairs that led to the kitchen and more divine cookie aromas. A trunk and other boxes took up part of the area, which had been created from the attic space above the kitchen add-on, as far as I could tell. Separated from the rest of the room by a small screen was a single metal bedframe that had been painted white, covered by a tired patchwork quilt with tucked-in hospital corners, and a battered suitcase under the bed.

"Why is there a rope across this room, Jasper?"

"I am not sure. That is an old quilt, and the fabric could rip if you sat on the bed, I guess. My mother had to mend a cushion downstairs that someone leaned against. There was no rope before, though."

"Before what?"

"Before the mess. Now, be very careful because these stairs are hard to walk down for some people."

Jasper was leading me away from the maid's room, toward the enticing smell of cinnamon and nutmeg. That wasn't the only reason I was eager to follow him. I wanted to know what he meant by "mess." We navigated the even narrower maid's staircase and found our way into the kitchen. There, a woman with dark hair pulled back in a bun, and a coverall apron that reminded me of Hilda Ogden from *Coronation Street,* still couldn't hide how attractive she was. She looked up at us with Jasper's dark eyes and smiled at her son.

"If you wash your hands, you can help me with the cookies, Jasper. Good day," she nodded to me, somehow taking in that I had been adopted as a non-raptor. "I trust Jasper has been giving you the tour of the upper floor? This would have been the job of the Rutherfords' maid, although Mattie Rutherford was reputed to be a very good cook and she definitely won ribbons at the summer fairs for her rhubarb relish and crabapple jelly."

"Hello, it's nice to meet you. My name is Randy Craig, and I am actually working on researching material for Rutherford House, the newer one by the university. I came out here to see the ways in which the newer house was modelled on the Rutherfords' first house. Jasper's tour was terrific."

"Ah, well, then, you're practically family," she laughed. "Why don't you have a chair and I'll pour you a cup of tea to go with your cookies?" When I was about to demur, she hurried to add, "It would be so nice to talk to a grown-up who wasn't looking after twenty-seven wriggling, bored nine-year-olds. They'll be here soon enough, believe me." Jasper's mom, who told me her name was Nola, poured tea for both of us into spectacularly thin, large porcelain teacups that had a pearlescent sheen to them.

"It's a real lesson in opposites, working here. You have all this knuckle-reddening work, with no mod cons, and then you sip your tea in the most impossibly elegant teacups, and pin on brooches with semi-precious stones as a matter of course. I am not certain we came out the winners, we women of the next century."

"Well, it wouldn't necessarily be the same people getting their knuckles raw, would it? I mean, houses these days don't accommodate a maid's staircase, although I guess there are live-in nannies and au pair rooms in fancier houses. But I mean, most people today cook their own meals, wash their own clothes, and do their own dishes, instead of relying on servants to do that for them."

"I agree, we have gotten rid of the servants, but with them, we've lost touch with the elegance. I don't have anything this delicate at home from which to drink my tea, do you?"

I thought of my old, weathered Kliban cat mug, and wondered whether it would qualify as a collectible, if not an antique. Regardless, it certainly wouldn't match a Limoges teacup for elegance.

"You make a good point. How did the Rutherford servants do, though, on the scale of Royal Doulton to tin mug?"

Nola laughed. "Oh, I'm sure they were a lot closer to tin mug than we want to portray here. There is a huge egalitarian streak in Canadians that rebels against the concept of unfair treatment, I've noticed. For instance, have you been to the Fort today?"

I admitted that I hadn't, but that I had visited in the past.

"Well, if you'll recall, there is a tiny door cut inside the big doors to the Fort, the ones that are usually open. When an interpreter tells people that the usual practice was to keep the inner doors closed and direct potentially hostile natives, who were coming to trade, to use the small door and trade through the iron-barred window, people tend to bristle with the unfairness of it all. And yet, they never seem to question the fact that the entire structure is built inside a massive palisade."

I laughed and reached for a cookie, noticing out of the corner of my eye that Jasper had commandeered the floor area in front of the warm stove and was munching contentedly on his second cookie, too.

"I see what you mean. So, do you have to downplay the maid's role when visitors come to Rutherford House here?"

"Very few of them make the connection, to tell you the truth. A few of them have asked if that is where a maiden aunt or Mrs. Rutherford's widowed mother slept, when they see the maid's room upstairs."

"Oh yeah, speaking of the maid's room, I noticed that it has a rope across it. Jasper was mentioning it didn't used to, but that there had been a recent mess?"

Nola shot a troubled look over to where Jasper was sitting and then back at me. I sensed she didn't want to continue in front of her son, but I wasn't certain why. Was she afraid of saying something that would scare him, or something to me that he knew to be untrue? I was even more interested in what her answer might be now, so decided to play along to make life easier for Nola Peacocke, and changed the subject to deflect attention from what I really wanted her to talk about.

"I've been working on a website for the House to go along with their book about the centennial of the House's being built. I went out to the Ukrainian Village, to get a feel for the girls who may have come to the big city to work in the private homes and hotels."

Nola saw and seemed to approve of what I was doing. She nodded and poured us some more tea.

"We haven't been to that park yet, though we should go. Do you have any idea when they are going to be closing up for the winter?"

I wasn't sure, but wrote down the URL for the Ukrainian Village for Nola. I also put my phone number on the piece of paper, as I had a sense that she was someone worth pinging this kind of research on. She had, after all, been living the life for the past few months. Nola folded up my offering and put it in the pocket of her apron.

We talked about volunteering at the Fort, and how working in the fall for the school tours differed from the regular summer tourist times. After a few minutes, Nola asked Jasper if he would mind positioning himself in the front parlour so that they could know when the school group was headed toward them. He obliged, after reaching out to take a final cookie from the plate on the table.

"Don't you ruin your lunch, young man," his mother intoned, but his grin back at her made me realize this was some sort of private game between them.

Nola confirmed it as he left the room. "I swear he has a tapeworm. I have never seen anyone eat as much as that child."

"Boys are always hungry, aren't they? Just wait till he is a teenager. I had a colleague who had to put a lock on the pantry door because her boys were honestly eating them out of house and home. She would budget for grocery money monthly, and they would gnaw through half the mortgage payment, too."

Nola laughed and shook her head.

"No, I can't imagine Jasper getting that bad. I mean, where

would he put it? But still, I never have to worry about his ruining his appetite!"

She wiped her hands on her apron as if she was drying them of mirth, changing the smile on her face and even the set of her shoulders.

"Now, what I didn't want to dwell on while Jasper was in the room was that there was a break-in to this house a couple of weeks back, and some of the artifacts were tossed about."

"What Jasper called the mess," I said.

"Yes, that is what I called it because I didn't want to spook him and I didn't really want it to loom in his mind as something to chat about with visitors, either. For one thing, you don't want to spread the word about how easy it might be to sneak into the Park, but for another, you want people to feel safe when they are here."

"Do you feel safe?"

"Why not? It's not as if there actually is anything here, and I don't think anything was stolen, either."

"What did they mess up?"

"Mostly the maid's room. The bedstead was overturned and the trunk opened, and one of the baseboards had been pried away from the wall. That was the extent of it. They put up the rope so that people wouldn't go in while the baseboard, which had to be repainted, was still wet, but I think they decided to leave it up as a deterrent, since there really isn't anything you can't see from the other side of the barrier. It's not as if you could swing a cat in there, after all."

"Not many maids in the habit of cat-swinging, I'm guessing."

Nola laughed, which did a lot to disperse the mood of gloom that was descending upon us.

"No, I expect they had had enough of carpet beating throughout the day." She pointed to the rather lovely object near the back door. It was about the same size as a tennis racket, but instead of net, it had a curlicue design. "That is what she would have used, after dragging the carpets out, on her own, and draping them over the clothesline. The harder you hit the carpet, the more dust and grime and dirt would fly out, likely right into your eye. Whenever I think of that whole process, I tell you, I go home and hug my Hoover."

Nola stood up, after offering me another cup of tea, which I refused. I could tell the moment was over, and she was getting ready for the onslaught of children who would be asking questions about the stove and learning how butter was made. Nola cleaned off the table from our teatime, sliding the leftover cookies onto a larger plate she had set aside for the school group.

Jasper called out to his mother from the parlour.

"I see them coming from Egge's."

22

The school group was on the move, having had their first class in the upstairs area of Egge's Barn. They were likely to be a bit restless and rambunctious, but Nola and Jasper would be ready for them. She had lined up ten pint jars, which Jasper was helping her to measure cream into. As he put the lids on each jar, Nola set out several baking trays and started to mix dry ingredients into a large bowl.

"The kids will be shaking these jars to make butter, which will separate from the milk after about fifteen minutes, and then they can spread their homemade butter onto fresh biscuits."

"Hot biscuits and fresh butter is wonderful," Jasper sighed. "Are you going to stay, Randy? You could have a butter jar, too."

"Thanks, Jasper, but I probably should be getting out of the way. I think I'll just pop up and take a couple of pictures of the rooms upstairs, to use as comparisons to the ones at Achnacarry, the new place, and then I'll head out. It was lovely to meet you both and thank you for the tour"—I nodded to Jasper—"and the tea and cookies." This time I smiled at Nola.

"We'll keep in touch, Randy. I am interested to know how this project will turn out." She patted the pocket she'd popped my phone number into.

"Thanks! You never know, I may be back."

Jasper's face lit up in a grin, which turned the possibility to certainty in my mind. You never knew, maybe I would get him to teach me some of his expert jacks techniques.

I went back up the little maid's staircase, which was just as well, since I heard the first steps of feet on the front stairs. Nola was expecting twenty-seven nine-year-olds. It sounded like a marauding army, coming to pillage.

Now that Nola had mentioned it, I could see the slight difference in paint colour on the baseboard closest to the doorway of the maid's room. Otherwise, there was nothing to indicate that there was any hiding place at all. There were three hooks set on the wall behind the doorway. Perhaps, in the Rutherfords' day, there would have been a washstand in here as well, for her own pitcher and ewer, or maybe she was allowed the use of the indoor plumbing along with the rest of the family. But aside from the colour in the patchwork quilt, there was nothing bright and personable about the room.

I didn't suppose it was an original quilt, though it looked old and worn enough to have been used well and washed thoroughly more than a few times. From my work around Rutherford House, I was beginning to understand the difference between the concept of preserving sites due to their cultural significance, their architectural significance, or their historic importance. There were all sorts of standards that had to be considered when deciding on what plan of attack the historic site committees would aim for, whether it be restoration, rehabilitation, or preservation. It reminded me of a dinner conversation I'd once had with a museum curator who explained the dilemmas inherent in the preservation of our history. She had used, as an example, the rope used to hang Louis Riel. Embedded in the fibres of the rope were bits of skin and traces of blood and sweat, which would break down over time and eat into and erode the rope. To preserve the rope, it would be optimal to clean away this organic residue. Of course, once you removed the actual bits of Riel, did you still have a valuable historic artifact? Or did you just have a rope? Would it be better to have a disintegrating noose in a glass case? Or would preserving forever the actual rope make more of an impact on generations to come?

Questions like these made me glad I'd not chosen a curatorial path. I had enough trouble picking out which socks to wear in the morning. I knew that many of the artifacts in Rutherford House, the brick rendition, were actual Rutherford-owned items. But here in Fort Edmonton Park, with so many visitors and school groups coming through, it was likely this wasn't really one of their old quilts. And why should it be? The province was likely awash in old quilts. I had three at home myself, made by my grandmother.

This room, though plain and utilitarian, seemed cozy enough. It wasn't as girlish and bright as Hazel's room, of course. I thought back to my earliest exposure to what a working-class young girl could expect when coming to a new position, which was, of course, Anne Shirley's delight in the room Marilla and Matthew Cuthbert had prepared for her. There would have been little to delight even the most imaginative Anne here.

Working backward from my original tour, I took the front stairs down to avoid the throng whom I could hear avidly shaking jars of milk in the kitchen. One of the parents who had volunteered to shepherd them was standing in the front room, checking out the harmonium. She looked startled at my appearing out of nowhere, but I smiled and held out my camera at her, the international sign for "I'm a harmless tourist." Of course, since she was chaperoning minors, that same gesture could have equally been interpreted as the international sign for "I'm a pervert hoping for lewd shots of your children."

I must have looked harmless because she just smiled and nodded as I let myself out the front door. It was brisker outside than it had been in the warmth of Nola's kitchen. I did up my jacket, but it was a lovely day nonetheless. I decided to wander down 1885 Street to see if there was anything open along that way, and to stretch my legs. It had been a long time since I'd been down to Fort Edmonton Park.

Unlike the Ukrainian Village, which was spread out with lots of walking required between buildings, Fort Edmonton was filling in to be a bustling little town in its own right. While there was a large empty space still open on 1905 Street, where the tent city got set up in the summers to show how desperate people had been for housing in the earliest boom time, there was very little real estate open on 1885 Street. From the sample homesteading spike through to Ottewell's Farm, both sides of the street were lined with interesting shops, a church, and early homes.

I wandered down past the old hotel, the general store, and a saddler and crossed the street over to the Ottewell Farm. The last time I had been to the Park, there had been a covered wagon set on the corner, bridging the timeline between the Fort days and the settlement time. It had been a hot day, and the interpreter, a feisty girl in a calico dress and grimy apron, had crawled out from under the wagon, where she had been resting on a thin mattress she'd dragged out of the wagon. She gamely discussed the compartments and ingenuity of the wagon, with sweat running down the sides of her face. In her interpretive scenario, she and her husband had been coming over the Carlton Trail, but he had taken ill somewhere near Yorkton and was buried there. She figured there was nothing for it but to carry on, as they had the paperwork affording them a homestead near Fort Edmonton. She wasn't certain how she would manage to clear the land and fence it in accordance with the homestead laws all on her own, but perhaps she would meet someone eventually who would wish to share the life. All the while, she poked up the fire she had made near her wagon, and set the coffee pot to swing over it. She pulled out a tin mug, dipped it into a pail of water she had on hand, and wiped it on a towel before offering it to me.

I hadn't taken her up on the coffee, but it was testimony to her acting and interpreting that I recalled so much of our exchange even now. The wagon wasn't there; it had probably been taken away into storage for the winter. I was noticing a few signs of the Park's preparing for their annual Spooktacular, as well. They ran a two-day extravaganza of scary Hallowe'en fun, stretching from candy and games for little kids in the airplane hangar on 1920 Street to zombies and horror houses on 1885 Street for the older ones looking for a thrill. Houses with precious artifacts were locked up, but Lauder's Bakery was a favourite for creating a haunted-house effect, especially as there was a clear entrance and exit for the unwary to pass through on their way to meet the undead.

I walked down the gravel road toward the Fort, which loomed up on my right. It was very impressive with its upright palisades surrounding the big house, whose roof I could see peeking out above the walls. I tried to imagine it standing on its own, on the promontory of land where the Legislature grounds now were, just about where the north side of the High Level Bridge began. If you were paddling up the North Saskatchewan River, and you caught sight of that, how would you feel? After days and weeks of solid nature, with no roads or houses or any other sign of western civilization encroaching, would these walls appear to you as the equivalent of the bright corona of city lights after miles of dark highway?

It was to the Park's credit that they had managed to situate their sightlines so that relatively few modern buildings were spotted on the horizon. From various places in the Park, a visitor could imagine himself back in a time with no power lines or river-edge mansions to mar the effect.

It was particularly true from where I stood now, at the Indian Village edge of the Fort. I had been told it wasn't open, but I walked down toward the Fort gates anyhow, mostly to see for myself the little door that Nola had mentioned. There it was, cut into the door, with a threshold at least two feet off the ground, so someone entering would have to clamber over the lintel. There was very little that was inviting about it, and yet, through doors like this, the history of European infiltration of the largest part of North America was forged. The river ways of Canada brought the fur traders of the North West Company and the Company of Adventurers of the Hudson's Bay Company further and further to the source of their wealth, the native trappers themselves. Just like every major hotel in Canada was situated near a railway, every major city was camped on a river.

I patted the door once more, for luck, and turned to walk my long way back through the history of Edmonton. By the time I made it out to the bus stop on Fox Drive, it was the beginning of rush hour, and a bus came right away. As I waited on the platform at South Campus for a train, I calculated that I had travelled 163 years in about an hour.

23

The Jaque family had not wanted a public funeral for their
daughter, so the staff of Rutherford House had not been
given a chance to congregate and deal with their own grada-
tions of grief. Perhaps that was why I saw several of the permanent staff members in the chapel of Old St. Stephen's College
for the somewhat delayed memorial service for Mr. Maitland.
That is the worst thing about losing someone in circumstances
that warrant a police investigation. The time before the body is
released to the funeral home creates an awful limbo in which
grieving hangs with no release. Funerals may be dreadful ritu-
als, but they somehow serve the purpose to purge and release all
those tragic emotions.

St. Stephen's College was a suitable place for the funeral of a
provincial archivist, since the stately building, which had been
one of the first on campus, was now the home to the provincial Historical Resources Management department. I wondered
if Mr. Maitland had specified that he wanted his service there.

Nestled into the east wing of the main floor of the building, it was small enough to make the small number of attendees seem to swell in rank. A plaque listing members of the college who had died in wars hung on one wall, and muted stained glass windows ran down another. A central aisle was flanked by several rows of blond pews, which were all facing an apse that was one elevated step up. It was all muted and restrained and comforting, like so much of the United Church.

The service was officiated by the principal of the present St. Stephen's College, which was now housed in a small two-storey building at the south end of the old college grounds. He gave a short homily, led us in prayer, and then turned the pulpit over to several people who read psalms and spoke about Mr. Maitland.

Even his close friends seemed to touch on the aspects of his character I had found immediately endearing, so it occurred to me that Alastair Maitland had been one of those totally authentic people who had delivered the same open features to everyone he met. He was fair, kind, interested, a stickler for detail, loyal to a fault, and a creature of habit. One friend spoke of his irritation at having to find a new place to buy his shirts and bow ties when the Woodward's department store closed—after a hundred years of business. While this brought smiles to several people around me, a full-throated laugh came when it turned out Mr. Maitland had reluctantly taken his business to Eaton's. When they also closed their doors almost immediately, he had stocked up on several bow ties and crisp white shirts from the Bay and held his breath.

The more I heard from his friends, the greater my indignation over his death seemed to be. While I am, of course, a big fan of John Donne and pay lip service to that whole concept of "each man's death diminishing" the collective, in practice, it's not something that really tracks with me. Most of the time, the knowledge of someone's demise warrants a sigh. If I hear of an accident taking several lives or a situation where some madman mows down a park full of teens, I will take note, of course. But it is rare that I actually feel the loss, that the chasm opens up and I understand the vacuum that has occurred in the firmament.

In an article about why she stooped to write mystery fiction, Dorothy L. Sayers, the great Dante scholar, said that murder was the one crime whereby society became the victim, as part of it had been rent, and in order to create a whole cloth once more, the murder must be solved and the living victim avenged. Any other crime could be dealt with by the victim him- or herself, which is why lesser offences created a voyeuristic impression in crime literature. I was beginning, there in the small chapel, surrounded by polite friends of a buttoned-down little man who had lived alone and trod gently, to understand the concept of the hole created by the loss.

We all stood to sing the final hymn, "Jerusalem," which was still in the old blue United Church hymnals tucked into the pews, as this was, after all, a historic site. The late autumn sun hit the windows, sending dazzling purple and golden lights across the room, and I heard a sniffle behind me. Though it had been a very polite service, it seemed somehow good that nice Mr. Maitland had someone crying over his passing.

We filed out the back door of the chapel and made our way

to the main entrance of the college building. Although the lobby area was obviously a government office space, effort had been made to maintain the integrity of the building. The minister had positioned himself next to the woman I had learned during the service to be Mr. Maitland's sister. She and her husband shook hands with people, and it was only polite to wait in line to do the same. I didn't presume she would whisper an invitation back to their house for refreshments to anyone like me, a person she didn't know, and I wasn't wrong on that count. She smiled distantly as I explained my tenuous connection to her brother and she thanked me for coming. Within minutes I was out on the street, facing the Fine Arts building and wondering whether to pop into HUB for a cup of Java Jive coffee or just head home. Navigating the stairs in my go-to-meeting heels just seemed like too much bother, so I looked left for buses, crossed the street, and wended my way sadly home. This sort of rite just took it out of me. Someone seriously needed to put the "fun" back into funeral. Steve had offered to come with me, but I had not taken him up on it. After all, people usually didn't go to the funerals of people they didn't know, and it wasn't as if he had to scan the crowd for suspects. His partner, Iain McCorquodale, had been there, at the back of the chapel, covering that task.

I was now back in my apartment, shoes kicked off and a cup of tea on the lamp table beside me, massaging the balls of my feet and pondering great philosophical questions, the sort that melancholy funerals bring out. Would I die alone and would I draw more than forty-five people to a memorial? When should one set down requests pertaining to one's own funeral? Should they be filed with one's will? Why didn't I have a will?

Mr. Maitland was my age, or nearabouts, likely no more than ten years difference, if that. As he was so trim and dapper, it was hard to peg him. Somehow, even though he couldn't have been anticipating being killed by someone trying to rob the Archives, he had all his paperwork in order, and his family was able to set a perfectly appropriate service into motion at the drop of a hat.

No one expects a twenty-year-old to be the first one in the family to die, which might be a large part of why Jossie's family wasn't having a service. No matter how I tried, there was no way I could imagine the gut-punch of learning your daughter had been killed during the course of her boring little job.

Her parents had likely brought her up carefully, ferrying her to play dates and dance classes, sending her to summer camps, and attending school plays. They had warned her against calling attention to herself with her giggling girlfriends at bus stops. They had supported her choices of classwork at university. They would have restrained themselves from commenting on her choice of boyfriends. They had taught her to look both ways when she crossed the street, and to never leave her drink untended at rowdy parties. They had likely done everything right. And, during the course of her part-time job, taken to earn some money while at university, they had lost her.

My research into the Rutherford maids was likely romanticizing my posthumous recollections of Jossie. Having just come from Mr. Maitland's funeral didn't help, either. And maybe the pressure of having to get the website mocked up in time for the board meeting this coming week had taken its toll. Whatever the cause, I found myself weeping. Not just a few magical movie tears sliding down my cheeks, either. This was one of those sinus-clearing, eye-burning emotional releases. I stretched my hand out for the tissue box and in the process dumped my phone, a notepad, and several pens onto the floor. Heedless, I curled up on the chesterfield in the fetal position and cried. At some point, I hooked the afghan in the corner with my toe, dragged it up over myself, and fell asleep.

I woke up drained, but clean. Not certain I wasn't about to feel a headache, I sat up gingerly. So far, so good. I used the tissue wadded in my hand to wipe my nose and looked around. A mound of spent tissue lay on the floor in front of the sofa. My tea was cold. My phone's battery had come off and was lying beside the rest of the phone. Two paperbacks, several loose pieces of paper, and a ruled notepad were in a heap in front of the end table. It looked like raccoons had come in and tossed the place while I'd been sleeping.

I padded into the kitchen for a plastic grocery bag and came back to clear my mess. I stuffed it full of soggy tissues, picked up my books, reattached my phone, which almost immediately buzzed to let me know there was a message waiting for me, and reached to pick up the loose paper still on the floor.

One of the sheets was blank, but crumpled. I crumpled it some more and popped it in the garbage bag, hoping David Suzuki would never find out.

For a minute I sat there, perched on the edge of the sofa, bag of refuse in one hand and cup full of cold tea in the other. The sun had set while I'd been napping. It said a lot for the ambient light of the street lights on 109th Street just east of me that I could still navigate my apartment. I shifted the bag to my other hand and flicked on a light, then quickly closed my blinds, just as my parents had taught me to do. Then I went into the kitchen to throw away the evidence of my meltdown and make a sandwich.

24

Steve was spending quality time with Iain dealing with Mr. Maitland's murder, and I was inured to the thought that I wouldn't be seeing much of him for a while. The weekend went by in a blur of apartment cleaning, Hallowe'en candy buying, and outfit choosing for the upcoming showdown with the board. Some people get all geared up for summer by spring cleaning, but the new year so surely begins in the fall for me, programmed as I am by the school and university year. This year's mild fall and my lack of connection to a course syllabus had delayed my instinctual need to clean my cupboards, but it had finally caught up with me. I had the windows open to catch the drifting smell of bonfires and dry leaves, and had cleaned out the freezer compartment of my fridge, replaced the shelf paper in all my kitchen cupboards, washed the windows and wiped down the venetian blinds, turned the mattress of my bed, and was on my third load of laundry. I had swept all the floors and was in the process of dragging throw carpets outside to thwap them against the side of the garbage-bin shed. The next step would be to wash the floors, and then closet myself in my bedroom and shift my wardrobe choices from summer to winter by hauling out the under-the-bed tubs of sweaters and woollens, and folding up the tee-shirts and cottons.

Hitting the mats against the trash-bin stands was good therapy, as long as too much grit and dust didn't fly back into my eyes. I wouldn't have minded one of those carpet beaters from the first Rutherford House for this chore. I looked about as good as Hilda Ogden on a bad day, which was why it was so great to see Roxanne and Chef Bryan standing just a few feet away from my back entrance, dressed to kill. They had obviously been for lunch at the High Level Diner and looked just as pained to see me. Well, no wonder; it's not often that you see the hideous shadow self revealed in one of your co-workers. I shrugged apologetically and called out, "house cleaning," as if that would explain my grimy capris, bleach-spotted oversized shirt, and headscarf. Roxanne offered a brittle smile and a small wave of her hand. Bryan looked as if he was going to walk over to see me, but I noticed Roxanne tug on his sleeve and stop him.

I would have stopped him, too. Women understand that other women do not want to be caught looking their worst, and even if saving me face had not been her motive, I silently thanked Roxanne for her tact. I waved again and dragged my somewhat cleaner mats back inside with me, leaving them to their stylish weekend date.

Now I had something to think about as I mopped the floors. I had no idea Roxanne and Bryan were seeing each other socially, if that indeed was what they were doing. Of course, if they weren't, then why had they been out for lunch together? And for that matter, if they were out together, who was working their shifts this weekend at Rutherford House? Bryan was normally always there when Marni was on duty, and Roxanne took over for her, usually on Sundays and Mondays. Weekends were a busy time for tours, but the Arbour Restaurant seemed to score its steadiest clients during the weekdays, when ladies of leisure could go for lunch without being bothered by the hoi polloi. Marni tended to take one weekend day and one weekday off, to balance the supervisory needs. So maybe she had switched with Roxanne this week. But I had always seen Chef Bryan with Marni, so something about seeing Roxanne with him in the Diner's parking lot just didn't sit right.

It wasn't a crime, though, and for all I knew it would be cleared up with a word or two from Marni when I saw her on Tuesday. I got back to the business of cleaning, and by the time the sun set, my entire apartment was gleaming. Citrus smells from the kitchen were vying with the lavender cleaning supplies I'd used in the bathroom, and surfaces shone brighter as I switched on the lights to counter the dark. Pleased with myself, but exhausted, I decided to treat myself to a movie. I flipped through too many choices on the television and briefly considered renting one from iTunes. Then I recalled there was a double feature of the original and remake of *The Italian Job*, one of my favourite movies, playing at the Garneau Theatre around the corner. I had never seen the remake. I dumped my cleaning duds into my now empty laundry hamper and pulled on clean jeans and a mauve sweater I hadn't worn since the previous winter, which made it feel new again. It smelled faintly of cedar from the bag of chips I kept in the corners of the plastic bins.

I contemplated calling Steve, but he had sounded a little brusque on the phone the last time we'd spoken, a sign that he was under some stress from work. I didn't want to add to that and make him feel as if I was feeling neglected. Relationships were a tricky business, and the hassle involved in reading invisible cues and navigating metaphoric minefields were probably the main reasons for the medieval rise in convents and monasteries. I brushed my hair, pulled on my leather jacket, and grabbed keys and a twenty from my wallet.

Pretty soon, I was ensconced in my favourite seat in the upper part of the cinema, revelling in movie popcorn and dreamy blue eyes. All in all, it was a nice way to end the day. I never felt odd about going to the movies alone at the Garneau or the Princess, since they seemed to cater to film buffs rather than people on dates. That was one of the best things about living so close to campus, of course. The lifestyle of the average student was one of solitude and much of the area catered to that. The local Safeway sold smaller trays of meat and single-portion-sized deli meals in greater quantities than other groceries in town. They also, of course, carried more Kraft Dinner and their soup selections skewed heavily to tomato and cream of mushroom. They knew exactly who was cooking for the first time in basement suites and starter apartments within a ten-block radius of their store.

I shook a few kernels of popcorn out of the cowl of my sweater and headed for home by popping out the front-left exit of the cinema. From there, I was about thirty yards from my apartment. If they hadn't put up the fence between the parking area and the yard of the duplex between my apartment and the cinema, I'd have been able to see my window. I hurried along the back lane to the rear entrance of the apartment, passing the place where I'd seen Roxanne and Bryan earlier.

I made sure to close the outer back door firmly. Every now and then, a homeless person would manage to sneak in if the latch hadn't firmly caught. All the mayhem I'd witnessed in the movie was making me feel "urban cautious." Satisfied, I made it to my apartment door, key still in hand.

There was no need for a key. My door was standing open. I pushed it slightly to reveal a mess of foam and feathers and paper. Someone had done their own cleaning job on my apartment.

As horrified as I was, I wasn't a cop's girlfriend for nothing. Staying in the hall, I reached into my jacket pocket for my phone, which had been turned to silent during the movie. I hit 911 to report the break-in, then dialled Steve. I told him I would wait for him in the hallway, and obligingly sank to the floor, leaning on the wall across from my ransacked apartment. No one from the other apartments on the main floor popped their heads out to check, which made me think the looter must have been pretty silent. Or, maybe they all thought I was still heaving things around, cleaning house, since I'd been strenuously perky all day.

Or maybe they were all dead in their bathtubs.

Lucky for me, the police arrived before I could freak myself out too much.

25

Using the key I had given him, Steve appeared from the back door of the apartment building at about the same time that the officers on call entered through the main doorway, using some master key, I supposed. Or maybe the building's front door had been wedged opened, as often happened. For all I know, that was how the thieves had got into my apartment.

I rose to my feet, sort of creakily, with Steve's help. Sitting on the floor wasn't the best thing for my knees, especially in the evening. Between the joint stiffness and my sudden shivering, likely brought on by shock, Steve had to prop me up a bit and I clung to him more than I'd anticipated.

I had once had my university office ransacked, and it had been Steve then, too, who had comforted me and seen me through the sense of violation one feels when one has been invaded. Thank goodness for his presence in my life, because I wasn't sure just how people managed this sort of thing on their own.

While I don't mean to usurp the words from those who have had far more violent and horrific things happen to them bodily, I was once again shaken to the core by the sense of violation and molestation that came with having my personal space and belongings desecrated and mauled by some strangers' hands. Paper, presumably from my desk drawers, was strewn everywhere. The cushions of my chesterfield had been sliced open diagonally and the foam yanked out in hunks. The feathers seemed to still be coming out of my bedroom, but that was likely the heating vent pushing the erstwhile contents of my duvet on air currents. One of the officers on the scene mentioned that I was lucky to have been out when the Huns arrived.

I supposed I was, though standing in the middle of the ruins of my apartment, I didn't feel particularly lucky. Once they had dusted for prints and photographed the scene, I was asked to determine what, if anything, was missing. To do that, I'd need to start clearing away some of the mess.

"You can file a complete list later, Randy," Steve said, and the other officers nodded. "Right now, they just want to know if there is anything major they can search for, if they manage to stop someone suspicious."

I leaned over to pick up a damaged book from the floor. While I was bent over, I gathered up some of the papers at my feet, shuffling them messily into a pile. I would have to go through them all, and probably would still not make any sense of them. Material from my last job was mixed up with notes on Rutherford House and I even noted an early draft of a thesis chapter on Margaret Ahlers, which had been stored in the bottom of my filing cabinet, spilled over the floor.

What had they been looking for? Was this just plain vandalism? Or had they targeted more than one apartment? I looked up and noted that one of the officers who had initially been examining the living room mess had disappeared. Steve noticed my look and read my mind, as usual.

"Officer Dugo is checking with the other residents to see if anyone heard anything, or if anyone else's homes were vandalized."

I nodded. "Well, it's hard to say, because as you know, I have an awful lot of stuff in this small apartment, but off the top, I can't find my laptop or the remotes for the TV and PVR, and this may sound weird, but there is more china missing than seems to be broken here." I pointed to the built-in glass-doored shelves that created a half-wall between the kitchen and dining area. The doors stood open, and there were a couple of plates smashed on the floor below, but I had owned several bits and bobs of old glassware and china, which were teetering between collectible and antique. The pink glass condiment jar and several of the teacups seemed to be missing, and the green Depression-ware platter that had leaned up against the back wall of the cabinet was no longer there.

"They stole your china and your laptop?"

"I know that sounds weirdly specific, doesn't it?" I headed into the kitchen and opened the canister cupboard, where I kept my flour, oats, sugar, and rice. Beside the rice jar was an envelope in which I kept a small stock of cash for emergencies like late-night deliveries of Chinese food. It was still there, with $90 in tens and fives. So they weren't after my hoard of money. On the counter was my Magic Bullet, which might only cost $40 at London Drugs, but was worth millions to me in terms of smoothie ease. Between it and my self-sharpening paring knife, I could make practically anything.

I moved back into the living room, trying to see in my mind what it had looked like before I'd headed off to the movies. All that work to make my personal world clean and organized for nothing. Just as I had felt calmed by the order instilled, this chaos was making my head throb, and the tears began to stream down my face.

How could I even operate the television without the remotes? Why would someone take remotes without the machines they operated? Steve answered that by showing me that the set and PVR and DVD player had all been unplugged, but not yet carted away.

"You might have surprised them, babe. I'm just glad you didn't walk in on them."

"But how could I have surprised them? I was at the movies."

"Maybe they knew that? Maybe they were watching you leave your apartment."

I shuddered. Somehow, the thought of someone spying on me felt even more repulsive than someone breaking into an anonymous apartment and destroying it. Had this been personal?

"So they took what they thought was valuable and easy to sell. But they left actual cash, which wasn't all that well hidden, and didn't take all the electronics they intended to. They also had an eye for antiques. I wonder if..." my voice trailed off as I walked into the ruins of my bedroom. The thieves had pulled apart my duvet and dumped it at the end of my bed. My underwear drawer was dumped into the middle of my bed. The thought of someone having pawed through my panties made me gag a bit, and my immediate urge was to throw them all away and head to Zellers for some nice cotton briefs. But Zellers was gone and so was my feeling of security.

The jewellery box I had inherited from my grandmother, a black wooden box with a Japanese cherry tree painted on the top, had been tossed onto my bed, as well. Her gold wedding bands had rested in the bottom of that box. I could find neither, though most of my casual costume jewellery and two amber rings were still there. Defiantly, I put on both rings. How dare they consider these not worth stealing?

Steve and the officers were still in the kitchen and dining area, so while I was alone, I checked my personal wall safe, the brass plate of my bedroom-light switch. I flicked it to the right, revealing a tiny space under the wiring box. My spare flash drive and safe deposit box key were still there. I flipped back the plate and tapped it for luck, wondering idly if a Jewish god would find that profane, and then checked the medicine cabinet in the bathroom. Since I didn't require any expensive or narcotic medications, I didn't think much would have been taken, and I was right. Instead, the jerks had dumped all my ibuprofen and TUMS into the sink, under the misguided possibility that I hid uncut diamonds or microchips in the bottoms of the bottles.

I sat down on the side of the tub and yanked a bunch of toilet paper off the roll to wipe my eyes and blow my nose. Steve stood in the doorway of the bathroom, saying nothing. I don't know how long we stayed there, but eventually one of the officers came to speak quietly with Steve.

"Randy," Steve said, patting me on the knee to bring me back into the real world. "We should go. I'm going to take you to my place tonight, and we're going to seal your apartment up. The crime scene boys will be back in the morning to go over everything. We can possibly pick up a print here or there, since they've been through everything."

"When will I be allowed back in?"

"Likely by tomorrow, but you can stay with me as long as it takes, hon. C'mon. The sooner we are out of here, the better."

He reached out his hand and I pulled myself to standing. I was directly across from the medicine-cabinet mirror. My face looked bruised, what with my mascara puddled under my eyes and streaks of tears down to my chin. I swiped the back of my hand across my eyes, and pushed my hair out of my face. There was nothing I could do to set things straight tonight, either to my apartment or my looks. People were dying around me. My world was no longer safe. Everything felt off-kilter and out of step. The falcon probably couldn't even hear the falconer.

The officers locked up behind us and taped the door. We left out the back way.

26

I signed a short statement for Steve to take in to the station for me before we went to sleep, and when the morning came, he left me to stay in bed at his place. I was supposed to go downtown to see the Widows in the afternoon, but the events of the previous day had left me feeling fragile, as if my skin was made out of tissue paper and I was in danger of ripping and leaking with any sudden movement.

Why would anyone destroy my apartment? What could they have been looking for that wasn't right out in plain view? Was it just wanton fun on the part of some crackhead breaking in to find something to sell for a fix? Or was all that mess and ruination meant as a further insult to me personally? Was it a message?

That last possibility seemed silly. Who the heck did I think I was to anyone, particularly anyone criminal? For the past few months, all I had done was research Rutherford House. No big secrets, no big pay-off.

And yet, it was my connection to Rutherford House that had brought me into contact with two murders within the space of a couple of weeks. That couldn't just be coincidence, now could it? First Jossie, then Mr. Maitland, and now my apartment.

Thank goodness for Steve. I felt safe locked away here in his condo, which I loved. His living room looked out on to the river valley and was the very best place from which to watch the annual fireworks on Canada Day. He had decorated it in brown leather and wood, with highlights of bright throw cushions and one crazy quilt of an upholstered chair. Being Steve, he had one long wall of the living room devoted to bookcases, which was one of the reasons I was devoted to him.

I padded out of the bedroom, which he kept tidy by keeping furniture to a minimum. I had pulled the duvet straight on the bed and closed the closet doors. There was coffee still in the carafe, but the little light on the coffee machine was off. I touched the glass of the carafe, which was cool. Taking a cup from the cupboard above, I poured cold coffee and set the cup in the microwave. I needed to shower and dress and have something to eat before I could even think what to do next. I leaned against the counter of Steve's kitchen, waiting for the beep-beep that let me know my coffee was heated.

Steve had left the day's newspaper and a note on the other side of the counter, where he had two barstools tucked up for kitchen seating. I got my coffee, doctored it with milk from the fridge and, grabbing a banana, walked around the counter to sit down and see what he had to say. I could barely remember him leaving that morning.

The note was short and sweet, reminding me to lock the deadbolt when I headed out and telling me there was strudel in the fridge. I slipped off the stool and went to check whether the nice policeman had been telling the truth. Sure enough, a third of a plank of strudel was sitting in the second shelf, in a plastic bag. I pulled it out and cut a generous portion, which I decided to also warm up in the microwave. While it was heating, I checked Steve's freezer and found some fancy vanilla ice cream. Breakfast of champions.

Now, armed with *apfelstrudel* à la mode and a cup of Rwandan roast, and feeling mighty cosmopolitan, I was ready to tackle reading the newspaper.

There, of course, was nothing about the desecration of my apartment. I hadn't thought there would be, unless it was in the form of a "crime spree hits Old Strathcona area of town" sort of story. The canvassing of the rest of the apartment owners in my building had not shown any other break-ins. Four of the people on the main floor had been at home, but of course the man next to me was quite deaf, and hadn't heard anything from my apartment, a situation I normally found comforting.

Only two of the six tenants upstairs had been at home, but none of the empty apartments had been ravaged, leading the investigating officers to consider the crime to be targeted at me in particular. And the situation of one little academic researcher in the heart of what had been called Canada's Murder Capital just last year, didn't warrant a news story.

There were some stories of interest on the cover, though. Apparently, someone had tied in the recent unsolved murders of two working adults to mean that parents should panic about their children's safety when trick-or-treating this upcoming Hallowe'en. The mega-mall had announced there would be treats delivered store to store for little ones too small to do outdoor treks, and the annual Spooktacular at Fort Edmonton Park was highlighted as a family alternative. Other related stories further inside the paper dealt with not allowing masks as part of the costume, to keep eyesight at a maximum, commentary on the safety of sparkly makeup, the need to ascertain all candy was factory sealed, and how to examine it for tampering.

Somehow, as Hallowe'en grew as a commercial activity, with people decorating their homes as splashily as they did for Christmas, though obviously along a slightly more garish and ghoulish theme, the joyous anarchy of the event had diminished. Not that I had ever been one of those rascals out egging windows and toilet-papering trees, though I had secretly delighted in that sort of trickery. For me the old flickering candle in the malevolent jack-o'-lantern and a bowl of candy handed out in placation provided far more of a preteen high than did blinking plastic headstones and stick-on blood spatters on the screen doors. Mostly, just being out in the dark without one's parents was enough of a thrill for the twelve-year-old set. For the younger ones, it was all about the candy.

Maybe I would head down to Fort Edmonton for their Spooktacular event. It was anachronistic, of course, and one was likely to encounter a zombie bride walking down the street just as easily as a turn-of-the-century bobbing for apples game being held in one of the houses, but there would be fewer street lights and more potential for anarchy.

I checked the paper. The Spooktacular ran for the three days before Hallowe'en. I turned Steve's note over and wrote "Wanna do this with me?" and drew a large arrow pointing left. I folded the paper to the Fort Edmonton ad, and placed the note strategically, before heading to the washroom to clean up and head downtown.

The Widows were happy to see me and made all the right noises when I told them about the break-in to my apartment. Linda said something that hadn't occurred to me till she mentioned it.

"Are you going to feel safe there once you've cleaned it all up?"

"I really don't know. I didn't stay there last night. But as soon as the police are done with it, I have to get back in there to start cleaning up the mess."

"Well, in the meantime, you don't have to worry about tomorrow's presentation," Judy pronounced, patting me sympathetically on the arm. "I think we have got it totally under control for you."

"You bet we have. Sit down here and let us walk you through it," Linda joined in.

I sat down, prepared to be amazed. I always loved what the Widows came up with. Their sites were clean and simple, but deceptively so. A lot of work went into the background of making things flow smoothly.

"We've mocked up the website into our sandbox, meaning

that you can offer a secure URL to your board members so they can actually paddle around in the site themselves, if you like. Otherwise" —Judy clicked her mouse and pointed at the Smart Board on the wall in front of us— "you can just lead them along with you in a demo. Either way, it's set to show."

The site was fantastic.

A shadowy brick background framed a central film on the splash page of the site.

"We have a bypass built in here," Judy said, pointing to the scripted "returning visitors" note at the bottom right of the screen. "But we wanted it to start as the default to underpin the concept of how magnificent and different the House was for its time and place."

The film began with a wide, establishing shot of prairie that moved toward a belt of aspen parkland marking out the river valley. It morphed into a sighting of palisade wall, presumably Fort Edmonton, then a sod shack with a little goat standing on the top of its green roof. This became a full-sized split log cabin, then a small clapboard house, and finally a view of the wooden Rutherford House now situated down in the historic park. There was a pause of about five seconds, and then the picture broke into a thousand little tiles and spilled down to the bottom of the screen, leaving a majestic vision of Rutherford House as it stood today, looking out over Saskatchewan Drive. It radiated majesty and dignity, the way the cornerstone of one of Canada's major universities should.

The title RUTHERFORD HOUSE appeared at the top of the screen, and a set of ornately filigreed radio buttons faded in on the left, letting the viewer choose to go to Family History, House History, Timelines, People, Hours, Arbour Tea Room, Friends of Rutherford House, Special Events, and Contact Us. I looked questioningly at Linda, who nodded, and I proceeded to mouse my way through all the sections of the site.

I especially loved the House History section, which consisted of a blueprint layout of each floor of the house. When the cursor rolled over a room, a photo of the room as it appeared now sprang onto the screen, as well as a portrait of the pertinent Rutherford. If you were to click the portrait, the site took you to the Family History section.

"This is amazing. Will it all load this quickly, wherever?"

"It should," nodded Linda. "We have deliberately tweaked things to be sure that everyone, regardless of platform and capacity, gets the same upload. After all, many of the people checking out a site like this will be tourists, some of them still using dial-up Internet, who are checking out the possibilities before booking a trip to Alberta. It just wouldn't do to lock them out or hang up their computers in the loading stage, right? It's perception as much as ease. Who would feel comfortable going somewhere they felt too backward to navigate?"

I thought of my initial attempts to feel comfortable in cities like London and New York, where my adrenalin went into warp speed while I tried to find the bus route back to my hotel, and smiled. The Widows were amazing. By making a tourist website über-easy to deal with, they were subliminally offering a welcome to Alberta as a destination that would provide a relaxing pace along with amazing vistas and sites. It was no coincidence that Marshall McLuhan had been born in Edmonton. These girls knew in their bones that the medium was the message.

They went on to explain that they had imbedded all the photos used as tiny pixels in previous layers of the site, so that they were loading invisibly behind each window of text or substance.

"The opening montage will run a bit slower on older computers, but we went with really bright, clear images, so we could run them at a lighter resolution and save on some upload time that way." Judy was obviously proud of the measures they had taken, and rightly so. They both looked at me, as I maneuvered my way through the layers and intricacies of what was only a mock-up of what the real site would be.

I was delighted, and told them so. I was especially glad that they'd had the foresight to put all the interactive elements within the secure area for the Friends of Rutherford House to play around with in peace. Having spent time monitoring a public chat site in the past, I had no desire to play bouncer while my fate was being decided by a non-Internet-savvy board. The Widows beamed, looking more like sisters than work colleagues.

"Do you think it would be gilding the lily to introduce another character to the site?" I asked. Judy grinned broadly.

"You mean, the maid? We took your notes at the back of the notebook and sort of ran with that, as well." She clicked the mouse onto a tiny teacup in the corner of the screen. "We set it up as a sort of Easter egg extra, and you can also get here by clicking either the back door on the blueprint or through the paragraph on servants in the People section."

The columns on either side of the front door dissolved and a regular green wooden door appeared, and then opened. Using the arrow buttons on the keyboard, Judy took the tour of the kitchen, then went up the back stairs and into the maid's bedroom and parlour. The Widows had obviously left their loft at some point in the last week, because some of the photos appearing were not the ones I had provided. The bedroom, while ostensibly the same, had a more personal, lived-in air to it. A needlepoint pillow, with red and white Ukrainian embroidery, sat on the bed. A thin gold chain with what was possibly a crucifix attached hung from one of the bedposts, as if someone had taken it off before going to sleep, and on back of the door was a green hat with two long pheasant feathers, suitable for wearing on one's day off when one went as far away as one could to forget the servitude of the previous week.

"Where did you get the extra elements?" I asked.

"Do you like them?" Linda asked.

"They're perfect. It's just what was needed to bring the maid to life."

"CGI is an amazing thing," smiled Judy. "We were hoping you'd get a kick out of it. The whole idea of making the maid's world a different view of the house was a blast. We wanted to make the distinction without it being a politically-charged upstairs/downstairs sensibility. After all, the Rutherfords were lovely people; it's not as if we wanted to start a class warfare issue. But the whole idea of layers and levels to the way a historic site speaks to people is vital, I think."

They were absolutely correct. It brought to mind the time my parents and I had visited my mother's cousin in Coventry. We had gone to see the great Cathedral, as one does. The new cathedral was built alongside of the bombed remains, and there was a cross made of melted nails supposedly crafted by a verger from the ruins of the World War II bombing. There was a display of wartime photos, along with other art that strongly evoked world peace, in the new, modern cathedral, and a summertime re-enactment of the Coventry Mystery Plays in the body of the old cathedral. We stood there, watching theatre our ancestors would have watched from pretty much the same vantage point, but it wasn't until great-cousin Betty said, "You know, my mum and dad were the first couple married here after it was consecrated a cathedral," that I actually felt a familial connection to that lovely place, which had been sacrificed by Churchill for the sake of the Enigma Code. Vows had been taken here and promises shattered.

That's the magic of a historic site that allows the visitor in to find his or her own connection. Rutherford House might be a bastion of high society to those coming to see the premier's home, or for others it might be a nostalgic visit to the site of their grandfather's fraternity hijinks. But for some, it would be a valid reminder of their grandmother's hard work in a new land, baking, polishing, and cleaning for the rich ladies, and holding on to a dream of her children and their children standing side by side with every Edmontonian. And we had found a way to honour that.

I was sure the board was going to love the site until my mind flashed to Greta Larsen with her pinched little face and my certainty dropped a point or two. Judy and Linda must have sensed my shift in confidence because their eyebrows went up questioningly. I smiled and shook my head.

"It's perfect. You two are amazing."

They preened a bit and then got busy providing the URL to their test site, log-in prerequisites and, in the event of a power outage during the board presentation, a printed version of the site. These women thought of everything. When I left their office that afternoon, I was loaded for bear.

As it turned out, it was just as well I was.

The next morning, Steve was still up and away before me, though my inner alarm clock woke me closer to my normal time. It was just as well, as I had a long day ahead of me. Besides, the phone would not stop ringing.

The board meeting was to begin at seven. Marni had suggested we meet for supper at five. Steve had called right before Marni to tell me I was allowed to re-enter my apartment, so I figured I would do some cleaning at the apartment before joining her at the High Level Diner. I got ready for a day of grunt work, but packed my satchel full of the sort of talismans I needed to feel professional at the board meeting, along with the flash drive and the laptop the Widows had loaned me. As for a professional-looking outfit for later, I hoped there were some elements of my wardrobe passable for the meeting, and that not everything had been damaged by the intruders.

I was in luck there. Though they had pulled and ripped clothing off the hangers in my closet, it was all in a pile on the floor below. I also had a box of winter clothing still under my bed, which I had been meaning to change out the week before but had been too lazy to do so. I left it where it was, so that I could clean up the feathers and detritus outside the closet first.

The mess at Rutherford House had been nothing compared to this, but at least I was prepared for the pervasiveness of the fingerprint powder. "Experienced at crime scene cleanup" — another useful thing I could put on my resume. It took three hours of back-breaking, non-stop work, but by early afternoon I had nine black garbage bags filled and tied by the door, the floor scrubbed, and the laundry humming down the hall, and had called some rubbish removal workers to come and wrestle the broken chesterfield off to the dump. I had put some of my CDs back in their cases, setting aside a pile that seemed too scratched to save. I would test them when I wasn't quite so fragile myself. Books had fared better, but only because most of them had been well-used by me already. It was hard to tell whether their spines were cracked due to being flung on the floor, or because they'd spent a week spread-eagled on the arm of a chair. I had gathered them up into piles, but was considering sorting them alphabetically since they were all in need of re-shelving anyhow.

Although it didn't seem as if I'd made much of a dent in things, barring removing most of the feathers and kapok, I decided to call a halt around three o'clock, since I needed to shower and change in time to meet up with Marni. The bathroom smelled strongly of the new soft plastic shower curtain I had hung earlier, which was just as well, because otherwise it would have reeked of bleach. I unwrapped a new bar of soap and hopped into the tub.

I wasn't sure how I felt about being back in the apartment. It was unnerving to be stuck behind the opaque shower curtain, for one thing. The curtain they'd slashed and tossed into the tub had been clear plastic with cartoon fish swimming across it, and my minor claustrophobia had been assuaged by being able to see out. This replacement had been purchased quickly at the Safeway, along with the bleach and rubber gloves, and grocery stores weren't known for their home-decorative sensibilities.

It wasn't just the shower curtain, though. I had been edgy all morning, closing and locking the door every time I went out with the laundry basket just to head ten feet down the hall. A car revving on its way down the alley startled me as I washed dishes, causing me to gouge my hand with a potato peeler. This ground-level apartment was not a secure place, and it had been violated. I knew I didn't want to stay here on my own tonight. I wondered if and when I was going to get over that feeling.

I dressed as well as I could for the board meeting. A blue trouser suit with just a thin thread of pinstripe hinted at, a rust tank top with a touch of lace at the hem, and an orange, brown, and blue scarf tied loosely around my neck made me feel businesslike and mature, which I would have to be to sway any naysayers on the board. I wasn't sure how many people would be there this evening and, of those who showed up, how many were opposed to the website project. Still, armour was useful for building self-confidence and deflecting all but the most singular attacks. And boy did I need some confidence.

Marni was already at the restaurant when I got there, which wasn't much of a surprise since I had gone back to the apartment twice to make sure all the window latches were secured and that the front foyer door was pulled tight and locked. She waved at me from her table by the east window.

I sat down heavily, realizing in that way one does only after finishing a task that I hadn't stopped in too long. Marni lifted her eyebrows.

"Hard day?"

"Hard couple of days." I filled her in on the break-in at my apartment and my efforts of the day.

"God. Are you going to stay there tonight? Or are you still dealing with the cleanup?"

"I have to buy a new mattress before I can actually stay there again. They slashed up both my sofa and bed. The box spring is still okay, but I'm not sure they sell those separately."

"Have you considered one of those daybeds, the sort that pull out to a full-sized bed?"

"I'm not entirely sure there would be room to pull it out to full size in that room," I laughed. "I honestly have no idea what they were thinking when they built those apartments. The ones in the front are bigger, and the rooms are proportionately larger all round. Then you get in the back six apartments, and it's as if they decided they'd be housing skinny spinsters."

"Well, some of those daybeds have drawers underneath them, meaning you wouldn't necessarily need a dresser in the room. That might make the footprint a bit smaller." Marni obviously knew her Swedish furniture.

I shrugged.

"I am still not certain I will ever feel comfortable staying there again. What wasn't vandalized was stolen. I might move."

Marni look concerned but not surprised.

"You might want to visit a counsellor, just for a session or two, you know. I've read that the violation felt by this sort of invasion can be pretty devastating if you don't tackle it."

"I might," I said, picking up my menu. "I am so lucky to have Steve to turn to in situations like this. He says I can stay with him as long as I want, which is not exactly the way I wanted us to move in together, but for the moment I am extremely grateful."

The waitress arrived to take our orders. While I was longing to order an alcoholic ginger beer, I figured it would be best to have my wits about me this evening, so I asked for a large glass of water with an order of their black bean chili. Marni opted for their veggie burger, saying she was a sucker for their homemade relish and ketchup. After we placed our orders, she excused herself to use the washroom, and I took an opportunity to check out the new artwork hanging about the restaurant.

An artist with a bold eye for colour and line had created a series of architectural studies of Edmonton. I was especially taken with an entry to the High Level Bridge on a narrow, wide canvas. A series of stained glass pieces hung from the middle beam of the restaurant, creating a glittery half-wall between the tables on either side. The waitress brought my water and Marni's coffee just as Marni reappeared.

"So, I gather we have a mock-up presentation for this evening to show the board, anyhow, right? The robbers didn't get that, as well?"

I shook my head.

"No, they didn't get that. Hard to steal something off an intranet. I have a link to the site I can open, and we can present to them if you have the technology." We discussed the various ways we could provide the best means of showing the website to the board to gain their buy-in to the project. While some of them were older, this didn't necessarily mean they were unversed in computer usage. On the other hand, the fear of looking awkward might set them against the site if they were asked to reveal their less-than-stellar skills in front of the others.

Marni suggested that I link her laptop to the projector in order to show the overall site to the board as a whole, and that we could set my loaner from the Widows up on the sideboard for individual members to tap on for a one-on-one experience.

It should work. I was still worried about the antagonism to the project from Greta Larsen, and asked Marni if she thought it had spread to others.

"From what I can tell, most of the folks are not against the idea of a website or of attracting more traffic to the House. There is a quirk in some historic boards and societies, though, which is the hope to gain funding to preserve a place or artifacts but not allow access to the general public. That's a tendency I keep having to fight against here to greater or lesser extents."

"You sure you don't mean Greta or lesser extents?" I grimaced and Marni laughed.

"Finding that happy medium between preservation and

education is what we're all about. And for the most part, this board feels that way. However, there are two or three people who value peace and tranquillity more than rubies, and they will bend to the path of least resistance in order to prevent any disagreements on the board."

"And how do you approach them? Do they side with the person being an oasis of calm, or do they vote with the louder, abrasive person in order to placate her and bring back the calm?"

Marni laughed. "There's the million-dollar question. Good luck figuring that one out tonight!"

Just then our food came, and I realized as the aromas wafted under my nose how hungry I really was. I pushed aside the cilantro garnishing the swirl of chili, guacamole, and sour cream, and stirred the cheese into the beans. Alternating bites of toasted cornbread with big spoonfuls of chili, I nodded appreciatively to the waitress and then to Marni, who was attacking her burger and home-cut fries with equal gusto.

The restaurant had filled up while we were eating, and after paying the bill, we edged along a substantial line of people waiting to get in. The Diner didn't take reservations, and people obediently lined up for the chance of eating there. More original art hung along the line-up wall, and several local entertainment newspapers and brochures were stacked near the door. I nabbed a small, folded version of the *Nightlife* poster that showed concerts and plays a month in advance.

Once we were on the sidewalk, we turned left and took the sidewalk hidden from the High Level Bridge traffic by the large caragana hedges still in full leaf. In just another month, they too would be bare, though still thick enough that an observant driver would only catch a glimpse of a colourful parka, unable to discern who was walking there.

The sidewalk met up with the stairs from the bridge, which opened onto the keyhole start of Saskatchewan Drive as it wound down along the campus. A block of private residential houses led to a block of university-owned buildings, ending with my old office from my teaching assistant days. We crossed the street and strolled along the side of the Humanities Building and there, in the setting sun, was Rutherford House, gleaming.

"It must have been amazing to see it here, before the Tory Building or Bio Sciences were ever built, standing on its own on the side of the river valley. I mean, I know that there were houses along here where Humanities now sits, but they were double lots and wider apart."

"Yes, if you walk along the HUB parking lot a block south of here, you can still see the stairs going up to the individual paths for the houses that used to be there, and they're farther apart by far than houses sit today. When it was being built, of course, the thought was that it would eventually become the premier's home, looking across the river at the Legislature, each building majestically claiming a bank. But by the time it was done, Rutherford was no longer premier, and he had turned to the university as his major interest."

By this time, Marni had unlocked the front doors. We had a half-hour head start on the earliest bird of the board, but she had already set up the dining-room table with pens and blotting pads at each place, so that no one would scratch the oak.

I busied myself by plugging in her laptop where she suggested and opening up the projection screen at one end of the room, while Marni went off to get water pitchers and glasses for the centre of the table.

I counted eleven places, and wondered if Marni had heard whether all the board would be there. If the chair didn't vote, and two of those places were for Marni and me, that mean that I had to persuade at least five people to continue to support my livelihood this evening. I wasn't fooling myself that I could win over Greta Larsen; whatever bee she had in her bonnet had already poisoned her against my endeavours. What I had to hope for was that her way of thinking wasn't contagious.

I logged onto the Black Widow site and entered my client number into the password box. The splash page bounced up. I hit pause and then maneuvered the timer back so that when I hit the return button, the board would have the full experience of entering the Rutherford House site. Our theory was that, after the meeting, board members who wanted to play with the site could do so on Marni's laptop or mine, individually.

Marni had everything set up and was wiping her hands on the sides of her black-and-grey shift dress as the bell signalling the opening of the front door sounded. She smiled at me with a forced gaiety.

"It's showtime," she whispered, and headed out to the foyer to greet the first board member.

I positioned myself in the back corner of the room, as far from the head of the table as it was possible to be. I didn't expect to be sitting at the table itself, but Marni had insisted. Still, I didn't want to be conspicuous. I would be on the block enough this evening as it was.

People streamed in, greeting each other with familiar pleasantries. It was hard to tell how well anyone knew each other, if they socialized outside this connection or whether they were united only in this context. All of them were polite but slightly puzzled by my presence, so I figured they had all been on the board long enough to know each other by sight. Marni stood in the doorway from the lobby, like a gracious hostess. Greta Larsen came in, glowered at me, and took a seat close to the front, leaving the end seat vacant, presumably for the board chair. He soon arrived, and the air in the room got a little bit more oxygenated.

Walter Karras had retired from public service years ago, but was still doing his part for the province he loved. He had been the Deputy Minister for Culture back in the halcyon days when the government had recognized the value in supporting the arts. Film production money had flooded in, with everyone from Richard Donner to Ang Lee taking advantage of Alberta vistas. Artists and writers were supported with seed grants, historic sites were saved and sustained, and museums and festivals were born and flourished. Mr. Karras had a park and a theatre named after him, his portrait hung in bronze on the "culture wall of fame" in the Citadel Theatre foyer, and he and his wife were ambassadors for several charitable foundations.

I had not been aware he was the chair of the Rutherford House foundation till I had begun this project, but I wasn't in the least surprised. I just wished he, as chair, could have a vote in what happened tonight. He was renowned as a fair-minded and forward-thinking person. I couldn't imagine him not being in favour of a website celebrating the centennial of the House and luring people to learn more about our history and artifacts. However, unless it was a dead-heat tie, the chair did not cast a vote.

When the entire board was seated, water glasses poured and clinking with ice, Mr. Karras cleared his throat and brought the meeting to order. The agenda had been emailed to everyone prior, and they each brought a binder or notebook computer along, complete with their own set of minutes from the previous meeting and agenda. This was looking better. Not a single Luddite among them. I wouldn't have to argue against those who were still pretty sure this whole Internet thing was just a fad that would blow over soon enough.

The meeting ticked right along, and I watched with admiration as Mr. Karras managed to keep people on track while allowing everyone his or her say. It was a masterful talent at work. My project was number six on the agenda, right before new business, but the discussion of the possibility of a new boiler utilizing the present duct system took no time at all, as did the reflection that hollyhocks for the side bed, while accurate to the time, would not have been indicative of Mattie Rutherford's own personal style. Lilies of the valley were approved for the front beds as being both representative of the time and adaptable to a north-facing garden. One of the women brought up the fact that their leaves were poisonous but this was shot down by a younger man who maintained that it was the personal responsibility of parents to keep their children from gnawing on foliage in public places. I snorted at the image, but while Mr. Karras twinkled his eyes at me from the end of the table, no one else, even the man who had said it, seemed amused. I shut up quickly and looked down at my notes.

In no time at all, it was my turn. Mr. Karras introduced the item on the agenda, smoothly overriding Greta Larsen, who seemed about to speak, by handing off the point to Marni.

Marni stood and walked to the sideboard, where we had positioned her computer that I had synched up to the projector.

"As part of the centennial celebrations, and in a bid to position Rutherford House as a prime destination when making tourism decisions, we have commissioned a website project that will highlight both the personal and social history, as well as the architectural interest in Rutherford House. To that end, we have hired Randy Craig as the researcher/writer/designer for the project. We are presently at the midway point of the project and hadn't anticipated requiring a mock-up of the site, but Randy has kindly provided us with a sense of where the initiative is going, to answer questions brought by individual board members regarding the need for the project."

She didn't look in Greta Larsen's direction, but I noticed that two or three people around the table couldn't help but do so. I wondered if they were cowed enough by her negativity to vote with her, or whether Marni and I would be able to somehow persuade them to hold their ground against the woman I was beginning to think of as an evil fairy.

"Rutherford House holds such a special place in our collective conscience, which is represented by its ties to the City, the Province, and the University. What we hope to show through this interactive website is the place it holds for all walks of Alberta life, whether or not we are concerned with the preservation of history or connected somehow to the Rutherford family themselves. We want to show how Rutherford House should matter to all of us." And with that she hit the "return" key.

The website opened with the sweep up toward the main steps of the House, after establishing the postcard-perfect front view. The front door opened and the computer stilled. Across the bottom of the screen appeared the words: *Welcome to Rutherford House*. At the foot of the open door appeared the word: *Enter*.

Marni beckoned to me.

"I would like to turn over this preview tour of the site to our researcher/coordinator for the virtual museum project, Randy Craig." There was polite applause as I got up and went to take over the mouse from Marni. I smiled nervously at my small but important crowd. These people held my livelihood in their hands this evening.

"Good evening, folks. What you are seeing is a mock-up of the eventual site. There is still quite a long way to go to get all the information seeded and bells and whistles operating. That said, what we do have so far is a pretty fair rendition of where the project is headed." I pointed at the screen at the end of the room. "This is the splash page. The viewer clicks the open door to enter and finds him- or herself in the foyer. It's an intuitive approach tied to the physical reality of a tour of the House, which is the reason most people come to the site."

I clicked Enter, and the screen dissolved into the foyer of the House, with the magnificent staircase as the focal point.

"However, here is where the choices of the site begin to happen. I didn't want to limit the person coming to the site to be just looking for directions to us or to hours listed. Alternately, I didn't want it to sit there as just a repository of data. In order to be useful and of additional value to the experience, a website needs to be kinetic, rather than static, and it has to be multifaceted. So, we have a marriage of the two."

I moved my cursor from left to right, showing how the view on screen did a 360-degree tour of the foyer.

"Click on any of the entries you pass in this circuit, and the screen will take you into that room. This is modelled on the principles of computer game movement, so it should be intuitive to the majority of viewers under the age of forty coming to the site. I am still determining whether or not to label this function for other visitors' ease. As you can see, just a slight touch of the mouse or your laptop thumb pad would generate movement, so it wouldn't take much for anyone to be conversant with the method.

"Meanwhile, at any time during our tour, there are ways to move out of the physical tour and into a more educational aspect." I clicked on the picture of Premier Rutherford hanging in the study. The screen changed to a page with a lot more script, interspersed with photos from the Archives, detailing Alexander Rutherford's biography.

"A back-click will take you back to the room you left to continue your tour, or you can always start at the beginning again, by clicking the little House in the top right of the screen. There are at least three Easter eggs, the term used for hidden information accessed by a click or a rollover, in each room. As well, if you roll over the stairs in the foyer, from top to bottom, you access the menu to all the paths." I ran the mouse downward, revealing the scripts tidily written on the riser of each step.

There had been some oohing and aahing, and now I received a small burst of applause. This was going far better than I had feared, and Marni was beaming at me from the other end of the dining room.

"I also have a section built in for your board to use for your own convenience." I clicked on the right newel post and a user ID box appeared. "Entering this restricted area, you can put up your mandate and vision documents, list your meetings, record and store your minutes, and set your upcoming agendas."

Mr. Karras looked very impressed with this section, as did the woman next to him taking minutes. I was thinking I had things pretty well in the bag when I saw Greta Larsen move her hand up. I nodded to her cautiously.

"And where is the information most people would be coming for? The times the House is open to the public, the address, the parking information? It seems to me with all the fancy elements you're playing with here, you've forgotten the essentials."

Mutely, in the face of her obvious antagonism, I moved my mouse to the doorway, where a smiling, costumed Roxanne stood by the guest book. I clicked on the sign next to the guest book, and the dates, times, and applicable fees appeared. I clicked the guest book itself, and an online feedback box, with two or three questions that would net interesting demographic statistics, was found. I back-clicked and hit the 100th Anniversary sign that was framed and sitting on the shelf behind the table. This opened up to a full history of the House, with a timeline running along the left side of the essay you could scroll through. Hyperlinks in this essay stood out in blue, linking back to places in the virtual tour, essays specific to each person important to the House, and in some cases, to outside sources. Not all of these were active, as the site was still housed in the intranet sandbox of the Black Widows. I didn't want to hover here overmuch, but felt it should be noted by those willing to vote with Greta Larsen that the ordinary aspects of a historic site website had not been ignored or overrun. Instead, we had incorporated them into a more dynamic design, which could add to the interest.

Greta Larsen looked nasty when thwarted. I had a feeling she wasn't done yet. That sense of animosity made me stumble a bit over my next words, but I covered it with a cough.

"So there you have the sneak preview into the centennial site. I hope it excites you as much as it does me, and that you will continue to support this project. I think this effort will put Rutherford House solidly into the top ten things to see when coming to Edmonton, making it an easy sell for travel agencies, Travel Alberta representatives, and self-researching tourists. And of course, for those closer to home, this site will also highlight the Arbour Restaurant and Tea Room." I clicked into the restaurant area, and then clicked on the menu in the server's hand. Up came a list of dishes and prices, along with the hours of the tea room and telephone number for reservations.

"If we want, online reservation booking can be connected right here."

Mr. Karras cleared his throat, which seemed to be his understated answer to using a gavel.

"Thank you, Randy, for a most informative tour of the site. I am very impressed with all the work you have done to date, as I am sure we all are. I also appreciate your putting this together ahead of time, to answer the questions of those of us who couldn't quite imagine the scope of where you were taking the project. We will be discussing this further as a board, and will be getting back to you very shortly with our decisions about the future of the project."

It was obvious that I was to be dismissed. Thankful that I hadn't bothered to set up the laptop I'd brought, I headed to the back of the room to pick up my coat and satchel. Marni saw me to the door.

"I will call you with a full report later. I could tell they were very impressed."

"But if Greta sways people to her side, I could be out of a job by the end of this meeting."

Marni looked pensive. "I will remind them of the kill fee on the project. They would have to pay you for everything you had already completed, plus 20%, and have nothing to show for it. I don't think most of them would like that, just to satisfy Greta. She still hasn't made a case for why she doesn't want Rutherford House to join the twenty-first century, either. Anyhow, don't fret."

Marni promised to call any time before midnight, and I left for the bus terminal at the other end of HUB Mall. I was going back to Steve's condo to await the results.

As I walked along the path outside the three-block-long covered mall and housing unit, I wondered what the heck I would do if the board decided to drop the project. When I had first come to this campus, I had been sure I was going to enter academe and come out the other side as part of the system, teaching undergraduates and writing thoughtful chapters about interesting research. It had looked like such a decent and satisfying world.

It still looked like that to me, though it was obviously not a world that wanted me as part of it. I had scrabbled to get sessional classes to teach, but the stress of never knowing how many courses you could count on, coupled with the lack of a pension or security, had worn me down. I had hoped that my last job would have been turned into a permanent position, but the Department of Ethnomusicology, which was housed across the quad I was passing, in the old Arts Building, had drawn in its horns and decided it couldn't afford a permanent web researcher.

This gig for Rutherford House was a temporary and finite one; I had known that going into it. However, I couldn't deny that I had been harbouring the sort of pipe dream that if it made a big enough splash, I could parlay that sort of success into a steady gig with either the university's public relations department or the provincial government's tourism section. Now, if that sour little bad fairy had her way, all my work to date, and all my chances of advancement, would be scuppered.

Once I made it to the bus line, I texted Steve, letting him know I was going to catch the bus to his place. He messaged back that he was en route, and why didn't I wait in front of St. Stephen's College where he would pick me up. I texted back my appreciation and headed around the corner to where he would be able to pull his car in and retrieve me.

Aside from Rutherford House, St. Stephen's was the only other designated historic site found right on campus, though I seemed to recall that Emily Murphy's house had a plaque on the outside and student housing on the inside. Between the two samples of nineteenth-century grandeur lay HUB, which embodied a late-twentieth-century idea of the future, the sort you see in Tom Baker-era *Doctor Who* shows. It was a wacky juxtaposition, but I sort of liked the jumble of buildings that comprised the U of A. I especially liked the dignity of St. Stephen's College. While no tours ever took place there, the chapel in which Mr. Maitland's funeral had been held was open to the public, and the two main floors of the building and the base-ment housed government offices.

The upper three floors were no longer accessible, I'd been told. Once upon a time they had been dormitory rooms for nurses and Methodist theologians, with a basketball court on the top floor, but apparently the government had determined it would be too costly to haul everyone out of the building to revamp all the floors, so instead the doors to the upper areas were locked and bolted.

I paced along in front of the green area, trying not to look like I was eager for a ride. Three taxis idled in line, and another car sat darkly at the end, likely a kindly mother waiting for a teen doing a night course. It would be nice if they would fix up the upper floors of St. Stephen's. That way, there might be light behind the lovely stained glass windows up at the top. I couldn't figure out for the life of me why the architect had decided that stained glass would augment a basketball court, but so be it. Maybe he had originally envisioned the chapel up there, and someone else determined it wouldn't do to make all the dons and profs climb five sets of stairs for morning prayers each day.

Steve pulled up and blinked his lights at me. With the talent of a long-time detective, he quizzed me about the board meet-ing, while deftly weaving between the waiting cabs, turning back out past the Timms Centre for the Arts, and out of the university area. Although his condo wasn't far in terms of crow flight, with one-way streets and such, it took some maneuvering to get us into his underground garage.

When we were finally upstairs and safely locked in, I could relax. I took the beer he handed me and walked out onto his balcony in my sock feet. For a late October night in Edmonton, it was still quite balmy. This was the sort of Hallowe'en season children in Alberta dream of, where they can wear shoes with their impressive costumes and venture all through the neighbourhood seeking anonymity, candy, and praise—instead of rushing and huddling in snowsuits in front of doors that slam shut as quickly as possible. I hoped the weather would last till the end of the week.

The thought reminded me to ask Steve about the Spooktacular at Fort Edmonton. It was one way to get Steve to take a look at the site of what Jasper Peacocke had called "the mess," the break-in at the first Rutherford House, without there being a hue and cry from his boss about sidelining investigations with my interferences. Besides, what could be more romantic on a date night than wandering around a historic park in the dark in costume?

Steve joined me on the balcony. "Twoonie for your thoughts?"

"Wow, inflation has hit Canada, eh?"

"Well, they've discontinued the penny."

I laughed. "I was just thinking of asking you to go on a date to the Hallowe'en Spooktacular down at Fort Edmonton."

"On purpose?"

"Does that mean you don't want to?"

Steve looked out over the dark river valley toward the iconic skyline of downtown across the river.

"Well, I don't know. I suppose it could be fun. I always thought it was more of a family thing."

"They promote it as a fun-for-all-ages event."

"That's code for 'no one will mind if your kid pitches a tantrum while you're there,'" Steve said drily. "Oh heck, why not? Are we going to dress up, too?"

"It could be fun, but I have to see what I still have that might work. I will let you know on that front after my stint at cleaning tomorrow."

We clinked beer bottles and, after finishing our drinks, headed back into the warmth of Steve's apartment, sanctuary from the chill of the night.

Marni had called around ten to let me know the board hadn't reached a decision yet, since Walter Karras had countered Greta Larsen's motion to have my whole project cancelled with a suggestion that each board member go home and play with the website available through the Widows' sandbox test site for a day or two. Then he would personally call them and determine their informed opinion.

"Now, this may mean that Greta spends the next two days pouring poison into the ear of everyone on the board, but it could also mean we have a chance. In the meanwhile, I have to get ready for Hallowe'en at the House. Are you in for that?"

I mentioned that we were doing the Spooktacular at the Fort the next evening, but could be available for her event. I was a little surprised at the planning, though.

"I thought the magic evening was supposed to be the only Hallowe'en activity at the House for the season?"

I could almost hear Marni shrugging over the line.

"It was going to be, but you wouldn't believe the number of people calling to see if there was going to be something happening, so we decided to put together a turn-of-the-century Hallowe'en, complete with carving turnips and other traditions brought over from Scotland."

We talked a few minutes longer while I doodled in my pink daily reminder book and then hung up. Steve had the electric fireplace going and had brought a pot of tea and two mugs to the low-slung table in the living room. I curled up on his couch, grateful for the sense of relaxation and safety he had conjured, and told him about the Rutherford House event.

"I don't blame her for cashing in on the interest, but it's ghoulish interest in the site of a murder, I'm betting, that has people calling and wanting to head over there at Hallowe'en. I doubt you're going to be luring the brain trust to the house that night."

I laughed. "No more than we will be consorting with tomorrow down at Fort Edmonton at the Hallowe'en Spooktacular," I said, allowing the last word to turn into several extra syllables of "oo."

"That is true, but there you have the added benefit of having gloriously anachronistic Klingons running a blind maze."

"Klingons? As in *Star Trek*?"

"Where else would you find Klingons? Faulkner?"

"Well, this should be even more interesting than I was anticipating. Any more ideas on dressing up for this event?"

"On the whole I think we should be comfortable. None of the buildings that will be open will be all that warm, and mostly we will be outside. There are wagon rides, I think, and a lot of wandering around in the dark streets, dodging the odd zombie and ghoul."

"You make it sound so appetizing."

"I know, right? I should really be writing for Travel Alberta instead of case reports."

Steve let me lean on his shoulder, and I stared at the fire licking the ersatz logs and coals while he leafed through a magazine. Fire mesmerized me, fake or real, controlled or wild. I hated to watch fire acts at the Street Performers' Festival and walked away immediately if someone lit a torch to juggle, twirl, or swallow. It was something too primal to play with, and I couldn't even imagine being entertained by the teasing of the flame. But otherwise, I'm hooked. I figured they only invented television for people who didn't have fireplaces in their homes.

Television had clued into that, too. There was a cable station that, instead of running Christmas programming in December, would devote hours to a film loop of a crackling wood fire, so that people like me could tune in and snuggle up to the hearth. Things like that made me happy to know I wasn't the only oddball out there.

I had probably nodded off and mini-jolted back awake a couple of times, because Steve suggested we head to bed. He followed me down the hall, turning off lights as we went. I was tired enough that a wooden bench in a railway station might have held some appeal, but as I sank into his high-thread-count sheets, part of me was resisting how easy it could be to just let Steve step in and save the day.

Tomorrow, while sorting out a warm costume to wear for our

sojourn in the Park, I would also consider what I was going to do about my apartment. Was I ever going to feel safe living there on my own again? Was it time to find a new place? Was it time to think about moving in with Steve on a permanent basis?

I looked around the sleek man-cave room he had created for himself, but my last waking thoughts were lost as sleep claimed me.

30

Steve had an early call, so I woke to an empty place once more. I showered and raided his kitchen for coffee and cereal. He had left me a note on the counter, saying he would call my cell later, but that he figured he would pick me up from my place on the way to the Park, since I'd told him the night before I'd be there, cleaning and putting together a costume.

I read the newspaper while eating breakfast, which didn't take too long. It was as if newspapers had just given up the fight against online news sources and were content with tying together an assortment of stories taken from the wire. Gone was the local breaking news, gone were the reviews by Edmontonians and enthusiastic coverage of local events. The surfeit of car ads was still around, though. Maybe that was how newspapers survived, one car ad at a time.

I slurped the last of my coffee, blessing Steve for spending that little extra for freshly roasted beans each week, and tidied up my presence in his world before heading out to walk back to my apartment.

The day was bright and crisp. All the leaves had turned orange and gold but not all of them had fallen yet, thanks to a remarkably calm autumn. Sometimes, the green would have barely faded when the winds arrived, and we would have bare, bony trees way too early for my liking. There were enough leaves on the ground to produce a satisfying crunch as I strode along, listing in my head any cleaning supplies I should stop to pick up on my way there. I'd used up pretty much all of the cream bleach and could stand another pair of rubber gloves, so I popped into Safeway. I also bought a loaf of sprouted-wheat bread, some sliced turkey, and some equally thinly-sliced Swiss cheese, figuring I would be hungry enough for two sandwiches after another morning of cleaning.

There were letters visible through the grille of my brass mailbox at the front of the apartment block waiting for me. I unlocked it, clutching my grocery bags in my other hand, and stuck the mail under my arm in order to relock the mailbox door and retrieve my keychain hanging from it.

After I let myself into my battered apartment, I set the mail down on the kitchen table and unpacked my groceries. Looking around, I took a deep breath and stalled. There was still so much work ahead of me, no matter which direction I looked, that I lost all energy, and almost collapsed into the nearest chair. This was not the sort of attitude for getting things done. I reached for the mail, anything to seem to be doing something. Besides junk mail, there was the new IKEA flier, which I set to one side, thinking I might need to make a trip out there for new, unbroken furniture. I had one letter from the university requesting a substantial gift to my alma mater, another from the kidney foundation, and a pamphlet from the Full Moon Folk Club listing their upcoming winter concerts. Under that was a thick, white envelope with my name and address printed with a strong black ink. The left corner had only an address, no name. I opened it with some curiosity. It was from my insurance company.

I had sent in my claim the morning after the burglary, on Steve's suggestion, and I guess having a police report to include did the trick, because in my hands were a very solicitous letter and an equally substantial cheque. While my premiums might spike as a result of this claim, I couldn't fault them on coming through for me. There was enough in the cheque to equip me with a new laptop, some functional furniture, completely new underwear, and CDs and DVDs to replace those scratched and broken. Or I could get really minimalist in my middle age and spend it all on Australian red licorice from the Bulk Barn.

The zeroes lined up on the cheque galvanized me, which probably says something really dreadful about my character. If I was going to get a new start, I might as well clean up the detritus of the old chapter. I spent the morning sorting through the apartment, cleaning and replacing books, teacups, canned goods, ornaments, and clothing that were intact, and bagging possessions that were irreparable for quick removal. By lunchtime, I had cleared away all evidence of the break-in from the main room. Of course, most living rooms are equipped with places to sit, and this was conspicuously absent in my room.

Still, the books were on clean shelves, the walls were washed, the blinds were straight and clean, the pictures were hanging back where they belonged, and there was even a pile of magazines stacked, doctor-office style, on my coffee table.

My kitchen was easier to deal with, and I had managed to clear away most of the broken glass the day before, so scrubbing the shelves and restocking them didn't take quite as long as I had feared.

While eating my sandwich, I jotted down a list of things I would need from the grocery store. It was strange to be writing down things like mustard and flour, but the people who had trashed the place had been thorough. I had to restock staples right from the beginning, like I had done when moving back to Edmonton for grad school.

After lunch, I tackled the bedroom. It was easier to move around without the bed in there, which I had dragged to the back alley and leaned against the rubbish-bin shed, but having no place to put the things I had folded and sorted made things a bit more complicated. I brought in one of the kitchen chairs so I wasn't constantly leaning over to pile things on the floor.

The underwear wasn't torn, but the sheer thought of marauders having touched it was enough for me to toss every single pair of panties into a green garbage bag. The same held true for the bras, though I popped the newer ones in a blue bag for the Goodwill. I took the opportunity to sort through my socks and tossed the mismatched pairs, the ones that had shrunk, and the blue knee socks that always scrunched their way under my arch in the time it took to walk to the bus stop. If I was going to have to shop for clothing, I might as well get some new socks while I was at it.

I had pulled the basket of odds and ends from the top shelf of my closet and was sorting through it when I remembered I had to think up a costume. I didn't want to be too standout noticeable, but of course, when it came to Hallowe'en, that might mean not wearing a costume at all. It would be chilly, wandering around Fort Edmonton at night, so I wanted my costume to be several layers' worth of warm.

I supposed I could layer on several sweaters and an overcoat and go as a homeless person, but that would be insensitive in the extreme. Not that I figured too many homeless people were going to be at the Spooktacular, objecting to my insensitivity. But some politically correct person would get in my face, I was certain. If everyone who got pompous over things said in jest actually did something tangible to make the world a better place, I wouldn't mind their wet-blanket comments so much. But it seemed to me they were just in it to make sure no one looked to be having fun. Not that I particularly wanted to dress as a homeless person, mind you. For one thing, where was I going to find a shopping cart and how would I get it down to Fort Edmonton? No, I didn't want to hurt anyone's feelings, and of course by that I meant homeless people, not bleeding hearts. Them I wouldn't mind twitting. How the heck did they know how homeless people saw themselves anyhow? For that matter, how did pirates feel on Hallowe'en?

This sort of thought, while mildly entertaining and certainly diverting, wasn't getting my apartment cleaned or my costume planned. I leaned against the bedroom wall and sank down to sit on the floor. From this vantage point I could still see some feathers from my gashed pillows under the dresser, but on the whole, the place was looking better. Not homey and cozy, but clean. It looked like an apartment one was leaving and cleaning in order to get back the damage deposit. With no upholstered furniture, everything I owned was either a table or a bookcase. I really did need to schedule a trip to IKEA, and soon.

I looked down to my right at the plastic under-the-bed box I hadn't yet opened. For some reason, the marauders hadn't bothered to ransack it. Perhaps they had determined, since it was made of clear plastic and clearly full of sweaters, it didn't contain whatever items of value they were searching for. Perhaps they had just pooped out by the time they got around to it. I reached over and clicked open the lid, releasing a scent of cedar from the little wooden chips I'd placed in the corners of the box. We didn't get a lot of moths, but I purely loved the smell of cedar.

It was about time to get these clothes back into circulation anyhow, as the nights closed in and the weather dipped. I reached for my green pullover from the Pitlochry woollen mills I'd visited just after high school with my parents on our massive trip to the United Kingdom, and held it to my face. Not overpoweringly cedar-smelling. Good. I didn't want to remind people of planked salmon wherever I went.

I set the sweaters out on to the floor mat and repacked the storage box with the tee-shirts and shorts I had folded and stacked. That done, I had room in two of the dresser drawers for my sweaters. Once this switch was made, the place looked cleaner, and I closed the closet door and moved back into the main room.

I was never going to think of a good Hallowe'en costume. My whole brain felt addled. Maybe it was the break-in, or the uncertainty of whether or not my project was going to continue, or Mr. Maitland's death, or Jossie's, but nothing in my world felt sorted.

Steve, as usual, had played his cards pretty close to his vest, so I wasn't sure how his investigation or the linked investigation was going, or even if they were actually linked. All I knew was that until some answers started floating to the surface, I was going to feel similarly to this sense of disconnectedness.

A lot of things would be better in my life if Greta Larsen hadn't showed up in it. She hated my project, she was there the night Jossie had died, she was known to Mr. Maitland, and I'd seen her one of the days I'd been to the Archives. For all I knew, she was the one who had trashed my apartment. On the other hand, Roxanne had never masked her dislike for me, either, and she had been right outside my back door the day my apartment was ransacked and she had been there the night Jossie had died, as well.

Mind you, there were other people who were connected with both Mr. Maitland and Rutherford House. Marni, for one. Mr. Karras, the board chair, even with all his charm and celebrity, might have had a reason to kill. For all I knew, the mysterious magician that no one seemed able to find had done them both in because they'd discovered the secrets to his disappearing budgie trick.

I tried to place each of my disparate suspects in all three situations, because no matter what Steve said about assumptions, I could not for the life of me believe that things weren't connected. I could picture Mr. Karras at the House and the Archives, but not at my apartment, though I suppose he could have just looked my address up in the phone directory. Marni, I could see everywhere, purposeful and deadly efficient. I could see her bending rules and morality to fight for the future of the House, I just couldn't figure out why she might want everyone dead and me robbed. Roxanne I could imagine doing nasty things, mostly because she was just so negative and sour about everything. But again, I couldn't sort out a motive for her. I could see Greta having the will to kill Mr. Maitland and Jossie, just because she exuded that sort of meanness, but as old as she was, she would have really had to surprise either of them, and I wasn't sure she could pull off a robbery.

I snorted, in spite of myself. Thinking of Greta Larsen, all done up downtown-style in black with a balaclava, made me laugh. In my mind, her cat-burglar suit emphasized her doughy spare tire, and her mean little eyes squinted through the woollen mask as she bent to tie up her sensible walking shoes. Okay, so I really couldn't picture her as being responsible for my apartment break-in. I honestly couldn't see one little old lady making that much mess in that short a time.

Thinking of Greta in black sparked the idea, and I wasn't sure why I hadn't come up with it before, surrounded as I was by the evidence of the break-in. I could dress as a cat burglar for Hallowe'en. It would be practical and warm and not terribly distasteful, and I could likely put it together from stuff I was planning to toss anyhow.

I texted Steve my idea, and he responded enthusiastically, determining that he could put together a convincing "cop" to my "robber," thereby making us one of those infuriatingly cute couples who match outfits.

The irony, of course, did not escape me, but wasn't that what Hallowe'en was for? To confront our fears and overcome them? Nothing like inhabiting the role of burglar to truly overcome its power to make me afraid. Thanking my internal Dr. Joyce Brothers, I went to work sorting out a costume. I busied myself by finding the darkest clothes I could find, laying out a pair of black jeans, socks, and runners, as well as a black turtleneck, hoodie, down vest, tuque, and gloves. I tucked a pair of clear plastic gloves I'd been using for cleaning into the vest pocket, along with a large suction cup hook taken from the side of the fridge, and a protractor, which I thought could pass as glass-cutting tools.

I retrieved a black knee sock and a dark pair of pantyhose from the half-full garbage bag in the bedroom, and cut off the legs of the hose for over-the-face masks. I used the scissors to hack two eye holes out of the knee-high and rummaged in a drawer for a large safety pin. If needed, that could work as a sort of lone ranger/cartoon robber mask.

I was set, and the beautiful part of it was that I wouldn't need to carry a purse. My keys and wallet could fit in the inner pocket of my vest.

Now that my costume was finalized, I could hardly wait to get changed and ready for the night ahead. I glanced at my watch, only to realize it was still only three o'clock. Steve wasn't coming to get me till six-thirty. I looked down at the costume, laid out as if the robber inside had somehow dematerialized, leaving only her outer layers. It was going to be great.

I busied myself for the rest of the afternoon by dragging out more garbage bags and setting the recycling near the door. Once my books were back on their shelves, I made a pot of tea and pored over the IKEA catalogue for half an hour, dog-earing pages that held possibilities.

I was pretty sure I was going to opt for the daybed with the drawers under it instead of a regular bed, which might leave me more room to move around most days and yet able to pull out to a full-sized bed on nights when Steve stayed over.

A loveseat, rather than a full chesterfield, would be a better fit for my living room, too. I had been bequeathed the behemoth that had previously dwarfed my apartment, and while it had been a nice place to curl up, it was sort of exciting to think of moving into a new look.

With new furniture, perhaps the little apartment would feel larger and different enough that I wouldn't have to move away to feel safe again. I had called the landlord, who had promised to have two new locks installed this week, along with bars on the back window.

It wasn't that I didn't love Steve. I just didn't think I was ready to commit to sharing space wholeheartedly yet. If ever. I knew of two or three people who were in long-term relationships, one set even married twenty-some years, who maintained two households. I was pretty sure that was one of the secrets to their happiness.

I would have to think about whether or not I did want to stay in my apartment, though. My default position was lethargy, when it came to moving. I wanted to be certain I was comfortable enough in my space to live there with ease. As soon as the locks were installed, and I had a bed bought, I would move back to see how I felt. I re-examined the furniture I had bookmarked.

It wouldn't hurt to get the items I was thinking of, as they were sensible bits of furniture that could move with me, should I decide this place held too many bad vibes.

Baby steps.

I cleaned my teacup and took my costume bits into the bathroom to change. By the time Steve showed up, looking like a motorcycle cop from some movie with Sidney Poitier, I was ready.

He had on his brown leather jacket, aviator sunglasses—which would be useless to him within five minutes as the sun was setting sooner each night here along latitude fifty-three—a tan shirt, and darker brown trousers with a stripe down the side. His old handcuffs were jangling on his left hip, and his leather holster was snapped shut over what he demonstrated was his camera.

"I figured there would be some pretty cool costumes down there."

He had done well. If you didn't know him and what his day job really was, you'd just think it was a really good costume. There was nothing overt stating "Edmonton City Police." In turn, he admired my burglar outfit, including the glass-cutting tools.

"I had halfway considered a stick-up note, but decided I was going for more of a second-story look," I said and Steve nodded.

"Yes, it reads. Who knows, maybe later in the evening, I could put you in handcuffs for greater verisimilitude." He leered a bit and I swatted him.

"And this would be at the Fort or home in your apartment, Officer?"

"Wherever you might consider resisting arrest, I would say."

"Where did you get those, anyhow? Don't you mostly just use twist-ties these days?"

"They're not twist-ties, they are highly effective plastic restraints and way lighter to lug around, let me tell you. These babies are what I was issued in '87, when I first joined the force."

"Well, I hope you still have the key for those."

"I have never taken it off my ring." He pulled out his keys to prove it. There on the ring, amid his car keys and condo keys, I could see a tiny, shiny silver key. It's so funny what people keep close to them as talismans.

"You know, this is going to be fun, I think."

"You bet it is. A Hallowe'en in Edmonton without snow. What more could you want?"

31

The folks who had organized the Spooktacular had out-done themselves. There was signage at the train station entryway that laid out the map of events for the evening. "Fun without fear" was the name of the game in the hangar for parents with small children. Their Spooktacular would be indoors, warm, and well-lit, and would consist of candy-toss games, a maze made out of hay bales, storytelling, face-painting for those who hadn't already come dooded up, and a craft area.

Further along, on 1905 Street, was the middling spooky area, for those of fainter heart. A fortune teller was set up in the fire station, and she must have been good because there was quite a lineup. Bobbing for apples was happening on the main floor of the Masonic Hall, and tours and tales were happening in Firkin House and Rutherford House.

The interpreters who during the day despaired of people coming in to hear about the "Firkin ghost," a completely spurious story, were vamping it up this evening, boasting theirs was the only truly haunted building in the Park and that we should all come and feel the vibrations of the dead. While I had no illusions that ghosts were floating among us, it was silly fun to go through the house, which was decorated with jack-o'-lanterns that grinned at us from every conceivable landing and mantle.

Rutherford House was another thing altogether. I looked for Jasper and his mother, but perhaps she had decided he was too young for the festivities. More than likely, Jasper was too logical to play such inane make-believe. Interpreting history was one thing, but scampering about in the dark looking for walking spirits would seem farcical to a boy of Jasper's intellect.

I made a special point to show Steve the upstairs rooms of Rutherford House, in particular the maid's room, which had been burglarized recently. There were ropes across all the doorways this evening, which was just as well, because the crowds coming through, while not rowdy or obnoxious, were high-spirited and more intent on their own fun than the preservation of artifacts. It was hard in the evening light to even see where the new baseboard had been repainted, and he shrugged as he turned to me. It was hard to show any sort of connection between some vandalism here and a murder at the brick house.

We had some apple cider and pumpkin muffins at the Henderson Farm House at the end of 1905 Street, then strolled to 1885 Street, which was guarded at our end by a pair of burly gentlemen dressed as a Viking and a Jack Skellington.

"Beyond here is Horror Hollow, and you enter at your own risk," intoned the Viking. "No children under the age of sixteen may come through here, unless they are accompanied by their insane, unfeeling parents."

I laughed.

"Good work," Steve commented. "What do you do if younger kids try to sneak in?"

Jack Skellington checked around to make sure no one else was within earshot.

"We eat them," he grinned.

Knowing we weren't going to get a straight answer from these two, who were having too much fun, we held hands and walked through between them. At first, there didn't seem to be much difference between the two streets, although 1885 had no street lights, a fact which played with the perspective of the length of the street. Not all the buildings were open, but I could hear screams from the Jasper House Hotel (the one Jasper Peacocke had so adamantly explained he was not named for) and could see a line forming to get into the haunted house tour. This had been reviewed on the radio as rivalling Madame Tussaud's for startling and scary. I wasn't sure those attributes were actually attractions, but Steve was excited to find out, so we compromised by agreeing to look at the rest of the street before entering the hotel.

Dodging a zombie bride who appeared from behind McDonald House with blood and gore congealing on her lacy gown, we headed for Lauder's Bakery, which during the summer sold cookies, cinnamon buns, and bread. It was the best place to be if you loved the smell of sugar and yeast.

Tonight, it was a different sort of thing on the menu. The

Cannibal Café was serving a stew, and in the dim anteroom we snaked through to get to the eventual display, we could see a pile of body parts flung into a heap, supposedly waiting to be added to the stew. I recognized one of the mannequins in the pile from the store across the lane and presumed some of the others came from the costume-making department, a full-time, ongoing production house in the Fort.

I just about hit the ceiling when one of the body parts moved and reached out to us, moaning. It was a young woman, her eyes made up to emphasize their sockets. Steve reacted by taking a picture. I guess when your profession is to deal with real horror, you don't get quite so jittery and squeamish by the make-believe.

A head in the display case opened its eyes and winked at us when we were finally in the bakery proper. After encountering the moving body pile, I wasn't quite so edgy, so I just winked back. The stew, being stirred by a slender girl in ghoulish makeup and a hair net, was not getting any takers after we'd seen the set-up of human components, but the staff must have been heating something like beef stew nearby because the dry-ice-clouded cauldron smelled appetizing in a terrible, awful way.

The zombie bride was drifting back in the other direction, and we wandered up and down the street, taking in the costumes of our fellow visitors and those of the crew working the Spooktacular. I figured most of them would be interpreters and volunteers who had grown close during the summer months the way summer camp staffs tended to. This event which was taking place a couple of months into the school year would be a welcome reunion for most of them.

Volunteer families, like Jasper and his mom, might be involved as well. I could imagine that many of the children who had grown up volunteering at the Park would end up applying to work here during the summertime. Although it was relatively out of the way, transit-speaking, it seemed as if it would be a great place to work when going through school.

The haunted hotel wasn't as terrifying as Steve might have hoped, but that was just fine by me. Things jumped out, and people loomed but didn't touch, which seemed to be the unspoken rule of scaring. Various dioramas of tortured people were set up in the rooms of the hotel, and then a trip down to the basement, where the mad scientist's lab was set up, capped things off. Trying to get down the stairs in the gloom of the emergency light was probably the scariest bit for me.

Once we were back out on the street, there was only one more thing to experience: the Fort of Fear. The concept seemed to be that as one moved further and further back in time, things got progressively more frightening.

Tonight, the Fort had been overtaken by zombies, which was sort of the same concept a television horror show took a few years back — just one of the many films that had been shot in the Park, which offered such a nice setting, complete with accurate old-time housing and a lovely lack of power poles and anachronistic elements in the distance. As long as the cameraman didn't aim across the river at the million-dollar houses perched on the river valley, you could approximate almost any era.

I wasn't sure I wanted to be accosted by zombies in a confined area like the Fort. I didn't much care for the bride on 1885

Street, and she had been rather innocuous in her creepy way. Steve, however, loved zombies, so we held hands and headed through the pitch dark of what was normally the Fort garden and Indian camp, toward the entrance to the Fort.

The gates were shut, and we had to climb through the trading door cut into the larger wagon door. Torches were flickering in the quadrangle ahead, and I moved a bit more quickly toward them because according to my limited knowledge of their lore, fire was not the zombies' friend.

A guide met us at the corner and explained the rules of the game. Zombies had infiltrated the Fort, and we were attempting to round them up and contain them, as our ammunition was very low and we didn't want loud noises to bring more out of the forest beyond.

I could have done without him intoning "forest beyond." Steve grinned.

We were supposed to wander about the Fort, much as if we were touring it on an ordinary summer day, except that it would be dimly lit, and lumbering gory creatures would possibly jump out at us. If they did, we were to turn toward the quad immediately and let the zombie chase us to the holding pen. Every time we managed to corral a zombie, we would be given a sticker.

I almost bumped my head trying to get away from one in the lower floor of Rowand House, the chief factor's impressive house with windows whose glass panes had been brought upriver from the east, suspended in molasses barrels. That was a fact most western Canadian kids knew by heart, even if they'd never tasted molasses.

Steve and I each got a sticker for the first zombie, but only he got one for the one that chased us from the icehouse, around the side of the bachelors' quarters, because the two of them moved so fast I was left in the dust. I looked inside the long building that had housed the unmarried fur traders and ran into two girls who were nervously giggling and screamed when they saw me, even though I had no blood on me.

Steve came back, preening with his two stickers, and we set off for the carpenter's house and the archway through to where the York boats had been built. Two zombies shambled into sight, and we waved at them as if we were manic matadors and then turned and ran, luring them toward the centre of the quad. We each got two stickers and were told that was enough to trade for hot chocolate at the trading window by the entrance to the Fort.

I had a hunch they had to get us out and disperse their zombies before the next batch of visitors made it as far as the Fort of Fear, but that was fine with me. While the actuality of the zombies and haunted houses and ghouls was not totally terrifying, the concept worked on you incrementally, and it was getting to me to be out in the middle of the dark in the middle of a historic park where there was poor cellphone reception and no escape from the chill in the air and one's own imagination.

Steve, ever sensitive to a situation, suggested we head for home. Since the train wasn't operating, we hitched a ride with a wagon driver, who dropped us off by Egge's Barn at the far end of 1885 Street, close to Jack Skellington and the Viking. From there we decided to walk back, and with every step we took, things got lighter and sillier and a whole lot easier to take.

I wondered what it was about our desire to scare ourselves that impels us toward spook shows and amusement park rides and extreme adventure holidays. Here I was, having been a near witness to a murder and had my house broken into and possessions stolen, who in my relatively short lifetime had been shot at, stalked, pushed down a set of stairs, locked in the dark and left for dead, paying to be titillated and terrorized. How crazy was that? Who actively sought out that sort of sensation? Not me. And yet, here I was, dressed all in black, walking with my police pursuer down a gravel road on a chilly fall evening, feeling pretty good about life.

"That hot chocolate could have gone further," said Steve, reaching into his pocket for his keyfob, as we approached his car. "Want to grab a bite?"

"Where? I am not walking into the Diner dressed like this."

Steve laughed.

"Well, I am betting Earls would welcome costumes, this time of year."

I shrugged. He was probably right. Earls, especially the one on campus, positioned itself as the party place, but I had a feeling it was a way more happening place back in the day when the Oilers were a winning team. They had gone through several manifestations since the chain had morphed from the old Fullers Restaurants I had known and loved in my youth, sporting huge parrot statues for a time, to the chalkboard-and-chrome minimalism of the present.

What the heck. Earls it was.

The woman seating us complimented our costumes and led us to a table by the window across from the Timms Centre. This was just as well—it meant I would be far likelier to order dessert than if we'd been at the other window, facing the diabetes research building. While Steve scoured the menu, I looked around at the crowd. He had been right, there were several other people in some form of costume or other, either on their way to or from a Hallowe'en party. I spotted a penguin, a gypsy, and the twins from the Tintin books at one table, and another couple dressed as Sonny and Cher down the aisle from us. The folks who weren't in costume seemed a bit nonplussed by our fervour for the season, but it felt pretty good to be on the side of the joiners this time. I adjusted my tuque and ordered mushroom soup and a brownie sundae.

Steve must have worked up an appetite rounding up all his zombies, because he ordered a steak, baked potato with all the trimmings, and a brownie sundae of his own.

Our food came quickly and the service was pleasant, which seemed to be the underlying secret of Earls' success. After we had chewed over the various elements of the evening, our conversation wound itself back to the break-in at my apartment and the situation at Rutherford House.

I told Steve about the need to work the following evening at the House.

"That's bound to be unnerving, isn't it?"

"How do you mean?"

"Well, how many times have you worked an evening event since the girl got murdered in the guest bath?"

"You had to put it that way, did you?" My laugh sounded tinny even to me. "I was there last night for the board meeting."

"But that wasn't a working event. I really wonder at the wisdom of running this thing on Hallowe'en."

"I think it has something to do with Marni's worries that the board is going to shut down the special events end of things. She wants the events to show a profit and demonstrate an interest in the House, so that the place can be seen as self-sustaining, meaning the tea house and special events could keep the day-to-day expenses humming along without a big outlay from the province. The less investment required from outside, the more autonomous the House can be."

"What do they want autonomy for? Doesn't being a historic site come with some provisos? Like not being able to upgrade the wiring and all that?"

"Oh, it's more complicated than that. Your building can require upkeep that is vital, like a new furnace or weeping tiles or something like that, but grant monies would be targeted to specific items like newel posts or stained glass. If you can demonstrate that the public sees you as an important site, through turnstile counts and money spent, then you have a bit more say in how money is spent and what you do."

"So Marni wants that sort of autonomy and the board doesn't?"

"No, of course the board wants that sort of success, too. They are just divided on how to achieve it, and what it would look like once achieved. I think there are people on the board who resent people walking around the House, causing wear and tear on the floorboards. They would like to see the place turned into a shrine only very few can visit. Then there are others who just don't think Marni can pull it off, so they gainsay everything she attempts. There are a few who are solidly on her side—the chair, for instance—so it's not a complete battle all the time."

"And she wants another event so soon after the disastrous one why?"

"You know, aside from one brutal murder and the disappearance of the magician, that was a pretty good event. Oh god, what am I even saying?"

Steve chuckled while cutting off a piece of steak.

"Yeah, the old 'aside-from' conundrum. Funny how that sneaks up on you."

"Well, if that is the last event ever set in Rutherford House, Marni might as well pack things in now. She has to do something to erase that from people's minds as their memory of Rutherford House."

Steve shrugged. "So what's up with this event?"

"All I know is that it's a Hallowe'en party of some sort, set in period. Marni wants me there as moral support and probably because she needs the extra pair of hands. I will get minimum wage plus food, which is all to the good, since I still have no idea whether or not the board is going to allow my contract to continue. I knew I should have negotiated a stronger kill fee."

"Kill fee? Not exactly the sort of thing you want to be saying to a cop."

"It's a freelance term meaning the money owed you if the publisher decides not to go with the piece they've commissioned. You need to get compensated in some way for the work you put into the project, so your contract has a set kill fee, or amount they will pay you if they decide to terminate the contract."

"Kill, terminate, contract. This just gets better and better."

I laughed. "You're just teasing. I know you've heard me use these terms before."

"Maybe," Steve allowed, "but not while you're dressed like a jewel thief."

I had eased into the evening so well that I had half-forgotten my costume. Now that I had my tuque, gloves, and mask off, it seemed more counter-culture than criminous. Steve spent enough time around me in uniform that his costume had just blended into the norm. However, to people seeing us from a distance, we were the perfect Hallowe'ening couple on the town. Thinking about it made me feel good, the way I had felt earlier in the year, when Steve had taken me out for a romantic dinner on Valentine's Day and we were surrounded by other dining couples. I had felt as if I'd hit my mark, and was feeling the same way tonight. We were doing the right thing at the right time, being on the inside of the situation rather than on the outside looking in.

Lots of people would probably roll their eyes at my bizarre yearnings to be normal, status quo apple pie, but when you don't fit tidily into societal boxes most of the time, discovering yourself fitting the bill can provide a tiny thrill.

Steve was demolishing his dinner while I indulged in my meditation on self-awareness, then signalled for the bill as I pinched up crumbs from the table and dropped them in my empty bowl. Something winked off in the distance, distracting me from what Steve was saying. I peered closer to the window, to avoid the mirror-glare from the lights inside. What had I seen?

Steve cleared his throat in the time-honoured signal of "pay attention to me, you moron" and repeated himself.

"So, you ready to go?"

We had parked in the lane in front of St. Stephen's College, where Steve had picked me up, and in the dark, the college loomed high and forbidding.

I stared up at the stained-glass windows, wondering yet again why someone would put such glory in a basketball court. To the left, down one level, a light came on in one of the windows on the fourth floor—one of the sealed-off areas.

By this time, Steve was at the car, holding the passenger door open. Silently, I pointed to the light in the window, but down low, close to my body, just in case someone was watching us from a darkened window up there. Steve, bless his heart, looked where I was pointing instead of spending useless moments ask-ing me what the heck I was doing.

His eyebrows shot up, and he closed the passenger door.

"There shouldn't be anyone up there at any time," I whis-pered, "and that just doesn't look like a safety light to me."

"Me either," Steve agreed. "Thing is, there is not a lot we can do other than phone it in."

"Is Iain on duty tonight?"

"You think he'd like to be called out to investigate a potential break and enter? We'll be lucky to net a peace officer."

"Really? In a provincial historic site, on campus, just weeks after the death of two people involved in history and archives? I think it might be a bit more of a priority."

"It's just about time for the bar patrols on Whyte and Jasper Avenues to begin. Sending a car out to check on what might possibly be a workman's light left on or a safety light is not going to be a priority in anyone's mind."

"What about us?"

"What do you mean 'us,' Kimo Sabe? I am off-duty and you are, if you recall, a civilian. A civilian dressed as a cat burglar. Try to imagine the headlines if a patrol car *did* manage to arrive to check out the light."

"Okay, so what do we do?"

Steve shrugged. "I guess we could inspect the perimeter and check for any break-in that we could then report."

"That sounds good. Let's go." I made to stride off toward the front doors, but Steve caught my arm.

"Not in the light. Come this way." We turned away from

where the car was parked and headed south down the street the way we'd come. When we got to the lane that led to the parking lot between St. Stephen's and the Education Building beyond, we ducked into the shrubbery and hostas next to the building. There was a door halfway visible at the basement level, and Steve clambered down five stairs to try it out. It was locked, and the windows beside it looked sturdy and painted shut. We sidled on around the back of the building.

Here, too, the windows we could reach were closed tight, in the way of modern buildings. The college had been retrofitted, but surely in that way not for the better. Windows that could open were something I craved in a building. I was pretty sure they hadn't retrofitted corresponding air conditioning into St. Steve's when they sealed out all the air.

Whatever the case, no one had gained entry through a window.

Steve was checking the annex, hanging back a bit from the wall jutting out so as not to obliterate any footprints there might be. There were no doors to check, so we walked a bit further out.

It made me nervous not to be hugging the building, as this way we were more obvious to passersby and could be reported as suspicious ourselves. Mind you, we could claim plausible deniability if we weren't creeping along, too, so it was a classic six of one, half a dozen of the other toss-up.

Steve stopped still as we got to the corner of the T-shaped annex that jutted out the back of the college. I butted into him slightly and he held his hand up to keep me from saying anything. He pointed ahead of us.

The fire escape ladder had been pulled to the ground. Someone was in St. Stephen's College. Someone who had no business being there.

33

I looked at Steve and could see him mulling over all the argu-
ments he had made against calling in the mysterious light.
We had found evidence of a possible breaking and entering or,
on the other hand, an instance of negligence by custodial staff,
or even a malfunctioning element of an elderly building. The
fire escape could have slipped down on its own.

And I could be Laura Secord. As far as I was concerned, there
was nothing about this situation that could be explained away.
Someone had broken into St. Stephen's College. Worked up as I
was against people breaking into places, I didn't even weigh the
odds or take time to consider the fact that I don't like ladders all
that much.

I put my hand on a rung above my head and began to climb.

I heard Steve mumbling something into his cellphone below
me, and he hissed at me to wait a second. I quietly clambered up
another three rungs so he couldn't pull me down from my perch.
Maybe we could write it off as youthful Hallowe'en hijinks if we

were discovered. I just hoped I'd put on enough moisturizer this morning to pass for youthful in the dark.

I felt the ladder shudder and realized that Steve had begun to climb as well. I started up again.

"So help me, Randy, this is not going to end well," I heard him whisper. There was nothing I could say in reply, and the whole situation was too scary to do anything but concentrate on the metal rungs under my gloves, flaking paint and rust into my nostrils.

So I stayed silent and I climbed. The ladder went on through a hole in the fire escape balcony at the third floor. I stepped off it gingerly, testing the metal of the flooring. It seemed sturdy, and I could see an open window, two over from the ladder. This was where the entry had been made. I waited for Steve to reach me, which didn't take long. I pointed to the window and he nodded. Somehow, we had moved to hand gestures for communication without consultation. I held up my hand to stop him, pulled my phone out of my pocket, and turned it to silent. He nodded again and smiled grimly. He pointed to himself and then me, and I agreed to that order of entry. Taking a deep breath, Steve moved toward the window. He stood beside it, and then peered in before climbing over the sill.

I followed suit. We stood in darkness, with some ambient light flowing in behind us from our access point and some further ahead coming from the transom window above the door. We were in a very small room, one of the abandoned dormitory rooms, from what I could figure. There was an alcove that must have been the closet, and some pretty beaten-up linoleum on the floor. The door was halfway open and possibly jammed on the bubbled-up flooring.

Steve pointed at the doorway and then at himself. I nodded again. This "Me, Tarzan" concept was a little dated, but on the whole, I was not averse to letting him go first into the fray. The whole exploring of unwarranted lights in St. Stephen's College was seeming less and less like an idea I should have pursued. Still, Steve had called it in, so presumably we would soon be joined by some sort of patrol team. We just had to keep our cool and not get shot or put a foot through a rotten floor joist in the meantime.

Steve poked his head out into the hall, listening for a noise that would tell us which direction to turn once we left the relative sanctuary of our entry room. He waved behind his back and then moved through the doorway.

Okay, so was that a wave of "stay where you are"? Or one that indicated "come on and follow, things are fine"? Words, not actions, were my business. This was why my major had been English, not semaphore. I shrugged, because action seemed called for, and followed Steve. On the whole, I would feel safer with Steve in the middle of a firestorm than on my own in the dark in a creaky old building. So, truth be known, it wasn't an act of bravery on my part.

We crept down the hallway to the right, heading south. Since the only light we had was coming through the transom windows from the rooms at the front of the building, facing the street and its lights, we stuck to the darker side of the hall, using the light to guide us. Steve stopped as we neared the staircase, which must have been situated in one of the towers. The fire door had been wedged open with a block of wood.

Our target was either above us or below us. Of course, he or she could be right behind us, having tricked us into thinking he or she had left the floor. I thought a minute and then pointed down. Steve cocked an eyebrow at me. I nodded, more vigorously. He smiled and nodded. Down we would go.

It made sense to head downward, to the only floors where human activity took place. For one thing, anything a thief wanted would be down there, rather than up here in the deserted floors. There was nothing left here; even the toilets had been removed from the lavatories.

For another thing, we had not heard a single footstep overhead, which indicated to me that the person we were after was below us. I was just hoping our own footsteps hadn't sounded like the baby elephant dance above the bad guy's head.

Any minute now, with luck, we would be hearing the front door open and Steve's back-up would be entering to check things over.

Any minute now.

Steve had mimed the need to walk at the edges of the staircase, to minimize creaking. I followed him around the newel post and pointed back toward the darkness that denoted the second floor. The fire door here was likewise blocked open. I wondered if spare pieces of wood had been lying around on the unfinished floors, somewhere Steve and I hadn't spotted them in the dark, or whether the burglar had brought his own shims, knowing they'd be needed. If so, did that mean that he or she had been in St. Stephen's College before, during the day? I made a mental note to tell Steve when I wouldn't have to play charades to do so.

By this time Steve was already through the door and into the hall. I could see a bit better on this level as the fire-exit sign above our heads produced some light, and there was a spill of light from a meeting room down the hall that was equipped with glassed-in half-walls. We went forward carefully, again trying not to announce our arrival with too many creaks and rustlings. Surely, the person we were seeking was on this floor, or else why had the door been shimmed open?

A car radio blared outdoors and a motor was gunned. It startled me, but also calmed me down a bit, making me realize we weren't that far from the ordinary world. If we could hear that sort of noise from a demonstrative jerk outside on the road, then we'd be likely to hear something inside the building, too. We just hadn't yet.

Steve had been trying the doorknobs of each door we passed, and none of them had yielded. We were pretty much all the way down at the north end of the hall, and from what I could tell we were alone on the floor.

An office at the end was also glassed in, possibly the bursar's office in the college's past. I wondered if whoever had that place now appreciated doing his or her work in a goldfish bowl. I supposed a door that closed was better than working in a cubicle.

A shadow moved on the back wall of the glassed-in office. It was momentary and when I blinked it stopped, so I wasn't positive I'd actually seen anything. I touched Steve's arm and pointed. His face was too much in shadow for me to read his expression, but I could sense its questioning look. If I had seen something move in there, then we had already been spotted. Otherwise, why the stillness now? And if I hadn't, then trying to get into that office would likely create enough noise that our presence would be telegraphed to the other intruder in no time flat.

Steve backed up, motioning for me to retreat alongside.

We made our way cautiously back to the stairwell and crept down another level, to the main floor of the Heritage department. Steve pressed down quietly on the door bar, which proved to be unlocked. So, really there was no indicator to let us know whether our intruder was still up on the second floor or here with us on main. We moved to the rotunda, which had some street light spilling through the windows by the doorways and red security lights high in the corners. I wondered if our movement had been monitored somewhere, and whether security forces had been mustered as a result.

Somehow, I thought not. The fire escape, oiled and silent, and the door shims placed where they were needed made me think that this entry had been pretty well planned in advance. We had just stumbled upon it by chance, seeing a light in a window where it shouldn't have been. I figured the red lights were likely just for fire emergencies, and moved a bit closer to Steve.

Although I had heard the street noises before, Steve was far more attuned to what he was listening for. He moved to the front doors and opened them for two uniformed policemen.

Behind them, in a nicely tailored suit, was Steve's partner, Iain McCorquodale.

Iain looked us over from head to foot and smiled broadly. We were never going to live this one down. Steve shrugged and grinned back. He moved into a huddle with the officers and briefed them on what we had discovered.

"The entry was on the third floor, rear, and we think we may have seen movement in a closed office on the second floor, but the door was secured and we backed off. We haven't yet searched this floor."

"We have a car at the rear of the building, so if anyone has made a break for the fire escape, we'll have them. Let's see whether we can flush out any quail," Iain said. "Any idea who or what they're looking for?"

"No." I shook my head. "But with all the incidents around historic sites, to see a break-in here seemed a bit too weirdly coincidental."

"Right. Well, even if it's a squatter, we have to deal with that. This old place could go up in smoke with the wrong usage." Iain deployed the two uniformed policemen to search the main floor and then meet him on the second floor. He must have radioed the security people to overwrite the alarms, because we walked up the north staircase, where a sign warned us the doors were alarmed— an anthropomorphic choice of words that normally amused me.

I pointed the way to the office where I had been sure I had seen movement. The door was still closed, so Iain, using his master key, opened it carefully. He had his Taser holster open as he moved into the room, reached the desk lamp, and flicked it on. He looked around and then beckoned us in.

"What do you see? Can you say anything is missing?"

We joined him in the middle of the office. It would be impossible to tell whether someone had ransacked the place or not because of all the paper piled everywhere. There were at least seven piles of file folders stacked on the desk, two more on each of the four filing cabinets along the wall, and three boxes stuffed with rolled-up maps and posters beside the desk. A visitor's chair had a stack of books on it. Two filing drawers were open. One desk drawer was slightly open as well.

I stepped back and almost knocked over another pile of books behind me.

"You'd have to get in touch with the person whose office this is to tell you that."

Steve laughed. "How can anyone get anything done in this sort of disorganization?"

"Well, not to defend a packrat, but there may well be some sort of organizing principle here that we just can't see."

"Really," said Iain. I was betting this sort of mess made Iain's skin crawl. I had once seen the glove compartment of his car, and it was indexed.

"Well, it's possible that whoever works here does know where everything is."

"Okay, I'll grant you that. But you looking around, do you think your intruder was in here?"

Maybe I'd watched too many Hammer horror films in my lifetime, but I wasn't positive I hadn't seen a shadow move when

I was in the hallway. If I was correct, then the source of the shadow had to have been standing right by the open file drawer. Steve agreed with my estimate and Iain wrote something in his notebook, saying he would make sure they contacted the owner of this office to come in and inventory things from that area specifically.

All three of us left the office. Iain's cellphone vibrated and he answered. He listened for a minute and then swore.

"The officers found a window in the basement that had been forced open. It must have coincided with us turning off the security, which the perpetrator may have been counting on, or it could have just been a nice little gift. Whatever the case, you were on the money and there was a break-in. I'll call in a forensic team and secure the place now. You can give your statements tomorrow if you like. I assume"—he smiled, looking at me—"that your prints are on file?"

"Yes," I grimaced. "Staff Sergeant Keller insisted the last time."

Iain and Steve laughed at my discomfort.

"Well, some government wonk is going to thank you tomorrow for being so observant tonight." Steve patted me on the shoulder and then squeezed me to him. "Cheer up, Randy. Keller already has your picture on the boards for both murder investigations. This is just going to be gravy."

They weren't making me feel any better. Their boss looked daggers at me any time I got mixed up in an investigation. A look from Keller was deterrent enough for me. They should just put threatening pictures of him up all over the subways and bad areas of town, a surefire way to keep crime down.

Steve and I left by the front doors this time and headed for his car.

Once inside the car, I pulled off my tuque and scratched the top of my head. We were not that far ahead in any way. I was still camping at Steve's place. We had added a wrinkle to the puzzle rather than solving either crime currently clouding my world. And on top of everything, my job was still on the line, with no word from Marni.

Steve was pulling into the underground parking of his building when I realized that Marni might have called me while we were cat-burgling. I reached into my long trouser pocket, where I'd slid my phone, keys, and debit card. I pressed the button on my phone to light up the face of it, and noticed a couple of text messages. The first one was from Marni and said cryptically, "Call me in the morning." That could mean anything. Worrying about that all night wasn't going to make for an easy sleep.

The next text message was even more unsettling. It came from an unlisted number and was a combination of photo and text, which would incur me an extra charge. I was curious, though; I rarely got anonymous spam on my phone, since very few people had my number and I never gave it out to businesses. I clicked it open. The picture showed Steve and me in the hallway of St. Stephen's College. He was looking to the right and had his hand out, pointing toward the stairway door. I, on the other hand, seemed to be looking straight into the camera, like the proverbial deer in the headlights.

The light was low and the image was dim. The text was crystal clear, though. It said, "Keep out of my way."

34

Steve sent the photo immediately to Iain's cellphone, along with a terse explanation, and to the forensic team at the station. We were told to bring my phone in so they could try to trace the sender, though they were holding out only faint hope. Burner, or disposable phones, something I had only ever heard about on *The Wire*, were becoming more and more popular with both travellers and criminals right across North America.

We drove to the station, dropped off my phone, and then went back to Steve's. I was too wound up to crawl into bed right away, and felt grimy besides. I opted for a shower while Steve made us hot chocolate. By the time I got out of the bathroom, skin scrubbed and pores wide open, wrapped in his green terry robe and a towel turban, the chocolate was steaming out of oversized pottery mugs at his kitchen counter bar. Steve decided my idea was a good one, so while he was off having his shower and I was waiting for the cocoa to cool a bit, I pulled his grocery list pad and pencil over to see if I could make sense of any of the recent events.

The stand-out thing to me was that if everything was tied together and connected, then whoever was responsible for Jossie's and Mr. Maitland's deaths and for breaking into St. Stephen's College had to be one and the same. But it was more than that. Whoever had been in St. Stephen's tonight knew exactly who I was. In the dark. In disguise. And to top it all off, they had my cellphone number.

I could count on one hand the number of people who had my number. Steve had it. Marni had it, because she was a texting fiend, but I had specifically asked her to list only my landline on the employee contact list. Denise had it. My folks had it written down somewhere for emergencies, but had never used it. Hell, I hardly used it. Steve had insisted I get a cellphone, and I had to admit it came in handy from time to time. I felt more secure with a means of communication always available, the way Albertans feel more secure driving throughout the year with a blanket and candles and a shovel in the trunks of their cars. To me, it was a just-in-case device. Most calls I made were still by landline.

Steve slid onto the stool next to me, wearing plaid pyjama bottoms and a grey tee-shirt, his hair spiked up and towel-tousled. He slurped his hot chocolate and pulled my half-baked list toward him.

I had written my cellphone number and my contact names.

"I don't think your mom was hiding in St. Stephen's College tonight, for what it's worth." Steve grinned at me.

"Thanks, I'm glad you find her to be of unblemished character." I scrunched my face back at him.

"Yes, that, and the fact that she and your dad are out visiting your cousin Fay somewhere on the Miramichi."

"Well, there is that."

"And I cannot see Marni being responsible for this, in that chasing you away from things is against her own self-interest. Of anyone associated with Rutherford House, she is the one least likely to be creating a stink. And it's not me, because, I would like to point out, that is my profile in the photo."

In spite of everything, I laughed. "They teach you that sort of amazing deduction in police school?"

"Pretty good, eh?"

We deliberately aimed our conversation at lighter topics, trying to settle ourselves before heading to bed. I made a stab at determining what my schedule would be for the next day, but it was amorphous. I had to call Marni, check in with my apartment, and go to IKEA. Whether or not I stayed there, I would still need a new couch and bed.

Steve would be working, so I figured I would call Denise and see if she would come and help me decide which element of Swedish functionality I should haul home. It would be a full day, trying not to think about having been in the sightline of a killer.

I had heard it said that when you walk in the river valley, chances are you will be seen by at least one wildcat, but you will not see any. I presumed the intention was to make you feel terrified walking there, but Steve tried to make the case that it was meant to demonstrate that wildcats were typically afraid of humans rather than being predatory. I pointed out that a woman in town as well as a couple of people in Canmore had been attacked by cougars while jogging along well-marked trails. His argument was that the runners had surprised the cats by coming upon them silently, and that they should have been wearing bear bells to herald their arrival. Bear bells just make me think of ice cream trucks, announcing delicious treats on their way. Nature and I were not meant to co-exist without a certain edge.

Licking the last of the hot chocolate from his lips, Steve decreed it was time for bed, so I hung my hair towel back in the bathroom and traded his robe for the lovely crisp sheets he favoured. Instead of changing to flannelette sheets in the winter months, Steve used a heavier weight of duvet with a fuzzy cover. It made sleeping there feel like one was encased in a s'more, all smooth and warm and toasty.

Usually, Steve would leave the bedroom drapes open, letting the downtown lights act as a pretty backdrop. Tonight, he had closed off the panorama, making both of us feel a little less vulnerable to prying eyes. He could talk a good story, but this action told me that the photo warning had got under his skin just as much as mine.

The next morning, we woke to Steve's alarm, and for the first time I felt the encroaching presence of winter. Lights were still shining in the dark across the river valley as we drew the curtains back, and the sun didn't make any inroads until an hour after Steve was gone and I was ready to get going myself.

The air was crisp with the smell of dry leaves. I walked through the neighbourhood, one block in from the river valley road, to keep a distance from the rush-hour traffic. Here, houses had begun to set up their Hallowe'en decorations, which were a bit more muted than I was sure they would be in communities with a younger demographic. Black and orange streamers, a jack-o'-lantern or two along the stairs, and orange bags sporting faces and filled with leaves indicated who would have a bowl of candy ready in the evening.

I stopped at Remedy for a pistachio chai latte to take with me to my apartment. There was no mail delivery yet, so I headed down the long hall to my apartment and opened the new deadbolt they had installed the day before. Even with all my cleaning and sorting, the space seemed foreign to me each time I stepped across the threshold. The people who had trashed my apartment had stolen its soul along with my laptop.

Speaking of laptops, that was something I was going to have to replace pretty darn quick. The Widows had been nice enough to loan me one till the insurance money came through, and I had now deposited the insurance cheque, so I could afford it, but I wanted to savour the sight of that large a number in my account a bit before depleting it all once more. Still, I needed to work.

I called Denise from the phone at my desk in the dining area of the apartment, sorting through the closest pile of papers stacked there as I waited for her to pick up. There is nothing like the odd break-in to make you realize you store too many useless papers. I vowed to create a better system for storing tax-worthy receipts, and to be more rigorous with my recycling from here on in.

Denise answered and agreed to come get me for an IKEA date, if I sprang for meatballs. It sounded like a very good deal to me. She said she'd need about an hour, so I continued to clear the desk area. I was soon done with the surface of the desk, and two of the three desk drawers were nearing some semblance of order. One of the local Szechwan restaurant's take-out menus was all I would need, so I tossed three others in the blue bag filling up beside me and tacked the first on the corkboard to the right of the window above my desk. Things were going to be very tidy in my new life.

I pinned the menu at the bottom of the corkboard, which also held three postcards—two from my folks and one from a friend who was flaunting her research trip to Peru, a map of the university libraries, a brochure of Rutherford House, and a list of phone numbers. At one point, I had industriously typed all my frequently used phone numbers and printed them on a sheet of green paper. Scrawled at the bottom was my own cellphone number, so that I would remember it.

I stared at my bulletin board.

That was how the phantom photographer had discovered my cellphone number. Whoever we had been searching for in St. Stephen's College last night was the same person who had trashed my home. The robbery was connected to the murders of Mr. Maitland at the archives and Jossie at Rutherford House. It was all one big ugly situation, and I was somehow right in the middle of it.

35

I called Steve to let him know about my cellphone number, and he promised to pass the information on to Iain right away. Apparently they were done with my phone there, anyhow, as they couldn't do much more than trace the anonymous call to the cell tower that accommodated the university. Since most students didn't even bother with landlines anymore, and in every HUB apartment at least one cellphone was being used, it wasn't much of a trail. He suggested we drop by on the way to IKEA to get my phone, which the techs had charged up for me. All part of the service.

Denise pulled up behind the apartment and honked. I waved through the kitchen window and hurried to lock up. Pretty soon we were tooling down 109th Street, on our way to the south side police station. Denise had the hardtop on her creamy Volkswagen Bug, but I was pretty sure she was going to be pulling its quilted tarp over it soon and leaving it in the garage she rented. Denise refused to drive in the winter, citing poor road conditions and good public transit.

It was nice to drive today, though, since everywhere we were going to visit was the hell and gone on the edge of town. After I picked up my phone and gave Steve a quick kiss, Denise and I headed south on 99th Street, which turns into Parsons Road just where it gets twisty. Eventually, Parsons Road led us right into the belly of the beast known as South Edmonton Common, an area of big-box stores and strips, each with its own parking lot, all jumbled together next to the highway. Traffic to this area—where IKEA, the mega-discount grocery store, several outlet stores, a huge cinema complex, Indigo Books, the Wal-Mart on steroids, various electronics and home furnishings stores, restaurants, and Home Depot had all sprouted—was so dense that the city had to cough up tons of money for an overpass system to alleviate the snarls and accidents occurring from shoppers going headlight to headlight with commuters and traffic from the airport.

It was a place I liked to avoid, mostly because people drove on its streets as if they were parking lots and in its parking lots as if they were on the street. Besides, when I shop in suburban Edmonton, I really prefer to do it in the relative climatic comfort of a mall, rather than having to move my car every fifteen minutes when wandering to a different store.

However, for our purposes, South Edmonton Common was the only place to go. The only IKEA in town was on the west edge of the development. We decided to go there first, since I didn't want to risk leaving a pricey computer in Denise's car while we shopped for furniture. I figured that if I rented a van to drive my purchases home, I could stop by the Apple Store on the way out.

The parking lot at IKEA was already full, and it wasn't quite noon.

"Don't let that spook you. It's so vast in there, we probably won't see anyone," said Denise blithely, as she locked her little car with a friendly beep of her keychain.

I wasn't quite so sanguine about the lack of other shoppers. They couldn't all be registered in the ballroom play area. We took the escalator up to the showroom floor and headed straight for the living-room sofas.

Denise also figured I should look at loveseats, to maximize the space in my tiny apartment.

"They did you a favour, wrecking that old chesterfield you had. I know you loved it, but it dwarfed your space." She moved toward a flowered overstuffed two-seater with high arms and plunked herself down on it. "I could see you curled up here very happily. The colours aren't overpowering, and you could easily get a solid-coloured chair to complement it. And, if you do choose to move to a larger space, you could always come back and buy another loveseat."

She was right. It was comfy and would fit better into my apartment. Not only that, it was at least two hundred dollars less than I had been budgeting, so I could indeed get a chair to match. And, should I choose to merge furniture with Steve, it would look great in a corner of his second bedroom/den. I noted the bin numbers with my golf pencil and we moved on to the chairs, where I wrote down the numbers for a PÖANG chair and head cushion.

Before long, we had snaked our way through the display

floor, picking up some cardboard boxes to store things on the upper shelves of my bookcases and a couple of matching picture frames. Denise had been right about it not feeling overly crowded, but there were still enough people that we had to line up for our Swedish meatballs with lingonberry sauce.

While we were eating, I filled Denise in on our Spooktacular evening and the spookier still St. Stephen's College adventure after that.

"I cannot believe that Steve let you go in after a bad guy," she said. "Isn't he always the one trying to make sure you are well out of dangerous situations?"

"What were we supposed to do?"

"Duh, I don't know, wait for the cavalry to arrive?"

I sliced through my last meatball, sopping up gravy with it. "It seemed like the right idea at the time."

"Yes, well, now it seems like you've painted a big target on yourself for someone who doesn't seem to have any trouble killing people who get in his way."

"That's something I'd rather not focus on," I said.

"I'll bet you would rather not. But it's all honing in on you, isn't it? What you have to sort out is why. What sort of knowledge do you have that the killer wants? Or what sort of knowledge do you have about the killer that the killer doesn't want out there?"

"What do you mean? I don't know anything about the killer."

Denise looked thoughtful. "I doubt that. You were there when the young woman was killed during the magic show. You were a regular at the Archives the week the archivist was killed.

You may know something or have seen something the killer doesn't want you sharing."

"What could I know? I was on the main floor when Jossie was killed upstairs in the guest room."

"Were you? I thought you were eating in the maid's room with the magician."

"Well, that is where I was when dinner was going on. I was downstairs when the body was found, and there's no way to pinpoint to the minute when she died. The last time I saw her was when we were hanging up coats as the guests arrived."

"And the two of you were together there right up till the magic show?" I could tell Denise was getting into Trixie Belden mode; like most professional researchers, there was little she liked better than solving a puzzle.

"Well, Jossie had to run upstairs to get another umbrella stand from the attic, but she was back pretty quickly." I closed my eyes to try to see the order of events more clearly. "Then Marni announced the magic show and the guests moved into the parlour. I was standing near the piano for that. I put the cover over the keys so no one would make any noise while the show was on."

"And did you see Jossie in there with you all?"

"The police asked me that already, and I really had no idea. It was a very well-attended event. I know that some of the actors were mingling with the paying guests, in order to see the magician at work. He was amazing, you know."

Denise nodded. "I remember seeing Dafoe da Fantabulist on TV all the time when I was younger. What got me was how quiet he always was. I had been reading about how patter was used as a deflecting element, to keep the audience from paying attention to the sleight of hand, and most magicians tend to use a running line of talk—well, except Teller, of course. But Dafoe was doing that here in Edmonton long before I'd ever heard of Penn and Teller. I thought I'd heard something about his having a speech impediment, which is why he never spoke on camera."

"This was the first time I'd ever seen him, but he certainly didn't have a stutter or lisp or any such thing when we ate supper together. He seemed very pleasant, although I have to admit it took all I had not to pester him about magic tricks."

"You not pestering him was probably what put him at ease," laughed Denise. "Can you imagine always having to discuss your work, even on your off times? It would be like being a doctor at a cocktail party, being asked to diagnose aches and pains over drinks."

"Well, you are always happy to discuss Shakespeare at the drop of a hat."

"Shakespeare is different," Denise sniffed. "Everyone has the right to my opinion."

I laughed, because Denise was the least pushy scholar I knew.

"Well, anyhow, I suppose I could have been right down the hall from Jossie getting killed, which would get Stephen Dafoe off the suspect hook. But she could already have been killed by then, or she could have been downstairs eating her supper."

"The coroner would be able to tell if she'd eaten supper," noted Denise, popping a meatball into her own cast-iron stomach.

"I suppose so. It's not something Steve shares with me."

"I guess not. Have they combined the investigations yet? Jossie's and Mr. Maitland's?"

"I'm not honestly sure about that either. But you think they are connected? The whole method of killing is different."

"I've never been overly fond of that as a reason against, in mystery novels. This whole idea that some methods are more of a man's or woman's purview is so sexist and out of touch with the modern equalities. And to think that murderers always use a consistent pattern gives brute, amoral monsters a lot of cerebral credit." Denise took a drink of coffee and wiped her lips with her napkin. "If I needed to kill people, I would use what was at hand. Maybe he snuck up on Jossie, so he didn't have to do so much damage in order to kill her. Or maybe he didn't have his hammer at Rutherford House that night."

"You think for sure it was a man?"

"Okay, there you have me, getting all sexist. I suppose a woman could break another woman's neck. I wonder just how much upper-body strength you would require. Maybe just some basic martial arts training would do you."

This was getting us nowhere, even though talking things over with Denise did make me feel a bit easier about the craziness I'd become involved in. Somehow, having her give voice to the possibilities and patterns made them less insane and outrageous. If she could discuss them, like Alice's six impossible things before breakfast, they took on a veneer of ordinariness that made them just a little bit less scary.

We cleaned our table and headed down the stairs to the pick-up area. Lucky for me, everything I wanted was in stock and, flatpacked, could be tied onto Denise's car, with the handy little Ikea cardboard triangles to support the cartons. We decided to go with that, buying only the living-room furnishings today and coming back another day for the daybed and mattress, rather than renting one of their vans, which I would then have to return to IKEA on my own and bus back to the university area alone. After all, I didn't need a bed yet. I wasn't quite ready to move back to my apartment. I was hoping that being able to sit and work in the living room would help to entice me back.

Denise sat in the parking lot at the Apple Store, to keep watch so no one walked away with my living room suite. It was probably just as well, as it focused me to get in and get out again. I knew the basics of which laptop I wanted. I could splurge a bit, since I wasn't going to replace the desktop model. I figured I could pick up cheaper USB cords to attach to my printer and my camera elsewhere, so I was in and out again within twenty minutes, which had to be a record for that electronic funland.

While Denise helped unload the cartons from the roof of her Bug and bring them into my apartment, she demurred about helping build the furniture itself, citing a meeting she had to get to with a grad student. I felt a pang of regret, watching her drive away, that I hadn't persevered and done my PhD, so that I too could have grad students. At the time, I had been more enamoured of the eager freshmen I could teach with an MA under my belt. I had no idea then that colleges would decide that doctorates were necessary for the teaching of first-year students, but when unemployed PhDs were wandering about for the taking, I guess they saw their chance.

The huge cardboard pack held the underpinnings of the sofa, which the bag of fabric and cushions were then pulled over like a glove. I managed to get the structure together with no problem, but ended up breaking two nails pulling at the coverlet. Once it was done, though, it was worth it. The chair, in contrast, was a straightforward breeze, which I think is the English translation of "pöang."

I folded up the cardboard and hauled it under my arm out to the recycle area of the rubbish bins. When I got back to my apartment, it felt homey for the first time in a week. Maybe I really could stay here.

Too grimy to sit on new furniture, I had a quick shower and changed into clean jeans and my sweater with the bear pattern. Now for the fun stuff. I made a pot of tea and took the lovely shiny white Apple box to the new sofa. The plug-in was close enough that I didn't need an extension cord, which was another good thing about a smaller couch. I'd have to remember to tell Denise.

Within minutes, I was up and running. My email, when I logged in, held more than three hundred new messages. I decided to read them later, and continued to set up my bookmarks and docking station for shortcuts to applications and programs to my liking. The operating system was two generations ahead of my old laptop, so there was a bit of a learning curve, but the keyboard was so amazingly comfortable that I found myself luxuriating in the sensory newness of it all.

It occurred to me to download the material from the Widows' flash drive I'd been carrying around in my wallet. I went into the dining area to retrieve my purse and noticed my phone was blinking, indicating new voice mail.

I poured another cup of tea and pressed my codes into the phone, pulling a pad of paper and pencil closer in case I had to write anything down. The first message was from the Widows, asking how the presentation had gone and letting me know they'd made some more tweaks to the back-stairs walk. I made a note to call them, though I had been putting things off till I'd found out what the board had decided.

It seemed I would know pretty soon. The second message was from Marni asking me to call her as soon as I got the message. I checked the time and realized I'd used up the entire afternoon. I would be seeing Marni in another two hours for the Hallowe'en event. But she sounded insistent in her message.

Marni answered on the first ring.

"Randy? I'm so glad you called. I have news. Like I told you, Greta Larsen went hammer and tongs against the project, but I think you must have charmed Walter Karras, and he in turn must have charmed the rest of them, because he managed to swing the board into thinking about the ways in which the virtual visits to the House would both extend the reach of the history outward and preserve the House from excessive wear and tear. He made them think it was their duty to make it possible for Maori children to wander through on a school tour without leaving their classroom." Marni laughed. "Greta never stood a chance."

"So we're good to keep on going?"

"We're gold, Randy. The board moved to extend the project and make you a permanent curator of the virtual Rutherford

House. They're going to explore the budgetary possibilities and approach you officially next week."

"Permanent? As in steady money?"

"You bet! It would be a part-time position, but long ranging. I guess the idea is you'd be available to respond to email questions, and would do ongoing research to add to the website as you went along, providing a new article or element every couple of months or so."

"Wow." It sounded like a good thing, but I would have to crunch the numbers and see if being tied to the House would be a sound economical step. What sounded like an easy task might become onerous if I had other projects on the go. I would read the fine print of their offer and weigh my options. At the moment, though, the green light on all that we had already achieved was what I wanted to focus on.

Marni seemed to agree. "Anyhow, the big news is that you're good to go on the anniversary project, and all the work you have already done is validated. Congratulations, and I am so sorry you had to be put through that waiting game. I honestly could just kick Greta."

I was curious. "Do you have any idea of her reasoning for hating my project so much? I mean, what could her motivation against it have been?"

"Greta is just a genuinely unhappy person. She objects to everything, as far as I can tell. She hated the new tablecloths for the teahouse, she voted no on the change of Sunday hours, I am pretty sure she tried to scupper my being hired. If it weren't for the Larsen family's stature, I doubt she would be on the board at all."

"Is she on other boards?"

"She is on the symphony board for sure, and I think she was on the museum's transition committee. Her family, or at least her late husband's, has been in Edmonton forever, and she sees it as her duty to carry on the positions her mother-in-law held. To hear her tell it, the Larsens invented Edmonton, and she's certainly inculcated her grandson to think that. You only have to spend five minutes around him to sense the entitlement reeking out of him. I know nothing about Greta's own family, but if you ever want to hear about Ivan Larsen coming west, just get her started."

None of that made any solid sense as to why she would decide to hate my presence in Rutherford House, but I figured I'd won that round and wouldn't worry any further about Greta Larsen.

Marni and I finished off the call with a promise to get together properly for drinks in a week's time, once the Hallowe'en season was done. I was half hoping she was going to let me off the hook for her event that evening, but no, she stressed, sounding regretful, we needed all hands on deck as much as we needed the money the event would bring in.

I decided to call the Widows back in the morning and get ready for the event. I grabbed my black tights, black skirt, and white blouse, and popped into the bathroom to change, since I still didn't have a replacement blind for my bedroom window. It occurred to me that I would need to deal with that, if I was going to sleep here again. I made a mental note to get a blind along with the daybed when I ventured back to IKEA. The Swedes were going to be able to retire on me this week, that was for sure.

36

Marni had managed to round up several of the part-time staff to help out with what she was dubbing "Frat Time in the Old Towne Tonight." One of the Greek fraternity houses had decided it would be fun to have an old-fashioned Hallowe'en party, complete with bobbing for apples, candy crafts, ghost stories, and a costume contest. They were selling tickets to the evening, raising money for some charity, and providing the food. The House got a flat fee for hosting and staffing up the place.

Marni's decision to go for it had to do with erasing the stigma of the last event and getting back on the bandwagon. I could see her reasoning. You didn't want people to constantly be thinking of Rutherford House as the place where the young woman had been killed in the guest room, especially if they were thinking of booking a wedding venue. Of course, it helped that Finn Larsen was on the organizing committee. I wasn't sure whether it was his powers of persuasion or Marni's attempt to get back on his

grandmother's good side that had ultimately made her acqui-
esce to the idea.

It was sort of weird to be back in my serving clothes, waiting for the evening to begin. Two of the organizers from the
frat were hauling in a galvanized washtub toward the kitchen
area. This was the only place Marni was going to allow the apple
bobbing, since it was guaranteed to generate a mess. She had
provided two oilcloth tablecloths for them to set up on.

The teahouse had been divvied up, with tables in the interior
area devoted to decorating pumpkin-shaped cookies with icing
and candy corn and sprinkles; stringing mountain ash berries
into necklaces to ward off witches; and decorating domino
masks with feathers and glitter. The sun porch tables each had
on it a bowl of Hallowe'en candies. Most of the tea services had
been left downstairs, and all that remained upstairs behind the
counter was glassware.

I was beginning to wonder if I'd misheard the concept and
that somehow the fraternity was running a party for orphans,
but Marni assured me it was for university-aged children.

"It's Finn's idea," she said, pointing to the lanky fellow I'd
seen accompanying his scowling grandmother a couple of
times. Tonight, he looked younger somehow, even dressed as
he was, in a double-breasted suit and devil horns. "The idea is
that nostalgia for one's youth can start even in youth itself." She
shrugged. "He may have a point. I have to admit, this looks like
it could be fun."

They were both right. The guests began to arrive within the
hour, paying their twenty-dollar entry fee and accepting their

four different-coloured tickets entitling them to one apple-ducking try, one cookie to decorate, one mask, and one beer. Additional beer tickets were for sale at the sun porch. There weren't many coats to hang, which was surprising, given the coolness of the weather and skimpiness of the outfits. Most of the girls had opted for the micro version of their costumes, and there were plenty of "sexy" nurses, milkmaids, mice, molls, police officers, and gypsies. The guys had shown some imagination, going for more than ripped-shirt zombies. The classy devil was standing with a six-foot Winnie-the-Pooh, while a remarkable Tim the Enchanter, complete with little white stuffed killer rabbit, sat in the parlour talking to Pop-eye and a roll of Life Savers.

Finn the devil had been right. The kids, allowed to indulge in childlike delights, made the most of it. The craft tables were in demand, and while a few people sat in the beer area, most mingled, sitting for a story or two before heading out to explore the house and get more candy. One girl with ruined makeup and wet hair proudly crunched an apple as if she'd ascended the Olympic podium.

Marni was monitoring the upstairs while I circled the main floor and Roxanne patrolled the basement. The kitchen was closed, and we had packed the gift shop away by covering the tables with sheets. The fraternity exhibit was accessible, though it occurred to me that the partygoers were not in any mood for a history lesson. Roxanne could dream, though. For the most part, the guests were using the basement only when they had to use the washroom. Roxanne had been required to shoo one overly amorous couple back upstairs, but she seemed more than up to the task.

I was having an easier time of it, even with the number of open artifacts on my level. The dining room was being used as a pass-through area, with no activities focused there. As a result, the glass cupboards holding the set of Limoges dinnerware seemed safe. The storyteller in the parlour was also watching out for the furniture and ceramics, and the bartender had his eye on the glassware in the sunroom.

I had to ask a Bugs Bunny not to take one of Mr. Rutherford's law books from the shelf in the study, but that was the extent of my hardnosedness. The door monitors had a people-counter ticker with which they were tracking the number of ghouls and goblins allowed into the House.

On the whole, things seemed to be in pretty decent order. Or so I thought.

Marni had locked the doors to her office and the attic, to set some additional boundaries, and she had closed the gate to the sewing area in front of the doors on the second floor. As she had said, the last thing she needed was a drunken Juliet on the balcony, which had been deemed structurally compromised in the last architectural audit.

She had stationed herself in the guest room, to deter too many gawkers from doing stupid things in the former crime scene.

It was understandable that there would be curiosity seekers, and likely the savvy frat devil had booked the House for that very reason. Everyone wants to rubberneck in some way when something that horrific happens. It had occurred to me that this whole party might have been concocted in order to profit from the prurient curiosity about the murder, but Marni had assured me the booking seemed innocent.

I made another quick trip back to the kitchen area to ensure that water spillage from the washtub of apples wasn't spreading across the floor, but a Dr. Who (the one with the fez) and a Jersey cow, complete with udder, were wielding a mop and bucket to maintain safety at the bobbing station. The cow seemed also to be in charge of taking tickets.

The mask station was empty, and only two cookie decorators were still at it. A group of thirty or so young people was congregated in the sunroom, drinking beer and laughing. Several girls were perched on laps.

The storyteller in the parlour had a small crowd enthralled. I stepped through the doorway and positioned myself close to where I had been the night of Jossie's murder, when the magician had been performing in this room.

"It was during the building of Achnacarry that the accident happened, as I'm sure you've heard people remark." The storyteller, a large woman dressed as a gypsy, with swirling skirts and silver chains and a purple headscarf, leaned toward the group at her feet. "No one had seen a house this size west of Winnipeg, and the brickyard was put on double shifts to manufacture all that was needed for the task. A master mason had come from Toronto and several younger men of the area were happy to sign on as apprentices.

"At first, it was a happy place to work. Time flew, the weather held, and the foundation was dug and set in record time. The plans were true and elegant, and all the workers felt a certain pride that they would all their lives be able to point across the river to the brick house on the edge of the university and say, 'I helped build that house.' That's why no one anticipated what happened after the accident."

There was a bit of rustling, and I realized it came from a few of the young women edging closer to the boys beside them. The deep, mellifluous voice of the gypsy storyteller was painting a picture that felt a little too real.

"It may have been the wind or the weather, it may have been that the worker had been drinking the night before, it may have just been very bad luck, but one of the masons fell from the scaffolding and landed on the sharp edge of saw lying below, slicing off his arm. His wails and the shouting of the men on that side of the building brought the whole crew to his side. They staunched the bleeding and bustled him down to the ferry site as quickly as they could to get him across to Edmonton, where the hospital was. It wasn't until they arrived at the hospital that they realized not one of them had thought to bring along his severed arm, which the doctors said was a shame, as the fellow might have stood a chance of reattachment, had they acted more quickly.

"One fellow offered to go back and get the limb, but the doctors assured him it would be too late if he weren't back within the hour. Now, it was barely possible to get down into the river flats and across the North Saskatchewan by ferry in half an hour's time, but he was sure it was worth a try. After all, what could a one-armed mason do? So off he went and made it back to the worksite in just thirty minutes. If he could get the arm, wrap it in something and get it back to the hospital in the same amount of time, there might be a chance. He raced over to the scaffolding.

"The arm wasn't there."

One of the girls gasped and I swear I saw a young man dressed like Bugsy Siegel shudder.

"The man searched everywhere, frantically shouting for whoever was still on site to tell him what had been done with his friend's arm. But no one had kept track of it, so anxious were they all to get their bleeding colleague to the ferry.

"The man was frantic, and the clock was ticking. If some animal had come by and taken the arm, it would be gnawed and mauled by now, but if he could spot it quickly enough, then perhaps reattachment would still be feasible. He searched the bush near the worksite, looking for a trail of blood that might indicate which way an animal had dragged the limb.

"There was nothing at all. An hour or two later, the man returned to the hospital, dishevelled and depressed. The doctors hadn't waited for him past the hour, but had cauterized and stitched up the nubbin at the elbow, doping the poor fellow with morphine to dull the pain.

"While the injured man lay in the hospital across the river, his wound knitting up, work continued at the House. The walls went up with one less apprentice laying the bricks, and things were never quite as jolly as they had been. Though no one mentioned it, the men kept their eyes peeled for the missing arm as they went about their work.

"The young mason with one arm was released from hospital and made his way back to the worksite. People were happy to see him, and they all stopped what they were doing for the moment, to greet him, pump his good arm, and pat him on the back. But there was nothing for him to do. Even stirring the mortar was a job for two strong arms.

"But one arm and a nubbin can, with determination, tie a noose. The young man hanged himself in his rooming house in Old Strathcona, and the arm was never found.

"Now, it's not considered a haunting of the House itself, but every so often, joggers on Saskatchewan Drive nod to a young man in loose denim trousers and a work shirt with one sleeve pinned up, standing in front of Rutherford House, as if admiring the lines. And," the gypsy paused, sweeping the room with her hooded eyes, "on an otherwise calm and windless day, you can sometimes hear a rustling at the side of the house, a sweeping of the bushes and a tossing of the earth, and a voice can be heard ever so faintly, crying, 'Have you seen it? Have you seen the arm?'" The gypsy sat back up straight and clapped her hands, breaking the spell she'd woven over the crowd.

People laughed in that way they do to cover their shock or fear. Sensing the storyteller wanted a break, the crowd clambered to their feet and dispersed to other activity centres. I hung back, wanting to check on the windowsills behind the curtains, to be sure no glassware had been perched there. When the room was empty, the gypsy stood and stretched. I noted she was much taller than I had at first estimated. Sitting, she had been hunched over, drawing in her audience. She also had enormous hands for a woman.

I must have been signalling all these observations with my expression, because the gypsy smiled and said, in a somewhat lower voice than she had previously been using, "Hello, Randy."

It was like one of those plastic puzzles where you slide the squares one at a time to get the picture. The tiles rearranged themselves, and instead of an old gypsy woman, I found myself staring at Walter Karras, with a kerchief on his head and bangles and skirts swirling about his body.

"Marni roped me in, and I thought it would be good fun to see how many people I could fool. I borrowed the costume from the Walterdale Theatre. What do you think?"

"I think it's remarkable. You fooled me."

Mr. Karras took a mock bow. "Since they stopped the Klondike Melodramas, I've not had much of a chance to indulge my inner thespian. This was fun."

"You're quite the storyteller, Mr. Karras."

"Call me Walter, please."

"All right, Walter. That last story, about the suicide of the workman, was that true?"

He smiled. "No, I am afraid there are no juicy ghost stories associated with Rutherford House. I adapted a story that used to be told with relish out at a summer camp where my son worked, and tossed in some historic elements to make it something of a learning experience."

I laughed. All most of the kids had taken away with them

was that they would never talk to an amputee standing on the sidewalk in front of Rutherford House, just in case.

"I was trying to find some way to deflect attention from the grisliness of what happened upstairs," Mr. Karras continued. "It would be so sad to me if everyone focused on that poor girl's death here in the House as the main attraction. It would rob the House of its value historically, and it would diminish the tragedy of her death for her parents and family."

I nodded. "I hear you. I'm pretty sure ticket sales are so brisk exactly because of Jossie's death, but on the whole, they've got over that allure pretty quickly and just moved into party mode."

"And that is exactly as it should be. This House is a living museum. It is more than just the home of the first premier, after all. It was a fraternity house for a while, housing another premier in his university days. My eldest brother lived here for a couple of years when Peter Lougheed was in residence. And now, it's been a historic site for a good long time. There are probably a handful of girls here tonight who had their birthday parties here, dressing up and having tea and playing croquet on the front lawn."

Taking advantage of his loquaciousness and the lack of party-goers in the room, I decided to ask Mr. Karras what his thoughts were about the events of the past couple of weeks. Maybe an outside view would prove useful.

"Do you think the deaths of Jossie Jaque and Mr. Maitland are connected? I can't help but tie together everything that has been happening, including the robbery in St. Stephen's College, but I just can't see how it fits."

"Robbery at the College? I hadn't heard about that." Mr. Karras looked very concerned, which endeared him even more to me.

I recounted the bare bones, and he tut-tutted appropriately.

"I can certainly see how you would connect the dots. But, realistically, isn't it rather a stretch to imagine a crime spree over something connected to Rutherford House?"

I decided to go out on a limb. After all, I had no idea what the ties and possible loyalties were on the board. But Mr. Karras seemed so sympathetic, and Marni's mention that he had helped sway the board into keeping my project going pushed me to get his take on Greta. I couched my question without naming names, trying for discretion, but Mr. Karras was no dummy; he'd know exactly who I was talking about.

"Do you think someone negative on the board might be behind all this?"

Mr. Karras arched one eyebrow, and a new coldness seemed to enter his eyes.

"I know the people on the board of the Friends of Rutherford House to be upstanding members of this community, giving their time and energy to preserve our history and heritage. I cannot imagine for one minute that anyone on our board could be suspected of such crimes and I hope I won't hear of such rumours being spread. If you'll excuse me, I must go change."

It was as if I'd crossed an invisible line and made a serious faux pas. I felt numb and hot in the cheeks, and knew I was flushing with embarrassment. I mumbled an apology and went out into the hall, almost bumping into Winnie-the-Pooh. Lucky for me, he had his back to me, talking to someone, and the dimness of the hall—and his likely blurred vision through the large fuzzy head—meant he couldn't see my face with its telltale signs of shame.

Thing is, I wasn't really certain why I had been snubbed so severely. Up till that point, Mr. Karras had been perfectly willing to discuss hypotheticals. It was only when I clumsily linked Greta to the crimes that he had stiffened.

Why was that?

37

Marni was still shaking her head at the bad taste of a young woman posing in the tub with her head lolling over the side while her friend took her picture. She was relating how she had sent them out of the room and chastened them with a tongue-lashing, before deciding to close the guest room bath door for good.

"I don't know why I didn't think of that sooner, just lock the door." She grinned ruefully. "The curator in me overrode the caretaker, I guess."

We were having a cup of tea after cleaning up the aftermath of the party. I was waiting for Steve to come get me as he had promised, and Marni was hanging out with me till he arrived, which I appreciated. For all Mr. Karras' assurances that no ghosts lingered around Rutherford House, sitting alone in a historic house on Hallowe'en night was my idea of a spooky setting for a horror movie, an old 1970s one, with Dean Jones in the cast.

I had told Marni about my discussion with Mr. Karras, and she had tried to settle my mind about his change of attitude toward me.

"He is really behind the project. Don't worry about him changing his mind about that. As for his pushback on Greta, you have to give him props for standing up for members of his board, right? On the whole, that's the sort of loyalty you want to have for your project, and I tell you, once he has said he supports you, Walter Karras supports you all the way. That's why he was here tonight, and why he popped in to the magic night for a while, too. I'm not sure I'd have the energy to push for some of the things I have done here if it weren't for his good will."

I was somewhat mollified, but it still smarted to have been put in my place so definitively. I don't think anyone since my grade-school piano teacher had ever made me that sorry I'd said something.

"Well, I will be back in touch with the Widows tomorrow and figuring out when to get a full-scale website up and running. I have about another week's worth of research to do before setting up the first three of the five sidebars, but we can launch with 'watch this space/work in progress' signs on a couple of links, so I'm not worried about that. What I want to figure out with you sometime when you have an hour or so is the information for the interactive parts—bookings and registrations, that sort of thing—and then we can chat about the kids' area and the blog section."

I had been wrestling with the best ways in which to make the website a kinetic area that people would return to on a regular basis. My thought was to have Marni take on a regular weekly update section, where she could post funny things that had happened, a historical fact or two, and her thoughts about an upcoming event. She had such a quick wit and love for Rutherford House that I couldn't see it being too onerous a task for her, and it would mean return visits to the site, generating more foot traffic to the House.

Marni shrugged and laughed. "What's one more thing to do, my list is already a mile long and around the block. You'll have to show me a way to make the entries without risking breaking all the links and ruining the Internet."

I grinned back at her. "Yes, I will make it so you can't break the Internet."

Both of us jumped a little when the bell rang.

It was Steve, coming to take me back to his place. I gave Marni a quick hug and grabbed my bag. She came along behind me, turning out lights and locking the door.

Steve kissed me and greeted Marni warmly. "Happy Hallowe'en, ladies. Feel like heading out to smash some jack-o'-lanterns?"

"I think I'll leave that to the junior high kids," Marni laughed and turned down the little side path to her car, parked behind the House.

"Have you been working your regular cases, or is everyone on extra patrol tonight?" I asked as we walked down the path to Steve's car, crunching leaves beneath our feet. Soon the snow would come, but the tiny pink fairies and cardboard and tinfoil robots had won tonight, with a lovely dry Hallowe'en for their hijinks. I reached into my pocket for one of the mini candy bars I had picked up for Steve.

"We weren't as busy as you might think. I think they put extra patrols on Whyte Avenue and downtown, and there are cars out in the suburbs doing slow drives, but on the whole, I would rather work Hallowe'en in Edmonton than, say, Stanley Cup finals or Canada Day. The kids are happy, the mayhem is minor and diffused right across the city, and there is candy involved."

We were stopped at a light, and laughing as two Trekkies and a Dalek crossed in front of the car. A university party was letting out somewhere, I figured.

"More likely just starting. Parties for twenty-somethings don't even get going until around ten-thirty, eleven."

"How come?"

"Iain figures it has something to do with the combination of later hours in the bars and the nine-to-ten-o'clock closing hours for stores. It used to be that only restaurant workers and actors would party in the late hours. Now, it could be pretty much anyone."

"No wonder there's such an outcry about the bar scene on Whyte Avenue, if it doesn't even get started till right around my bedtime."

"Oh Randy, you have no idea. The street you see when you shop there on a weekend afternoon turns Felliniesque around two in the morning. Drunks smoking outside the entrances to bars, then meeting up and fighting with other drunks who've been fermenting in other bars. Girls dressed up for a night on the town puking in the gutter next to grubby guys living rough and hoping for a handout. It's not the Edmonton you or I really want to know."

We were in Steve's parking lot by now. Even with the added foot traffic of happy, costumed drunks, we'd made it back to his place in less than ten minutes, which was an added bonus to living on Saskatchewan Drive.

I hadn't even found a moment to tell Steve about my furniture purchases, so we unwound with some green tea. I prattled on, trying to make my work with Allen keys sound entertaining. Steve seemed to be listening, but I had the sense he wasn't totally with me.

While I wanted to ask him if something was bothering him and give him the opportunity to unburden himself, I wasn't certain that sort of thing was within the bounds of where we were allowed to go. I had to admit it hurt whenever Steve said he couldn't talk about something to me. Even if I knew logically that his job came with restraints on divulging information, it seemed to indicate a lack of trust, underlining the chasm between us when it came to his job and the security of the Western world.

It wasn't as if he thought I was going to run out and tell people about cases he was working on, I knew that. Still, he would get a look in his eye and clam up, and I would know that we'd wandered into dangerous territory.

The problem was that I often felt as if I was wandering about in that same territory without much of a map. I could use a bit of information from time to time, even just a landmark or two to watch for. But Steve had taken an oath; besides, Steve's boss would have his badge if he thought my boyfriend was indulging in "pillow talk" with me. Even so, this barrier made for stilted conversations from time to time.

The silence between us wasn't uncomfortable, but I strove to fill it anyhow. I recalled something I had been meaning to ask him, tickled to life by my evening at Rutherford House.

"Did you guys ever talk to that magician again?"

"Stephen Dafoe?"

"Yes, the fellow who did the real magic act the night of the mystery play. I was patrolling tonight from about the same vantage point I had that evening, and I got to thinking about how he had been able to move around the House without people seeing him."

"I thought you said he went out the window."

"Well, I was pretty sure he did. He had curtains up in front of the windows, at any rate, but who knows, that could have been an illusion, too."

"No one can move through walls, Randy, not even a magician. But no, we haven't tracked him down. I am pretty sure they are still looking for him as a person of interest."

"Does that mean 'suspect'?"

"Not always, though with the way the papers hype the term, we'll have to begin to come up with another phrase soon, or we'll have vigilantes beating up witnesses all over the place. What makes you ask about Dafoe?"

"He's a loose end, I guess. Maybe something Mr. Karras said. And in some way, I think he was connected to Jossie, which makes him interesting."

"Connected? How do you mean?"

"We were organizing ourselves for duties that evening, and I guess Marni wanted to give everyone a chance to see the shows, either the actors or the magician. I remember asking Jossie if she wanted to work the main floor and she said something about having seen Dafoe before and not needing to catch his act. She said something about having known him when he taught at a magic school."

"Jossie was into magic? That's the first anyone has mentioned that as a possible connection."

"You would think, eh? But no, I don't really think she was. She had a sort of eye-rolling attitude to it all, at least she did that night. I think she was really just there for the extra money the part-time job brought in. She seemed far less interested in the machinations of the entertainment than the rest of us were. Even the dishwasher was a bit star-struck by the actors wandering about. But she just seemed to be there to do a job."

"I think she was an economics major."

"And that explains anything?"

Steve shrugged. "I'm just saying. Thing is, why would an economics major know anything about magic school? Did she have a brother or sister studying to be a magician? Were her parents circus people?"

"You would think that Detective Howard might have uncovered that sort of connection by now, if it existed."

I had a vision of Jossie, dressed in a blue blazer and plaid skirt, surrounded by a family in sequins and spandex. While it sounded like a great concept for a TV sitcom, it didn't quite fit my idea of what she had been like. I hadn't known her well or all that long, but she had made enough of an impression for me to be able to weigh possibilities.

"Okay, so Jossie knows the magician from before. And Greta Larsen hates frivolity at Rutherford House. And the magician is missing. And Marni is worried about her tenure at the House. And Mr. Karras wants you to either back away from Greta Larsen or focus on her so you'll miss seeing something else he's worried you'll remember. None of which brings us any closer to why Jossie was found dead in the bathtub."

"I was thinking about the whole tub aspect."

"The tub is important?"

I glowered at him. "A cop I know once told me that everything is important. As I was saying, there may be some significance to her being found in the tub because, unless you are familiar with the House, you wouldn't think there would be a tub there. After all, it's a turn-of-the-century house and unusual in that it has any plumbing at all. Secondly, it's the guest room, and a slightly smaller version of the Rutherfords' room. There is no tub in their room, just a walk-in closet. So, if you hadn't combed the property beforehand, you wouldn't expect to find a place where you could conveniently ditch a body, right? Meaning, it had to be someone who knew the House well."

Steve smiled and poured me more tea.

"Good theory, but not necessarily sound. If it was a crime of chance, taking place in the guest room, the tub would be a happy discovery rather than a targeted body dump. Or, take into consideration the fact that people do tour the House and may have been there before without being on the board or staff, and some may have done so even before the dinner."

I shook my head. "Not before dinner. Marni had the staircase roped off. I had to move the cord to get the actress and myself upstairs to scope out her location for the murder mystery."

"And she decided to go in to the walk-in closet?"

I nodded.

"After seeing the tub in the guest room, I presume?"

My face fell, literally. I could feel my jaw take the brunt of it. There is some truth to every old saying, I guess.

"You think that Tanya Rivera murdered Jossie? Why?"

Steve laughed. "No, I am not saying that. I was just pointing out that lots of people might have known about that quiet little tub room tucked away in the guest room. And it's not as if the body wasn't discovered pretty quickly."

"Yes," I nodded slowly. "But maybe it was hidden away just long enough."

"Long enough for what?"

"For whatever time the killer needed."

"So, Jossie was killed to get her out of the way of some other action that needed to take place."

"Because she was in the way."

"Or she had seen something she shouldn't have."

"Or she knew something that would piece together the puzzle after the fact."

"But her death was the crime. Nothing else happened. Nothing was stolen."

"Nothing that we know of. Has the complete inventory been turned over yet?"

I nodded. "I am pretty sure Marni sent it over by courier on Monday or so."

"And who completed the inventory?"

I shrugged. "I guess just Marni, but she would have a catalogue for comparison."

"And where would that catalogue be kept? The Archives?"

"I doubt it, though that would tie things up really nicely, wouldn't it. No, as an active historic site, it's more likely the catalogue would be housed with the provincial office."

"Which is where?"

I looked at him and again felt the shift happen where puzzle pieces seemed to slide around to create a new design.

"In St. Stephen's College."

Steve smiled. "I thought as much. Whoever we disturbed last night may well have been making his or her way down to the historic sites offices to steal or alter that catalogue, having gained an easy entry from one of the shut-off floors."

"So something may be missing from Rutherford House?"

Steve looked grim.

"If it is, then your present boss may not be as much of a stand-up gal as she'd like you to believe."

I sagged a bit, both because of the hour and the thought that Marni might be capable of theft, subterfuge, or worse. Steve noticed and suggested we head to bed. The minute he said it, the accumulated efforts of my day caught up with me and I yawningly agreed.

All I recall is heading toward Steve's bedroom. I may have been asleep before my head hit the pillow.

38

The next morning, I woke up before Steve, who refused ever to set an alarm on his days off. I got out of bed quietly and went to the kitchen to start coffee and raid Steve's wealth of granola. He had seven or eight different blends and types, from regular-grocery-store boxed muesli-styled cereals to several bags of exotic nuts and dried fruit in with the oats. And to look at him, the average person would guess steak and eggs were his regular fare.

While I was eating at his breakfast bar, I pulled the notepad he kept beside his phone over to me. It was a burnt-orange stickie pad. An erasable pen, Steve's secret to success at crossword puzzles, was next to it.

Instead of a to-do list, I found myself writing out all the criminal things that had happened in the last couple of weeks, one per stickie. First came Jossie's murder. The death of Mr. Maitland came next, unless you counted the missing diary of Mrs. Rutherford, which I did, so it got a stickie as well. There was the "mess" in Rutherford House in Fort Edmonton, too, which young Jasper Peacocke had told me about. Might as well put that on a stickie. The break-in at my apartment. The intruder at St. Stephen's College. I wondered if anything had been stolen from there. I wrote the question on a stickie. For that matter, was anything else missing from the Archives? Stickie. Pretty soon, I had quite an accumulation of paper squares on Steve's counter. I cleared away my bowl and spoon to make room for some sort of organizing principle.

If we supposed everything was connected, it might be useful to put events into chronological order. I flipped the stickies around so that the Fort Edmonton loss went before Jossie's murder, and the possible thefts from the Archives and St. Stephen's were attached to their break-ins. Even written out and organized, there was no order to be seen.

I decided to add a few more things that we knew. The magician was missing. Jossie knew the magician. The person who had been in my apartment had been the St. Stephen's intruder, because he or she had my cellphone number. Mr. Maitland had known everyone related to Rutherford House, because they all turned up at his funeral. Greta Larsen hated the Internet, and as an extension, me. The inventory for Rutherford House was at St. Stephen's.

I looked at all the stickies I'd now used. I would have to think about buying Steve another pad. How the heck could I organize them? Things were all over the map now.

I decided to group things that had to be connected, like the break-in at my place and the cellphone photo from St. Stephen's.

I placed the inventory under those two squares, as a maybe. I then grouped the Rutherford House murder, Dafoe the magician, Greta Larsen all in a clump. I linked the Archive grouping next, with the loss of Mrs. Rutherford's diary between that group and the Rutherford House cluster. I was pretty sure my laptop had been stolen because of its connection to the website construction at Rutherford House, so that went below Rutherford House, meaning I had to move the whole St. Stephen's grouping under there.

It was possible to see links between all the major incidents. Every grouping of stickies connected to another, but it was all conjecture. What if there were two murderers and a completely separate thief, all working with distinct and unique agendas? It could be. Edmonton had, after all, lived down the moniker of "Murder City" once, after a spate of drug-related murders had taken place in an immigrant community. Maybe we could expand and be known as the "Crime Capital."

My hypothesis was possible, but not really probable. For one thing, if three different criminals were operating within my vicinity, it stood to reason that they'd be tripping over each other. Was there really that much honour among thieves, that you would just smile and nod when another criminal was on your turf? I didn't think so. But still, maybe everything wasn't related. Maybe, if I were to take one or two squares out of the mix, as coincidence or some weird sort of karma, everything would come clearer and I'd be able to see plainly who the murderer was.

Because, when it came down to it, no matter how much I

hated the fact that someone had trashed my wonderful little sanctuary of an apartment, murder was the absolute worst.

I went back to my stickies.

Which one could I remove?

I looked at the clusters.

The first one, standing on its own, represented the purported thefts from the original Rutherford House down in Fort Edmonton Park. While it seemed a long shot to be taking something an earnest five-year-old had told me at face value, I'd put Jasper's testimony and perspicacity above that of many adults. Besides, the Park wasn't the most secure place in the universe. Although they had watchmen and patrols, no fence is entirely impregnable, and it would be hard to maintain historical integrity with a load of state-of-the-art security wires everywhere.

I believed Jasper. There had been a break-in. I just couldn't for the life of me figure out what could have been so valuable in a historical display.

The only other solitary stickie was the Greta Larsen note. I couldn't in all conscience attach it to any of the others. As much as I disliked Greta, I wasn't about to tie her into a crime just to get her out of my hair. It would be pleasant, though, to be shot of her hovering over my project, trying to get it cancelled.

I pulled the stickie pad toward me. Maybe my project fit into this mix somehow. I wasn't sure where to put it, but seeing "virtual museum" on a stickie, right in the middle of the lot of them, made me feel as if some fat spider was going to crawl out and get me if I wasn't too careful. As the nominal fly, I was going to have to be very careful not to get stuck in this puzzle if I didn't want to be a statistic on the final stickie.

I heard stirrings from the bedroom, and preemptively poured Steve a cup of coffee. He came out, fuzzy-headed and adorable, wearing his terry robe and padding slowly in his bare feet. He looked grateful for the coffee, and after a swallow or two, seemed to focus. His eyebrow arched as he took in the countertop awash in rust-coloured squares, but he came around to my side to read what I'd written.

The nice thing about Steve was that I rarely had to fill in the blanks. He always managed to tune into my wavelength effortlessly.

"Trying to see how all the crimes are connected?"

"Having all these things happen so close together seems like just too much of a coincidence."

"This is the one that bugs me." He pointed to the cluster near the left, dealing with Jossie and the missing magician. "Jossie knew the magician. Walk me through it again. How do you know she knew Dafoe?"

"She said something about him working at the magic school, or being from the magic school, or something like that. I figured she meant a business here in town, though at the time it surprised me that a teenager would be all that interested in magic. I don't know, it's not the 'in thing' anymore, is it?"

"You never know," Steve shrugged. "Penn and Teller have shows all over TV and on YouTube. And there are all those punk-danger magicians these days. For all I know, magic could be the latest greatest thing."

"Okay, so say she hangs out at a place called the Magic School, because she's some sort of Harry Potter fanatic. And she sees Dafoe da Fantabulist at this place, either performing, if it's some sort of club, or buying something, if it's some sort of shop, or teaching tricks, if it's some sort of training centre." I was stretching to try to find a reason. "So, if she sees him, does he see her? Is this the sort of place where a teenage girl would stand out? Was she memorable? Did she see something she shouldn't have?"

"What we really need to do is ascertain where exactly the magic school is," said Steve. "If we were to begin with the idea that it's a proper name, how would we begin to look it up?"

"We could come back at things from the other direction—focus on where Jossie was from, and where she could possibly have come across a place called Magic School."

Steve nodded. "Good idea. If we follow the same process with Stephen Dafoe, we should eventually come up with where their paths bisect."

"Look at you, all woke up and sounding mathematical."

He groaned. "Not quite awake. But give me ten minutes in the shower, and I should at least be human." He wiggled his eyebrows suggestively. "Care to join me?"

Showering together is one of those things that sounds a whole lot sexier than it ever turns out to be. Having bruised my knee on a tap once too often, I shook my head and told him to go ahead, but to leave me some hot water.

"That's the beauty of high-rise living, Randy. The hot water never runs out."

Steve padded off to the bathroom, leaving me to ponder the

stickies and figure out how I could trace the path of one dead young woman.

Marni would be able to give me her home address from her work application. The Rutherford House form asked for applicants' permanent addresses as well, since so many of their part-time employees were students who sometimes had to have a last cheque mailed to their parents' home. Could it be that Jossie came from the same small town as Dafoe?

He didn't live in Edmonton proper, as I recalled. He had mentioned something about a forty-minute commute, but I wasn't positive in what direction. For some reason, I had pegged him as coming from the northwest, but that could have just been because his name sounded French to me, and there was a whole enclave of Franco-Albertan towns, starting with St. Albert, just to the northwest. Or had he actually mentioned St. Albert? I really needed to start doing daily crosswords and eating zinc and all the other things purported to aid memory.

I would certainly be happier knowing where Dafoe was at present, as well as where he was from. How could someone disappear in the middle of a criminal investigation and not be suspicious? For that matter, how could anyone disappear in the middle of a criminal investigation? With all the GPS tracking on phones, monitoring of ATM transactions, and CCTV cameras about, I had long ago figured that Big Brother had effectively tagged and branded most of us. So, how could the police have lost track of someone like Dafoe?

Well, if anyone could elude discovery, it would be a magician, I supposed. But only the most naïve innocents wouldn't consider how their actions and movements might be perceived when the police were involved. Or maybe not. Having been on a list of suspects in the past for a crime where I was totally innocent, it occurred to me that I had not over-thought what the police might construe my choices to mean. Maybe Dafoe had innocently gone on an off-the-grid vacation.

I was hearing more and more about that. People ceremoniously stripped themselves of cellphones, tablets, computers, and watches, then took off to the lake or the mountains for some total down time. I imagined little trays of buzzingly annoyed rectangles of various sizes, all vibrating in anticipation of getting their hooks back into their owners.

I pulled out my own little rectangle and texted Marni, asking her to check into Jossie's home address for me and any other information she might have on her application or résumé, such as schools she had attended. Then I flipped open my computer and sent an email to a friend from grad school who was working for the province. Emmanuel had done his history thesis on place names in Alberta before and after the railroad. Chapters of it had been published almost immediately in *Canada's History,* when it still had the much more evocative title *The Beaver,* and he had been hired to some sort of provincial cross-ministry task force between Culture and Infrastructure, to research and record naming across the province. If anyone could find me a Magic School, it would be Emmanuel Aleba.

Steve came back into the kitchen, shiny and dressed, and offered to make French toast. I figured I had five minutes for a quick sluice in the shower, so I raced off to get cleaned up for the day.

I got back to the kitchen to find that Steve had rearranged my stickies onto one of his oversized lap trays, so that he could set out the breakfast dishes. I moved the lap tray onto the couch, leaning it against the back, so it appeared like a miniature whiteboard in one of Steve's investigation rooms.

He had placed the stickies in six tidy rows, rather than clusters, and in each row, the thefts were stuck at the bottom, with a bit of space between them and the other squares. It made for an interesting balance—murders on top, and thefts below.

"Food's ready," Steve announced, so I tore myself from the patterns and went back to the bar chair. Steve's French toast was to die for. It was fluffy and crisp at the same time, and there was a secret ingredient that he wouldn't divulge. I could taste the nutmeg and vanilla, but there was one other taste at the back of the tongue. Someday, I figured, I would catch him adding it to the bowl and the jig would be up.

"Do you think Jossie saw something happening she shouldn't have, when we were all at the House that night? Or was she killed because she knew something about someone? Like something from the magician's past that he didn't want anyone in Rutherford House talking about?"

"Maybe she had seen his show before and knew how one of his good tricks was done?"

I shook my head. "A) I don't think a magician would actually kill anyone over a trick. B) I don't think anyone would actually go to the effort of telling people how the trick was done, because who really wants to spoil someone's entertainment? And c) well, you never met her, but I can't really imagine Jossie spending her energies on trying to figure out a magic trick. Most young people these days seem both sneeringly judgmental and bored out of their minds as they're talking to you. Magic tricks wouldn't have been her style unless they were approached ironically. Come to think of it, I have no idea what her style would be. She mostly exuded polite blankness to me."

"Sounds like a real princess," Steve laughed.

"I know it sounds harsh." I nodded. "But I used to get students like her a lot in first-year English courses. They were annoyed that they had to take a prescribed course, and that resentment seemed to colour everything for them. Half of them could be won over by the material or the enthusiasm of the other students who actually enjoyed English, but some of them sat and stewed in their own juices the entire semester."

"Okay, so she was a typical teenaged cypher, in the wrong place at the wrong time." Steve flipped another sizzling piece of eggy-bready goodness in the frying pan while I mopped up stray bits of maple syrup on my plate with my last bite.

"Maybe. Or maybe her knowing the magician from before was enough. Maybe he was trying to erase that element of his past. Or maybe she reminded him of someone else back home. An older sister, an aunt. People look alike in families. Maybe it wasn't Jossie at all that he was worried about, she was just a reasonable facsimile thereof."

"We're now presuming Dafoe was the killer, then?"

"Why not? It's not my case."

"Speaking of not your case, what about the Archives murder? Have you got any further on Mr. Maitland's death? And more importantly, when I was making the stickies this morning, it occurred to me to ask you, was anything else missing from the Archives?"

"It's tough to be connected to a case, because I am never totally sure what it would be all right to discuss with you and what really should be off-limits." Steve looked pained, which was the last thing I wanted to do to him. Just as I was about to tell him to forget I'd said anything at all, he spoke.

"We have a forensic archivist in, going over the collection along with the folks doing the inventory. The vaults were locked prior to the assault but there was still enough material on the hold shelves for us to wonder if something had been taken. She is doing spot checks for materials that should be in the collection, in terms of statistical averages. We're working on an inventory of their lists and catalogues, but we figured, what if the thief knew to remove the cataloguing trail, along with whatever he or she took? So many of the things in the Archives are listed as 'box of papers' that it's almost impossible to guarantee we'll even know for certain if anything was removed and if so, what it was." He smiled. "But we're doing our best."

"I'll bet it's not Keller's priority, though."

"Well, no, he is mostly concerned with being able to get a murderer off the streets. It doesn't do much for a city's morale to have an unsolved killing, particularly one with no ties to drugs or gangs. It's one thing to read about crime that will never affect you if you stay away from certain neighbourhoods or lifestyles.

It's quite another to have someone killed in the lobby of a public building, where anyone with a question about genealogy might pass through. No, Keller doesn't like it at all."

My phone trilled its little three-note tune declaring I had a text message.

It was from Marni and read: "J was from Eureka. Must be near Ponoka, because she attended Ponoka High School and Mecca Glen School before that. Does that help?"

I texted back a quick thanks and closed my phone. I hate people looking at their phones when there is food on the table. Steve had popped another piece of French toast on my plate and was now sitting next to me, enjoying his own.

"Jossie was from south of here, near Ponoka somewhere."

"Farm girl?"

"I guess. Not sure what else is out that way, once you're past the car lots in Wetaskiwin."

"Well, it doesn't really rule anything out, because once they can drive, most rural kids find their way into town for concerts and dance parties on the weekends through high school. That close to Edmonton, she'd have likely known her way around pretty well."

"Still, it places her geographically in a location where she could have known something about Stephen Dafoe that most folks here in the city wouldn't have been privy to. That is, if Dafoe came from that neck of the woods, too."

Steve pushed his plate away, sated. "So if that is indeed where the magician comes from, too, we possibly have two people who might conceivably have known each other from near Ponoka.

What about other folks at the House? There is only a danger of information leaking out about you if there is someone to leak it to, someone that you don't want knowing it. After all, Jossie told you she knew Dafoe, so if it was you he was hoping the information wouldn't get to, he wouldn't have solved anything by killing her. If it was someone else, though, then stopping Jossie from talking was still worthwhile."

"Or maybe Jossie knew something about another person in the House, and we're just focusing on the magician because she actually talked to me about him. If she could make a statement like that about Dafoe, who knows what she could say about someone else? And if that other person didn't want, say, the magician knowing there was a connection between them, maybe that explains why Jossie had to die."

"That is getting almost too confusing for me to follow," Steve laughed. "And I have to get to work pretty soon. What are you doing today?"

"The last thing Marni said to me last night was not to come in today, and I'm taking her at her word. I have an article about Cecil Rutherford to read, and then I was thinking about seeing if Denise was free for an early dinner. What about you?"

"I'm on call for the next three days, but I could meet you after work as long as I keep my Blackberry on. Keep in touch and I'll track you down later, 'kay?"

"Okay. Hey, you get going and don't mind the dishes. It's the very least I can do, and lord knows I'm all about doing the very least I can!"

Steve kissed me and grabbed his keys from the brass bowl

under the wall phone. I spent the next half hour putzing about the kitchen, cleaning and polishing. It was a nice-sized kitchen for a condo, but I wasn't all that certain I wanted to move my trusty potato peeler into the drawer alongside Steve's shiny knives and cheese graters. I still hadn't determined whether or not I could handle living in my violated apartment, let alone whether I was ready to start cohabiting. Too many decisions, right in the middle of all this flux; I determined to put off thinking about Steve's generous offer.

I poured myself the last of the coffee and swirled warm clear water into the glass pot to rinse it out. Wandering back into the living area, I pulled the drapes open wide, as the sun was starting to make a dent on the early morning darkness. This winter encroachment of darkness really depresses newcomers to the north, but those of us who have lived here most of our lives figure that on the whole, it's a fair trade off for the long, warm summer days we get at the other end of the year. Besides, who wants to be outside in the early morning chill of November? Even without a first snowfall, temperatures had been dropping significantly. When the sun had warmed things up enough, around two or three in the afternoon, we'd be unbuttoning our jackets and wishing we hadn't decided to layer quite so much that morning. Then, by about six, we'd be bundled up with scarves wrapped round our necks and gloves on once more. And we'd all be congratulating ourselves on not having to wear boots quite yet.

At least the rain seemed to have stopped for the season. I recalled all the umbrellas coming into Rutherford House the night Jossie had been killed. She'd even had to run up to the attic to find another umbrella stand.

Had I told anyone that tidbit? I don't know that I had even recalled it myself till just now. What if Jossie had stumbled across something she shouldn't have seen while she was on her way up to the attic or back down?

What would she have seen, though? The attic door was located close to Marni's office door, so she'd have been nowhere near the maid's quarters where the magician and I had eaten our meals later on. She might have seen one of the actors figuring out where their plot-line would take them. She might have over-heard Marni talking to someone in her office or on the phone. She might have seen someone in Marni's office who shouldn't have been there.

I went to my laptop to send Steve and Detective Howard a quick email, before I forgot. I didn't want to presume that I was handing them the clue that would unlock everything, but I fig-ured they ought to know that Jossie had indeed been up in the attic and around the upper level of the House before the event had begun.

After I sent it, I checked my incoming mail. Emmanuel, bless him, must have been in to work early, because his work email was in the "From" box.

```
FROM: emmanuel.aleba@goa.ca
TO: randy.craig@telus.com
SUBJECT: Magic, Alberta
Randy! It is wonderful to hear from you; it has
```

been far too long since we have connected. I trust you are well and prospering.

Your question about magic school is intriguing and makes me wonder if you have decided to become a wizard in your spare time. While I cannot help you with trade names of businesses (you may want to look into the City of Edmonton records for the registering of such), I do have a Magic School for you. It is no longer in existence, but at one time, there was a town called Magic in Alberta, not far from Edmonton. It was along a line of towns that melded into one district, that was then renamed as an acronym of the towns that had been absorbed, in geographical order (this is something so dear to my heart, in that I spent an entire summer researching towns named sequentially along railroad lines).

The towns, beginning with Magic, then Eureka, then Calumet, Climax, Concord and Asker, became "Mecca Glen." I presume they determined three Cs in a row were untenable. Mecca Glen is near Ponoka, almost an hour's drive southeast of Edmonton.

Until 1949, there was a Magic School in existence. I believe the building is still there, though it is no longer a school proper.

I hope this helps you in some way. Are you

```
still working for the Folkways music people, or
have you moved on to yet more exciting endeav-
ours? I look forward to catching up with you
eventually. Hot toddies near a fire, soon.
```

```
    Yours,
    Emmanuel
```

Emmanuel, for all his English-as-a-fourth-language furbelows, was a treasure. I made a mental note to buy him a hot toddy soon, and fired off a quick thank-you email to that effect.

Magic. Eureka. Mecca Glen.

Eureka, indeed.

39

I sent Steve another email, cutting and pasting most of Emmanuel's information into it, then went to brush my teeth and make the bed. I called Denise to set up a time for me to take her to dinner to pay her back for her help with the living-room furniture. Generously, she offered to first drive me out to pick up the daybed and mattress I'd decided on.

"Then we can walk over to the High Level Diner and you can treat me to a bowl of their black bean chili."

"It's a date."

I had a couple of hours to kill, so I decided to walk up to Whyte Avenue from Steve's condo and window-shop my way down the strip. So many shops were changing as the tenor of the avenue evolved. A fire a few years back had destroyed an entire corner, which had grown back as a modern approximation of a vintage building, containing interesting hat shops and small companies. Several more bars and nightclubs had also newly come to Whyte, making it a less salubrious place to wander in the evening than it had been in the past.

While the best time to be on Whyte Avenue was a summer Saturday, there was enough of a small-town feel to the eccentric and mom-and-pop shops at the eastern end to make it interesting. I looked at amber displays in a jewellery store window, and duvet and pillow posters in the next window. Cupcake shops warred with each other for what I had presumed would be a pretty small demographic, but with enough icing-laden cupcakes their customers could get a whole lot larger. Boutiques were squeezing out some of the older shops, but the Army and Navy, a funky cut-rate department store, still held its own, resilient to change. I ducked in to browse the women's side of the upper floor before heading downstairs to check the housewares.

I had spotted some lovely duvets and pillow sets at IKEA, but I figured I could do a lot better price-wise somewhere like the Army and Navy. They were fully stocked on mattress pads and covers, and the variety and colours of towels were overwhelming for a store this size. I found the sheets aisle and spent twenty minutes deciding between stripes and flowers. I finally went with the flowers, since I figured they would complement the high white ends of the daybed I'd decided to buy, making it look even more like it came out of a German fairy tale. I also noted a couple of duvet covers that might work, but that purchase could wait. I got two sets of the sheets, as the daybed used two twin mattresses and a spring device to bring one mattress up from under the other like a drawer. I also picked up a set of king-sized pillow cases and pillows. So much for not loading myself down for the rest of the walk down Whyte Avenue.

The cashier bagged my merchandise and I continued my journey west on Whyte Avenue. I was across the street from some cute gift boutiques and card shops, but laden with purchases as I was, I resisted the urge to cross the street. I wouldn't even fit down their aisles.

I managed to stride along on the south side of the road quite easily, not getting in the way of too many people. I popped into the bank just before 109th Street, to check my balance and withdraw a bit of cash with which to treat Denise. My paycheque from the House had gone through to top up the insurance payout, so even with the drain of IKEA and Apple purchases from the day before, my account looked quite healthy.

I wondered if I would ever get to a point in my life when I would see a regular paycheque with benefits and a pension plan. Marni's intimations that the Rutherford House gig might become a permanent one held a great deal of promise, but only if it would pay enough to make it worthwhile. If I had to add on other contracts to make up the difference, I'd be juggling timelines and requisite hours for the rest of my life, which didn't sound like fun. This gypsy life of contract-to-contract existence was a young person's game, and something in me was made for more security. I might have to knuckle under and find a civil service job one of these days, before I became a cat food-eating statistic. While you couldn't actually starve to death in the social service safety net that was Canada, being poor and old was not a fun thing anywhere on the planet.

I was standing at the bus stop on 109th Street, just past the drugstore on the corner where Denise had told me she would pick me up. There were fewer buses roaring in to a stop here since the LRT had started to carry a lot of the southern load, but there were enough that I wondered if her little cream Bug would be accordioned between them. I needn't have worried. She sailed in easily when no buses were in sight and laughed as I shoved my assortment of puffy bags into the back seat.

"You've already bought the pillows, so I guess we really have to get you a bed!" she declared, and took off as soon as she heard my door thud closed. I was still strapping into my seat belt, it seemed, when she was already curving off 109th to get to the thoroughfare that took us once more to the big blue store.

"How are things going? Was Hallowe'en terribly spooky after everything that happened there?" Denise was the best listener, and she prompted with interested little grunts as she drove expertly through the traffic. I filled her in on the party and on my insights into the connection between Jossie and Stephen Dafoe, the magician.

"The Magic School, not the magic school?" echoed Denise, effectively enunciating the capitalization. "Of course, that makes sense. So you think the magician may have murdered her because he realized she could reveal something about him? Or another person murdered her because they realized there was this possible connection between her and the magician—and whoever it was didn't want that connection to happen?"

"Right, I guess." The truth was I hadn't managed to think my way through everything that clearly. I was still basking in the glow of realization that there had indeed been a Magic School at all.

Denise sat up even straighter. "Randy, you don't need a bed. What you need is a road trip!"

And with that, she drove right past the overpass exit to IKEA, and down the highway toward Ponoka.

40

I contemplated texting Steve to let him know where we were headed, but instead I just promised myself not to be too obvious about anything or get into any trouble, and then slid my phone into my satchel. Denise was asking me to get out a map from her glove compartment, where three tidy maps sat under a pair of stylish leather driving gloves the colour of the Bug. She was the only person I knew who actually used a glove compartment appropriately. There were times when I just wanted to be Denise.

The road to Mecca Glen lay just east of Ponoka proper, and it looked as if we'd be best taking the first exit to Ponoka and carrying on along that route once we were off the Queen Elizabeth II Highway. I was a little nervous, since I'd never been east of the highway except to go to the Tyrell Museum in Drumheller.

From Denise's map, I could see that most of the towns between Edmonton and Red Deer were located on the older Highway 2A, which ran relatively parallel to the QEII and which, until the

Queen's last visit to Alberta, had been called Highway 2. While it consisted of four lanes of zippy transit between Edmonton, Red Deer, and Calgary, it wasn't much of a scenic route—unless you liked cows and canola.

"So, let's try to work this out," Denise demanded, her eyes never leaving the road and her driving mirrors. "How do we know this place is the hub of all things nefarious?"

I laughed. "We don't, and I'm not even certain there is a nefarious web of intrigue happening. It could be just a perfect storm of tragic coincidences."

"But you don't believe that."

"No. No, I don't." I took a breath and folded the map so that Ponoka and Highway 53 were in the uppermost section. "Jossie, the murdered girl, came from Eureka, the town next to where we are going. I think she had seen the magician before. She told me so, although I wasn't clear on what she meant at the time. I thought she must have meant she had caught his act at a club, or something like that. But it can't be a coincidence that a small town called Magic is right down the road from one called Eureka, can it?"

"It's worth looking into," Denise agreed. Well, she had already agreed wholeheartedly by devising this semi-crazy plan to drive off to who-knows-where to play girl detectives. We were making good time, passing the sign to Wetaskiwin and chugging southward. I was keeping my eyes peeled for a sign to Ponoka.

"I am figuring that either Dafoe killed her to keep anyone else from knowing his connection to Magic, the town, or that someone else killed her to keep her from saying something that

Dafoe would immediately understand because he came from the same area. The only thing is, I cannot imagine what on earth anyone could say that would be worth killing that person to keep quiet about."

"That's because you and I are on the moral side of the fence," Denise snorted. "Lawbreakers, sociopaths, psychopaths all have an entirely different fix on what or what not can be said or shared. They're on a different wavelength, so the energy you are expending trying to understand 'why' is energy wasted. The only way to clear up the situation is to find a logical course of events. Attempting to justify any of them might be crazy-making. After all, can you imagine killing someone?"

Denise had a point.

"So why can't the police just question the magician and his relationship with the dead girl?" she asked.

"He's gone missing, apparently." I indicated the turn; Denise dutifully got into the right lane and aimed for the exit ramp that led to the highway overpass. "Steve, of course, doesn't know everything to do with the case, as it's not his, and besides, he can't share every little thing with me, but they haven't been able to find Dafoe since the night of the murder."

"Really? Then why don't they have a manhunt going on? You would think the press would be going crazy over something like that. They love to post photos and wax on about 'persons of interest to the police' and all that."

I wasn't sure why they were playing that aspect so low-key, either. "Maybe he's not a person of interest. Isn't it possible that he could have satisfied all their questioning the night of the murder and been struck from the list of suspects there and then? After all, the detectives dealing with the Rutherford House murder have not questioned me again, either." Thank goodness. I had actually been a suspect once, and it was not a nice feeling.

Denise nodded thoughtfully. We had slowed down quite a bit driving through Ponoka, which was charming in a clean-little-prairie-town sort of way. There were signs declaring it a winner of Towns in Bloom, but since the municipal flower beds had all been cleaned up and turned over for the winter, we were just going to have to take their word for it. A sign on 39th Avenue declared this the route to Highway 53, so we kept going past the Stampede grounds. I made a mental note to come back some time to make a day of it in Ponoka; it seemed like a nice little town.

"Okay, so if we think everything is connected, what can we extrapolate? There are a lot of thefts on your list and two people taken permanently out of the way. What did they know that the murderer wanted hidden? What thing or things was the murderer after wherever a theft took place?"

I tried to think of a connecting principle, like a shiny cord running through my memories, linking all my sticky notes and shaking them into a smooth line of cause and effect.

"Well, I think perhaps the thefts are not successful. Whoever it is has been looking for something and hasn't found it yet. If you line them up chronologically, you have the first Rutherford home in Fort Edmonton Park being broken into, then Rutherford House itself. The murderer might be just covering up his tracks. I haven't heard whether Marni had an official inventory done after the murder, because, well, you know, there was a murder, and that sort of keeps you from thinking about theft. Then there was Mattie Rutherford's diary, which no one but me believes is missing. Then the break-in at the Archives, which was also the occasion of the death of Mr. Maitland. He, I believe, was killed so the thief could get unrestricted access to the Archives."

"But he knew all the players," Denise pointed out.

"What do you mean?"

"Well, you said he was telling you about Greta Larsen, and Marni and people from the House were at his funeral with you. Maybe he did know something about someone. I'm just saying."

I nodded. "Maybe. But it could also be that he was just in the wrong place at the wrong time. Like Jossie." I was counting on my fingers. "So if you add on my apartment and St. Stephen's College, we have six thefts or break-ins. And we are not even certain that the thieves took Mrs. Rutherford's diary. Mr. Maitland might have removed that from the rest of the carton for reasons of his own. As for the possible loss of an inventory catalogue, that is just conjecture. Steve hasn't got back to me on that."

Denise pulled onto a highway lay-by to let a truck with huge round hay bales get some distance. The place reminded me of car trips with my folks, when my mother would run around to the trunk to get a thermos out of a quilted plaid plastic picnic bag, and my father would embarrass me with deep-knee-bend calisthenics to "avoid phlebitis." This roadside stop was partway up a hill leading to a promontory of sorts above the highway. There was enough parking for about four cars; near the crest of the hill was a stone cairn, delineating a provincial historic point of interest, next to a trash barrel with uninteresting graffiti sprayed on it. At least they hadn't tagged the sign, which resembled a huge gravestone with a tall grey granite stone bisecting a long red granite stone. I got out of the car and walked over to the sign.

MECCA GLEN. The grey sign told of the merging of the six townships and included a legend with a list of symbols and their meaning. The red granite held a carved map that indicated where each of the towns had been and what significant historical sites had been there. The problem was, there was no Highway 53 shown on the carved map and no convenient YOU ARE HERE star in their list of symbols. For all we knew, we might have driven right through the vanished towns of Magic and Eureka without even realizing it.

On the other side of the granite monument was etched a picture of pioneers tilling the soil with oxen. Pictures like that always made me perversely thankful for microwave ovens and supermarkets.

Denise came up behind me and spoke the words I was thinking. "Damn, well, I guess we have to turn back and see if we missed something. I don't remember passing a school, but we were talking and I have to confess I was focusing on not being ground up under the wheels of that hay truck. What do you say we head on, maybe four kilometres or so, and stay on the lookout for the Magic School? If we don't find anything, we can always turn back. There is bound to be a museum in Ponoka that would have some information about it all. We're not far from there. They will have a proprietary interest, I'm sure."

I agreed and we hopped back in the Bug and pulled back out onto the two-lane highway.

"So," I said, "picking up our train of thought about what might have been stolen, I would be willing to go out on a limb and say something pertaining to the Rutherfords. If it were just an artifact of the time, the thief wouldn't have bothered with the Archives. I think it's information that he or she either needs for a specific purpose, or wants no one else to have, for whatever reason."

"Sounds eminently reasonable," Denise teased.

I grinned in acknowledgement and went on. "So, let's think about who is involved and match them to either needing something or wanting something to stay hidden. First we have Dafoe, the magician, who could probably steal anything he wants from right under your nose. He was hired by Marni, but recognized by Jossie, and spent his dinnertime with me. If he had been trying to steal something, why did he stick around for dinner, talking to me?"

"He could have been looking for a secret treasure buried in the walls or under a floorboard, and talking to you was misdirection."

"That's what I was thinking, as insulting as it is to think that talking to me wasn't a scintillating experience but just a cover."

"Or he could be totally innocent and sincerely interested in good dinner conversation."

"But if he's so innocent, then where is he now?"

"He could be so totally innocent that he's gone on vacation and doesn't even know this is happening. Or maybe he is down in Mexico, performing nightly at some resort hotel."

"Maybe. I'm not so sure, and I wish he'd checked in with the police before he left if that's the case."

Denise slowed. We had come to the Mecca Glen School site. It was a nice modern building, with a very cool-looking playground off to one side. Because it was surrounded by trees, we hadn't seen it from the road or from the hilltop cairn, which was really saying something in this remarkable valley, where you could see for miles. Denise pulled into the parking lot and stopped the car.

"We might as well look around here, don't you think? Maybe there's someone who could figure out where things used to be."

"What, like go in and check with the principal?"

"Why not?"

"Well, it looks like hardly anyone is here, is why not. Look at the parking lot."

There were three cars in the lot.

"Well, let's knock anyhow."

"We can do better than that." I pressed the institutional button that mimicked the doorbells of private houses and heard the obnoxious buzzing reverberate through the halls. I was willing to bet several little boys had been punished for pressing that buzzer at recess.

While we were waiting for someone to come to the door, Denise picked up our conversation about suspects.

"Okay then. So, Greta wants to maintain family decorum for the Rutherfords and Dafoe wants to steal a secret treasure. Anyone else on your list of suspects?"

"Well, aside from person or persons unknown, I guess Marni is the only other person I've been wondering about."

"Your boss? Classic."

"Actually, she's a good boss. She was just born to manage people, I think."

"But you think she might manage one or two of them into the grave from time to time?"

"I think she is a highly motivated person with bigger fish to fry than running a historic house. She's so full of energy she almost hums, and I'm not quite sure what she's doing is what could be perceived as a dead-end position."

"So you're saying she's suspicious because she seems too good for where she is."

"Does that sound stupid?"

I didn't get to find out whether Denise thought I was stupid or not because just then someone came to the door. He was probably ten years older than us, wearing dark green trousers and a matching shirt tucked into them, looking like every plumber and workman I'd ever seen before the invention of Carhartt overalls. I suspected he was the school's custodian; just to be certain, I introduced myself and Denise and asked if there was someone we could speak to about the history of the school in relation to the Magic School.

"We don't want to interrupt school, though."

The man laughed.

"Can't do that today, no how. It's what they call a PD day. The kids get to stay home and sleep off their Hallowe'en candy rush, and the teachers have gone into the city for a daylong course. No one here except my cleaning staff and the librarian."

That accounted for the dearth of cars in the parking lot.

"Do you think we could talk with the librarian?" asked Denise.

It was as if he had just seen Denise for the first time as she spoke, and I could see his eyes refocusing on her, the way men's eyes always did.

"You might as well come with me and meet her. For all I know, she might have some idea of what you want." He opened the door a little wider and ushered us into the hall. The overhead lights weren't on, but all the classroom doors were propped open and sunlight streamed through into the dim hallway.

He introduced himself as Mike and led us past bulletin boards full of bright orange and brown paintings and collages of leaves, the first fall artworks of the children. A tall trash bin on wheels stood in the middle of the hall, filled with orange and black streamers and construction-paper pumpkins.

Mike nodded to it as we past. "We had a costume parade and sock hop for the older kids."

The school was built like a lower-case T, and we had come in at the bottom of the stem. We were headed up to the junction of the cross bar. The gym lay in front of us, the office to the right, and the library directly across from the office. We had passed eight classrooms. I presumed the staffroom was somewhere behind the general office. All in all, it was a tidy little school.

Mike knocked on the library door before trooping us in, to give the librarian a heads-up, I supposed. Working in a deserted school had to be a bit spooky; I wouldn't want anyone sneaking up on me, either.

A woman came toward us from between waist-high shelving stacks of books.

"Yes, Mike? Oh, hello. May I help you? My name is Rhea. I'm the teacher-librarian here at Mecca Glen." She smiled, a bit puzzled to see two strange women checking out a rural elementary/junior high school. I could see her running through different scenarios, possibly trying to shape a welcoming face to greet the new lesbian couple who had moved out of the city to raise their edamame- and quinoa-fed children. I spoke quickly before she said something that would make us all uncomfortable.

"Hi, my name is Randy Craig, and this is my friend Denise Wolff. We're here doing a bit of research on the Magic School and wondered if you could tell us something, anything, about it? I've been working for a provincial historic site, putting together an interactive website for them."

"And you want to connect to other points of interest? Of course. Were you hoping to tour the school today?"

Denise piped up. "You mean it's still standing?"

Rhea laughed. "Last time I looked. It's right out back."

Denise and I looked at each other and laughed as well.

"So much for our map-reading skills," Denise said. "I was pretty sure we had already driven through what had been Magic before we got to the hill."

Rhea nodded. "The map on that cairn is really misleading. I wish they'd drawn in Highway 53, but they based it on a 1912 survey map, and the highway didn't come through here till around 1940. I'm not sure it was paved till the '50s." She nodded to Mike, who had gone through a door into the office and reappeared with a single key on a keychain. "I'll turn off the alarm, Mike, but perhaps you could reset it before you leave today?"

It sounded as if Rhea alone would be showing us around the old school.

We left the big building by a side door between the library and the gym, and crunched our way down a pebble gravel path around the back of the gym.

There, among a grove of trees, was a schoolhouse that looked very much like the one I'd seen at the Ukrainian Village. A set of stairs led up to the entrance, which had a small bell tower overhead. Rhea unlocked the door and stepped quickly to a numberpad just inside, disarming whatever alarm would have sounded. I couldn't imagine who would have heard it, beyond the folks in the Mecca Glen School office, but perhaps that was enough. The alarm was there to keep out students with petty vandalism on their minds, not to repel thieves after a massive treasure.

Because there was no treasure here to be found. A mannequin dressed in an early-twentieth-century dress stood at the front of the classroom near a blackboard filled with beautiful copperplate writing. The contents were a couplet from what I was pretty sure was a Shakespearean sonnet but would check with Denise later, a complicated algebraic equation, and a list of the colours of a rainbow prism in order, along with a couple of simple arithmetic problems.

Rhea saw me looking. "The idea is to show people just how encompassing a Grade Eight education really was. So many of our elderly generation today have alternated between being ashamed of getting only so far in school and bragging about getting so far with only a rudimentary taste of schooling, but really, in the days of the teacherages and one-room schoolhouses across the province, a Grade Eight education was nothing to sneeze at. You'd have enough poetry memorized that you could provide a quote for any occasion, and the capacity to memorize would hold you in good stead throughout your life. Your mathematical abilities would allow you to buy the right amount of seed for whatever size your fields might be, or enough paint to cover the barn, or an eye for laying out a dress pattern in the most efficient configuration for fabric use while still matching the seams. You would be able to make change and recognize when you'd been shorted, know the capitals of all foreign countries and thereby understand the news, read the weather from your science-class cloud identification, and write polite notes for any occasion. There was nothing second-class about the education you received here, by any means. If you had no need for more book-learning, you were set for life."

It was a spiel I figured she had recited several times. I could see her being a very good storyteller, which had to be a prerequisite for being a librarian. Rhea walked us through the display, which took up the front quarter of the schoolroom, and showed us some of the books set open on the desks.

"There would have been upward of thirty or forty desks set up here, with children ranging in age from five to seventeen. School would have begun later in the year than we're used to, so that the older children could help with the harvest, but by mid-September, they'd be coming to school on horseback or walking across the fields with their lunches in lard pails."

"This is wonderful," I said. "Is it open to the public in the summer? Or do you rent it for special events at all?"

A quick frown passed over the librarian's face. "We do rent it out when we can. The display can be packed up relatively quickly, and the desks line up under the window, leaving a good-sized space for meetings and the occasional performance. Local council meetings used to take place here, too. In fact, that cupboard back there, which at one time was the teacher's bedroom, holds folding tables and stacking chairs. There's not all that much call for it, though. People tend to favour Ponoka if they want a meeting of any size, or else they vote for meeting in Edmonton so they can shop at the Bulk Barn before they return home."

"I don't suppose there was ever a magic show here, was there? I mean, it would be sort of cool to hold a magic show in the Magic School."

Rhea smiled.

"There was—for just that reason—and not that long ago. It would have been May, I think. School wasn't out yet, because I had a poster for it in my library and there were leaflets for the kids to take home. How did you hear about it?"

"A girl I knew told me she had seen a magician at the Magic School, and it took me ages to work out what she meant. I thought she was talking about something like the Magic Castle in Las Vegas, but when I heard about there being a town called Magic in Alberta, everything clicked into place."

"Very few people even know about us, unless they're from these parts. People just tend to refer to it as the Mecca Glen area."

"She may have been from here, I am not sure. She was a university student, and I guess they come to Edmonton from everywhere. Did you ever know of a Jocelyn, or Jossie Jaque?"

The librarian's eyes clouded over.

"Yes, I knew her. She was my niece."

41

It was more Rhea Jaque's graciousness than my diplomatic skills that got us through the next ten minutes. I was embarrassed to be caught playing at Nancy Drew in front of a grieving relative. Denise, who hadn't said a word besides a muttered pleasantry when we had first arrived, abdicated all responsibility beyond being the driver and provided no back-up at all.

I gave Rhea a very brief rundown of my connection to her niece's death and what had brought us out here. I didn't want to cloud the issue, so I didn't add anything about the break-in at my apartment or the death of Mr. Maitland so close on the heels of my working at the Archives. I didn't want her to start thinking I was somehow the reason her niece was dead.

We left the Magic School of the 1920s and headed back to the contemporary Mecca Glen School, where we had coffee in the staffroom. Rhea might have felt more comfortable in the sanctuary of her library, but all but one chair in there had been designed for much tinier behinds.

"Jossie couldn't find any work in town last spring; or rather, she didn't want to go back to the restaurant downtown where she had waitressed the summer before, because the chef was sort of a sleaze. So she had come home for the summer. I couldn't afford to pay her, but she did some volunteer work for me in the library and with the end-of-the-year concert, after helping her dad seed. She was also a big help getting the magic show advertised."

"So she would have been known to the magician, you think? If he saw her again?"

Rhea nodded. "Oh yes, I would think so. The show was a fundraiser for the museum foundation, and Jossie was very committed to that cause. She helped him set up his show and fed his budgie, and I think she even met up with him to get posters out ahead of time. The whole idea was to generate more traffic out to the school, to make it more of a tourist attraction, you know? My mother, whom Jossie adored, had been a teacher in the Magic School when she was first starting out. Jossie used to love to hear her grandmother's stories about growing up in the Peace Country and going to Normal School to become a teacher and then travelling all over the province teaching. In those days, I don't think teachers stayed more than two or three years in any one posting, and my mother was probably flightier than most. She had such an urge to see the world. Of course, then she met my dad at the rodeo one summer, and that was that."

"So you're from around here?"

Rhea nodded.

"My mother loved it here. My dad's family had settled in

Eureka, and so Mom named our cat Archimedes. Her favourite joke was to point to the offerings he would deposit on our front porch every morning and say, "Poor Archimedes spent all night looking for an honest mouse."

I wasn't sure all this reminiscing was getting us anywhere.

"So you became a teacher-librarian like your mother? Was Jossie's mother likewise inclined?"

Rhea shook her head. "Jossie is my brother's girl. All my brother wanted to do from the day he could walk was ride a tractor and have coffee at the Co-op. He was born to be a farmer. I was the black sheep and ran off to Europe to see all the things my mom had never got to, but even prodigal sheep eventually come home."

Denise, who had been sitting silent for a while, finally spoke. "So Jossie helped out with the magic show here, then goes back to university, gets a part-time job at Rutherford House, and helps out with a magic show there? Somehow, that just seems too coincidental."

Now that she said it out loud, it did seem a bit strange to have such symmetry. Of course, Hercule Poirot would have loved it.

It was Rhea who refuted Denise's objections.

"Coincidences are just patterns that haven't been explained. It seems quite clear from my viewpoint. Our magic show was quite successful, and generated quite a bit of interest with the government department that oversees heritage buildings. I had to submit a description of the event for their matching grant program. That application included Mr. Dafoe's name and particulars, including the costs of hiring his performance, which was really very reasonable. I can imagine someone seeing that report and considering him for another fundraiser in a heartbeat."

"Well, that would account for the magician being at Rutherford House," I agreed, "but it doesn't quite explain why Jossie would be there."

Denise backtracked a bit. "Actually, I can imagine that part. Once someone works at one of these places, they see the potential for jobs at other places that the average person wouldn't see. It's like waiters knowing they can find a job in a restaurant wherever they go. I've had plenty of students who spent their summers working at Fort Edmonton, then head off to grad school and end up taking summer jobs at Upper Canada Village or Plimouth Plantation." She shook her head. "So, it could be just a clear parallel effect of the magician getting on the heritage-site gravy train while Jossie took a part-time job doing something she was already trained to do. I just wonder if she was the one who suggested hiring the magician."

I shook my head doubtfully. "I don't think she would have had Marni's ear, really. As ladders go, she was pretty much just up from the dishwasher, rung-wise."

I stopped and looked quickly at the dead girl's aunt. "I'm sorry, I didn't mean to belittle her offering to the place."

Rhea Jaque looked sad and old, especially around the eyes, but she smiled and set me at ease.

"No offence taken, don't worry. We are grieving the loss of our girl, but we're not in the process of beatifying her. She was nineteen and working as a servant at a historic site. She wasn't refining cold fusion."

There didn't seem to be anything more to learn from Ms. Jaque, and we had taken up most of her afternoon. We thanked her profusely as she walked us back out of the school to Denise's car.

Denise, who had an unerring sense of direction, decided to take a couple of back roads leading toward the secondary highway, which she figured would be quieter at this time of day than the QEII. We were quiet on the way home, listening to the remastered and reissued CD she'd been excited to share with me, the provenance of which she had been delighted to explain. Now, she drove efficiently and calmly, tapping her fingers on the steering wheel and letting me think.

We turned off the highway into the city at the Ellerslie turn-off just as the last sounds of *Procul Harum and the Edmonton Symphony Orchestra* trailed off to recorded applause. I smiled at Denise.

"Coincidences are just patterns we haven't recognized yet? Do you buy that?"

Denise shrugged. "Sometimes a cigar is just a cigar. Why, what are you thinking?"

"I'm thinking we have got to find that magician."

To make up for not taking me to IKEA, Denise had loaned me her guest air mattress—perfect for when you don't want company to stay too long—and I spent the early evening inflating it and setting up an approximation of comfort in my barren little bedroom. I was improvising a bedroom blind with two beach towels pinned over the window.

The entire room looked different from the vantage point of eight inches off the floor—smaller and more oppressive. However, I was determined I was going to try to stay in my own place that night. The longer I put it off, the less likely I'd be to get back on that particular horse, and I couldn't think of a less salubrious reason to move in with someone than the thought of being too afraid to live alone. Nope, if Steve and I were going to make that move, it would be for good and for proper.

Thinking of Steve made me realize I hadn't connected with him all day. I deliberated whether I should text him or send him an email. Somehow, texting felt more intimate. I rolled off the air mattress and onto my knees in order to get up, much the way I imagine one would have to get out of a low-slung sports car. Grace in action, I tell you.

I texted Steve, saying I'd been out of town and had some interesting tidbits to add to the mix, and that I'd be at my place tonight. I heard back from him almost immediately, as my cell-phone rang his call through before I'd even had a chance to put it down. I guess he thought calls were more intimate.

"Where 'out of town' were you?"

"Denise and I drove out to a little place between Ponoka and Bashaw, to see if we could find the Magic School that Jossie had mentioned."

"And did you?"

"Yes, as a matter of fact, and I think you really have to put more effort into finding Dafoe da Fantabulist, because he is way more entwined in this thing than we first suspected. He worked a show out there where Jossie was volunteering, so if she knew him, it's a sure thing he would recognize her."

"And did you find out how the organizers of this show got hold of the magician in the first place? Were you talking to someone who may have turned around and tipped Dafoe off the minute you drove away?"

I thought about Rhea Jaque and her sad eyes. "I don't think so. Jossie's aunt seemed more invested in her niece's end of things."

"Interesting, kiddo. I am not sure Howard and Gibson talked to an aunt, probably just the mother and father. And sometimes, at that age, they are not the best sources of information on their teens. I'll pass this on to them. But geez, Randy, don't go running around playing girl detective on your own, okay? Do I have to remind you that there is a killer out there?"

"No, but thanks. It's that sort of thing that makes me feel all cozy and secure on a dark November evening."

"Well"—Steve's voice was warm—"you don't have to stay there tonight, you know. I could come pick you up after my shift."

I wavered, thinking of Steve's nice sheets and lovely view and secure door system. Then I thought about my toaster full of crumbs and my lowly dishpan and ratty bedroom slippers I wore only when I was on my own. I needed to be home.

"No, that's okay. I should get back into the groove and there's no time like the present."

We made a date for Steve to take me out to IKEA on the weekend. I figured that was only fair, since he should get a chance to weigh in on the bed I'd be buying. I was determined to continue living on my own—I wasn't planning to go into seclusion.

In northern Alberta, we pay for our glorious long summer days by living in gloom by about five o'clock from October on. Now, as we entered November, we considered every day without snow a victory—but dry times made everything darker, because the snow cover reflected street lights and allowed for more visibility. Additionally, being on the east side of the building enhanced the sense of darkest night, even when it was barely seven o'clock. I flipped all the venetian blinds closed, to keep from feeling as if I was living in a fish bowl, watched by killers unknown, and puttered about making myself a later-than-usual meal. I fashioned a tasty sandwich from cold cuts and cheese between two slices of dark rye bread from a bakery along Steve's end of Whyte Avenue, an area that had long ago been dubbed Little Berlin for its collection of German restaurants and delis.

A pot of tea and fat sandwich in hand, I made my way into the living room, hoping to find something on television to take my mind off my own life. I flicked through the channels, figuring out as I went how to navigate the universal remote Steve had picked up for me, and happened upon a rerun of Penn and Teller's *Fool Us*, a show that had run in Great Britain a year or two earlier. It seemed as if magic acts were on the rise again. Perhaps they had never gone out of style. I tried to remember exactly when it was that the Doug Hennings of the world had stopped looking exciting and the David Copperfields had started looking cheesy. Of course, my perception was just based on television. For all I knew, magic acts were alive and well and keeping Las Vegas solvent.

I clicked the channel button a few more times and settled in to watch a local newscast. It didn't hurt to be informed every now and then. A contest was afoot to name the new LRT lines, an MP in Ottawa had been caught for the third time sleeping during question period, and the weather girl warned that we might get snow in the coming week. Now that I knew what was what, I turned off the TV and took my plate back to the kitchen.

The day's adventure had brought Jossie's death back to the forefront for me. Too much had happened in a very short time. It was hard to believe that anything could make the violent death of a young woman lose its impact, but there it was, just one of the things clamouring for attention in my tired brain.

One of the reasons I hadn't been focusing on her death was that nothing about it had seemed to implicate me, whereas the Archive thefts and the death of Mr. Maitland could quite possibly be connected to my research. The break-in at my place was probably tied to the research, too, since I was pretty sure that whoever had trashed my place, or ordered it trashed, was really only after my laptop.

I wondered if they'd managed to decode my password by now.

That was one thing Steve had never had to chide me about, locking up my information. I chose passwords that were combinations of nonsense words and numbers, with capital letters randomly dotted throughout. I might be lax about turning the deadbolt on my front door, but backing up my work and creating strong passwords were second nature to me.

I had read somewhere that the program to decode a password took approximately two weeks to run and you would need a computer with enough juice and a variety of connecting cords to run it. The computer techs in Steve's precinct had a couple of workstations set up for just that purpose, I knew. So, unless Staff Sergeant Keller had stolen my laptop to see where I'd turn up next to ruin his day, I figured it was not going to be easy for the thief to get at the inner workings of my laptop.

Luckily, whoever had broken in hadn't found either of the back-up flash drives I used. One of them was on my keychain and had been with me all along. The other was in my serendipitously discovered hiding place, which they hadn't found: the small crevice behind the light switch in my bedroom.

I had taken off the switch plate when I was stripping the hideous wallpaper border that the previous tenant had put around the doorframe. Behind it, I found a small switchbox with an inch on either side of it, carved out of the plaster and lath. Rewiring the place seemed to have included the replacement of larger boxes with their more modern counterparts. Whatever the case, leaving the bottom screw out of the plate made it easy to flip it sideways and stash valuables in the leftover space.

Thinking about my little bolt-hole made me wonder again about the enigmatic maid about whom Mrs. Rutherford had written in her missing diary. Where could a girl like that store a love letter or a cache of savings in that plain little room in someone else's home? Had she really been a thief?

I wondered if anyone had checked behind the switch plates there. I knew that some of the wiring had been upgraded, but I was pretty sure that only the main floor and the office upstairs had been done. The lights upstairs still went on and off by means of the old-fashioned button pushes, rather than a flick switch.

Could there be enough room inside one of the larger, older switchboxes to store something precious? Might a maid have pried off one of the plates and hidden something behind an electrical outlet or a light switch? Before I drifted to sleep, shutting my eyes to the ceiling that was way too far away for comfort, I put "take a screwdriver" onto my mental list of what to pack before heading over to Rutherford House to meet up with Marni in the morning.

43

While I slept hard, as my dad would have said, my dreams were all over the map. Even while I showered and dressed, my mind was still swirling, trying to pick out the real from the fantastical. Answers to the puzzles that had appeared so clearly just an hour ago in my sleep were now tantalizingly hidden just around a corner.

I was close to figuring something out, though. I could feel it. If I got a chance to poke around in the maid's room at Rutherford House, things might start to come clear.

I tried to recall whether it was the magician who had suggested we sit in the maid's parlour or whether I had done so. Or had someone else steered us there, out of the way of the actors and their shenanigans?

I had certainly not felt the need to show the back rooms to Tanya, the actress who needed a semi-hidden place to be found dead. She hadn't even gone near the back of the house, as I recalled.

Was it Marni who had asked me to take Mr. Dafoe's food up to the maid's sitting room?

Did it matter? We weren't even sure that Dafoe had anything to do with the death of the waitress, let alone the murder of the archivist and the various thefts of seemingly unimportant historic artifacts.

He had been upstairs. I had been upstairs. Tanya Rivera had been upstairs. And, of course, poor dead Jossie had been upstairs. Marni may have been up and down several times to her office, for all I knew. Greta Larsen and her grandson certainly knew their way around the house and could have gone up while people were being served their dinner. The same held true for Mr. Karras, and who knew how many other guests who might have known the House well. Roxanne had been there, looking baleful in the basement corner, likely worrying about the Limoges china in the dining-room cabinet.

Maybe it would be easier to figure out who hadn't been there, and then work backwards from there. I sighed and grabbed my jacket and backpack, locking the door behind me.

The sky looked like snow, with that grey edge to the overcast that most westerners can spot. If it didn't snow today, it would begin soon. Of course it would. It was November in Edmonton. I didn't have to sound like the *Farmers' Almanac* or a gnarled old woodsman to predict snow. But, nonetheless, Mother Nature was making a pretty good job of sending out advanced warning.

I made it to Rutherford House by way of Saskatchewan Drive, instead of heading to HUB and grabbing a coffee on the way. Marni could spring for English Breakfast tea, I figured, since this was marginally earlier than I normally got up, let alone attended business meetings.

I was a little curious to discover what she wanted to see me about, but even more interested in checking out the maid's room for hidey-holes. I saw Marni's car tucked in behind the House, but no cars pulled into the angle parking out front. I checked my wristwatch and realized it was still two hours before opening time. I figured Marni would let me in the front door if I rang, so I pressed the button and waited.

The entryway had a vestibule and then another door beyond that, making it impossible to hear if anyone was coming. I gave her what I figured was the requisite amount of time to get from the back of her office upstairs to the front door, then I rang again.

After a while, I switched to knocking on the door, putting my hand on the handle for emphasis. The knob turned in my hand and the door swung open. Okay, for anyone who has watched one too many horror movies, that was creepy in and of itself. It was even creepier knowing how rigorous Marni was about maintaining security at the House.

I contemplated calling Steve or the police station but recalled our discussion about whether or not we should call in suspicious activity at St. Stephen's College, and I figured an early-morning call to say my boss had left the front door to a public historic site open was perhaps an overreaction. It was a Saturday morning meeting, not a dark midnight rendezvous.

I told myself to get a grip and stepped into the dim house. The lights weren't all that plentiful in Rutherford House to begin with, and whoever had left the door open hadn't bothered to open the parlour drapes, which might have let in some ambient light. Of course, it was a rather grey day out there to begin with.

"Marni?" I called out, hoping my voice didn't betray my edginess. I knew she was touchy about the idea that people were going to shun Rutherford House as a scary place to visit after the murder. It wouldn't do to prove her correct, right off the bat.

"Marni?" I called again, and was rewarded by a thud from somewhere overhead. Great. The house wasn't haunted, it had just turned itself into a two-storey Ouija board.

I headed for the stairs toward the noise I'd heard.

"I'm here, as requested, boss lady," I chirped, trying to fill the silence. I thought I heard another thump coming from the front of the house, in what would have been Mrs. Rutherford's sewing area. I hurried up the stairs and made the turn to find Marni tied up and gagged and lying on the floor. It looked as if she had tried to wiggle her way toward the door out to the balcony and had managed to pull herself into a semi-sitting position. I opened the small wooden gate that had been erected to keep schoolchildren from touching the displays and bent to reach for the duct tape covering her mouth.

Before I could tear it off, I noticed her eyes go wide, staring at something behind me. I froze; for some idiotic reason, the thought popped into my head that there was a bear behind me. I turned to see what she was looking at.

All I could see was the double barrel of a shotgun pointing directly at me. It took a moment or two for the rest of the image to come into focus, since the horror of seeing a gun, let alone having one pointed at me, is a complete shock, something most Canadians have no concept of, except on television.

"Don't move," said Greta Larsen, who spoke just as my eyes and mind began to take in the bigger picture. "Move over there and sit down on the floor."

Marni made a noise in the back of her throat, which I took to be encouragement to follow this order. Never let it be said that I did not respect the power of a firearm. I dropped immediately to the floor and scuttled back into the corner Greta had indicated. Beside her loomed the tall young man who had been beside her when I had first seen her at the magic night and who I'd last seen dressed in devil horns at the Hallowe'en bash. Even in my terror, I could recognize a family resemblance. This was her grandson, Finn Larsen. Whatever genes Greta had brought to the Larsens, they had certainly won out.

"What are you planning to do with us?" I asked, immediately regretting I had even spoken. Why would I want to make the person with the gun pointed at me start planning her next move? Particularly when her next would probably be my last?

She motioned to the young man, who came forward with a roll of duct tape, and told him to tear off a piece and stick it over my mouth. So much for civil discourse. This was obviously going to be a one-sided conversation.

He tore off a piece of tape, and I recalled the pain of waxing sessions as he patted it roughly over my mouth.

"Now put your hands in front of you, wrists together."

I could see that Marni's hands had been taped together behind her. Greta was apparently directing affairs, and improving as she went along. I noticed the largish bump on Marni's forehead. Maybe hands behind the back was too much effort. Greta had probably cold-cocked her before her henchman had bound her.

Finn had the tape stuck on my left wrist and was holding my wrists together. Greta aimed the gun at Marni's head, effectively keeping both of us still. In a few strong twists, the young man bound my hands tautly together. Now that I was immobilized, Greta put the gun down at her side and young Lochinvar ripped the rest of the tape roll off my wrist. He pulled my feet together and wrapped them quickly too, which was even more uncomfortable, because the seams of my jeans dug into my ankles as they winched together. He then bound me at the knees, making it pretty much impossible to stand without a great deal of rolling, balancing and hopping, none of which could be done gracefully and silently while there was a gun aimed at me. I sat, hogtied and uncomfortable.

I looked over at Marni again; she rolled her eyes, which I took to be some form of apology. I tried to smile at her in encouragement, but all that did was pull at the duct tape, making me wince. Wincing at a fellow hostage does nothing to foster encouragement. Marni's eyes began to well up with tears, and I realized she had already come to the conclusion that we were coming to a conclusion. Greta Larsen and her grandson were going to blast big shotgun holes in us, and we were going to die here in the sewing alcove of a historic site in Edmonton, Alberta.

There was absolutely nothing about this scene that I was willing to accept as my last. I had a lot still to do with my life. I had bills to pay, continents to visit, a man to marry.

It is amazing how the barrel of a gun can focus one's priorities.

Greta had picked up the gun once more and was standing before us, moving it back and forth toward each of us, as if it was a willow stick and she was witching for water.

"I have had about all I can take from you two meddling girls. You think you can come here, turn everything into Disneyland, and bring the world tromping through this old house."

I was not sure what she was talking about, but Marni was moaning softly to my left and generally letting me know she was not going to be much help for anything. It was up to me to divine whatever meaning I could from Greta's ramblings that would give me an idea of how to get out of this mess alive.

"You couldn't leave well enough alone, could you?"

I shook my head, trying to seem abject enough for her.

"No, you had to dig and dig. You wanted to name names and make everything 'tangible' so that the modern generations could feel the 'people' behind the history." Greta was waving the gun in time to her pronouncements, and I wondered vaguely if she really was speaking in iambic pentameter or if it just seemed that way because of the force of the weapon pointed in my face.

"Well, let me tell you, you live-everything-on-the-computer-no-privacy people should think about what you do. You step all over others, people who don't want their dirty laundry hung out in public, who want to just let the past remain buried and the future to be the only thing to worry about."

I had no idea what she was talking about. I got the idea she was mocking something Marni had once said, because I could hear the air quotes around some of the words she was tossing in our faces, but she was still making no sense. What really worried me, though, was that her movements with the shotgun were getting more erratic as she spoke. Finn was standing behind his grandmother, with a look of loathing that matched hers. I couldn't see appealing to his better nature. He seemed to be right onside with whatever Greta had in mind, and I had a fair idea what that entailed.

She was winding herself up to shoot us, I was certain of it.

My puzzlement about what she had said must have read on the half of my face that wasn't covered in duct tape, because Greta looked at me impatiently, as if I was a surly nine-year-old who wasn't obeying her wishes.

"I am talking about all this website business, and bringing people into the House who aren't concerned with the Rutherfords. Always, you are trying to make them learn more."

Why was this a bad thing? Surely, that was exactly why the board had hired me to work on the virtual museum. Surely that was what museums were all about. Why was Greta even on the board if she didn't approve of museums? I realized she was still droning on, and the gun was still punctuating her words with its metronomic pattern between Marni and me.

"More about the times, about the people they met with, about the maids they hired." Greta's voice took on a keening wail. "Why couldn't you just leave well enough alone?"

All of a sudden, like a kaleidoscope shifting, pieces of what she was saying began to fall into place. I wasn't completely aware of every nuance, but I was beginning to see why Greta Larsen hadn't wanted my website and its new focus on the activities of the other staircase coming to light.

She must have seen the dawning realization in my eyes.

"That's right. My mother was a maid here in Mrs. Rutherford's day. She was fourteen when she came to work for the family. She helped them move to the new house and was kept on, helping out with all the tea parties that Mrs. Rutherford and Hazel and Mr. Cecil's wife got up to while Cecil was at war. Can you imagine being a maid in a house with three grown women pulling at you in different directions? Still, she was a good maid, and she worked her way up to becoming the real housekeeper."

Finn's face took on the look of an acolyte who was finally hearing the secrets of the Grail. Somehow, this was the crux of the matter, why this family was so intent on closing down my project.

"She might have gone on to become a matron at an old folks' home or a head housekeeper for one of the big hotels, later, with a good reference. But one of the young men from home, who drove deliveries from Edmonton to Smoky Lake all summer long while the roads were good, started courting her. She got herself pregnant, and when she finally began to show, that was it for her career. No matter that hers had been a strong back and quick hands and a quiet step on the stairs. No matter that she had worked for them for years."

Marni moaned again. I was beginning to think she might have a concussion from the bump on her head. Greta kept talking. I kept listening, mesmerized by the gun, but also beginning to see the girl Greta was obviously pining for. Her mother who had stood here, perhaps in this very spot, and been chastised for loosening her stays and her morals. The words in Mrs. Rutherford's missing diary were coming clearer.

"In the middle of the night, she was taken to the ferry, and off on the road back home. She and my father didn't get too far, though. No one was sure whether it was the bumping on the road, or her working so hard through her time, or being a bit older than usual for a first pregnancy, or her girdling herself pretending she wasn't gone, but the pains started before they were well away. She began to shiver and get ill, and they took a room along the Fort Road, at the old Transit Hotel, so that she could be seen by a doctor. Just that visit would take all she had managed to set aside from her wages, her nest egg. And they couldn't save her in the end. The baby came, and the man who loved her took her home in the back of his truck, with me swaddled tight in a hotel sheet and wedged into an apple crate lined with his winter sweater."

Marni was silent beside me. I wasn't sure whether it was the power of Greta's delivery or that she had finally succumbed to unconsciousness. I wasn't about to lose eye contact with the madwoman pointing a shotgun at me to check.

"They buried her at the edge of her father's farm, because in that three-street town she came from, where there were four fat-domed churches and no forgiveness, she wasn't allowed in the cemetery. And that's the history you want to broadcast to the world."

Greta's voice had a shrill edge to it. Her cause was so justified in her mind that she was projecting the kind of fervour you would hear from an earnest student actress cast as St. Joan. And we all know how well that turned out.

"The sort of story that made a little motherless girl the butt of every cruel joke in the playground, that made her move to the city as soon as she could—away from the father who saw in her only the woman she had killed with her own birth. That made her fearful any time someone mentioned the town she came from or the family she fled. That's the history you want to celebrate?"

The shotgun was moving up and down for emphasis, and it occurred to me that it might not have been the wisest course of action, getting her started on justifying her actions. There was nothing I could do to stem the tide, though. Any placatory noise or motion I might make could be misconstrued and cause her to pull the trigger.

"That's why I needed to see the diary you found. Alastair Maitland called me after you and he had talked at the Archives. I think he'd always suspected something about my past and my interest in the Rutherfords. I had the idea he was going to blackmail me with the diary he'd pulled from the box you had been looking through. But," she shrugged, "he didn't have a chance. Finn shut him up, didn't you, boy?" She acknowledged her henchman with a nod. My eyes flicked over to his, and saw growing horror in his face.

"There was a locket that my father used to speak of, that he had given to my mother before I complicated matters, a locket she didn't have with her when she died. He always thought she had sold it, and believed that betrayal to be a sign that she really was the tawdry woman that the rest of the town and her own family had painted her, even though he was the only one she had given herself to. That made growing up such a joy, let me tell you."

Marni's eyes were still closed. I hoped she hadn't passed out. You weren't supposed to let someone with a concussion go to sleep. Of course, shooting them with a twelve-gauge was probably not all that health-inducing, either.

"I don't think she sold it. I think she put it somewhere for safe-keeping, and that's all we were looking for when that twerp of a girl found me up in the attic. I was not trying to steal artifacts that belonged to the Rutherfords. I am not a thief! I was merely looking for what was mine by right."

I had sent Jossie up to the attic to get another umbrella stand. She had said nothing about seeing Greta rummaging up there. She probably had thought nothing of it. Greta was a board member and fully entitled to be wherever she wanted to be. I wouldn't have been suspicious, either, if I had been the one to see her. But Greta was so tied up in knots about the secrecy of her mission that she had broken the girl's neck, or had her sidekick do it, rather than let her tell anyone what she had seen Greta doing.

If they could snap the neck of an innocent girl and show no remorse for bludgeoning Mr. Maitland and leaving him in a pool of his own blood, I realized with a chill that bit into the marrow of my bones—and a solid lump that felt like someone had dropped a brick into my gut—that Greta was going to kill us, here and now. She had nothing to lose, from her viewpoint, and neither did her grandson. We had become the reason they were forced to commit all these heinous acts, and we had to pay for it. After she had dispatched us, they could continue to conduct a thorough search for her mother's locket. I considered following Marni's lead and passing out, so that I didn't have to be around for the painful denouement.

Would it be painful? Or immediate? I tried to imagine the size of a hole that big a shotgun would blow in a person at this close range. My next thought was that it really didn't matter what size the hole was.

With all this running through my mind, it was a moment or two before I tuned in to the argument Finn and Greta were having.

"You said it was a great secret that could ruin the family, Grandma. You said it would ruin us."

"Exactly. Your grandfather was a Larsen. It would never do for him to have married a bastard. It would have closed society doors to him and to all of you. We have to be sure it is never spoken of, never broadcast."

"But Grandma, you said it would ruin us. I thought you meant your mom had killed someone or stolen something important from the Rutherfords. I helped you because I thought it was something criminal, something that would blacken all our reputations."

"Finn, be quiet. This was something that could sully reputations, all the way to you."

"No, it couldn't, Grandma. No one cares anymore. Some people are even proud they're bastards. Look what you've managed to do, how far up the social ladder you've climbed—it's not even worth mentioning, let alone killing for. Oh, Grandma, why didn't you tell me before?"

Greta drew herself up as tall as she could, and even without the shotgun in her hands, she would have terrified me. She was like a Valkyrie, icy and driven.

"Not worth mentioning? This shame is what shaped me, and what I spent a lifetime hiding. Who are you to tell me what is worth mentioning? Do you think you'd be here if your father had been shunned in society? Reputation is everything!"

It was as if Finn had woken up from a trance. He lunged for the shotgun, but Greta anticipated his move and whacked him across the face with the barrel of the gun, felling him on the stairs.

Suddenly I heard Iain McCorquodale's voice ring out from the stairs: "Police! Put down the gun and put your hands up!"

My head shot up in time to witness Greta whirl around. Steve and Iain were positioned on either turn of the staircase, guns drawn on her. She aimed the shotgun at Iain and pulled the trigger. The blast echoed that of Steve's handgun, which dropped Greta where she stood. The shotgun must have tilted upward as she fell; the blast missed Iain, but brought the entire stained-glass skylight down in shards on Finn's, Iain's, and Steve's heads.

I closed my eyes and joined Marni in la-la land.

44

The upper lobby and stairs must have looked as if a Sam Peckinpah movie had been filmed there, but aside from Marni's concussion and a nasty gash on Iain's scalp, we walked out of there relatively unscathed. Physically, that is.

Finn was being held for the deaths of Jossie and Mr. Maitland and for the break-ins at both my place and St. Stephen's. While I was pretty sure his grandmother had coerced most of his behaviour and likely joined in quite a bit of it, he was proving himself to be Greta's kin through and through, maintaining a solidarity against invoking the past.

The folks from the Alberta Serious Incident Response Team had become involved, due to the officer-discharged weapon. As a result, while Marni and I were questioned extensively, it was days before I learned anything substantial. Steve had to attend counselling for several weeks, a mandatory requirement of discharging his firearm. On the whole, even though Greta was the first person he had ever killed, I don't think the incident had too much of an effect on his psyche. She had been showing no signs of remorse for her actions, which was the standard sociopathic behaviour that police officers are sworn to protect the rest of us from. The tableau of her swinging a shotgun back and forth between two helpless citizens was enough for Steve to compartmentalize the shooting of a little old lady into a line-of-duty necessity.

I had never been so happy to learn of his second sense when it came to me. Somehow, my not answering my cellphone and Greta's having pulled Marni's office phone out of the wall earlier had been enough to make his spidey senses go haywire. When he found out Iain had called over to confab with Inspectors Gibson and Howard—and had learned that they'd been narrowing down connections between people in the Rutherford House context and those who were cross-referenced on the gun registry, the information of which luckily had not yet been bulk erased by the feds—he and Iain had jumped in the car to come talk to Marni and me. The fact that the other investigation was looking into Greta Larsen's background at the same time he and Iain were beginning to redirect their focus toward Rutherford House was enough for him to determine that my safety was at stake.

They had been just as leery of the door standing open as I had, and their stealth had allowed them to hear much of Greta and Finn's argument from the lobby area below. I was thankful they had decided to move when they did. A minute or two more and either Marni or I, or both of us, would have been severely aerated.

Marni's concussion sidelined her for three-and-a-half weeks, leaving the running of Rutherford House's day-to-day hours to the annoying Roxanne. Interestingly, she rose to the task, spearheading brisk pre-Christmas sales of trinkets and tree ornaments, and instituting the jolly good idea of Christmas cake teas to the Arbour Tea House for the beginning of December.

Meanwhile, the Black Widows and I soldiered on and managed to launch the interactive website, complete with a maid's-eye view of the house option that people could follow. The number of hits registered for the site was considerable, and I received a warm letter of recognition from the board with my final paycheque. So that was that. I never did get an explanation for why they had decided not to push for a full-time web curator, but figured it probably had something to do with Mr. Karras deciding I was some sort of malcontent for questioning him about board members. Well, it had been a limited contract to begin with, so technically I hadn't lost anything. And when I thought about the price Jossie had paid for coming to the attention of a member of that board, I counted myself lucky.

Poor Jossie, misjudged for her actions and discounted by all of us at one point or other, except for the one time it really mattered. I had assumed she was just a student logging in some part-time hours for extra cash, with no interest in her surroundings. Marni, on the other hand, had found her presence annoying, with her curiosity about the running of a viable historic site. And, of course, Greta had painted her as a threat, having been caught by her while rootling around in the attic after making the suggestion to hire a magician, yet another black mark against her in Greta's books. To Greta, she probably embodied all that was coming to peel away the secrets of her past.

In a funny way, Jossie and Greta had a lot in common; each of them had been drawn to the preservation of a piece of history because of a cherished relative. To them, history didn't need to be brought to life or connected, it was still a vital element of their lives. Jossie wanted to preserve the Magic School in honour of her grandmother's work there. Greta wanted to honour Rutherford House while blurring her connection to it. If only Greta had been able to see beyond her shame and appreciate the industry and bravery it took for her mother to leave the farm and head to the big city to work in a grand house. Maybe she'd have been a happier person. Maybe she'd have been a sane person.

We were all so quick to judge, to label. As historians, as researchers, as people. I hadn't been much better. Like the people who had judged Greta's mother first for her place in society and then for her unsanctioned pregnancy, I hadn't bothered to see anything more than a phlegmatic university student when I worked with Jossie. Had I taken any time for her at all, I'd have at least learned more about her connection to the Magic School and her part in the fundraiser.

As for the magician, Dafoe da Fantabulist was finally tracked down after he returned home from visiting relatives in Ontario. His disappearance, which had seemed the greatest illusion of all, was really simple once it was explained, like so many magic acts. Apparently, he had assumed that Detective Howard's interview with him the morning after the event had been all that was required of him. That's what you get, I suppose, from growing up with American television. If they don't tell you not to leave town, it doesn't occur to you to check.

It was the 7th of December when I crunched my way through the snow to meet Marni in the tea house for lunch. She had been back at work for a week, giving Roxanne a short break before the anticipated rush of carols and cocoa evenings, another of her innovative ideas. Roxanne might just have wormed her way into the events coordinator position.

Marni was looking less gaunt than the last time I'd seen her, and her colour was back to normal. She was also more serene, a generous byproduct of looking death in the eye and coming out the other side, I suspect. After the things we'd been through, I doubted that something like a late busboy or a missing tea delivery would ever ruffle her all that much again. ·

Marni poured our tea through the little silver strainer that came with the pot. There was no one else in the breakfast nook with us, and we could be at ease with our shared experience, about which neither of us had spoken to anyone but the police. Greta may have been wrong to think her reputation in the twenty-first century would have been smeared by having it known that her mother had been a maid who had been let go for being pregnant and unwed, but there was no real need to underline her family's sadnesses for the benefit of gawkers and tabloid journalists. Let the dead take care of the dead.

"So, they've pieced almost everything together for me," Marni said, adding a wedge of lemon to the side of my saucer and passing it to me. "I get that Greta was looking for a locket her mother had hidden somewhere in one of the houses, which accounts for her break-in at Fort Edmonton, though I have a hard time envisioning her shinnying up the chain link of the Park."

"That was probably Finn, though you have to admit Greta was pretty wiry and in great shape for a woman in her eighties," I said. "People underestimate the geriatric at their own risk. I have more of a problem with her managing to break Jossie's neck. That had to have been Finn, I would think, but the adrenalin of fear can push people to do amazing things. In a way, that was her worst crime, turning her grandson into a killer because she refused to tell him truthfully about her past. There she was, looking for a locket to keep quiet an illegitimate birth, and he was thinking he was hiding a hideous criminal family secret."

"I don't suppose we'll ever find the locket," Marni mused. "After all, it could have been long since found by some frat boy and given to his girlfriend."

"It could," I agreed. "But there was something I was going to suggest, something I had been thinking about before coming to see you that day."

I explained the concept of the hidey-hole, trying hard not to admit that I had one such in my apartment. Marni was skeptical, but we decided it was worth a look. The screwdriver I'd popped into my satchel that day was still in the bottom of my bag, and when we got up to the maid's bedroom, I went straight to the light switch, hoping to find a spot akin to mine at home.

I got the plate off with just a little trouble, after having to pry it up from the painted wall. I could hear Marni sucking her breath in through her teeth, mostly afraid my actions were going to necessitate another painting job.

There was nothing inside but the wiring and a dead spider.

I replaced the switch plate and rotated the little brass screws back into place.

"Well, it was worth a try," I said, shrugging my shoulders.

Marni pointed to the plate covering the one electrical outlet behind the tiny bedside table.

"What about that one? We might as well check, as we're here already."

We set the table to one side and unplugged the small lamp that sat on it.

I knelt down on the hardwood floor and set my screwdriver into the ridge of the screw. These screws hadn't moved in a long time, and I was pretty sure the grime I was finding went back a fair amount of time, too. Mrs. Rutherford would not have been impressed.

I really had to pry this plate and ended up wedging the screwdriver between the plate and the wall, trying to do so from the baseboard side of things, to minimize any marks I might make. Finally, the plate popped off, the dull metal of the switchbox making the plugs stand in sharp relief. At the bottom of the box was a folded piece of paper, which felt heavy when I pulled it out.

I heard Marni gasp behind me.

I unfolded the letter. Even after all these years, it was apparent that it had been folded and refolded many times. As I opened the final fold to read the sweet words written in the fading brown ink, a gold chain and heart-shaped locket slid into the palm of my hand. It was dulled and slightly brown-looking, making me wonder at the amount of real gold in the jewellery itself.

I turned it over to find the clasp, and there on the front of the heart was engraved the name GRETA. He had named his daughter after her mother and then punished her with his own tarnished memories.

"So this is what she was looking for?" Marni breathed over my shoulder. I held up the locket, the chain sliding between my fingers, as if it wanted to remain hidden, away from the light.

"Yep, this is it. Not worth the lives of two innocent people, is it?"

"Well, it could have been the Kohinoor diamond and not been worth that," Marni shrugged. "What are we going to do with it?"

I sat back on my heels to think. There was no way we would be able to find a grave on a private farm somewhere northeast of Lamont. There was no reason to turn it over to the police, as they had enough material on Greta Larsen to close both investigations with the event of her death. And there was nothing to link the locket to any great curatorial collection.

On the other hand, I had completely disagreed with Greta's reasoning that a focus on the maids of Rutherford House would be demeaning to the young girls who had come into town from the farms and nearby towns in order to better their lives and send money home. There was nothing shameful about honest work, and there never would be.

I looked at Marni and hung the locket over the wire bedpost, as the first Greta might have done before going to sleep. Then I screwed the plate back over the love letter in her safe place, and we went downstairs to finish our tea.

Acknowledgements

Without the generosity of people who are willing to help out and support me, it would just never happen. These acknowledgments are the very least I can do. They may also be the most you get, so there's that, too.

First off, thank you, Lorna Arndt, from folkwaysAlive!, whom I inadvertently left off the last list, but who championed the finished product anyhow. Thank you, Randy Williams, for doing everything in your power to make a little mystery novel about Edmonton folk music stay on the bestseller lists for such a long run, and for making the weekends easy, to facilitate the writing of this book. Thanks also to my father-in-law, Ron Williams, who bought out the entire stock of French Market chicory coffee and mailed the tins express-post when he learned my weekend morning tradition was running out. I swear, the book you are holding in your hands is fuelled by chicory. And thanks to the Ides of Lunch Ladies, who always know how to commiserate and when to cheer. Likewise, thanks to Cora Taylor, Martina Purdon, Marianne Copithorne, Barbara and all the Reeses, Stephen Dafoe, Bonnie Bramming-Dinelle, Timothy Anderson, Laurie Greenwood, Michael Rose, Garry Bodner, Brad Fraser, Lasha Morningstar, Caterina Edwards, Alice Major, Angie Abdou, Suzanne North, Gail Bowen, Linda Granfield, Stewart Lemoine, Jeff Haslam, Mark Meer and John Wright for being in my corner, in a variety of ways.

Brenda Manwaring, from Culture and Community Spirit, opened up locked doors of Old St. Stephen's College and arranged for a tour by Larry Pearson through the areas no one sees anymore. Peg Copithorne Tyler graciously brought those dusty floors to life with her memories and recollections. Jocelyn and Madeleine Mant allowed their brains to be picked about their collective work at Fort Edmonton Park and Rutherford House, and Laura Nichol and Alex Hamilton answered with alacrity whenever I needed a fact checked. Terry O'Riodan patiently explained the day-to-day workings behind the scenes at the Provincial Archives of Alberta. None of these people is to be blamed for me fixing, changing, switching, and rearranging any of the historical sites, offices, interior décor, rules, hours of operation, and artifacts.

I have to admit I did a lot of that. You won't be able to find a box of Mattie Rutherford's diaries at the Archives. You're not allowed to take picnic lunches into the Ukrainian Cultural Heritage Village. The Archives staff are far too professional to all take their vacations at the same time, and they aren't open on Mondays. Zombie tag isn't a regular occurrence at the Spooktaculars, though it should be. Please don't ask Stephen Dafoe to show you the trick with the hamster and the budgie. And I'm so sorry I didn't mention the Rutherford House Christmas cactus, but it's an October book.

Tom and Judy Peacocke, in a generous bid to support the Freewill Shakespeare Festival, which is also very dear to my heart, paid to name one of the characters in this book, who quickly became one of my favourite characters ever. They have also been supporters of the series from the start, and I am grateful for readers like them. I tell you, Randy Craig fans are top drawer.

This book, especially, has been a labour of love. My very first book-length writing was *The Northwest Fort: Fort Edmonton*, and I have spent many years wandering the dusty streets and boardwalks of one of the best historic parks in the world, taking visitors and visiting my working children. Thanks to my mother's twin urges of teaching and wanderlust, visiting historic sites is something our family always did, from Barkerville to Green Gables. I also want to thank the pioneer descendants of Mecca Glen, who placed a historic marker right where I was planning to invent one.

Those of you who wish to make historic visits based on this book will find your way easily to the Ukrainian Cultural Heritage Village, Fort Edmonton Park, and Rutherford House. And you should. These are great resources and all-around fun places. A couple of the other sites I made up of necessity; for instance, the Magic School, where my mother taught years ago, is an illusion worthy of its name.

I'd like to thank the several people who allowed their names to be used for suspects and victims. It was very pleasant to spend weekend mornings with your alter egos. And for those of you wondering why Jossie is the name I used for a victim, it was a compromise; she wanted to be a murderer, but I didn't think that would be seemly. After all, people always judge the mothers of murderers so harshly.

The folks at Turnstone: Jamis, Sharon, and Sara, are all lovely people to deal with who make beautiful books. I am very thankful they choose to make them out of words I've written. Sharon is so patient, prescient, and precise in her editing that the rewriting has nearly become the most fun part of the process.

As ever, a special thank you to my husband, Randy. Writing is a solitary task and without the right person in your corner, it can be a lonely one. Lucky for me, Randy is chief cheerleader, promoter, editor, first reader, and bottle washer. He's already getting me in gear to write the next one.

And of course, thank you, for reading and buying Canadian.

Janice

Sticks & Stones
by Janice MacDonald

How dangerous can words be? The University of Alberta's English Department is caught up in a maelstrom of poison-pen letters, graffiti and misogyny. Part-time sessional lecturer Miranda Craig seems to be both target and investigator, wreaking havoc on her new-found relationship with one of Edmonton's Finest.

One of Randy's star students, a divorced mother of two, has her threatening letter published in the newspaper and is found soon after, victim of a brutal murder followed to the gory letter of the published note. Randy must delve into Gwen's life and preserve her own to solve this mystery.

Spellbinding ...
—W.P Kinsella

Sticks & Stones / $14.95 / ISBN: 9780888012562 / Ravenstone

The Monitor
by Janice MacDonald

You're being watched. Randy Craig is now working part-time at Edmonton's Grant MacEwan College and struggling to make ends meet. That is, until she takes an evening job monitoring a chat room called Babel for an employer she knows only as Chatgod. Soon, Randy realizes that a killer is brokering hits through Babel and may be operating in Edmonton. Randy doesn't know whom she can trust, but the killer is on to her, and now she must figure out where the psychopath is, all the while staying one IP address ahead of becoming the next victim.

[Janice MacDonald] has managed to convey the inherent spookiness ... that a social cyberspace can invoke.
—Howard Rheingold

The Monitor / $10.99 / ISBN: 9780888012845 / Ravenstone

Hang Down Your Head
by Janice MacDonald

Some folks have a talent for finding trouble, no matter how good they try to be, especially Randy Craig. Maybe she shouldn't date a cop. Maybe she should have turned down the job at the Folkways Collection library—a job that became a nightmare when a rich benefactor's belligerent heir turned up dead.

Randy tried to be good—honest!—but now she's a prime suspect with a motive and no alibi in sight.

The Edmonton Folk Music Festival, the city itself and the fascinating politics of funding research in the arts lend a rich texture to this engaging mystery with the twisty end. If you enjoy folk music, you're in for an extra treat. Once again, Randy Craig is a down-to-earth, funny and realistic amateur sleuth: it's good to reconnect with her.

—Mary Jane Maffini, author of
The Busy Woman's Guide to Murder

I have been a performer at the Edmonton Folk Festival for 20 years. I always knew there were a lot of characters there, but until reading Janice's book, I never thought of the festival itself as a character, and a fine place for a murder mystery!

—James Keelaghan

Hang Down Your Head / $16.00
ISBN: 9780888013866
Ravenstone

Janice MacDonald holds a master's degree in English literature from the University of Alberta, where she has worked as a sessional lecturer, radio producer and bartender. She also spent a decade teaching literature, communications, and creative writing at Grant MacEwan College, and has held positions as both an online chatroom monitor and distance course instructor. A consummate folkie, she plays five-string banjo, fiddle, guitar, and piano, wrote the music and lyrics for two touring historical musicals, and has been a singer/songwriter. Janice lives in Edmonton with her husband Randy and is the proud mother of two glorious grown girls.